Moonlight Kin Vol. 2

Moonlight Kin 3: Nic

Moonlight Kin 4: Tristan

Moonlight Kin Vol. 2
By
Jordan Summers

Copyright 2015 Jordan Summers

Published by Smallbites Online Learning, Inc.

Moonlight Kin 3: Nic
Original Copyright 2014 by Jordan Summers
Moonlight Kin 4: Tristan
Original Copyright 2014 by Jordan Summers

ISBN: 978-1942237136

Moonlight Kin 3: Nic

PROLOGUE

A shadow of ash spread across the highway, staining the asphalt a deeper shade of gray. Fissure cracks appeared, threading their boney fingers wide until the earth bucked beneath Jerry Seaver's semi-truck. He clenched the wheel and fought to keep the heavy load from jackknifing on the road.

"Damn earthquakes," he muttered under his breath, but his heart continued to pound.

Thunder cracked in a cloudless blue sky. Jerry poked his head out the window. He squinted against the sunlight and looked around, but the only thing he could see was a green ocean of trees rocking gently in the breeze.

The fine hairs on his arms rose, along with the pressurization in the cab of his truck. Jerry's ears popped. His unease increased despite the natural beauty around him.

He wiped his hand across his grit-covered face and it came away moist. The highway stretched out in front of him with no cars in sight. There wasn't a town around for miles. Jerry was alone. The sudden change in the air reminded him just how isolated he was on this back road. Suddenly the shortcut he'd taken wasn't such a good idea.

He shifted gears and pressed his foot down. Smoke billowed out the semi's exhaust pipes as the engine strained to pick up speed. Jerry didn't want to be out here surrounded by oppressive woods any longer than necessary.

A half a mile in front of him the air shimmered like waves on a pond. It was too cool for the mirage to be heat rising from the asphalt. Jerry's foot eased off the accelerator and the truck slowed, but he wasn't about to stop. The glistening increased and the air yawned, opening wide to reveal its gaping black mouth.

"What the hell?" Jerry leaned forward to get a better look at...at...he had no idea what he was seeing. The sun gleamed off his red hood, but didn't penetrate the dark entrance ahead.

It wasn't real. It couldn't be.

"You're just tired," he muttered aloud.

Jerry rubbed his eyes and shook his head. He'd been driving for ten hours and hadn't gotten much sleep the previous night. He was determined to get to Vancouver today.

The crisp air worked to keep him awake, but wouldn't prevent hallucinations. This had to be one, because what he was witnessing didn't make sense.

He reached for his Red Bull and took the last sip. Moisture dribbled down his chin onto his shaggy beard. Jerry wiped his mouth with the back of his hand, then crushed the can and tossed it over his shoulder before grabbing another out of his cooler.

Jerry pressed the cold can to his forehead, then popped it open. He took a deep swallow, then checked to see if the *hallucination* still hovered above the road.

The tear had widened, revealing more of the gloom. If it got any bigger, it would swallow his truck. Something moved in the shadows. Fear plunged its icy fingers into him, locking on to his spine.

The gap expanded and someone—no, *something*—fell out, then the opening snapped shut.

Jerry was too close to stop and too scared to react. His truck barreled down upon the...he squinted...*creature*, striking the black mass. A loud bang filled the cab as the shadowy thing smacked the grille and flew through the air, landing on the side of the road.

He glanced into his side mirror to see where it had gone. The black creature rose, took a few steps, then collapsed in the lane.

Jerry crossed himself and prayed that it was dead. Whatever he'd struck wasn't human, wasn't of this world. He had seen where it had come from with his own eyes and he wasn't about to stick around to find out if it was okay. With his heart in his throat, Jerry shifted gears and tore down the road.

An hour later, he pulled his rig into the truck stop and washed the blood off the grill. By the time Jerry Seaver reached Vancouver, he had convinced himself that he'd imagined the whole incident.

1

Mindy MacDougal stopped her car next to the curb. Celina Gibson opened the passenger door and handed her the pepperoni pizza, then climbed in.

The aroma of tomato sauce, oregano, and sausage filled the small cab, making Mindy's stomach growl.

"I don't know if I can wait until we get to the house to have a slice," Mindy said.

Celina buckled her seatbelt, then reached for the warm box. "If I can wait, you can wait." She glanced at Mindy. "Isn't that Izzy's shirt?"

Mindy grinned. "Yep!"

"Can't believe she let you wear it. I tried to borrow it one time and she threatened to break my fingers."

"Yeah, Izzy is weird about sharing things. She never wants anyone to wear her clothes or use her stuff. Said it made them smell funny." Mindy laughed and put her blinker on, then pulled away from the curb. "If she didn't want me to wear her clothes then she shouldn't have left them in the closet when she moved out."

"I still can't believe she's gone," Celina said.

Mindy squeezed her hand. "I know you miss her, too."

Celina and Isabel had been best friends for a few years, then this last year Izzy pulled away. It was a pattern she repeated when anyone got too close. To soothe Celina's hurt feelings, Mindy had stepped in as a surrogate for her sister. She wasn't as good company as Izzy, but she did her best.

"She was always threatening to move. I just didn't think she'd go through with it. I mean, where else is she going to get such a sweet setup?" Celina asked.

"What do you mean?" Mindy glanced at her.

"You paid her rent. You did her laundry. You bought all the food. Isabel never had to do anything while you were around." Bitterness tinged her tone.

Mindy's face heated. "It was my choice. She never asked me to do any of those things."

"She never had to," Celina retorted. "Wish I had a younger sister like you."

Mindy sighed. How could she explain in a way that Celina would understand?

She hadn't always been the responsible one. There was a time when she and Izzy had been footloose and carefree. That was before Izzy's penchant for outlandish storytelling took a dark turn, before the expensive psychiatrists, before the psych meds, before all the experimental treatments.

Nothing their parents tried could eliminate Izzy's "visions" or quell her talk of monsters. To this day, her sister was utterly convinced of their existence.

The treatments did succeed in one area. They successfully changed Mindy and Izzy's relationship. Her role in the family dynamic evolved from close ally to her sister's keeper.

The change hadn't been easy for Mindy. At first, she'd chafed at carrying so much responsibility. She missed her freedom. She missed having fun. But there was only room for one bad girl at the table and Izzy had claimed the spot.

Now that Izzy was gone and Mindy was finally free, she didn't know quite what to do with herself.

Celina chewed on her bottom lip. "Did she at least say goodbye before she left?"

She did her best to hide her pain, but Mindy didn't think she was successful. "You know my sister. Goodbyes are so...responsible. She called you, though, didn't she?"

"Yeah, but she didn't tell me that she'd moved out," Celina said.

"Then what did she say?" Mindy asked.

"She told me to watch out for the monsters," she said.

Mindy rolled her eyes. "What's that supposed to mean?"

Celina shrugged and looked away, but not before Mindy saw fear in her eyes.

"Don't let her freak you out," she said.

"You know, this might turn out to be a good thing in disguise," Celina said. "You've been taking care of your sister for years. Izzy could do with a serious dose of reality."

Mindy knew she was right, but it would take some time to adjust to all the changes.

"She's your big sister. It's past time that she acts like it," Celina said.

"We're only a year apart," Mindy said. "Not exactly a huge gap."

"Doesn't matter. She's still older," Celina said. "Have you heard from her since she left?"

"She called Wednesday night, but I was at school," Mindy said.

"Did she at least leave a message?"

Mindy hesitated. "Yeah, sort of."

"Uh-oh. What did she say?" Celina asked.

Mindy sighed. "Maybe you can make sense of her message. She said the winds told her it was time to move on. That there was darkness coming."

Celina's perfectly shaped brow shot up. "The winds? Darkness? Last time I checked, wind didn't talk. And darkness"—she looked out the window—"comes every night. Did she tell you anything useful? Like where she was going?"

The question surprised Mindy. She thought for sure Izzy would've told her best friend where she was going. But one look at Celina's face made it clear that she hadn't. Weird. Should she tell her? She couldn't see any harm in letting her know.

"Apparently, the winds gave my sister directions to New Orleans." She laughed.

Celina gasped.

"What is it?" Mindy asked.

"Nothing," Celina said.

"Tell me."

"I just always wanted to go there. Izzy and I talked about it a lot. She said we'd run away there one day." Celina grew quiet. "Guess that won't be happening now. She'll fit right in down there."

That was what worried Mindy. What if Izzy didn't come back? What if there was no room in her 'new' life for her sister?

"I hope she's okay," Mindy said.

"You need to stop worrying about her," Celina said. There was sternness in her voice that hadn't been there a moment ago.

She was right, but the saying about old habits dying hard was true. "It's what sisters do," Mindy said quietly. She was surprised Celina wasn't more concerned given how much she knew about Izzy, but maybe she was in shock about New Orleans.

"I know you love her, but your sister is a flake. You have to live your own life now," Celina said. "It's past time Izzy learns to stand on her own two feet."

Mindy didn't want to think about Izzy anymore. It would mean examining her own sorry life. "So what's on the agenda tonight?" she asked.

"I thought we'd go for a Ryan double feature." Celina reached into her purse and pulled out two DVDs. "Dibs on Gosling."

"Man," Mindy said. "That's not fair."

Celina laughed. "Like settling for Reynolds is such a hardship."

Mindy glanced at her and smiled. "True. I wouldn't exactly kick him out of my bed."

"No woman with a brain in her head would."

Lights faded away as they drove out of town and made a right onto a back road that would eventually lead to Mindy's home.

Thick woods on both sides of the road swallowed what little light came from the headlights. Mindy cranked the radio and pressed on the accelerator. The miles rolled by.

Celina was doing her best pop princess impersonation when Mindy spotted the entrance to a long drive.

"Hey." She nudged Celina. "Is that the road you take to get to that club you're always talking about? Pits or something."

Celina stopped singing and looked out the window. "Yeah, that's it," she said reluctantly. "The place is called Sticks." She crossed her arms over her chest and sank down in her seat. "Izzy never really liked it. She said the place made her feel uncomfortable. She only went there a few times."

"Really?" Mindy asked. "I was always under the impression that Izzy liked it. Well, as much as she liked anyplace."

"No!" Celina said. "The only time she ever wanted to go there was when she had the urge to dance."

Dancing was one of the few passions she and her sister shared these days, but they rarely indulged in the activity at the same time.

"Can't believe that I've driven by the entrance so many times and never noticed it before," Mindy said. "For some reason, I could've sworn that you and Izzy told me it was on the east side." She was positive they had.

Celina laughed off her comment, then shifted in her seat. "You aren't exactly Ms. Observant," she remarked.

It was common knowledge around the animal clinic that Mindy was driven and focused, but only on work and school. What little time remained had gone toward caring for Izzy and protecting her.

Mindy stared at the entrance through her side mirror until it faded into the night. "Now that I know where it is I'll have to go," she said.

Celina cleared her throat and picked at the edge of the pizza box. "I'm not sure Sticks is your kind of place." She stared out the window as she spoke.

Mindy frowned. "What do you mean? You said it was fun. You told me there were tons of good-looking men. I know you've been going there just about every weekend with your friend Erin. Izzy went with you last week." She took a breath. "In fact, you've gone there with everyone but me."

"Isabel didn't have a good time," Celina said softly. "She hated it so much that she made me promise not to take you there."

Why would her sister do that? Mindy vaguely remembered Izzy coming home freaked out, but since that wasn't unusual, she hadn't been concerned at the time. Now she was.

Though she'd never shown it, Mindy's feelings had been hurt that Celina had never invited her to go with them to the bar. Had she asked, Mindy may have very well declined the invitation, but Celina had never bothered.

"Why would Izzy ask you to make that promise?"

"Why does Izzy say or do anything?" Celina asked, smoothly deflecting the question. "To find out the answer, you'd have to ask your sister."

They both knew that would never happen.

"Did anything unusual happen the last night you guys were there?" Mindy asked.

Celina readjusted the pizza box on her lap. "Not that I recall. It was a blast like always."

"Then I don't get why you and Izzy think I should avoid it," Mindy said.

"I can't speak for your crazy sister," Celina said. "But knowing you and knowing Sticks the way I do, I can honestly tell you it's not your type of place."

Why is Sticks great for Celina, but not for me?

Appearance-wise, they were polar opposites. Celina was tall, had long, dark hair, sun-kissed skin, a stunning face, and a trim figure that models would kill for.

Mindy had learned to live with being vertically challenged. Her curvy body was made for a different era—an era that didn't give side-eye to a woman who enjoyed eating a whole sandwich and a side of chips.

"Don't think you're going to get away with that answer without explaining yourself," Mindy said.

"You know what I mean," Celina said.

Mindy shook her head. "No, I don't. What exactly is *my* type of place?" She immediately pictured a library and rolled her eyes. How long had Celina and her sister been conspiring behind her back? It made her angry that between them they'd decided what was and wasn't good for her. How dare they after everything she'd done! She was the poster child for responsible behavior.

Celina's face pinched.

"Spill it!" Mindy wasn't about to let her off the hook.

Celina sighed. "You're more of a coffee bar kind of girl. Sticks is wild. Most nights it's a free-for-all."

Mindy's heart sank. "Are you saying I'm not any fun?" Celina wouldn't be the first one of her friends to imply she didn't know how to have a good time. Being her sister's keeper had left little time for a social life. The added responsibility had cost Mindy a lot of friendships over the years.

There were times, though—in the dead of night—that Mindy wondered if her sacrifice had been worth it. Wondered what would've happened if, just once, she had shrugged off her responsibilities and kicked up her heels.

Celina's brown eyes widened. "I didn't say you weren't fun," she insisted.

"No, you implied it." Mindy frowned as childhood taunts of "Monotonous Mindy" echoed in her head. She wasn't monotonous. Not anymore. She could have fun. There was no one to hold her back now. Tears unexpectedly made her eyes burn. She blinked them away before Celina noticed.

"I'm sorry. I didn't mean to hurt your feelings," Celina said. "It's just that Sticks isn't your typical bar. It's really rowdy. Fights are common. Most of the guys that go there are...*different*. You're used to hipsters, not the kind of chest-beating, blue-collar he-men that frequent Sticks."

Mindy glowered. "I like he-men. I just haven't met many in real life." Try never.

She wasn't lying about being attracted to those types of guys. Or *any* type of guy, for that matter. It had been a long time since Mindy had dated. Her dry spell now resembled the Mohave. She was willing to try anything at this point.

"And I enjoy going to wild places on occasion," she said.

Celina snorted. "Name one wild place you've gone to. Seriously, just one. Before you answer, I want the dates, too, because I can't remember the last time you went to a rowdy bar," she said. "For as long as I've known you, you've planned your 'impulsive' moments."

"That's not true."

"Yes, it is," Celina said.

Heat spread up Mindy's neck and into her face. She took her eyes off the road. "Perhaps if you'd invited me to go along with you just once, we wouldn't be having this argument." Her voice cracked.

Celina patted her arm. "I told you that Izzy didn't want me to. She made me promise."

"Well, Izzy isn't here anymore. This isn't about her. This is *my* life we're talking about, not my sister's," Mindy grumbled.

Maybe Celina and Izzy were right. Maybe she wasn't any fun. Maybe her sister had inherited all the fun genes in the family. That would explain why Celina always took her other friends to Sticks and left her at home.

Celina glanced out the windshield and slammed her hands against the dashboard. "Mindy, look out!"

2

They were going to die! And it was all because she didn't get invited to a bar. The black mass lying halfway in her lane grew larger and larger as she bore down upon it.

Mindy screamed and jerked the wheel to the right, missing the object by inches. Her tires screeched and her heart did its best to crack her ribs. She hit the brakes and the car skidded dangerously before coming to a stop in the center of the road.

She pressed a hand to her chest and looked in her rearview mirror to make sure no one was behind them. Darkness met her.

"What was that?" Mindy asked. She hadn't gotten a good look at it. She'd been too busy trying not to hit it.

"Not sure. A bear, maybe?" Celina slowly released the dash. "That was close." She looked over her shoulder. "Turn around so your headlights illuminate it. I want to get another look at it."

With shaky hands, Mindy managed a three-point turn. The massive animal came into view. "I think you're right about it being a bear." Nothing else outside the zoo could be that large. She couldn't see the beast's face, but its crumpled body was almost as tall as the hood of her compact car.

"No, it's the wrong shape." Celina squinted. "We need to get more light on it."

Mindy hit her high beams, illuminating the road and more of the animal.

They both gasped.

Whatever it was, it was massive. Really massive. "It has to be a bear. A grizzly from the size of it. There's nothing else in the wild around here that big," Mindy said.

"Buffalos are," Celina said.

"That isn't a buffalo," Mindy said.

"I know," Celina said. "Only one way to find out for sure."

Mindy squinted at the animal through her bug-stained windshield. "Do you think it's dead? It looks dead."

"Yeah," Celina said. "I think it's dead. We need to get it off the road."

Mindy glanced at her. "Have you been lifting weights without telling me? There's no way we're going to be able to move it, unless we cut it up."

Celina scrunched her nose. "Ew! I'm not cutting anything up. If need be, we'll hook your tow chain around it and pull it off the road. If we leave it there, someone's going to hit it and total their car."

"Looks like it's already been hit." Mindy checked the deserted road to see if there was a car lying in the ditch. "I don't see any wreckage." She also didn't spot any broken glass. "Maybe someone shot it."

Celina paled. "Let's hope not," she said. "That wouldn't be good for anyone involved."

It might not be good, but it was common for the area. Mindy pulled over to the side of the road and parked. She flipped on her hazards and kept her headlights trained on the animal.

Celina unbuckled her seatbelt and climbed out of the car. Mindy walked to her trunk and popped it open, then grabbed two pairs of latex gloves. She pulled a pair on, then handed the other set to Celina.

"I don't see a lot of blood." Celina moved closer to examine the animal. "Holy crap! It's still breathing."

The news startled Mindy. She'd thought for sure the animal was dead. "Get away from it," she said. "It might attack out of fear and pain."

Celina glowered at her. "I've been working at the animal clinic longer than you have. I may not be a veterinary student, but I know what I'm doing."

Mindy sighed. "I didn't mean anything by it. I just don't want you to get hurt."

School was a sore subject for Celina. She'd had to go to work to help support her parents and had never managed to finish high school. After they died, she'd eventually gotten her GED, but the achievement had done little to ease her insecurities.

Mindy had encouraged her to continue her education, but Celina had balked. She'd claimed that if Izzy didn't need a degree, then neither did she.

As excuses went, it was pretty sad. But not nearly as sad as the real reason Celina had no interest in going back to school.

The real reason she hadn't bothered to better her life was because Celina was waiting for a knight in shining armor to come and sweep her off her feet. It was a fantasy she clung to and it was just as real to her as monsters were to Izzy. Celina wanted that knight more than anything and wouldn't settle for less.

Years of looking after Izzy had taught Mindy that you couldn't change someone, especially once they'd made up their minds.

"I'm going to move in closer to see if it has any other obvious injuries," Celina said.

"Are you sure it's alive?" Mindy couldn't see any movement. Maybe what Celina had witnessed was the body settling after death.

"I just saw its chest rise again," Celina said. "I'm pretty sure that means it's alive."

Mindy took a deep breath. She wanted to point out that she was the one with the medical training, but didn't want to upset Celina any more than she already had. "Is it a bear?"

"No," Celina said. "It's canine."

"That's not possible," Mindy said. "It's too large."

Celina tore her gaze away. "Pretty sure the animal in the road is definitive proof that you're wrong."

Mindy ignored her sarcasm. "I don't have the instruments or equipment with me to tend its wounds and I don't have pain meds to ease its suffering."

"I know," Celina said. "Help me get it into the car."

Mindy glanced at the animal and then at her compact car. "There's no way it's going to fit," she said.

"It'll fit." Celina sounded so confident.

Too bad Mindy didn't feel the same. She hesitated.

"If we can get it to the clinic, then Dr. Fields might be able to save it or at least make sure it doesn't suffer more," Celina said.

Her friend was determined to save the animal. Mindy appreciated her tenacity, but found it odd since Celina had always kept her distance from all the animals that were brought into the clinic.

Up until tonight, Mindy was the only one who'd regularly rallied to save the animal kingdom. Maybe her passion was finally rubbing off on Celina.

Mindy approached cautiously. The animal was larger up close. Celina had to be wrong about the species. A quick cursory examination proved otherwise. What kind of canine grew to this size?

"Celina, I really don't think he's going to fit."

"He'll fit. Trust me."

She didn't think so, but Celina was right—they couldn't leave the creature here for someone to hit. Who knows how long it had been suffering. Mindy couldn't bear to see any animal injured and in pain.

"I'll move the seats forward." Celina raced to the car and adjusted the seats.

Mindy stared at the animal. She'd never seen anything quite like it. Its head was wide, wider than a typical canine, and it had a mouthful of sharp teeth. Sable fur covered its broad body. She glanced at its paws. They were canine in shape, but its claws looked like something more suited for a grizzly bear.

"I'm embarrassed to admit this, but I can't identify this animal." Mindy hadn't grown up in the area, so she wasn't familiar with every species, but thanks to school she had a pretty good grasp of the natural habitats of predators. "It sort of looks like a wolf, but it's too big and its head isn't the right shape."

The biggest wolf Mindy had ever seen had weighed 175 pounds. This one was *much* larger.

"Have you ever seen anything like it?" she asked.

Celina's gaze skittered away. "You grab the back end, I'll lift its head."

Mindy watched in horror as Celina whispered something in the creature's ear. The animal shuddered.

"Seriously, be careful," Mindy said. "I know you're trying to soothe it, but an injured animal this size can do a lot of damage." She glanced at her car. "I wish I would've thought to carry a muzzle."

"I doubt it would fit, even if you had brought one," Celina said.

Mindy glanced at the creature's mouth. *No,* she thought. *Probably not.*

After thirty minutes of grunting, dragging, and shoving, they got the injured canine in the backseat of Mindy's car. Surprisingly, it fit, when everything about its body said it shouldn't have. Maybe its size was deceptive due to the thick fur? At one point, Mindy could've sworn the animal was helping them, but it was just wishful thinking on her part.

Celina's knees touched the dash and the cold pizza box was crushed to her chest, as Mindy raced to the animal clinic in Breakbend, Oregon. Fifteen minutes outside of town, she dug her phone out of her purse and tossed it to Celina.

"Call Dr. Fields and tell him we're on our way," she said.

Celina punched in the number. "You know he's going to ask you to assist," she said.

Mindy glanced at her, afraid to take her eyes off the road for long at this speed. "Of course, that's my job. It's what I'm training to do."

Breakbend's lights twinkled in the darkness, illuminating the western facades covering the businesses on the main drag.

Mindy slowed when they came into town, but they still reached the clinic in record time. Celina pried herself out of the car and tossed the pizza onto her vacated seat. She was digging for the keys to the front door when Dr. Fields showed up.

"What do we have, Mindy?" he asked.

"Canine of some kind," she said. "Looks like it's been hit by a car, but it could've been shot. I haven't located any entrance or exit wounds, but won't know for sure until it's been X-rayed. We found him lying on the side of the road. We got out to move it and discovered he was still alive."

Dr. Fields poked his head into the car to take a look. His brow slowly furrowed. "Not a lot of visible blood, but no doubt there are internal injuries. Where did you say you were when you found it?"

"Off the highway. On the back road between Breakbend and Carson, not far from Telegraph Road. We were headed to my house."

"I'm surprised it fit in the car," he said.

"You and me both," Mindy said.

Celina came out of the clinic with a gurney.

"Help me get it on the table," Dr. Fields said. "Be careful. We don't want to do more damage."

Once again Celina and Mindy grabbed a section of the canine and lifted, then helped the doctor wheel it into the operating room.

After a quick set of X-rays ruled out a gunshot wound, Mindy pulled scrubs on over her clothes and administered the anesthetic under the vet's supervision.

"He's under," she said, monitoring its vitals, before making sure the animal received enough oxygen.

The doctor's frown deepened as he analyzed the X-rays for other injuries. "That's odd. Only one bone appears to be broken. Given its lethargic state, I expected the damage to be much worse."

"That's good, right?" Mindy asked.

"No, that means it's in shock. That can kill it just as effectively as an untreated injury. I'll have to open him up to be sure we're not missing anything vital."

Dr. Fields made the incision, then carefully repaired a couple of minor tears on one of the organs. After a thorough search to make sure he hadn't missed any other trauma, he closed the animal up and aligned the bone, then put a cast on the leg.

"Is he going to be okay?" Mindy asked.

"He should be, but I simply cannot explain his condition. With these minor injuries, the animal should've been up and moving around," he said, his expression troubled. "Albeit slowly."

"Do you know what it is?" Mindy asked.

"A mystery," he said.

"I mean, do you know what kind of animal it is?" she asked.

He pulled his bloody gloves off and tossed them into the HAZMAT container. "I'm not entirely certain," he said. "I've never seen anything quite like him, especially in the lupine family. It's almost as if someone bred a Russian wolf with a Caucasian Mountain dog, which would be hard to do without the wolf trying to kill the dog. But then again, those dogs are tough."

"I'm not familiar with that breed," Mindy said.

"It's also known as the Russian Bear dog for obvious reasons. The males can grow to be over two hundred pounds. They make perfect guard dogs."

"I can see why. I wouldn't want to take one on," Mindy said. "But this isn't Russia."

"No, but people have all kinds of exotic pets that they shouldn't own," he said. "I've pulled some of its blood for a DNA check. We'll know more once we get the results. In the meantime, let's get him into recovery. I think we have one cage big enough in the back."

"If he fit in my backseat, we can get him into the bear cage," Mindy said.

Celina watched through the small window in the door as Mindy and Dr. Fields wheeled the massive wolf toward the back room. She'd been eavesdropping on their conversation, so she'd heard the doctor order the DNA test.

She couldn't let them see the results when they came in. Celina had to get to them first, so she could switch them out with another canine. Since she received all the paperwork and documentation coming into the office, it should be simple enough to do.

The doctor and Mindy were baffled by the unique discovery, but Celina wasn't. She'd immediately identified the creature they'd found on the side of the road.

Sure, the animal looked a little different from the others. Less wolf, more monster, perhaps. Celina hadn't recognized it immediately, but once she'd gotten closer, she'd known.

She peered at it one last time before it disappeared into the recovery room. Its body was bigger and its head a few inches wider than the others of its kind. Its teeth looked longer and sharper, too. The only really surprising thing about the whole situation was that the animal was injured at all.

Celina had seen them in their other form many times. Watched them fight until they were bloody and almost unrecognizable. Each and every time they'd risen like nothing had happened. She'd always assumed they were invincible or close to it. The news that they weren't came as a relief.

No, there was no mistaking the massive animal lying on the table, but Celina couldn't exactly go in and tell them that they'd found a werewolf. A real, honest-to-goodness werewolf.

A thrill shot through her and Celina clasped her hands together. Today was her lucky day. She had prayed for an opportunity like this. Hoped it would occur. But deep down, never thought it would happen. Yet here it was laid out in front of her like a gift from above. It was a sign. The sign she'd been waiting for.

Izzy's warning floated in her head. *If you don't stay away from the monsters, they're going to end up killing you.*

Her best friend was wrong. Unlike Izzy, Celina wasn't afraid of these creatures. She understood them. They weren't all that different from humans. There were both good and bad ones. It was a distinction Izzy rarely made. She loved her best friend, but Celina wasn't about to pass up this chance.

It was the perfect opportunity to spend more than a single night with one of the Moonlight Kin. Be more than a chew toy that they nibbled on, rutted in, then passed around for others to sample.

Contrary to what those *Weres* believed, Celina wasn't anyone's plaything.

She tugged her shirt down to cover the scratches she'd received last week from her *date*. Marco had been a particularly energetic lover, but like the others, he hadn't bothered to call her after she'd gotten him off.

Celina had really thought that he liked her, until she saw him around town with another woman. Their eyes met, but Marco hadn't acknowledged her. She'd thought about confronting him, but Weres never responded well to aggression. Celina wouldn't have to worry about Marco after tonight.

A plan formulated in her head as she waited for Mindy to finish up. She'd nurse this one back to health and imprint her scent on it. All Celina needed to do was prove to the Were that she could care for it, make the creature feel indebted to her, then she would get him to claim her as his mate.

Mindy helped Dr. Fields get the animal into the cage. She stroked its head and cooed softly to it, to reassure the canine that it was safe.

"It won't wake up for a while," Dr. Fields said.

"I know," she said. "I just like to believe that it can hear me and knows that we're taking care of it."

He gave her a tired smile. "You have a good heart, Mindy, but I do worry about this job being too hard on you."

"I'm tougher than I look," Mindy said. A tongue brushed against the back of her hand. "He licked me."

Dr. Fields looked in the cage. "He couldn't have. He's still asleep and will be for a few more hours. You probably just brushed against his mouth."

Mindy frowned and looked at the snoring canine. She knew the difference between a lick and a brush. It had definitely been a lick. But since that type of thing wasn't worth arguing over, she let it go.

"I'm going to head home now."

Dr. Fields yawned. "Me too. See you in the afternoon."

Mindy glanced at her watch and winced. She was going to be a zombie in class tomorrow if she didn't get some sleep. The Ryans would have to wait for another girls' night. She looked at the animal and gave him one last pet, then turned off the lights.

"Goodnight, puppy," she murmured and left the room.

Mindy didn't see the black wolf raise its head. She didn't see its eyes begin to glow. She didn't see it lick its lips so it could taste her skin again. And she didn't hear it sniff the air, locking in her scent, so it would be able to find her again.

3

Gravel crunched under Nic La Croix's truck tires as he turned onto the long driveway. Trees and dense underbrush lined the road, leading him deeper into the woods. He ran his hand through his shaggy hair and the tension in his muscles released as wilderness surrounded him.

Nic didn't have long to enjoy the feeling. The tightness came right back as a steady thump, thump, thump reached his ears. So much for convening with nature. After a quarter-mile, the trees parted to reveal a crude gravel parking lot.

On the far side of the lot, a large wooden structure squatted like a toad against the tree-line. The roof slanted to the left and looked to be under imminent threat of collapse. Chipped red paint covered the front of the building, while ignoring the sides. The splash of color did little to disguise the building's deteriorated condition.

A flashing pink neon sign hung above the entrance to the bar. The first "T" and the last "S" of its name were burned out. Instead of spelling "Sticks", the sign now read "Sick."

The new name is more fitting for the shifter bar, Nic thought.

He stared at the crowded lot, debating whether to leave. The only parking spots left bordered the trees and were nowhere near the entrance. Not that it was a problem. The position would make it easier to get out when the time came. Nic looked at his watch. Not yet six o'clock and already packed. It would only get worse.

After a hard day's work, he wanted a beer, but Nic wasn't sure fighting the crowd would be worth it this close to the full moon. He glanced up at the sky. The sun hadn't set yet and the moon was already rising. Its pregnant appearance made all wolves anxious, but was especially difficult for the younger ones, who thought they had something to prove.

Restlessness snaked its way through Nic's body, leaving him edgy. The feeling was happening more and more lately, but had nothing to do with the moon and everything to do with not being bondmated.

Nic listened to the steady beat of the music and heard a crowd roar. The sound quickly morphed into howls. Blood simmered in his veins as he fought the urge to join in.

It had been two months since he'd moved off Aidan Fortier's estate and away from the pack. Two months since he'd sworn off fickle human females.

He'd always fallen too hard and too fast for his own good. It had gotten him hurt on more than one occasion, but this time had been the worst because he'd fallen for his Alpha's mate.

Nic couldn't bear to be around Aidan's mate, Jenna Dane, feeling the way he felt about her. Every day he watched her belly ripen with Aidan's child, and he couldn't help thinking what if...

It didn't matter that it was the man in him that wanted her, not the wolf. Pain was pain.

Next month Jenna would give birth, thanks to shifters' short gestation periods. Pregnancy wouldn't be possible if she wasn't truly Aidan's bondmate, but seeing her expectant, glowing, and happy only compounded his loneliness.

Maybe someday he'd get used to sleeping alone, but Nic had his doubts.

Once a pack animal, always a pack animal.

Being homesick for his pack was why he found himself at Sticks and not home at the little house he'd rented outside of town. The desire for a beer and to be around his own kind was a temptation he couldn't resist. Nic drove to the tree line and threw the truck into park, then climbed out. One beer, then he'd leave. Okay, maybe one and a half. It would take a lot more than that to impair a Were.

The music pumped hard, vibrating his chest as he strode toward the bar. There wasn't a cover charge for shifters, only humans. Not that many humans came out to this place or even knew about it. And the ones that did, knew the score going in.

Weres had groupies, just like rock bands. Their animalistic, insatiable nature drew them from hundreds of miles away. The humans who partied at Sticks came here for one reason and one reason only—to hook up with a shifter.

Nic wasn't looking for company, and he certainly wasn't looking for a fight, but he did want a beer. A nice cold one. For that, he'd put up with the loud music and the boisterous crowd.

"Hey, Derek," Nic said. "How's it going?"

The burly doorman grinned, flashing long canines. "Different day, same shit."

"I hear you. Lucien Bellard working tonight?" Nic asked.

His best friend bartended most nights, but he did get off work on occasion. When that happened, he didn't show up here. He took off for the mountains.

"Yep, he's behind the bar, keeping a close eye on the pups," Derek said. "A bunch of them came in earlier itching to test their claws. Remember when you were that young?"

Nic laughed. "Hell no! I was never that young."

Derek chuckled. "Me neither."

It was common for young Weres to come to Sticks. The place allowed them to blow off steam and test their skills. Pack life was all about hierarchy. Young wolves were constantly looking for ways to better their positions. Nic didn't have to worry about that anymore. He'd earned his spot in Aidan's west coast pack through blood, brains, and brute strength.

Nic leaned forward and waited for Derek to sniff him. It didn't matter who or what you were, everyone got sniffed on their way into Sticks. It was a surefire way to keep out the troublemakers and to identify the humans. If you weren't pack, you got your hand stamped with a wolf paw. It was an inside joke that only regulars recognized.

"You're good to go." Derek hiked his thumb over his shoulder. "You came on the right night. The band's supposed to be good tonight."

"Probably won't stay that long," Nic said. "Just here for a beer."

The bouncer shrugged, then gave him a look that said "suit yourself."

The inside of the bar was even more crowded than the parking lot. Most of the worn tables were already occupied, and the only stool available sat at the end of the long, polished oak bar. Weres lined the bar three deep. They kicked up sawdust beneath their feet as they waited to get served.

Nic made his way to the end of the bar and scanned the crowd. He didn't think many from Aidan's compound would be there, but it didn't hurt to check. He wouldn't mind shooting the breeze with a familiar face.

A dark head popped up above the crowd. Lucien waved to him, his green eyes glittering mischievously.

Nic nodded in acknowledgment. It had been a while since he and Lucien had had a chance to catch up, but it didn't look like that would change tonight.

Two pups knocked younger Weres aside as they pushed their way to the front of the crowd. Nic didn't recognize them, which didn't mean much since the west coast Moonlight Kin were spread out over several states, but he did recognize the type.

Impatience oozed from their pores. Some pups naturally fell into their pack position. Others fought for purchase. These two fell into the latter camp. Their stance screamed aggression. In a shifter bar, that was a good way to get your ass kicked.

Nic watched dispassionately as they stopped at the bar and waved money in front of Lucien's face. *I wouldn't do that if I were you,* he thought. His best friend didn't have a lot of patience for assholes.

Lucien's lip curled and a growl rumbled out of his wide chest. The Celtic tattoos that started at his neck and encased both arms rippled as he tensed. Smart pups took a step back to give Lucien space. The two with the money in their hands didn't move.

Some pups just had to learn the hard way.

A claw came out and speared the money, yanking the bills from the closest pup's hand. Lucien tossed the money into a tip jar, then yelled, "Next!"

The startled pup opened his mouth to complain, but must've got a look at Lucien's expression and changed his mind.

Nic sighed. He wasn't in the mood to put up with this kind of crap tonight. He turned to leave, but before he could go, a beer slid down the bar and stopped in front of him.

He looked over in time to see Lucien grin, then his friend went back to filling orders. The two pups who'd been flashing money glared at him. Nic raised his pint glass in salute, then took a deep swig. The cold, crisp flavor of hops and barley exploded on his tongue. He leaned his back against the edge of the bar and scanned the crowd.

Several groupies had already snagged a table near the front, close to the band. The location put them in the position to be seen by everyone, which Nic supposed was the point.

The band was still setting up their equipment. He couldn't tell if they were human or not. He spotted a few wolf paw stamps in the crowd, but not many. Nic made a mental note to avoid them and went back to enjoying his beer.

A few minutes later there was a knock on the bar. Nic turned to find Lucien smiling at him.

"You look miserable as ever," Nic said.

His friend had a perpetual smile on his face and took delight in the little things, especially if those things came in the form of aggravating a friend. But there was more to Lucien than that. Every once in a while the mask would slip and Nic would glimpse the darkness he kept hidden from the world.

Nic had never asked what caused the shadows. He figured if Lucien wanted to let him know, he would. Until then, he'd be there whenever his friend needed him and would continue to keep up pretenses.

"You're the one lurking at the end of the bar, my friend. How do you expect to meet anyone with that sour expression on your face?" Lucien asked.

"I don't," Nic said. "I'm just here for the beer and your stellar company."

Lucien laughed. "Then you're in luck, because tonight I am in rare form."

"I can see that." Nic indicated to the pups jockeying for position.

Lucien followed his gaze, and his green eyes glittered with deadly intent. "The problems they present can be easily solved with a quick trip around back."

"Is that what you plan to do later?" Nic asked, eyeing his friend.

"Ah, *mon ami*, I'm a lover, not a fighter. You know that." Lucien winked.

Nic snorted. Lucien was definitely a lover. He *loved* women. Nic had seen him with an endless string of ladies. One look from the dark-haired, green-eyed Frenchman and women fell to their knees. None of them stayed long, and that suited Lucien just fine. In that respect, they were polar opposites. Nic wanted nothing more than to have a mate to go home to at the end of the day.

As for not being a fighter, there was no way in hell his friend could ever convince him that was the case. The darkness in his green gaze was no illusion. He hadn't come by it from anything other than pain.

"What do you have to do to get a drink around here?" someone shouted.

The muscles in Lucien's arms flexed and his hands tightened on the bar. Lucien's nails lengthened, burrowing into the grainy fibers. Nic heard the wood groan under the pressure.

"You'd better get going, Lover Boy, before the crowd turns on you,"

Nic said.

Lucien glanced at him. "It wouldn't be the first time." His smile returned, but with a touch of melancholy. *"Au revoir, mon ami."*

* * *

Mindy stared at the lights in the distance and debated whether to turn her car around. Coming here had seemed like a good idea.

She'd told Celina that she knew how to have fun. It still irked her that Izzy had made Celina promise never to bring her here. Despite her irritation with the women, it had still taken Mindy two weeks to work up the courage to come.

Not that it mattered anymore. Izzy was gone and Celina no longer cared what Mindy did. She was too preoccupied with her new boyfriend, Slade. They'd been dating for a little over a week, which was positively long term for Celina. Every time Mindy saw them together, which wasn't often, they appeared to be joined at the tongue.

She was genuinely happy that Celina had finally found a steady guy, who liked her for who she was, but it also drove home the fact that Mindy went home to an empty house every night.

Mindy stared out the window. The only parking spaces left were by the woods far away from the entrance. Not the safest of locations. She should just go. This was insane.

No one in their right mind went to a bar alone, especially a woman. Wasn't she always telling Celina that? Yet here she sat outside of Sticks, considering whether to go inside.

Mindy tried to remember the last time she'd hit the bars. Between college classes and work, there hadn't been a lot of time to socialize.

If her calculations were correct—and they were—then it had been a year since she'd painted the town red. Okay, mauve. With her sister gone, she couldn't use Izzy as an excuse for not having a social life anymore. The music thumped and her body automatically swayed in her seat.

Just one dance, a little voice in her head whispered. *One dance won't hurt anyone.*

Neither Celina nor Izzy would ever know that she'd been there. Especially if she didn't stay long.

The music called out to her with its siren song. Mindy wanted to be the fun person she used to be before everything changed. She wanted to experience that kind of freedom again, if only for one night. Was that so much to ask?

She parked her car and climbed out. Gravel crunched under her shoes. Mindy glanced at her vintage pumps. They weren't made for traversing rock, but she saw no other way to get to the bar, unless she suddenly sprouted wings. Mindy apologized to her favorite pair of shoes, then toddled to the entrance.

Her footsteps faltered when she caught sight of the man checking IDs at the door. Barrel chested with arms the size of telephone poles, the man wore faded blue jeans and a ripped T-shirt that had some kind of biker emblem on it that she didn't recognize.

When his gaze landed on her, his light green eyes appeared to glow in the dark. The illusion only lasted a moment, but it was long enough for Mindy. Stories of monsters flooded her mind. She wanted to turn tail and run, but she wasn't dressed for sprinting. Mindy's knees locked in place.

How many years had she put her own wishes aside to cater to her sister's whims? How many lies had she told on her behalf? Mindy couldn't allow Izzy's dark fantasies to prevent her from living her life. Not anymore.

Instead of running, she forced herself to focus on her clothes. Mindy tugged at the skirt of her vintage red dress, though it already dropped below her knees. The nice outfit usually made her feel pretty and confident. But right now she'd willingly trade the dress and her favorite shoes for a comfy pair of jeans.

The doorman came out of the shadowed entryway and slowly approached.

Mindy quaked in her pumps and craned her neck to look at him. "You lost?" he asked.

It took her a moment to find her voice. "N-n-no. A friend told me about this place. She thought I-I-I'd like it."

One dark brow rose as he stared at her clothing. He didn't believe her. "What exactly did your friend tell you?"

Mindy's confidence wavered. Sweat laced her palms. She rubbed her hands along her skirt and swallowed hard. "Just that Sticks was a fun place." Her voice cracked.

He stared for a moment more, then shrugged. "Let me see your ID."

Mindy retrieved her license from her purse. Her fingers shook as she handed it to him. He sniffed, then returned her ID. The man settled back onto his stool and took out a stamp.

"How much is the cover charge?" she asked.

"Hold out your hand," he said.

She did as he asked.

He stamped a glowing wolf paw beneath her knuckles. "Have fun." The cheerful sentiment was ruined by his anxious expression.

"Thank you." Mindy put her license in her purse and stepped through the door. Her legs quivered when she saw the worn tables scattered around the room and sawdust on the floor. On the other side of the dance floor, a band was setting up their equipment.

Mindy tugged at her skirt again and waited for someone to greet her. After a minute, it was obvious no one was coming to show her to a table.

The music was louder now. It pumped out of the speakers, occupying the crowd until the live band started. The beat called to her, trying to lure her to the dance floor.

Mindy glanced around the bar. The place was packed and *exactly* like Celina described it. There were at least ten men for every woman in the bar, and most were exceedingly good-looking, especially the dark-haired, tattooed Adonis behind the bar. He was so gorgeous that he bordered on being pretty.

He smiled at Mindy and her knees went weak. She'd never be able to handle a man like him. Not in her wildest dreams, but flirting with the bartender never hurt.

She took a step forward and several heads turned in her direction. Mindy looked behind her, but there was no one there. The men sniffed in unison. She resisted the urge to do the same. She'd showered after work and put on a little perfume, but not too much. Or at least she'd thought so until she came in here.

Two guys broke away from the pack. Mindy giggled nervously at the metaphor, though it was fitting given the large group. They quickly approached her.

"Hello," the brown-haired one said. "My name's Marco. Marco Faretti. This here is Emmett."

"Hi. I'm Mindy." Every eye in the place was focused on them.

"You look like you could use a drink," Marco said.

Her hands trembled as she smoothed her dress. "Yes, I could." Mindy let them drag her to the bar. She had no intention of staying there long. Not with the music calling to her.

They passed a man with sandy brown hair and haunting dark blue eyes that she hadn't noticed when she'd first walked in. Though how she could've missed him was a mystery. He leaned against the bar casually watching everyone around him, including her.

Like the doorman and bartender, the man was big and unusually tall. His rugged good looks were understated, but striking.

The man smiled at her. The act transformed his face and stole the breath from her lungs. Marco and Emmett faded away, along with the rest of the bar. Mindy smiled back, hoping her nerves didn't show.

Outwardly the man appeared to be having a good time, but Mindy recognized lonely when she saw it. After all, it stared back at her every time she looked in the mirror.

His gaze stole across her, leaving heat in its wake.

Mindy's heart raced. It had been a long time since she'd experienced that kind of attraction to a man.

Emmett put his arm around her.

The move shocked Mindy, breaking the spell between them. She casually shifted until his arm dropped. Maybe he wouldn't notice.

Undeterred, Emmett did it again.

This time Mindy looked at him before lifting his hand and removing his arm from around her shoulders. She didn't want the man at the end of the bar to get the wrong impression, and she didn't want to encourage Emmett.

Just because he and Marco had approached her first didn't mean that they had dibs on her. No one had dibs on her. Mindy wanted to make that clear upfront. She was grateful that they'd been so nice, but her gratitude only went so far.

The man at the end of the bar continued to watch her. Without warning, he suddenly came to his feet and rounded the bar. His gaze never wavered as he made his way toward her.

Mindy took a deep breath to calm her nerves. In her mind, she ran through a dozen ways of how to say hello. Before she could put any of them into practice, his footsteps faltered and he stopped. His disarming smile slowly faded and he returned to his spot at the end of the bar.

What just happened? Had I inadvertently done something? Had Emmett's clumsy attempt to hit on me dissuaded the man?

The disappointment swirling inside surprised Mindy. She glanced at her clothes and wished once more that she'd worn something casual. This wouldn't have happened to Celina or Isabel. They both had the ability to wrap men around their fingers.

Game playing of any kind gave Mindy hives. She'd always been a "what you see is what you get" kind of girl, and she'd been okay with that until tonight. Now Mindy wished just once that she were someone different. The kind of woman that the man at the end of the bar wouldn't be able to resist. The kind of woman who was brave enough to approach him without throwing up on his shoes.

If only I were that kind of woman... Mindy sighed.

The music changed to a more up-tempo beat. Mindy slipped away from Marco and Emmett, away from the man at the end of the bar, and away from her troubles.

She strolled out onto the dance floor, where a few other girls were already dancing. Mindy allowed the music to seep inside her, until she could feel every note pulsing in her bones. Her body swayed gently at first, then found the rhythm.

When was the last time she felt this free?

Mindy couldn't remember. Didn't care. She let the music wash over her and move her body. Her hips swayed and she ran her hands down her sides as she rocked to the beat.

Nic couldn't tear his gaze away from the woman in red as she swayed provocatively on the dance floor. That vintage dress she wore accentuated her voluptuous curves and fair skin, making her appear luminous in the low lighting. Her fluid movements hinted at the passion she kept buttoned up behind that high collar.

She looked young—innocent, but he'd never been good at guessing anyone's true age. The woman rolled her hips and ran her hands over her body.

Drool formed in his mouth. Nic had to swallow hard to keep from embarrassing himself. Every muscle in his body tightened and his skin burned. He reminded himself again that this woman was human and not one of the Kin.

Nic watched her dance until the song ended. He was awash with disappointment when she slowly strolled back to the bar, back to the pups who'd been nipping at her cute kitten heels.

Mindy made her way back to the bar and ordered a wine spritzer.

"Nice dance," the striking bartender said, then grinned.

"Thanks," she said, but Mindy hadn't danced for him or anyone else. That dance had been for her.

The bartender quickly made her drink, then placed the cocktail in front of her. "If you need anything else, just ask for Lucien," he said.

She smiled and gave him a quick nod.

A moment later, Lucien added five more drinks to go with the first. "I didn't order these," she said.

He looked at her, his green eyes mesmerizing. "I know, *jolie femme*. They did." Lucien indicated to the men behind her.

"Oh." Mindy reached into her purse for her money.

Lucien stopped her with a light touch to her hand. "It's already covered."

A growl came from the end of the bar. Mindy turned to see who'd made the odd noise, and so did everyone else at the bar. The sandy-haired man she'd been attracted to earlier was staring at the bartender's hand with a mutinous expression on his face.

"Well now, that is interesting," the bartender said, slowly removing his hand from hers.

"Did he just growl?" Mindy asked. She couldn't have heard him correctly. People didn't growl.

The bartender blinked. It was the only indication she got that let her know that she'd surprised him with the question.

"I mean no offense when I say this," Lucien said. "But I think perhaps you're in the wrong establishment."

Mindy thought the same thing, but stubbornness kept her rooted in place. Isabel wasn't the only one in her family capable of having a good time. She was determined to prove to her sister, to Celina, and to herself that some part of the "real" Mindy still existed. All she needed was the chance.

"I wish people would stop saying that," she murmured.

Why did everyone think they knew what was best for me? She wasn't a child. She was twenty-five years old.

With a grim expression on his lovely face, he gave her a slight bow. "As you wish."

Nic watched the woman order a drink. Sparks flew as she and Lucien spoke. The attraction between them was undeniable. Almost as strong as what they'd experienced before he discovered what she was. Lucien touched her lightly. Nic's wolf grumbled before he could stop it.

Everyone turned to look at him with shocked expressions on their faces. Everyone but Lucien. His best friend was having a hard time keeping a straight face.

Lucien said something to the woman, then walked to the end of the bar where Nic stood. "It's nice to know that there's still some life in you, *mon ami*. I was beginning to wonder." Speculation replaced some of his amusement.

"Funny," Nic said. "What can you tell me about her?"

Why had he asked? He didn't want to know her, didn't want anything to do with her. He wasn't looking to hook up with a human, even one as delectable as her.

Lucien cocked his hip against the bar. "Not much," he said. "Just that she doesn't belong here."

4

The alcohol continued to flow, giving the men circling around Mindy liquid courage. She nursed her wine spritzer and danced alone a few more times.

The men grew more brazen. Marco and Emmett were determined to get her drunk and weren't above showing their displeasure over the fact that she hadn't touched the other drinks in front of her.

The man at the end of the bar continued to stare at her, but it was obvious he wasn't going to act upon their attraction. He'd made that perfectly clear. Once again, Mindy thought about approaching him, but the idea abandoned her when she noted his grim expression.

She'd never been good at reading people, only animals. People were complicated. Animals' needs were simple. It was why she'd gone into veterinary medicine.

Sticks continued to fill with people. The press of warm bodies around her made it hard to breathe. Emmett and Marco had been competing for the past hour to see who could get her to agree to a date. They were both beyond cute. Too bad they weren't her type. Deflecting their constant advances wore on her, and eventually she'd had enough.

Mindy pushed the last of her drink away and stood. She couldn't take it anymore. Celina was right. This wasn't her type of place. She waved goodbye to Lucien, then stepped away from the bar.

"Excuse me," she said to Marco and Emmett when she squeezed by.

"The bathrooms are down the hall on the right," Marco said.

"Thanks," Mindy said. "But I think I'm just going to head home. It was nice meeting you both."

"Don't go," Marco said. "You just got here."

Mindy glanced at her watch. She'd been there for over an hour. To a homebody, that felt like an eternity. "It's late and I have to work tomorrow. Thank you again for the drink." She didn't wait for them to respond. Mindy simply pushed past them and walked away.

She took a deep breath when she got outside. The air filled her lungs and cooled her heated skin. Mindy toddled across the parking lot toward her car. Her PJs and slippers were calling to her. Maybe she'd manage to get in an hour of studying before she went to bed.

"You're such a coward," she muttered. "You should've at least walked up to him and said hello."

It was too late now. She'd probably never see the man at the end of the bar again. Mindy was so lost in thought that she didn't hear the footsteps coming up behind her until they were upon her.

Marco and Emmett suddenly appeared out of the dark. "W-what are you guys doing?" She looked around, hoping someone was nearby, but they were alone.

"We wanted to make sure you got to your car okay," Marco said.

"Yeah, it's dark. Anything could happen," Emmett added.

"Thanks, but I'm already here." She pointed behind her.

Undeterred, the men kept coming. Mindy backed up and didn't stop until she hit her car. The second she touched the metal doorframe, the men caged her with their bodies.

"Guys, I told you that I have to go home."

"We thought you might be up for a private party. You know, just the three us." Marco ran his fingers along her arm.

Fear warred with anger. Was this kind of behavior why Izzy made Celina promise never to invite her to the bar? Ugh, she'd been so stupid. She should have listened to Celina and just stayed away.

"I think I'd better leave," she said.

Emmett moved in front of her door handle, cutting off her escape. "It's early," he said. "We won't keep you long. We can make it quick, so you can get home and have a good night's sleep."

"As appealing as that sounds, I'm not interested," Mindy said with as much sarcasm as she could muster. She could barely hear the words over her pounding heart.

Marco snorted. "If you weren't interested, you wouldn't have come here."

"I came here to dance," Mindy said. "Not to meet people."

"Come on, baby," Marco said. "Stop playing coy. Nobody comes to Sticks for the music."

"I do," Emmett said.

"Shut up," Marco said. "Nobody is talking to you." He ground himself against her so she could feel the bulge protruding from the front of his pants. "You'll have a good time. It'll almost be like dancing. Promise."

Emmett laughed. "At least it'll be memorable."

Marco met his gaze and smiled, then he licked the side of her neck.

Mindy opened her mouth to scream, but Marco clamped his hand over her lips.

"Shh," he said. "Save the screaming for later."

Nic was determined to finish his beer now that the woman in red had gone, but he couldn't shake the unease coursing through his veins.

He'd watched the pups follow her out. They could be just planning to party, but this close to the full moon there was a chance their hormones were overriding their good sense.

They wouldn't rape her. That crime brought an automatic death sentence from the pack. But they could become excessively aggressive while trying to convince her to do what they wanted.

He wasn't a white knight. And he certainly wasn't the type to rescue anyone. If a human came here looking for a good time with a Were, then who was he to interfere?

Nic swore under his breath and shoved his hand into his pocket to pull out some cash. He tossed the money onto the bar and waved goodbye to Lucien. His friend gave him a knowing smirk, then went right back to work.

He rushed out the door and headed through the parking lot. He didn't get far before he heard sounds of a struggle taking place. Nic bolted in the direction of the sound. He found the two pups clumsily groping the blonde and trying to convince her to go into the woods. Her brown eyes were wide with alarm and she stank of fear.

Fury overtook him and Nic growled low. So low that only the two Weres could hear him. Their heads whipped around to confront the threat. Matching sets of glowing eyes stared at him.

"Leave the lady alone," Nic said.

"Don't you have somewhere you need to be, old man?" the more daring of the two asked.

His friend shuffled his feet, putting some distance between him and the woman. Sweat broke out across his forehead and his Adam's apple convulsed in his throat.

At least one of them is smart, Nic thought.

Thirty wasn't exactly ancient, but he could see how a couple of twenty-somethings might think so. Nic didn't know these two, and they certainly didn't know him or they wouldn't be so mouthy.

"I'm not going to tell you again, *son*." Menace dripped from Nic's words.

"We're just having ourselves a good time. Aren't we, sweetheart?" The young pup grabbed the woman's arm, and she squeaked. "You need to move along before you get hurt."

At 230 pounds, Nic wasn't exactly a lightweight. Maybe the pup thought that since there were two of them that they could easily take him. It was a mistake they were going to regret. He might be naturally laidback, but he hadn't reached his position in the pack by being a pushover.

Nic's gaze shifted to the frightened woman. "Get in your car and get out of here."

She gave him a jerky nod and reached for her car door. The second she opened it, the young pup closest to her slammed the door shut. The woman flinched.

"You aren't going anywhere." His gaze never left Nic's as he spoke to her.

Nic shrugged. "Have it your way."

The pup farthest from the woman launched himself at Nic. Nic swung his fist, catching the pup under the chin. The Were flew through the air and landed on his butt. He shook his head, trying to clear it, and struggled to his feet.

Before he could right himself, the other Were attacked. His body slammed into Nic, taking them both to the ground. The pup got in a couple of good blows before Nic managed to throw him off.

Nic got to his feet, only to be punched in the face by the Were he'd taken down first. The blow caught him beneath the eye, slicing his skin open. Blood trickled over his face onto the front of his shirt. The next punch he dodged, but the pup's fist still managed to clip his ear. The move pissed him off.

"Enough!" Nic shouted, and tossed the pup at his friend. They collided, and both fell to the ground.

Nic faced the two young Weres, keeping his back to the woman. While he glared at them, he allowed a hint of his wolf to surface. The world turned to gray as his eyes shifted and his incisors lengthened. Power swept out in front of him, washing over them.

The two Weres paled and scrambled back.

"Go! Now!" The words came out garbled, but his meaning was clear.

"Come on," the smarter of the two said. He grabbed his friend's arm, dragging him away.

"This isn't finished," the brazen one shouted before he left.

Yes, it is, Nic thought.

Mindy never imagined that anyone would ever fight over her. "Cute" didn't inspire men to lay down their lives. Sure, she'd heard about fights happening and had seen them many times in the animal kingdom, when a male was fighting for the right to mate, but she'd never experienced it firsthand.

Celina had told her how thrilling the experience was. At the time, Mindy had thought Celina's need for constant drama and reassurance had led her to exaggerate, but she hadn't. At least not entirely.

Mindy couldn't deny the thrill skating along her spine or the sudden unwelcome surge of arousal. *What did that say about her?*

When her would-be savior had first arrived, Mindy wasn't sure if it was a good thing or if the situation had just gone from bad to worse. Now she had no doubt that he'd saved her life, or at least saved her from something truly unpleasant.

Her eyes were drawn to the play of muscles beneath his T-shirt as he watched the men who'd been hassling her leave. He was *magnificent*. Her gaze slowly lowered and the impressive view got even better.

Her heart continued to pound, but now it was from more than fear. And Mindy wasn't at all certain how she planned to handle that.

Between the impending full moon and the adrenaline pumping through him, Nic was having a difficult time maintaining a civilized façade.

Weres only fought over females for the opportunity to mate. His body hardened as bone-deep instincts attempted to arrest his control. Nic clamped down hard on his feral nature.

The breeze shifted, bringing her sweet scent to him. Sex was the last thing he wanted from a human—even one that smelled so delicious. He gritted his teeth and clenched his fists. He had to get his wolf leashed before he looked at her. His body was making demands that couldn't be met.

Nic decided his only recourse was to make sure she was okay, then leave before he did something they'd both regret. Nic took a deep breath and faced her, determined to get it over with. The second their eyes met, his resolve crumbled like clay in the hot sun.

5

Mindy was used to dealing with injured animals, not humans. So nothing could've prepared her for the jolt that struck the moment his dark blue eyes met hers.

Blood smeared his cheek and dust covered his shirt. There was something wild about his gaze, something utterly untamed. It drew her in when every instinct screamed at her to escape.

Mindy couldn't leave him. Not like this. Not after he'd fought to protect her. She pushed away from the car and tried to touch him.

"Don't!" The single word was torn from his chest as he grabbed her wrist. His hard, unyielding grip bordered on painful.

"You're hurt." She hesitated, then pressed on, drawn to the heat simmering in his eyes. The moment her fingers made contact with his taut face, the man groaned and pulled her into his arms.

His lips came down upon hers before Mindy could take a breath. He kissed her with such stark hunger that her body immediately went up in flames. The wildness inside her that had been dormant for so long flared to life and pushed aside all logic.

Mindy's body melted into his hard chest. Just for tonight, she didn't want to be the responsible sibling. She wanted to be someone other than "Monotonous Mindy." She wanted to be...herself for once.

She didn't notice that he'd released her arm until she'd wrapped her hands around his neck and sunk her fingers into his soft hair. By then it was too late to pull back.

Alarm bells rang in Nic's head. He immediately hit snooze and kept kissing her. He couldn't get enough of her sweet taste. He'd been prepared to let her walk away. Planned to make her leave. Then she'd gone and done the unthinkable. She'd touched him.

The heat from her fingertips incinerated his good intentions, sending them up in smoke. Nic pulled her into his arms and kissed her.

For one insane moment, he worried that he was no better than the Weres who'd been trying to take advantage of her. The thought unraveled when her blunt teeth sank into his lower lip and she ran her tongue across the tender bite.

Nic shuddered and his big body jerked, then his hands locked tighter around her. He kneaded her round bottom, then cupped her and lifted her off her feet. She fit perfectly in his hands, as if she were made for him. The thought ratcheted up his need, and Nic grew harder.

Despite her petite size and her vintage dress, the woman managed to wrap her legs around his hips. Nic groaned into her mouth as the ridge of his maleness collided with her feminine heat. If he didn't get inside her soon, his head would explode.

He carried her away from her car, away from the entrance to Sticks, to his pick-up truck. They were near enough to the tree line and far enough from the bar to ensure a level of privacy they wouldn't otherwise have. Still, Nic scanned the area with his acute senses to ensure they were alone before lowering his tailgate and setting her down upon it.

One hand continued to massage her lush bottom, while the other reached under her dress. He willed himself to slow, let them catch their breath and allow good sense to return, but he couldn't. It was like he was being driven by an unseen force that was determined to take, to seize.

Nic chalked his urgency up to the moon's influence, though he couldn't recall this ever happening before. His exploring fingers encountered lace, then struck moisture and scalding heat.

Just one taste. That was all he wanted. That's all he needed. He pulled his hand out and licked the moisture off his fingers.

Her taste burst over his tongue and he nearly dropped to his knees. Overwhelmed by the sensations, Nic growled in the back of his throat. He'd never tasted anything like her. So rich, so creamy, so addictively delicious.

Nic needed more. He hiked her skirt up and ripped her panties off. "I'll buy you new ones," he rasped, as her feminine musk surrounded them.

The heady aroma betrayed her eagerness. It also fueled the fire roaring through his veins. Nic's lips found hers once more.

He wanted to bury his nose between her thighs. Wanted to lick her depths until she quivered beneath him, begging him to take her, but Nic couldn't wait—and neither could she, if the needy whimpers coming from her throat were any indication.

He deepened the kiss, swirling his tongue around her mouth, trying to capture her essence. Each did their best to devour the other.

The woman pulled at his shirt and ran her fingers along his back, then grasped his ass and yanked him closer.

Her petals unfurled for him as he sank his fingers into her scalding heat. She instantly tightened around him. Nic waited a heartbeat, then added another finger and continued his intimate exploration. She felt like heaven and smelled like candy-coated sin. Nic couldn't get enough of her.

With a twist of his hand, he found her swollen flesh. He stroked the tender nub, driving her higher, leaving her teetering on the edge of oblivion.

"Please," she gasped.

Her begging didn't sit well with him. If anything, he should be the one groveling at her feet. Nic reached into his back pocket and pulled out a condom. He couldn't catch any human diseases, and one sniff told him that she was disease free. There was no chance he could get her pregnant. Weres could only procreate with their bondmates, and even then, they had to be marked. But the prophylactic would ease her mind.

Nic ignored the ache in his jaw and focused on the one in his pants. He popped the button on his jeans and his zipper hissed as he eased it down. Her hands were on him in an instant, taking his breath and making him weak. Nic gritted his teeth and prayed for strength to hold out long enough to get the condom on.

Mindy's body was on fire. She'd never been this brazen in her life. She'd also never wanted a man this much. If she weren't in total control of her faculties, Mindy would swear she'd been possessed. She had never understood what made sex such an all-consuming big deal—until now.

She pulled back from their kiss and saw him sheathe himself. His immense size obviously extended to every part of his body. For one crazy minute, she didn't think this would be anatomically possible.

"Wait!" Mindy held her hand against his chest as he positioned the thick head at her entrance. Was she really going to do this? Was this really her?

He clenched his jaw and his big body trembled, but her savior stopped instantly. "Have you changed your mind?" he asked, his expression pained.

Had she? Mindy stared into his dark blue eyes and found herself falling once more. No, she wanted this. Wanted him. Had from the moment she'd laid eyes on him. If only for tonight, she'd have him and be the kind of woman she'd always known she could be.

"No." Mindy shook her head. "Just needed to catch my breath."

"Thank the moon!" he said, then seized her mouth once more.

Mindy's thoughts scattered to the stars as he sent her sailing across a sea of pure sensation. He brushed her entrance, then ran himself up and down her moist cleft. Once he was covered in her juices, he pulled back and thrust forward, impaling her.

Nic swallowed her shocked cry, then tried to catch his breath as his body adjusted to the vise-like hold she had on it. He wasn't a small man, but he hadn't expected her to be quite so tight. Nic quivered as he tried to hold himself still inside her pulsing core.

For a moment, he'd thought she was a virgin and his heart had nearly stopped. She wasn't, but the woman was blissfully snug. Snug enough to let him know that it had been a while since she'd had a man inside her.

The realization left him feeling ridiculously pleased. He kissed her gently and slowly sucked on the tip of her tongue, savoring her passion, while he waited for her to relax.

Her body's grip on him eventually eased. Nic carefully rocked his hips to test her readiness.

She whimpered, then sighed.

The woman melted around him, while her big brown eyes shimmered with desire. Nic found himself drowning in their chocolaty depths, wanting to spend eternity there. All sense of self-preservation went out the window.

Lost in her eyes, he thrust again, gliding smoothly into her. She sank her fingernails into his forearms and tugged. Nic dropped onto his elbows. The move crushed the ripe swell of her breasts against his unyielding chest. Her nipples beaded instantly.

Nic pulled his mouth away from hers and nibbled on her earlobe. She hooked her ankles around him and canted her hips. He slipped further into her. Nic shuddered. The ache in his jaw returned with a vengeance and his lips automatically strayed to her delicate neck.

Her erratic pulse jumped beneath his lips. She was so soft, so sweet... so perfect. He licked the spot where her neck and shoulder met. The taste of her intensified and changed.

Nic's incisors lengthened. The urge to bite her was so strong that it burned through his soul.

Do it! an insidious voice whispered.

Nic jerked his head away.

His wolf snarled.

What was wrong with his beast? It shouldn't be doing that. It shouldn't *want* to do that. He couldn't believe how easy it had been to let his wolf take control and to forget that she was human.

The woman writhed beneath him. His lips found her pebbled nipples through her dress and he sucked hard. Nic wanted to bare her for his greedy eyes to feast upon, taste what his senses detected, but there wasn't time. It was far too dangerous with his control so tenuous.

His hands latched on to her full hips and he picked up speed. The first ripple struck. She sobbed and her body clamped down on him. The urgency inside of Nic grew. He couldn't seem to get deep enough or move fast enough to satiate his beast. Then, the unthinkable happened...

Nic began to *swell*.

At first he was too stunned to react, convinced he was mistaken. Once the shock wore off, panic struck. Nic tried to pull out, but he it was too late. His body had already locked with hers. He couldn't budge more than an inch in either direction.

"No!" he shouted, as the first of his orgasms struck, blinding him with passion.

Somewhere in the distance, Nic heard his wolf bark with laughter.

He was everywhere.

Mindy had no idea she could be so *full* and so hungry at the same time. His body blanketed hers, blocking out the stars. What they were doing was insane. She was insane, but Mindy couldn't bring herself to feel an ounce of regret. She couldn't manage anything beyond the searing pleasure he was giving her.

He surged forward, burying himself deep, and expanded inside her. The tremors that started a moment ago increased. The delicious shudders turned into quakes as her body erupted.

His hands latched on to her hips and he ground himself into her.

Mindy's back bowed off the truck bed as something exploded inside of her. She couldn't see, couldn't hear anything but the blood roaring in her ears.

He grunted and doubled his efforts. He wasn't thrusting as deeply as before, but he continued to ride her body like the hounds of hell were nipping at his heels.

He drove Mindy headfirst into another shattering release. As she tumbled over the edge into oblivion, she heard him bellow.

The sound morphed into something primal, almost animalistic. It made her ears ring, but Mindy didn't care. She was pretty sure she'd just died and gone to heaven.

6

Nic wasn't sure what just happened. One minute he'd been so lost inside her that the world had disappeared and the next his wolf had taken over. How long had they been lying here locked together?

No, not locked together. Not anymore. He could move again. What was he going to do? How could he explain that this should never have happened—had never happened before—when he didn't understand himself?

Nic expected to see contempt and accusation. At the very least confusion over what had occurred, since it wasn't every day a human experienced such a thing. But none of those emotions were visible. Instead, acceptance greeted him.

How could she feel that way after what he'd just done to her? Her selflessness only added to his sense of guilt. Nic took a moment to study her.

Her swollen lips, sleepy brown eyes, and mussed blonde hair made her look like a woman who'd been well loved. The sight of her stole the breath from his lungs.

She couldn't be the one. She just couldn't be. It wasn't possible.

He needed to think. Needed to get away from her to clear his head. Nic didn't trust himself. Didn't trust his wolf. He wasn't convinced any of this was real.

The woman stirred beneath him.

Nic took a choppy breath and pushed himself up. "You okay?" he asked, hoping his voice sounded steady.

Color flooded her face, matching her wrinkled red dress. She nodded. "That was amazing."

More like life altering, he thought, but didn't say so.

The sound of gravel crunching and music pounding came rushing at him. He remembered where they were and why they were here. They were still alone, but wouldn't be for long. Shame warred with embarrassment, but neither could contend with the confusion running rampant through him.

"I'm sorry," he murmured, and slipped out of her.

Nic helped the woman up so she could straighten her clothes. While she did that, he removed the condom and pulled his jeans up. He shoved the used latex into his pocket.

The woman buried her face in her hands. "I can't believe we did that here of all places. Anyone could've wandered by."

Nic wanted to reassure her that that wouldn't have happened, but he couldn't. The second he'd entered her, he'd been gone. Her body had transported him to another world. A world that felt dangerously like home. A world he didn't dare trust. He ran a shaky hand through his hair.

"I-" The word tangled in his throat.

"You don't have to apologize. You don't have to say anything. We're both adults. I'm just as guilty of poor judgment here as you are," she said.

She took a step and wobbled. Nic instinctively reached out to steady her, and the heat that had engulfed them reignited. He dropped his hand and asked for her keys. She handed them to him.

Nic walked her back to her car and opened the door. Out of habit, he climbed in and started the engine for her. The car sputtered to life, then immediately made a pinging noise.

He frowned. "How long has it been doing that?" Nic asked.

"A while," she said, unable to meet his gaze. "I'll get it taken care of."

He opened his mouth to offer to fix it for her, but closed it when he saw her mottled face. Nic climbed out and waited for her to slip behind the wheel.

There was no sense dragging the awkward moment out. It was obvious what this was. Anything else was a fluke of the moon. So why did he find himself lingering next to her door, reluctant to see her leave?

The wind shifted, carrying with it an all-too- familiar scent. Nic stiffened and slowly scanned the woods. He didn't spot the two pups, but they were there. Somewhere. How long had they been there? Had they been watching the whole time?

No! He shook his head. He would've known.

Something vicious snarled inside him and raised its furry head. It didn't want other Weres anywhere near her. Nic refused to look too closely at why.

"Drive safely," he said, and stepped back so she could leave.

Mindy was startled by his sudden change in demeanor. She could've sworn he'd been about to ask for her number or say something more. Why had he changed his mind? Did it matter? Her confidence seeped away as the wildness she'd experienced a moment ago deserted her.

"Um—thanks," she stuttered.

For a split second, his blue eyes glowed as he stared at her, but in a blink the light was gone.

"You don't have to thank me," he said, sounding tired.

"I guess this is goodbye." Her tone reeked of desperation. *Go! Now! Before you embarrass yourself even more.*

Mindy threw her car into gear and backed up. She needed to get out of here. Get away from Sticks. Get away from him.

He stood rooted in place as she drove away. The second she could no longer see him, something inside of her cracked and tears welled in her eyes. She stopped and banged her forehead on the steering wheel.

"Stupid. Stupid. Stupid," she muttered, then continued on.

Mindy replayed the events of the evening the whole drive home. She was sure the man had enjoyed himself as much as she had. Maybe more so. She rolled her eyes. Of course he'd enjoyed himself. He was guy who was getting laid. Except...it had felt like more than just sex to her.

She was aware that women and men viewed these things differently, but no matter how many times she examined what they'd done, she couldn't easily dismiss the connection she'd felt with...with...

Mindy sighed. Oh God, she didn't even know his name. Shame kicked her in the gut, leaving her winded. How could she have forgotten to ask something so important? She thought about turning around.

She glanced in her rearview mirror. The road behind her was dark and empty. It matched the hollowness in her chest. It was too late to go back now. He'd be long gone.

All this time, she'd envied Izzy's and Celina's wild streaks because she'd had to suppress her own. Mindy had finally let her wild side out, only to discover it wasn't what it was cracked up to be.

Sure, she'd enjoyed every minute with her mystery man and wouldn't trade the experience for anything. But Celina and Izzy had left something out of their adventurous tales. Something vital.

They'd forgot to mention how quickly the momentary highs would be replaced by crushing lows. The sharp edges of which only added to her sense of loneliness.

* * *

Nic arrived home to an empty house. The silence screamed volumes as he dropped his keys into a bowl next to the door and stripped off his clothes.

His chest ached. Nic rubbed the spot over his heart, but the pain remained. Didn't seem possible, but he was even lonelier than before.

The woman's sweet scent covered his body, making his heart race and his nerves tighten. He could still feel her velvet muscles gripping him and taste her honey on his tongue. He stared at the hard evidence protruding between his legs. He could deny it, but here was physical proof that he wanted her again.

Nic walked into the bathroom and turned the shower on, determined to wash her scent away—*wash her away*. He stared at the steady stream and watched it swirl down the drain. One quick scrub and she'd be gone.

For some reason, he couldn't bring himself to step under the water. Having her scent on him made it seem like he wasn't so alone.

"You don't even know her name," he snapped, overwhelmed by the sense of loss.

Nic shut the water off and walked to the sink. Clutching the sides of the porcelain, he stared at himself in the mirror. Blue phosphorescent eyes stared back at him accusingly and dried blood covered his face.

"You're wrong," he grumbled to his wolf.

His lip curled, exposing long canines.

"You've been wrong before and you're wrong this time! It's just the full moon." The words had barely left his throat, when Nic's head snapped back.

Fur rippled over his face and a snout appeared. His skin itched and stretched. Nic growled and shook his head, fighting off the need to complete the shift.

"You aren't in control. I am!" The garbled words ended in a snarl.

It took a couple of minutes for the fur and snout to slowly recede. By the time it was completely gone, the cut on his cheek had sealed and only a thin white line remained. That too would disappear in another day or so.

Nic washed his face and brushed his teeth, then went to bed. His skin smelled of her. The heady aroma was both ecstasy and sheer torture, but he needed it to get through the night.

7

Celina turned the television off when Slade stalked into the apartment. Every time she saw him, he made her breath catch and her heart skip a beat.

With his dark hair, tanned skin, and ridiculously long lashes, he bordered on beautiful. The sharp edge of his cheekbones and square thrust of his jaw kept the distinction at bay.

She glanced at the time. After midnight—again. "Where have you been?"

Slade looked at her, but there was no heat in his amber eyes. "Out."

"I made you dinner." She pointed to the cling-film- covered plate on the table. "It's probably cold by now."

The muscles of his broad shoulders rolled as he shrugged. "I already ate," he said, but sniffed the food anyway.

Celina rose from the couch and wrapped her arms around his trim waist. "What's wrong?"

"Nothing," he said, then tried to shake her off.

But Celina wasn't having it. She tightened her grip and clung to him. "You can tell me anything," she said.

Slade growled. "I said it's nothing."

Celina instantly released him. She could feel him pulling away emotionally and had no idea how to stop it. When she'd first brought him home from the clinic a week and a half ago, Slade had been grateful.

He'd wanted to know all about Breakbend and the culture. He'd watched tons of television and spent hours on the internet. It made her think he'd never seen it before, which wasn't possible unless he'd been living under a rock.

She'd helped him with everything she could given her limited resources. Afterward, Slade had been grateful. Grateful enough to sleep with her. He'd even hinted at them having a future together. The thought that that future might be slipping away terrified her.

Izzy's cryptic warning echoed in her head. Celina pushed it aside. Her best friend may be psychic, but she didn't know everything. If she'd ever experienced the passion inside a Were, she wouldn't be so quick to avoid them or so quick to judge.

"What can you tell me about the Moonlight Kin in the area?" Slade asked.

Celina blinked in surprise. "Not much. I'm sure you know more than I do, since you're one of them."

Slade glanced at her. "I'm not part of *this* group."

"Oh," she said. "I just thought..."

Impatience simmered in his amber gaze.

"What do you need to know?" An inkling of unease trickled down her spine. If he wasn't part of the Moonlight Kin, that meant he was trespassing on their territory. Wolves were extremely territorial. If the Kin detected Slade, he would be in danger.

"Is it normal for the Kin to run by Telegraph Road?" he asked.

Mindy lived on Telegraph Road. Hers was one of the few houses out that way. She'd got it for her and Izzy because the rent was cheap and she could keep as many animals there as she wanted.

What was Slade doing out there?

"It doesn't matter what I was doing. Just answer the question," he said.

Celina's stomach dropped to the floor. *Did he just read my thoughts?* She'd never heard of a Were who could do that. The idea was horrifying. Fear cooled her ardor.

"I'm pretty sure the Moonlight Kin only run on Aidan Fortier's estate," she said.

"Is he the Alpha?" Slade asked.

"Yes," she said, then amended her answer: "I think so. I've never met him."

"No surprise there. Alphas are *particular* about the female company they keep," he said.

It took her a beat to catch the insult. Celina stiffened. "What exactly do you mean by that?"

Slade smiled and kissed her cheek. "Nothing, sweetheart."

Celina wanted him—wanted this—so bad that she was willing to put up with a lot. That would change once they were mated.

A smile ghosted Slade's face as he pulled off his shirt and dropped it onto the arm of the couch. Her eyes devoured every inch of his bare skin. Celina had never seen a man built like him. He sported so many hard ridges and shadowed lines that he didn't look real.

His long, tapered fingers moved to the button on the front of his jeans. She'd had those fingers inside every orifice and still she wanted more, needed more.

Slade popped the button. The denim slipped an inch, riding low on his hips, exposing the indentations that hinted at greater perfection. He didn't seem to notice her physical response. Without a second glance, he walked into the bedroom.

Celina tried not to drool as she watched him go. The second he was out of sight, she glanced at the phone and debated whether to call Mindy.

And say what? Be careful, werewolves are sniffing around your house? Watch out, werewolves are real? She'd have her committed.

"Celina," Slade's raspy voice called out.

She recognized the tone immediately. He only sounded sexy like that when he wanted some, wanted her. The realization dispersed her doubts and bolstered her hopes.

"What, babe?" she asked.

"I'm hungry," he said, surprising her.

Celina glanced at the food on the table. "You want me to heat up the plate?"

"I don't want food," he said. "I want you to get your butt in here and take your clothes off."

Desire mingled with defeat. Celina couldn't resist his call, hadn't been able to from the start. Slade had come into her life and stolen her soul.

No, not stolen, she thought. She'd given it to him willingly. Wrapped it in a bow and handed her soul over, along with her self-respect.

Celina reached for the bottom of her T-shirt and pulled it over her head. She hadn't bothered to put on a bra, since Slade didn't like them. He wanted easy and fast access. She dropped the shirt onto the floor and slowly strolled into the bedroom.

Slade was lying on top of her white comforter with his back pressed against the wrought-iron headboard. He was gloriously naked, waiting for her. His tight fist encased his swollen flesh, emphasizing his arousal.

Celina gulped, drinking in the sight of him. He was big and thick. Everything about him was sheer perfection. "You're beautiful."

He ignored the compliment as if it were his due. "About time," he said, stroking himself. "This isn't going to suck itself."

Celina let out a desperate whimper and dropped to her knees.

"That's a good girl," Slade said, as she brushed his hands aside and grasped him, then slowly lowered her head.

8

The sun had barely peeked its golden head above the horizon, when Nic arrived at work the next morning. He punched in his security code and the large metal gate swung open. Nic pulled through and stopped, waiting for the gate to close behind him.

They'd had a security breach not long ago. Jenna Dane's "ex" had broken onto the estate and threatened to expose the Kin.

The problem had been dealt with swiftly, but he and the other wolves had become more vigilant about the pack's security.

The woods rushed by as Nic meandered down the long drive. The concrete and stone manor came into view as the trees parted and the road split in two. If he veered right, he'd go toward the circular drive in front of the house.

He went left. Most of Aidan's estate was still asleep, but the lights were on in the garage as he pulled his truck up and parked.

Nic walked in to find Josh Dubois and Bernie Macklemore already hard at work.

"Morning," Nic said, and went straight for the pot of coffee on the shelf.

Josh popped his dark head out from beneath the hood of the sports car he was working on. He was a wiry twenty-something who laughed as much as he talked and had the kind of energy that would shame that battery- operated bunny. "You look like crap. Must've been some night." Josh grinned and his youthful eyes danced with glee.

Bernie slid out from under the sedan he'd been adjusting and hauled himself to his feet with a groan. He looked to be a fit fifty thanks to his shifter genes, but was in all likelihood double that age. Methodical and wise, Bernie considered each word before he spoke. His gaze landed on Nic and his gray brow arched. "What happened to you?"

"Nothing." Nic avoided his gaze. "Had a little scuffle last night with some pups who were out to test their claws."

Josh laughed. "They aren't very bright if they decided to tangle with you."

Nic laughed. "They weren't," he said.

"Want me to talk to them?" Josh asked.

Nic shook his head. "They don't live here on the estate. I've never seen them before. Must be out-of- towners in for the full-moon run."

Bernie's eyes narrowed, but he said nothing.

Nic walked to the truck he'd been working on yesterday and set his coffee down on the floor, then slipped under the vehicle. He reached for a wrench to loosen the bolts. The wrench slipped from his fingers and dropped onto the floor with a loud clang. He picked it up, only to drop it again.

The third time the wrench hit the concrete, Bernie and Josh quit working on their cars and came to see if he needed a hand.

"Doing okay?" Bernie asked.

"Fine," Nic said through gritted teeth. He twisted the wrench and scraped a layer of skin off his knuckles.

Josh sniffed. "Ah, Nic, he said. "I don't mean to pry, but when did you start wearing women's perfume?"

Nic banged his head on the undercarriage. He muttered a curse, then slid out from under the truck. He rolled to his feet and walked to the neatly arranged wall of tools on the far side of the garage.

Bernie followed him. "Want to talk about it?"

Nic didn't look at him. Instead, he continued to examine the tools. "Nothing to talk about."

Bernie cocked his head. "If it's nothing, then where'd the perfume come from?"

Nic shrugged and kept his expression neutral. "Just a girl I picked up at the bar last night."

"She have anything to do with the scuffle?" Bernie asked.

Nic didn't answer.

Bernie stared at him for a solid minute.

Nic fought the urge to squirm.

"What's her name?" Bernie asked.

Nic's face heated. "Don't know. Doesn't matter."

"You don't know her name?" Bernie took a deep breath and slowly let it out. "How long have I known you?"

Nic looked at him in surprise. "What?"

"How long have we known each other?" Bernie asked.

Nic thought about it. "Ten years, give or take."

Bernie nodded. "Sounds right," he said. "In all that time, I can't recall you ever coming to work smelling like a girl you picked up at a bar."

Nic turned away, but Bernie caught his sleeve. He looked down at the hand and snarled.

Bernie's brow disappeared into his hairline. "Okay, now that we've established that she's not just some nameless girl you picked up at a bar, it's time to talk. Take a seat." He pointed to a stool in the corner of the garage. "Josh, run to the main house and get me a pastry."

"Nic, you want anything?" Josh asked.

"No thanks!"

The younger man nodded and strode out the door.

As soon as he was gone, Bernie leveled his gaze on Nic. "Now tell me what happened."

"I already told you," Nic said. "I got into with some pups and hooked up with a girl afterwards."

"You aren't a hookup kind of guy," Bernie said.

"Sure I am."

"No." Bernie shook his head. "You're not," he said patiently.

Nic shrugged. "I was last night."

"Hmm...interesting." Bernie got himself a cup of coffee. He made a show of taking a sip, then returned to Nic's side. "So let me make sure I have this right. You got into a fight—that may or may not involve a woman—then picked up some random bar girl to have sex with and didn't bother to ask her name."

"That about sums it up," Nic said. His jaw hurt from gritting his teeth so hard.

"I'm confused," Bernie said. "If it was such a fun night, and you certainly smell like it was, then why are you so grumpy?"

"I'm not grumpy," Nic snapped.

Bernie watched him closely. "You got into a fight. Found an easy lay. Sounds like a Were's idea of a perfect night."

"She wasn't easy," Nic said. She hadn't been with a man in a while. He was sure of that. Just the thought of her lying with another guy made Nic's head ache and claws flex.

Bernie scratched his chin. "You said she was a bar girl. If she was at Sticks, that makes her a Were groupie."

"I might have met her at the bar, but she was *not* a regular. Lucien didn't recognize her and she had no idea what I was," Nic ground out.

He didn't like that Bernie thought the woman was easy or that she was a groupie. She wasn't. Despite what they'd done in the parking lot, she was an innocent. Far too sweet for her own good.

"She didn't belong there. And she damn sure doesn't belong with me." Nic scrubbed a hand through his hair.

Bernie took another sip of his coffee. "I never said she did. It's interesting that you brought it up, though."

"Our beasts don't know everything," Nic growled. "They *can* be wrong."

"I've never known them to be, but I suppose anything is possible. We're proof of that." Bernie hid his smile behind his coffee cup.

"I need to get back to work," Nic snarled in frustration.

"Can I come back in now? I have your pastry." Josh poked his head in the door.

"Yes," Bernie said. "I've learned everything I needed to know."

Nic scowled at him.

"Jenna has a question." Josh set the pastry on the workbench.

"What does she want to know?" Bernie asked.

"I'll let her ask you herself," Josh said.

Nic didn't look up when Jenna Dane walked into the garage. His mind was too focused on the woman from last night. He'd been unable to think of anything else. Was she still sleeping? Or was she awake, regretting what they'd done?

Part of him did. While a larger half would do it again in a heartbeat.

Even though the night hadn't gone as planned, Nic didn't want her to regret their time together. He scratched his jaw. His fingers encountered stubble. He needed a shave. He needed a shower, but he couldn't stand the thought of losing her scent. He heard muttering.

"What?" he asked. It was then that Nic noticed Jenna standing next to him, talking. How long had she been there?

Somehow she'd squeezed her pregnant body between the truck and the tray of tools beside it. Her strawberry- blonde curls fell loosely down her back. She was smiling and stroking her stomach while she waited for his response.

"I'm sorry, what did you want?" Nic asked.

Jenna's grin widened. "I asked when you thought the truck would be ready."

"Uh." He reached for a tool and knocked the whole tray onto the ground. Nic flushed. "Might be a while."

Jenna's light green eyes twinkled. "Looks like it," she said. "Don't worry about it. We can use the SUV."

"I can probably have it up and running by the end of the day," Nic said.

Jenna touched his arm. "No rush."

There was a time when her touch brought him nothing but pain.

Now Nic didn't feel anything, and he had his one-night stand to thank for that. Too bad he didn't know her name and had no way of reaching her.

Jenna waddled out of the garage.

"Never thought I'd see the day you'd—"

Bernie hit Josh before he could finish the sentence.

Josh's brow furrowed and he looked at him. "What?"

Bernie shook his head in warning. He didn't want anything to spoil this moment. This was the first time Jenna had come into the garage and not left Nic tied up in knots.

He watched his friend slip back under the truck, totally unaware of what just occurred. Happiness filled him. It was about time the young wolf stopped obsessing over the Alpha's mate.

Bernie didn't know who Nic had met last night, but whoever she was, she'd changed his friend's life for the better. How long would it take him to figure that out and hunt her down? Hopefully not long. He wanted Nic to move back to the estate. Back home with the pack where he belonged.

Every time Nic inhaled, he smelled her honeyed scent and pictured her writhing beneath him. The aroma distracted him, but not half as much as the instant replay. He banged his thumb twice and lost count of how many times he'd dropped his tools.

After a few hours, he'd had enough. Nic needed to get some fresh air. Needed to clear his head. Needed to stop thinking about her, when there was a very good chance he'd never see her again.

His wolf surged to the surface and stared out through his eyes. It raised its furry head and sniffed the air. The woman's scent drifted deep into its lungs, then it sank back, hovering just beneath his skin.

He might be willing to walk away, but it wasn't.

"I'm going into town to grab some lunch." Nic headed for the door. "I'll pick up the cables we need while I'm there."

"The chef's putting on a big spread at the house. We don't need—"

Bernie hit Josh and glared at him. "See you in a few."

Nic nodded and strode outside. He climbed into his truck and started the engine. As he roared down the long drive toward the security gate, some of the tension in his chest eased.

Josh turned to Bernie after Nic left. "You want to tell me what's going on? I've never seen Nic so distracted. He didn't notice that Jenna was here."

"I know." Bernie grinned. "It's only going to get worse."

"What is?" Josh asked.

"Isn't it obvious?" Bernie replied.

Josh scratched his head. "Maybe to you." He grabbed the pastry and handed it to Bernie.

Bernie looked at it, sniffed, then wrinkled his nose. He tossed the confection into the trash.

"You better not let the cook see you do that," Josh said. "He went to a lot of trouble to make those fresh. I thought you wanted a pastry."

"No, I just needed to talk to Nic," Bernie said. "I wanted to confirm my suspicions."

"What suspicions are those?" Josh asked.

"Our friend Nic has found his bondmate," Bernie said.

Josh's eyes widened and he glanced at the door Nic had walked out of. "Why didn't he say anything? It's such a big deal. Definitely cause for celebration."

Bernie cocked his head and his smile widened. "Because I don't think he knows. At least not for certain."

Josh grabbed his stomach and hooted with laughter. "Oh man," he said. "Can't wait to see Nic's face when he finally figures it out."

Bernie chuckled. "Should be something, all right. In the meantime, cut him some slack. His wolf will really be riding him hard until he closes the deal."

9

Celina cornered Mindy the second she walked into the animal clinic. "Did anything odd happen last night?"

The humiliation over what she'd done came rushing back. Mindy couldn't meet Celina's penetrating gaze. "W-what do mean?" She rushed past the cheery light blue walls with the doggy and kitty pictures on them, and slipped into the office.

Celina followed. "Slade's a catch. I get it," she said. "I know if I find him irresistible, it's a safe bet that other women do, too."

Mindy had no idea how Slade figured into last night. "What?"

"If he dropped by your house, you can tell me. I won't be mad." Pain filled her eyes and she squared her shoulders.

"Celina, I don't know what you're talking about," Mindy said. "I haven't seen Slade since the last time he came by to pick you up after work."

"Swear?"

"I swear," Mindy said.

Celina deflated. "Oh, good." Her eyes narrowed. "Then why did you look so guilty when I asked about last night?"

"I don't know what you mean," Mindy said, then ducked around her.

"Mindy Catherine MacDougal, you just lied," Celina said.

"No, I didn't," Mindy squawked.

Thankfully, Dr. Fields walked in and interrupted her friend's interrogation. "Ready to begin?"

"Yes." Mindy glanced at Celina and smiled, then rushed off to scrub up.

Two spayings, one neutering, and a paw surgery later, Mindy came out of the back room. Dr. Fields had been kind not to say anything when she dropped three scalpels and handed him the wrong instrument—twice.

Despite vowing to never think about last night again, Mindy couldn't keep her mind off her mystery man. Her thoughts reveled in replaying each moment in vivid color. She could still feel his lips pressed against her neck, and the swirl of his tongue, as he tasted her skin.

Mindy fanned her face and pulled at the collar of her shirt, then walked to the thermostat to check the temperature. It was a balmy seventy-two.

Celina's gaze burned into her. She hadn't said anything more, but it was only a matter of time. Mindy sighed.

"The reason I look so guilty is because I went to Sticks last night," she murmured. "I just wanted to have fun. Feel free for once."

Celina's eyes widened and she came to her feet. "You what!"

"I know you told me that it wasn't my kind of place," she said. "But I had to see for myself." The temp in the room climbed higher.

"What happened?" Celina asked. "Are you hurt? Are you okay?"

"I'm fine." *More or less.* Mindy glanced at her, then looked away. "You were right. It wasn't my kind of place."

"Mindy, what happened?" Celina asked. "What did you see?"

Huh? "I didn't see anything other than a lot of good-looking men." *What is Celina talking about?*

"Just tell me what happened," she said.

"There was a fight. It was a mess," Mindy said. "Honestly, I'm embarrassed by the whole situation."

"You got into a fight?" Celina's gaze scanned her from head to toe.

"I can't catch a ball and you think I got into a fight? Seriously?"

"Sorry, I forgot who I was talking to," Celina said.

She'd confused Mindy with her sister. Celina did that a lot. It was a common mistake and only served to remind her how close this woman and her sister really were.

"Some of the men I met last night got into a fight." Mindy rubbed her hands over her arms. "I'm fine. Really. A man stepped in and saved me from a bad situation, then I went home."

"They were fighting over you?" Celina asked.

Mindy's brow furrowed. "You don't have to sound so surprised."

"Sorry. You sure you're okay?" Celina asked.

She wasn't, but not for the reason Celina was suggesting. "Positive."

"Who was he?" Celina asked. "The guy who saved you, I mean."

Mindy shook her head and sweat trickled down the side of her face. "Don't know. Didn't ask."

Celina frowned in confusion. "What do you mean you didn't ask?"

Mindy ran a hand through her hair, loosening her ponytail. "It all happened so fast that there wasn't time," she said.

Celina's frown deepened.

Before she could ask another uncomfortable question, the bell on the front door clanged. Mindy's heart jumped.

It's not the man from last night, she mentally scolded. *It's just a customer.* But that didn't stop her excitement or diminish the swell of hope.

They both walked into the waiting area to see who'd arrived. Celina's boyfriend Slade stood inside the door.

His light gold eyes drifted over Celina and settled on Mindy. He smiled when he saw her, a vibrant, welcoming grin that lit up the room. Mindy smiled back, but couldn't help feeling disappointed.

"Afternoon, ladies." Slade moved deeper into the lobby.

Celina's heart fluttered, but her elation faded when she saw who held his attention. "What are you doing here?"

"I thought I'd see if you want to go to lunch. I have a quick errand to run, but I'll be back in a few," Slade said.

Celina smiled. "Sounds good."

"Mindy," he said. "Have you done something different with your hair?"

Mindy touched the side of her head. "No, it's the same as it's always been."

He studied her appearance. "Hmm, you look different somehow," he said.

Her cheeks flamed.

Celina watched her closely, startled by her friend's response to such an innocent statement. Had she lied about him coming over? Celina shook her head. Mindy had always been a terrible liar. It was how Celina knew her friend had left something out of the story about Sticks. The question was, did it involve her boyfriend?

Slade moved closer.

Celina intercepted him before he could reach Mindy. She slipped her arms around his waist and snuggled next to him.

"You care to join us?" he asked.

Mindy glanced between Celina and Slade. "No, I have to study, but thanks."

Celina's relief was palpable. "You know Mindy, her nose is always buried in a book. She doesn't have time for socializing. Do you, Mind?"

"Nope," she said, and sounded suddenly sad. "No time."

Slade's amber gaze slid to Celina. "You should try following her example sometime." He kissed her before she could call him out on the insult.

Mindy glared at him, but didn't say anything. "I'll leave you guys to it."

Slade broke the embrace. "Don't bother. I have to run that errand. I'll be back in a few. Be ready," he said to Celina.

"I will." She preened.

Slade walked out of the clinic and headed down the sidewalk. The second he was out of sight, Mindy said, "You shouldn't let him talk to you like that. It's not nice."

Celina glanced at her, but couldn't hold her gaze. "He was kidding."

Mindy stared at her with pity in her eyes. "No, he wasn't," she said. "You deserve better."

Did she? There was a time Celina thought she did, but that was long ago. "I'd worry about your own boyfriend if I were you. Oh, that's right, you don't have one."

Mindy reared back like Celina had slapped her. Hurt followed her initial shock.

Celina rushed forward. "I'm sorry. I didn't mean it." She hugged her.

"It's okay," Mindy said, then pulled out of her embrace. "We're both a little stressed right now."

The phone rang as they walked back into the office. Celina picked it up.

"Breakbend Animal Clinic, may I help you?" she asked. Celina sat as she listened to the person on the other end of the line and took notes.

Mindy was about to check on their patients recovering in the back room when the bell on the front door rang again.

"I'll get it," she said to Celina, and walked back to the lobby.

Mindy stumbled when she caught sight of Marco Faretti. He stood in the doorway with a funny expression on his face. Was he sniffing the air?

"W-what are you doing here?" she asked.

He instantly stopped what he was doing and stepped forward. "It's so good to see you again."

"Slade, you're back fast." Celina came out the door behind Mindy. Her mouth dropped open and her expression changed three times before she managed to pull herself together. "Is this the man who saved you last night?"

Mindy slowly shook her head. What was he doing here? How had he found her? She hadn't told him anything about herself other than she was a student.

"How did you know where I worked?" Mindy asked him.

Marco smiled. The act transformed his handsome face into something truly stunning, but the beautiful mask no longer fooled her. He gave Celina a secretive smile, then said, "I asked around."

"Asked who?" Mindy wanted to know who he'd been questioning. Was it the man from last night? No, it couldn't be him. He didn't know her name.

"Do you want me to get rid of him?" Celina asked. There was hatred in her eyes. Hatred, and...*hurt*.

Mindy shook her head. "No, I'll handle it."

"Almost didn't recognize you, Celina," he said. "You look different with your clothes on."

"Where's your girlfriend, Marco?" Celina asked.

He reddened. "I don't have one. Never did."

Celina flinched.

"I just told you that." He gave her a snide smile. "You smell... *different*." Marco leaned forward and inhaled deeply. His nose wrinkled and something that looked strangely like fear flashed in his eyes. His smile vanished and he glared at Celina. "What have you gotten yourself into now?"

Celina stammered back. "I don't know what you're talking about. I have work to do." She walked toward the office. Celina hesitated in the doorway. "Leave Mindy alone. She's not like you—or me."

Marco's grin returned. "Run along, Celina. This doesn't concern you."

"I'm standing right here." Mindy scowled at them both.

"If you want, I can phone Slade," Celina said. "He'd have no problem getting rid of him." She glared at Marco.

"Who's Slade?" Marco asked.

Celina lost her bravado. "He's none of your business."

"It's okay," Mindy said. "I got this." She didn't want to make a bad situation worse.

Celina nodded and slipped out of the room.

Mindy turned to Marco. "What are you doing here?"

He glanced at the floor and looked sheepish. "I came to apologize for last night," he said. "My behavior was inexcusable. I'd like to take you to lunch to make up for it."

Mindy wasn't about to go anywhere with him. Not after last night. His sudden appearance only added to her anxiety. She wasn't entirely convinced that he wasn't stalking her.

"I appreciate the apology, but lunch isn't necessary." Mindy recalled the moment Marco punched her mystery man in the face.

Ignoring the hint, Marco grabbed her hand. He ran his fingers gently over her knuckles. "Come on, Mindy. Give a guy a break."

"Like you gave me when you tried to pull me into the woods? Is that the kind of break you're looking for?" Mindy tugged her hand away. His touch didn't feel right, didn't feel like the man who'd held her in his arms last night.

"I said I was sorry. What more do you want me to do?" Marco asked, then moved in closer, invading her personal space.

"Leave," she said.

"I don't know what Celina has told you about me, but I can guarantee that it was a lie," Marco said. "She and I have a history. We hooked up one time about a month ago. I found out afterwards that she hooks up with a lot of guys, so I cut her loose. It didn't mean anything, I swear."

Mindy bristled. "Didn't mean anything to you? Or to her?" She hoped the shock didn't show on her face. How could he be so callous? After his behavior last night, it shouldn't come as a surprise.

Marco shifted his feet and shoved his hands into his pockets. He glanced past her shoulder toward the door Celina had exited through. "It didn't mean anything to either of us. You can ask her. She'll back me up."

"So that's why you're here," Mindy said. "You think apologizing and asking me to lunch will get you laid."

His amber eyes widened. "No! You have it all wrong. I know you're nothing like her."

"Celina is my best friend. We have a lot in common," Mindy said, though it wasn't true. Celina was Izzy's best friend. They'd become friends by extension. She and Celina were close because of their common love for Izzy, but they had very little in common outside of work.

Marco's expression turned calculating.

"I think you'd better leave." Mindy made her way to the front door, leaving Marco no choice but to follow.

She opened the door and stepped out onto the sidewalk. Marco stopped in front of her.

"I think we got off on the wrong foot," he said.

"No, I'm pretty sure my first impression of you is correct," Mindy said.

* * *

Nic was driving along the backside of Main Street, attempting to avoid the tourists in town for a fishing tournament, when he saw the woman from last night come out of a light blue building on his left. His pulse jumped and his palms began to sweat.

She was even more beautiful in the daylight than she'd been under the moonlight. Her light blonde hair was tied back with a red scrunchie and she wore pink scrubs.

The clothes should've looked shapeless, but somehow managed to accentuate her lush curves. Elation quickly turned to confusion when he spotted the pup he'd fought coming out behind her.

The pup grabbed her hand and tried to bring it to his lips. Something dangerous and predatory rose inside Nic. He swerved his truck into the other lane and drove up onto the sidewalk. People scattered to get out of the way.

Nic barely noticed. He was too focused on the woman and the Were standing next to her. He threw the truck into park and jumped out. Nic strode down the sidewalk toward them before he'd formulated what he'd say or do.

The woman was looking at the pup, so she hadn't noticed him yet. She pulled her hand away and told him to leave. It was all the incentive Nic needed. He came up behind the Were and grabbed him by the neck.

"You heard the lady," he said.

The pup swung around. His eyes widened when he saw who had a hold of him. "You again? I thought we settled this last night?" He inhaled. His nostrils flared, and at the same time, his eyes narrowed.

Nic smiled, showing more teeth than was necessary. The pup had picked up the woman's honeyed scent on his skin. "I believe *now* it's settled," he said.

The pup muttered something crude under his breath, then took off down the sidewalk.

Nic watched him go, then turned to the woman. Suddenly alone with her, he was unsure of what to say or do. How do you ask the person you slept with their name without it sounding crass?

She broke the tension building between them by making a weak joke. "Seems like saving me is becoming a habit." She laughed.

Nic rubbed the back of his neck. *Say something. Say anything. Try not to stick your paw in it again.*

"Glad to see that your face is okay." She reached out to touch him, then seemed to think better of it and dropped her arm.

"It was just a scratch." Nic couldn't exactly tell her that he healed almost instantly.

"What are you doing here?" she asked.

"I wasn't following you, if that's what you're thinking," he said, and winced.

Her gaze lowered and she twisted her fingers. "I didn't," she stuttered. "I mean, I wasn't thinking that."

Her pained expression sliced him. Why was he acting like such a jerk? Nic never had trouble speaking to women. Ever!

"I came into town to pick up some parts. I'm a mechanic." He watched to see what her reaction would be to his announcement. He expected her nose to wrinkle or her eyelid to flicker. He expected to see some sign indicating that she preferred suits. She didn't have one, so he continued. "I was driving by and happened to see the pu—guy from last night hassling you."

She glanced up. "I don't know how he found out where I worked," she said. "I didn't tell him."

Nic could tell her exactly how the pup had found her. He'd followed her sweet scent right to the doorstep. The same scent that was filling his lungs and making him dizzy with desire.

"I'm Nic La Croix." He held out his hand. "I don't believe I had a chance to introduce myself last night."

She gave him a small smile. "Me either." She shook his hand. "Mindy MacDougal."

Her touched singed him. Nic's fingers itched to pull her into his arms. He wanted to taste those full lips again. They couldn't possibly be as drugging as he recalled. Before he could act upon the impulse, the door to the clinic flew open and a dark-haired beauty stepped out.

"Is he gone?" She looked up and her breath caught.

Mindy's brow furrowed and she nudged the woman. "Celina, this is Nic. He's the one I told you about earlier."

She'd been talking about him. The thought left Nic unduly pleased, but the feeling faded fast when he thought about what she could've been saying. He hadn't exactly treated her with respect. If anything, he'd behaved just as abominably as the pups. He had to do something. Say something to make the situation right.

Words tangled in his throat, refusing to come out.

"Nice to meet you." Celina eyed him with open curiosity—and undisguised interest.

"You too," Nic said.

Now that he'd taken a better look at her, Nic recognized the dark-haired woman. She was a regular at Sticks. She was also a known groupie who went out of her way to hook up with Weres. Which meant she knew what he was. Apprehension filled him.

Nic didn't think she'd out him in front of Mindy, but he couldn't be sure. His wolf protested inside his head as he made his excuses and left. Nic didn't get far before he turned around and walked back.

He pulled out his wallet. "Here's my number." He handed his business card to Mindy. "I'd be more than happy to take care of that ping in your car for you." He hesitated. "If you want, I could look at it tonight. Won't take long. Just call and leave your address."

Mindy looked at the card, not bothering to hide her stunned expression. "Okay."

Nic nodded and left again. Once more, he stopped short and looked back. "Call me if he comes back."

"I will," she said.

He smiled. "Don't worry, I'll take care of him," Nic said. "I'll make sure he doesn't bother you anymore."

Mindy was too stunned to reply. Her mystery man finally had a name. In her mind, she'd convinced herself that he couldn't possibly look as good as she'd remembered. She'd been wrong. If anything, he was more handsome.

She could get lost in those blue eyes. And no man should have shoulders like that or that tight of a butt.

The moment Nic was out of sight, Celina yanked her around. "I think you left something out of your story," she said. "Want to explain what just happened?"

"I'm not sure," Mindy said. All he'd done was speak to her. Yet her body continued to thrum.

Celina crossed her arms over her chest. "What's going on between you two?"

"Nothing, nothing's going on." The lie slipped from Mindy's lips. How could she explain when she didn't understand?

"Nothing?" Celina snorted. "Honey, that was the definition of something. I could've cut the tension between you two and used it to butter my bread. It was that thick. What do you know about him?"

The warmth on her face had to be coming from the surface of the sun.

"Whoa!" Celina said. "You didn't?" She studied her. "Oh my goodness, you did."

Mindy was pretty sure her heart was going to explode from the sudden rise in her blood pressure.

"I can't believe it," Celina said. "You of all people."

"I told you that I knew how to have a good time. You didn't believe me," Mindy said.

"Oh, honey, is that why you...?" Celina looked in the direction Nic had gone. "I didn't mean it. I'm such an idiot. Your sister asked me to take care of you."

Mindy snorted. "Izzy asked you to take care of *me*? Out of the two of us, she's the one that needs a keeper."

Celina hugged her. "Please tell me that you didn't sleep with him to prove a point."

Mindy bit her lip. Had that been the only reason? Maybe at first, but it had quickly morphed into something else. Something more incendiary. "That wasn't the only reason." She gave Celina a sly grin.

Her friend laughed. "Well, that's a relief," she said, then sobered. "You need to stay away from Marco. He's bad news. Serious bad news."

"You don't have to convince me of that," Mindy said. "What about Nic?" She held her breath as she waited for Celina's response. If her friend told her that she'd gone out with him, Mindy would be heartbroken, but she'd cut all ties with him.

Celina tilted her head, sending her long brown hair into her face. She absently brushed it back. "I don't really know him," she said. "I've seen him around town and at Sticks a few times, but I don't know anything about him. He keeps to himself." Her gaze fell away.

Mindy's heart slammed against her ribs. What wasn't Celina telling her?

"But?" Mindy asked, because she could clearly hear a "but" coming.

"Just be careful," Celina said. "Nic isn't like other guys."

"What do you mean?" Mindy asked.

Before Celina could respond, the phone inside the clinic rang and she hurried in to answer it.

Saved by the bell.

Mindy looked at the card in her hand. She should throw it away. Forget about last night. Forget all about Nic. That would be the smart thing to do. Too bad her idiot heart had other ideas. She took out her cell phone and punched in the number.

Nic picked up on the first ring.

10

Celina could barely hear the woman on the other end of the line over the pounding of her heart. She stayed on the phone only long enough for Mindy to walk into the office and see that she was still on a call. Mindy waved, then continued on into recovery area. The second the door closed; Celina took down the woman's number and disconnected.

Pressure squeezed her lungs until Celina couldn't breathe, while the sour acid of jealousy burned her stomach, leaving her hollow inside. Why Mindy? Why were so many werewolves circling around her friend?

Mindy had never been to Sticks until last night and yet two Weres had already shown up looking for her. She could chalk it up to coincidence, but Marco had all but admitted that he'd tracked Mindy's scent to the front door.

What happened last night? What had Mindy done to garner so much attention? Celina was tempted to ask, so that she could try it next time.

You have Slade, remember? Hopefully there wouldn't be a next time. As the thought filtered through her mind, Celina knew it wasn't true. She could feel him slipping away.

Celina had spent more weekends than she could count at Sticks. She'd spread her legs for every wolf who'd asked or shown any interest in her. She'd given them exactly what they wanted, in every way they'd wanted it, and her personal sacrifice had gotten her nowhere.

That was until Slade came along.

Bitter jealousy returned. He may claim he had no interest in Mindy, but Celina had seen the look on his face. She'd watched desire shimmer in his amber eyes. He'd had the same hungry look on his face as those other two Weres had when they looked at Mindy.

Tears filled her eyes. *Why her? Why not me?* It wasn't fair.

Mindy was cute and she had curves for days, but Celina was a true beauty. She'd been told so her whole life. Men were attracted to her and she was attracted to men. Bad boys were her fatal weakness.

When Celina had discovered that werewolves existed, she'd been cautiously intrigued. After sleeping with a couple of them, her curiosity morphed into obsession. Werewolves were the ultimate bad boys— thanks to their animal natures, which were never too far from the surface.

They had unbelievable stamina, incredible mouths, and were generous lovers. Best of all, they were overly possessive once they found and claimed their mate.

Celina's preoccupation with Weres had grown so much that being marked by a Were was all she could think about. And now, it looked like Mindy would achieve the goal before she did. The thought seared her insides, leaving her raw with anguish.

She loved Mindy like a sister, but it irritated Celina that she'd been able to garner so much attention without any real effort. The salt in the wound was that Mindy didn't know that werewolves existed.

Why would they be interested in someone so clueless? They were never quick to expose their secrets, but they had to know they'd have to eventually if they continued to pursue her. Unless of course they were just after sex.

Sex she could live with. It was an emotional attachment that would be unbearable.

Cold settled around Celina's heart. Maybe it was time she told

Mindy that her sister wasn't crazy. That the monsters Izzy warned her about were real. If she did that, Celina wouldn't have to worry about losing Slade or the other wolves coming around. Mindy wouldn't want anything to do with any of them.

11

Mindy made a quick trip to the grocery store after work before rushing home to get ready for Nic's arrival. She fed all her animals and talked to each one about their day, then put the cooked roast and potatoes she'd picked up into the oven to warm.

She threw together a salad and set the bowl inside the refrigerator. Mindy didn't know if Nic would want to stay for dinner, but she wanted to be ready just in case. She walked into her bedroom and found a dead mouse on her pillow.

"Hannibal!"

Her one-eyed orange tabby came strolling into the room. He rubbed against her leg, arching his back and purring with pride. Mindy rolled her eyes and scratched him behind the ears.

"You have to stop bringing me presents, or in your case, displaying your kills." She stroked him again, then picked up her pillow and carried it to the back door.

Mindy unlocked the door and tossed the dead mouse outside, then stripped the pillowcase off and threw it in the laundry hamper. She retrieved a clean pillowcase from the dresser drawer in Izzy's old bedroom and grabbed one of her sister's sweaters while she was at it.

With the clean pillowcase in place, she walked into the bathroom and turned the shower on. Mindy had just tugged on the end of her shirt when she heard scratching at the back door.

Hannibal was perched on her bed. Had Tart somehow gotten out when she removed the mouse? God, she hoped not. She did not need a litter of puppies.

Mindy dropped her shirt and walked down the hall. She moved the curtain aside and gasped. What was he doing here? She turned the lock and opened the door. The wolf-hybrid she and Celina had rescued stared at her with startling amber eyes. At first she was scared, then he whimpered.

"How did you get here, big boy?" Mindy slowly stepped out onto her small back porch and looked around. She didn't want to startle him. "Celina was supposed to have taken you to the preserve."

They'd decided that he wasn't someone's pet, but he also wasn't entirely wild. He'd obviously been around people at some point, but given his size it would be better if he had somewhere safe to roam.

He nudged her hand with his massive head.

Mindy's fingers sank into his thick fur. "Are you hungry?"

His tail wagged.

"Well, come on in. Let's get you something to eat."

Tart, her rescue poodle, came running out of the living room straight at them. Mindy had completely forgotten that she was loose.

She tried to cut her off, but the large, three-legged poodle was in heat and easily snaked around her. She immediately whimpered and spun around to entice the big male. If the hybrid mounted her, there was no way Mindy would get them apart without losing a hand.

The wolf-hybrid sniffed Tart's bottom and growled. The sound sent chills across Mindy's skin. Not the reaction she expected from a male canine, especially one who was part wolf. Tart yelped and scampered away. He watched her go, but made no move to follow.

"You are an odd duck, my friend," Mindy said. She'd never seen a male dog of any kind turn away a bitch in heat. "Let's get you some food."

His massive paws were silent as he trailed her to the kitchen.

"Sit," she said, then grabbed a plate out of the cupboard. Mindy pulled the roast out of the oven.

The hybrid shoved his nose between her legs and sniffed, then licked her jeans.

Mindy almost dropped the roast on his head. She quickly set the pot on the counter and grabbed his nose to move it away. "Watch it there, big guy."

She sliced a generous hunk off the roast and put it on the plate. The meat hadn't been in the oven long, so it wasn't too hot.

"Easy," she said, then lowered the plate to the floor. "While you finish that, I'm going to call Celina and find out what happened."

The hybrid gobbled his food down, then wandered back the way he'd came in. He sat next to the back door and whimpered to be let out.

"You're not going anywhere," Mindy said. "So get comfortable." She kept an eye on Tart to make sure she didn't try to entice the hybrid again.

Mindy punched in Celina's number. It went straight to voicemail. She was probably sucking face with Slade. She waited for the beep.

"Celina, call me when you get this message. I have the hybrid here with me. We need to talk." She disconnected the call and set the cell phone on the counter. The house was quiet—too quiet. She looked around.

Tart huddled in the corner next to the couch, trembling. There was a small puddle of urine beneath her.

"Terrific," Mindy muttered.

She poked her head in the hall to see what the hybrid was up to. A gentle breeze brushed her face. The back door was wide open and the hybrid was gone.

"How did you..." Mindy raced down the hall and ran out into the yard. She scanned the tree line, but there was no sign of him.

Mindy walked back into the house and stopped to examine the door. The glass and the frame appeared to be intact. Everything looked perfectly normal. Maybe she'd forgotten to close it properly and it had blown open? It was the only explanation that made any sense. It was either that or the hybrid had figured out how to turn a knob.

Her gaze swept the yard one final time, then she closed the door and locked it. Mindy didn't have time to go looking for him in the woods. Nic would be here any minute.

Mindy took a quick shower and put some makeup on, then slipped Izzy's sweater over her head. She tried on three pairs of jeans, giving each one the butt check in the mirror. None of them passed. She grabbed a pair of Izzy's and pulled them on. She should've known they'd be perfect.

She'd just tugged her shoes on when the doorbell rang. Mindy took a deep breath and glanced one last time in the mirror to check her appearance. It shouldn't have been so important, but she wanted to look nice for Nic.

"You look fine," she muttered, then wandered into the living room. Nic was early.

Eagerness is a good sign. Isn't it?

Mindy planted a smile on her face and pulled the door open. Her grin faded as she came face to face with Marco Faretti. Startled, she stepped back. Shock quickly turned to fear.

"What are you doing here, Marco?" She glanced up the road, hoping to spot Nic's truck in the distance.

"I came here to finish our conversation without being interrupted," he said.

Mindy's knuckles whitened from holding the door so tight. "Now's not a good time."

Marco's gaze started at her head and slowly worked its way down before reversing direction. "You going out? If you're heading to Sticks, maybe I'll see you there? We never did finish that drink."

Mindy shook her head. "I'm not going out," she said. "And I'm definitely not going back to that bar."

As was his habit, he crowded her with his body. "Why not? I thought you had a good time."

Scared, Mindy held her ground. "I think we remember last night differently," she said. "You need to go. I don't appreciate being stalked and I'm expecting company any minute."

Marco's amber eyes narrowed. "Is it that wolf from the Fortier estate?"

Wolf? Was that some kind of slang for a male slut? Mindy didn't keep up with modern slang, so she wasn't sure.

"I assume you're talking about Nic," she said.

"Is that his name?" His lip curled in disgust. Before she could respond, he continued, "I guess you are like your friend Celina after all. You know where to find me once he kicks you to the curb." Marco dropped down a step and his nose wrinkled. "Is Celina here?"

"No. Why?"

"Thought I smelled her," he said.

Mindy inhaled, but didn't smell anything other than the roast. "I don't know what you're talking about."

Marco poked his head in the door and dragged air into his lungs.

"What are you doing? I told you she wasn't here," she said. "You need to leave. Now!"

He scowled at her and walked to his car. He changed direction at the last second and slipped behind her house. Fear pulsed inside of her. What was he doing?

"I mean it, Marco," she shouted. "If you don't leave this second, I'm calling the police!"

At first, Mindy didn't think that he'd heard her, then she saw him sprint across the yard. His face was pale and his wide amber eyes kept scanning the tree line. It was a relief to see that he was taking her threat seriously.

Marco didn't stop watching the woods until he was behind the wheel. Gravel flew as he tore out of her driveway.

Mindy watched him leave. It wasn't until he was out of sight that she was finally able to let go of the front door.

Nic passed the pup on the road. There was only one place he could be coming from. Fear demolished his nervousness. He needed to get to Mindy. Make sure she was okay. He stomped down hard on the gas. Nic's truck roared as he raced down the road.

He found the address and hurried into the driveway. Nic threw his truck into park and jumped out, not bothering to turn it off. He leapt up her front stairs and pounded on the door.

"Marco, I told you to leave," Mindy shouted.

"It's not Marco," Nic rumbled.

"Nic?" Mindy opened the door. Her pale face and trembling hands said all he needed to know. "Sorry, I thought you were someone else."

"Are you okay?" he asked.

Nic didn't wait for her to answer. He simply pulled her into his arms and ran his hands over her body. He needed to see for himself that she was unharmed. What was the pup doing here? How had he found out where she lived?

She allowed him to comfort her for a minute, then Mindy slowly moved away. The awkwardness that had been there earlier in the day returned.

Nic cleared his throat. "I'll need the keys to your car. You still want me to take a look at it, right?"

"Yes, of course." Mindy lifted the keys off the hook beside the door. "Here." She handed the key ring to him.

"It won't take long," he said.

"Take your time," Mindy said. "I was just finishing up the side dishes for dinner. Would you like to stay? I made enough for two."

She was okay. He'd seen so with his own eyes. He should fix her car and leave, but Nic didn't want to go. He wanted to spend more time with her.

"Sure," he said.

"Great." She smiled, and his stomach fluttered.

Nic walked back to his truck. He could feel Mindy's eyes on him. Everywhere she looked, a wave of heat followed. He flexed his hands and turned off his engine before grabbing his toolbox. Twenty minutes later, he'd finished the minor adjustment to get rid of the pinging and had her car humming once more.

He dropped the hood and was walking back to his truck to put his toolbox inside when he caught a strange scent wafting on the air. Nic placed the toolbox on the seat and slowly shut the door. He raised his head and carefully smelled the area around him.

What was that?

Nic had never smelled anything like it. He stepped away from his truck and walked into the yard. The scent grew fainter. Nic frowned and switched direction. The breeze brought the odor again. This time stronger. He scanned the trees. Nothing moved. The hair on Nic's neck rose and the wolf inside him surfaced.

The door opened. "Are you done?" Mindy asked.

Nic nodded, but continued to stare at the woods.

"What is it?" Mindy stepped out of the house onto the porch.

"It's nothing," Nic said.

"Marco isn't back. Is he?" Her voice quivered.

Nic turned away from the woods. "No." He shook his head. "He's not around. You don't have to worry."

The relief on her beautiful face was palpable. "Good," she said. "I just wanted to let you know that dinner is ready."

"I'll be right in," Nic said. "Just need to get something out of my truck."

Mindy nodded and walked back into the house.

Nic waited until she was inside, then scented the woods once more. The odd odor was gone, but its absence didn't alleviate his unease. If anything, it made it worse.

As part of the Moonlight Kin, there weren't many scents he couldn't identify. He rubbed the back of his neck and walked to the house. The fact that he couldn't place this one worried him.

12

The second he stepped through the door into the living room, chaos erupted. Squawks, hisses, and barks collided in a glass-shattering cacophony. Nic was immediately hit with sensory overload.

Mindy's ranch-style house was neat and clean. Nic doubted a human would detect the various scents, but to a Were it was like taking a stroll through a zoo after a sinus rinse. So many scents. Too many. Including an unusual one that escaped him.

He held his hands over his sensitive ears and his eyes watered as he slowly looked around. Various types of animals were scattered throughout the cozy living room.

"Hush!" Mindy said. "What's wrong with you guys? Behave, we have company." She turned to Nic. "I'm sorry. They don't normally act like this. Have a seat while I check on dinner." She pointed to the rose-colored couch under the window.

Nic wasn't surprised by the uproar. A predator was in their midst and they didn't like it one bit. Between the scents and the noise, Nic couldn't hear himself think. The animals were making him edgy.

Still, he found himself sitting down. Nic told himself it was to be polite, but he was only lying to himself.

"Can I get you a drink?" She walked into what he presumed was the kitchen.

"I could use a beer." It was an understatement.

A one-eyed cat took one sniff of him and hissed. Its orange fur rose on its back and its tail straightened as it prepared to attack.

Nic bared his teeth and growled low in his chest. The cat snarled and ran into the corner under a side table.

Mindy's three-legged poodle showed no fear at all when it approached. It licked his jeans and whirled around to show him its butt, then proceeded to hump his leg. Nic tried to shake the dog off, but it was determined to entice him, since it was in heat. He groaned. This was a nightmare.

There was another loud squawk. Nic flinched and looked over at the cage hanging from a chain attached to the ceiling. A gray parrot cocked its head to look at him, then said, "Nice doggy." The comment was followed by a string of expletives that would shame a fleet of intoxicated sailors.

Movement in the corner of his eye drew his gaze away from the foul-mouthed feathered menace. A green, tailless lizard marched across the couch toward him. When it got close, it did a strange rocking dance that Nic was sure was meant to intimidate him.

He had to leave. This was too much. Nic shook the randy poodle off his leg and stood. Mindy came into the room as he was about to make his way to the front door. She was carrying two beers.

"Where are you going?" she asked.

He didn't want to hurt her feelings, but he had to go. "What is all this?" The question surprised them both.

Mindy set the beers on the coffee table, then walked over to pick up the cat cowering in the corner. "They're strays." She stroked the feline. "This is Hannibal. I named him that because he constantly kills things and presents the bodies to me." She pointed to the poodle. "That's Tart. She humps anything that moves."

"Go to your kennel." She herded the dog into a back room and shut the door, then walked back into the living room. "Now that her wounds are healed, I plan to get her fixed. Her owners abused her. It took me two months just to get her to the point where I could pet her without her flinching."

Nic looked at the parrot, who continued his foul-mouthed tirade.

"That's Perry. I'm pretty sure he has Tourette's syndrome," Mindy said.

It took Nic a second to register what she'd said. When he did, he threw his head back and laughed. "Tourette's?"

Mindy had the grace to look embarrassed. "It's not out of the realm of possibility. Animals tend to have a lot of the same issues that humans have. They have feelings. They dream. They have worth, though a lot of people don't believe so."

The flutter in Nic's chest turned into a full-on drumbeat. He rubbed the spot and wished more than anything that Mindy wasn't human. Her heart obviously held a lot of love for her menagerie. He could see it in the way she looked at them, the way she spoke about them. No doubt her capacity to love would extend to any relationship she had.

Longing, deep and fierce tugged at him. He had to get away from this line of thinking. It would only end in heartache and disappointment. He glanced at the lizard. "What about him? What's his story?"

Mindy scratched Hannibal under the chin. "That's George. He had an unfortunate accident that involved Hannibal." The cat purred at the mention of its name. "But they're friends now. Mostly."

"Are you keeping them for any particular reason?" he asked. It was normal for humans to have pets, but this was more than that.

Mindy frowned. "I don't understand the question."

"Why are they here?" he asked.

"Because they had nowhere else to go, and with Isabel gone there's even more room for them to roam," she said.

Of course she did. Nic sank back down on the couch. "Who's Isabel?" She was probably the animal scent he couldn't place.

Mindy handed him a beer, then sat in the chair across from him. Hannibal settled on her lap, but Nic noticed the cat didn't take its good eye off him.

"My sister."

"I'm sorry. Is she dead?" he asked as delicately as he could. He didn't want to dredge up painful memories.

Mindy laughed. "No, she's just-" she paused as she searched for the right word, "-eccentric. She ran off to New Orleans a few weeks ago to find herself." Mindy rolled her eyes. "Or something like that."

"Ah." Nic could tell there was more to the story, but he didn't press. "So how did this all start?"

"As you know, I work at the animal clinic in Breakbend," she said. "I'm also a full-time student at Clarkston Greenburg University. I'll finish at the end of this year." Mindy took a sip of her beer.

"What's your major?" he asked.

"Veterinary medicine. I prefer to work with animals. People can be confusing," she said, then sucked in her cheeks, as if doing so would draw the admission back inside her mouth.

Her ambition was admirable and her love of strays enduring. Thus far, the only *flaw* he'd found was her humanity.

"I'm surprised you found time to go out to the bar with that kind of schedule," he said.

Mindy brushed her shoulder-length hair back and suddenly looked uncomfortable. "I normally don't. Anytime I have free time, it's spent studying."

Nic couldn't smell her wonderful scent over her collection of critters, so he couldn't tell if she'd lied. "What brought you to Sticks?" he asked, though he wasn't sure he wanted to know the answer.

What if she knows what he is? What if the innocent act is just that—an act?

Mindy's brown gaze slipped away and she stopped petting the cat. "About the other night...I should apologize. I'm not normally like that. I'm sorry if I—" She paused. "Gave you the wrong impression."

Good to know, Nic thought. His relief was palpable, but she still hadn't answered his question. "Have you ever been to the bar before?"

Pink blossomed in her cheeks and spread down her neck. "No," she said. "A good friend told me about it."

Nic's brow rose. "Some friend," he chided, his voice harsher than he'd intended.

Mindy's eyes widened in alarm, then her gaze locked on him. "It's not like that. Celina is a good friend. She warned me not to go."

"But you went anyway?" He made it a question.

Mindy stiffened in her seat. "I'm twenty-five. I'm old enough to make my own decisions."

Nic held up his hands. "Darlin', you'll get no argument from me." Images of their carnal encounter flashed through his mind. Nic's body responded in an instant. He put his beer down and shot to his feet. "I forgot to check something in your car." Self-preservation drove him to the door.

"I'll set the table while you do that." Her voice petered out and she looked embarrassed.

"Sounds good," he said. "I'll be right back." Nic stepped outside. He hated that he'd made Mindy feel uncomfortable in her own home. It seemed like every time he opened his mouth, stupid came out.

He mentally cursed, then strode across the lawn toward her car. Nic fiddled around with the wires for ten minutes. Long enough for him to pull himself together, then he slowly walked back to the house.

Mindy wasn't in the living room and neither was her cat. She'd covered Perry's cage with a sheet, which quieted him down. George sat in an aquarium tucked in the corner that Nic hadn't noticed when he'd first come into her home.

"I'm in here," she said. "Did you fix it?"

"Fix what?" Nic asked, forgetting that he was supposed to be out checking something on her car. The house smelled like beef, along with the alluring scent of Mindy. He followed the sound of her voice into a small room off her kitchen.

Candles flickered on the table between two blue placemats. She'd positioned a roast at one end and potatoes and a salad at the other. His beer was sitting next to the roast.

"Take a seat," she said. "I hope you're not a vegetarian."

The thought made him smile. She had no idea what a carnivore he could be. "Smells good."

Mindy's hands shook as she passed the knife to Nic. "You want to do the honors?" She hated that she was so nervous.

He didn't hesitate. Nic took the butcher knife and quickly carved the roast. He lifted a couple of slices and placed them on her plate.

"Thank you," she said.

Mindy was still having a hard time believing that he was really in her house. She hadn't expected to ever see him again, but she was grateful that she did. It proved that she hadn't been wrong about their connection. There *was* something simmering between them. Something elusive, but tangible nonetheless.

Nic served himself, then waited for her to pass the vegetables. He didn't take many. The roast covered much of his plate.

"Can we start over?" she asked. "I know that's kind of a weird request, considering everything that's transpired, but I'd really like to begin again."

Nic looked up from his food and smiled. "I'd like that, too."

Mindy grinned. "My name is Mindy MacDougal." She held out her hand.

He took it gently. "Nic La Croix." Heat simmered in his blue eyes, leaving her breathless.

"So, Nic," she said, "tell me about yourself."

Some of the heat faded and his expression became guarded.

Unease settled into Mindy's stomach. "You aren't married, are you?"

Nic shook his head, sending his shaggy, light brown hair bouncing. "No. I wouldn't have... What I mean to say is, I wouldn't have been at the bar alone if I were attached in any way. What about you?" he asked. "Do you have anyone special in your life?"

Mindy played with her fork. "No, not for a while now. There really hasn't been time. What with school and all." *And looking after Izzy.* She placed her fork on the plate and picked up her beer. Mindy took a sip. The drink burned down her throat. "So are you from around here?"

"No," he said. "But I've been here for the past eleven years."

"Almost makes you a local," she said.

His eyes crinkled when he laughed.

Mindy loved the sound. It was deep, throaty, and infectious. From the creases next to his eyes, Nic looked like he laughed a lot. It made her want to say something funny just so she could hear him laugh again.

"You said you were a mechanic," she added.

Nic nodded. "I work on the Fortier estate. They have a big garage there." He watched her closely when he said the name.

Mindy wasn't sure what he was looking for, but he must've been satisfied with what he saw because he seemed to relax. "I'm aware of the place, but only because I think Celina mentioned it before. You said Fortier, right?" she asked.

"Yes," Nic said.

"Is the family any relation to the software mogul?"

"One and the same," he said.

"Ah, good for you," she said. "Thought the name sounded vaguely familiar. I don't really keep up with high-society news."

Nic took a deep swallow of his beer. "Has Celina ever been out to the estate?"

Mindy shrugged. "I don't think so, but I honestly wouldn't know."

"I thought you said she was your friend," Nic said.

Mindy's stomach tightened. "She is, but we don't do everything together. She's actually Izzy's best friend. We've always hung out together, but it's only recently that we've grown close."

"I understand," he said.

Did he? Did he really?

"Listen, about the other night." Mindy hated to bring the subject up again, but she thought it was necessary to clear the air.

Nic held up his hand. "Mindy, you don't have to explain," he said. "I don't normally do that kind of thing either."

She exhaled loudly, then laughed. "I guess we both were swept up in the moment."

"That's putting it mildly," he muttered. "I definitely got carried away." This time his blue eyes sparkled.

Memories of his rough hands gliding over her skin, his firm lips devouring hers, flittered through her mind. Mindy picked up her napkin and dabbed at the gathering moisture on her forehead.

"So," she said. "Have you always been a mechanic?"

"No, but I've always enjoyed tinkering on anything with a motor in it. Fixing cars began as a hobby and quickly became a profession," he said. "Does that bother you?"

Why would his vocation bother her? Mindy was genuinely confused by the question. "No, should it?"

Nic shrugged and put his fork down. "You just struck me as the kind of woman who prefers suits."

Her brow furrowed. "That's only because you don't know me very well." Did he really think she was so shallow? She looked at him. Maybe he did.

Mindy hadn't meant to give Nic that impression. Of course, it was hard to make a good impression, when you were flat on your back, half naked, sprawled across the bed of a pick-up truck.

He fidgeted in his seat. "I didn't mean anything by it. It was just an observation," Nic said.

"Well, you're wrong," Mindy said. "I've had to work for everything I've achieved." She'd had no choice, since Izzy's antics had bankrupted their parents. "I'm not interested in social climbing. I want to be a vet because I love animals, not because I have dreams of marrying a fellow doctor."

"Got it," he said.

They continued making small talk throughout the rest of the dinner. Despite the rough start, Mindy found herself truly enjoying Nic's company. When the meal was done, he helped her clear the table and wash the dishes.

After they were dried and put away, Nic said, "I'd better head out.

Thank you for the lovely meal."

"Thanks for fixing my car," Mindy said.

"It was the least I could do," he said.

He didn't owe her anything, but Mindy didn't want him to leave yet. "I picked up dessert." She opened the refrigerator and pulled out a chocolate cake.

Nic paled. "Sorry, I'm allergic to chocolate, but thank you."

Mindy was all out of excuses to keep him there, so she walked him to the front door.

13

Nic's gaze roamed over her face. This was it. Once he walked out that door, they probably wouldn't see each other again. It was the right thing to do. They were two different species. All that was left was to step out onto the porch.

He stared at Mindy. Throughout the whole meal, all he could think about was kissing her. His eyes locked onto her lips. They were full, rosy and just begging to be explored.

Nic slowly touched her hand and threaded his fingers through hers. He brought her knuckles to his mouth and pressed a chaste kiss to the back of them. He watched Mindy's breath catch and her pulse jump beneath her skin.

He tugged her hand, bringing her closer to him. "I want to kiss you," he murmured. "But I'm afraid if I do, I won't want to stop."

Mindy moistened her lips.

Nic groaned and closed his eyes. "Do you have any idea how beautiful you are? How *tempting*?" he asked. "I can hardly keep my hands off you. I should leave. It wasn't my intention to come over here and seduce you again. I really did want to make up for my bad behavior last night." He released her and turned to make good on his word.

Mindy caught his arm. "Don't go."

Nic almost didn't hear her above the blood raging in his veins. "I need you to be sure." It was a plea and a prayer.

"I'm sure," she whispered.

"Why you?" He leaned his forehead against hers.

Mindy laughed. "I've been asking myself the same question since last night."

Nic slipped his hand around her neck and slowly lowered his head, giving her plenty of time to move away—to escape him.

She didn't. Instead, Mindy's lips parted in welcome.

Nic seized her mouth, capturing her in a fierce kiss. The taste of her melted across his tongue. She was pure ambrosia. He followed the tantalizing flavor, exploring her depths thoroughly, wanting more. The room spun as he deepened the embrace.

Mindy's fingers fluttered over his chest, coming to rest above his pounding heart.

Nic's body hardened and his hands fisted in her shirt, bunching the sweater's material. Her skin heated. With the rise in temperature came the delicious, musky aroma of hot moist woman.

He broke the embrace, his ragged breath ripped from his chest. "Tell me to leave now and I might be able to go," he rasped. It was a last-ditch effort to save himself. To save her innocence from his dark world. "I'm not strong enough to walk away on my own." The confession scorched his soul.

Mindy's brown eyes dilated. She couldn't seem to catch her breath. She pressed her swollen lips together and swallowed hard.

"Please don't go," she murmured.

"I don't want us to regret this, this time," he said.

Her long lashes fluttered to conceal her eyes. "I don't regret the last time." She ran a hand over her arm and bit her lip. "Do you?"

Nic's denial was swift and fierce. "Hell no!"

If she told him to leave this second, Nic would. His stern expression said his offer was real. If that happened, there was a very good chance she wouldn't see him again. Panic hit, squeezing her throat. That was the last thing Mindy wanted.

Still, she didn't know much about this man. Was she really going to invite him into her bed?

He saved you from Marco twice. He fixed your car. He let Tart hump his leg. And he didn't run away.

That said a lot about his character. She stared into his dark blue eyes, watching the waves of passion wash over them. She could get lost in those eyes. It wouldn't take much to be swept away. Mindy was already halfway there.

"I don't want to be alone tonight," she said. "I'm tired of feeling lonely." This time it wasn't her wild side talking. This time it was the *real* Mindy baring her soul.

Nic shuddered as her words struck their mark.

"Me too." Nic cradled her face between his large hands and slowly tilted her head to capture her lips once more.

The kiss was so devastatingly tender that it brought tears to Mindy's eyes. With that one kiss, Nic conveyed all the emotions he kept bottled inside. Mindy tasted his fear, his need, his compassion, and his loneliness.

She also discovered a deeper, darker, wilder undercurrent. The last should've scared her, but instead she was drawn to it, drawn to him. Mindy savored every one of his emotions, grateful that he'd been willing to leave himself so utterly exposed.

He walked her backwards toward the hall, never breaking the kiss. Nic reached for the first doorknob he came to. Mindy stopped him before he could open the door.

"That's Izzy's room," she murmured against his lips.

Mindy grabbed his shirt and kept moving, taking him farther down the hall. The second door they encountered was cracked.

Nic pushed it open. A neat bedroom came into view. The only thing he cared about at the moment was the queen-sized bed with the rose-colored comforter and pillows piled high. The room smelled like Mindy. He flicked the light on and guided her inside, then kicked the door closed with his foot. As soon as he heard it click shut, Nic stripped her clothes off.

The sweater went first. It was followed by her jeans. By the time he finished, all Mindy had on was her lacy white bra and matching panties. She toed her shoes off, then stepped out of her pants.

Nic ran his fingertips over the swell of her breasts and watched her nipples tighten beneath the material. "I didn't get to see these last night." He slipped one finger under the strap and slowly slid it off her shoulder. "I dreamed about them. About you."

Gooseflesh rose on her arms.

"Cold?" he asked, knowing she wasn't.

Mindy shook her head. "Hot," she said. "If I get any warmer, I will be scalding."

"Then I hope you like the heat, darlin', because you're about to get a lot hotter." It was a vow Nic intended to keep.

He cupped her fullness, feeling the heavy weight of her in his hands. He brushed his thumbs over the front of her swollen flesh, loving the sound of her breath as it caught in her throat.

His lips found hers once more and he reached behind her. With a flick of his wrist, her bra gaped open and fell to the floor. Nic broke the kiss to look at her.

"Oh, have mercy," he said, then ran his tongue over the soft swell before capturing her nipple between his teeth.

Mindy gasped and clutched his head. Nic feasted on her flesh, turning it bright red. She was even sweeter tasting here. He latched on to the other nipple, making sure to give it equal attention. Mindy swelled before his eyes, ripening like a summer berry.

Nic sucked and nibbled until her knees threatened to give out, then he coaxed her onto the bed. Her blonde hair spread across the rose comforter, haloing her head. "I didn't get to explore you the way that I wanted to. I intend to make up for that oversight right now."

He grabbed Mindy by her ankles and pulled her forward until her bottom rested at the edge of the bed. He grabbed her panties and yanked them off, then dropped to his knees and inhaled. His head spun as her delicious aroma ensnared him.

Drool threatened to drip from his mouth as he carefully parted her legs to reveal her hidden cleft. She blossomed before him. His incisors lengthened and his eyes glowed. Nic's gaze dropped to keep her from seeing the effect she had on him. *On his wolf.*

Nic settled his wide shoulders between her thighs and slowly took his first real taste of her. Spice and honey exploded on his tongue. Nic's body instantly hardened to the point of pain. He dipped in again and her juices ran down his chin.

Nic wanted to bury himself inside her, experience the warm, tight embrace he'd felt the other night. But he wouldn't. Not yet. He wasn't finished tasting her, feasting on her yet. He wanted to sup on Mindy's flesh, devour her sex until all that remained was a deeply sated woman.

Nic stopped his gentle exploration and dove in with gusto. He licked, stroked, and worried her flesh with his teeth until she plumped beneath his firm lips.

Mindy's knees locked around his head and her thighs quivered. She tried to squirm up the bed when the sensations got to be too much, but Nic wasn't having it. He held on to her hips and slid his hands beneath bottom, tilting her to give him better access, then continued to feast.

She couldn't think. Couldn't breathe. Her entire world was centered on his amazing mouth and what it was doing to her. Pressure built inside her. A pressure the likes of which she'd never experienced before. Her hands clenched the duvet as she tried to hold on to her world, as it rotated faster.

Nic swirled his tongue around and around her until lights flashed behind her eyelids. Mindy's body bucked and she pressed her lips together hard to keep from screaming. She tasted blood and didn't care.

He sucked her between his teeth and bit down. The flare of pain amidst all the pleasure sent her spiraling over the edge, as the mother of all orgasms roared through her, engulfing her in flames. This time Mindy did scream Nic's name.

Mindy's cries rang in his ears as she rippled around his tongue. Nic couldn't stop the smile from spreading across his face. Mindy's legs dropped open and her body liquefied. She was everything he'd remembered and more.

Nic grabbed his shirt off the floor and wiped his mouth, then slowly climbed to his feet. He stared down at her. Mindy's pale flesh had turned a delectable shade of pink. Her nipples jutted toward the ceiling, all but begging to be nibbled on again. He watched her body quake. Nic would remember this moment for the rest of his life.

He repositioned her until she was further onto the bed, then Nic settled on top of her. He kissed Mindy tenderly and brushed the damp hair away from her face.

"You aren't finished yet. Are you?" he asked.

Mindy licked her lip and tried to speak. After a minute she gave up and shook her head.

"Good," he said. "Because I'm just getting started."

This time Nic didn't sheathe himself. He wanted to know what—if anything—would happen when they had sex skin to skin. He didn't expect a repeat of the other night. With his wolf firmly leashed, Nic didn't feel as out of control.

"I don't have any diseases," he said, kissing her again. "Are you on birth control?"

Mindy nodded.

"I know I'm asking you to trust me with your life, but I swear to you that I'd never do anything to put you in harm's way."

She stared at him for so long he thought she was going to reject him, then finally she answered. "Okay, but if you're lying, I will cut you up into little pieces and feed you to Hannibal."

"I'm not. Thank you for your trust." The words had barely left his mouth, when Nic surged forward burying himself inside her molten core. The sensation shocked his system, leaving him winded.

It was the first time he'd *ever* gone bareback in woman. That he'd done so with a human wasn't lost on him. It was...it was...*incredible*.

Nic held himself still and tried to catch his breath. Mindy's legs rose and she wrapped her knees around him, holding him close. Her level of trust made his heart soar. It also terrified him.

So far, so good. No odd reactions. No internal swelling.

For some reason, the thought that the whole thing might've been because of the full moon left him oddly disappointed.

You should be elated. This is what you wanted.

Nic rolled his hips and thrust forward, feeling her velvet muscles grip him. Fire burned down his spine and he had to fight the urge to rut like a beast inside her.

He found Mindy's mouth and continued his carnal invasion while he glided forward, embedding himself to the hilt. Nic shuddered. She was perfect. Everything about her seemed to fit. He pulled out until only the tip of him remained inside her.

Mindy whimpered and pushed down upon him, seeking more.

Nic's lips slid over her jaw as he easily slipped in and out of her fiery sheath. "I didn't think it would be possible, but it's even better tonight."

He concentrated on keeping a steady rhythm, so he could build the tension inside of her. He wanted to hear her scream his name again. Mindy tightened around him. Nic found her earlobe and sucked on it, feeling her core pulse in response.

He sucked harder until Mindy writhed beneath him and rocked her hips to meet him thrust for thrust. Her choppy breathing told him she wouldn't last much longer.

Nic hooked his elbows under her knees and lifted her legs higher. The position allowed him to go deeper. Mindy mewed, and her head thrashed from side to side as he pounded into her.

"I can't. I can't," she gasped. In the next breath, she convulsed, her body doing its best to milk him dry.

Nic kissed the side of her neck and felt a deep, primitive tug. His tongue swirled over the spot where her neck met her shoulder. While Mindy was coming apart in his arms, Nic was being pulled under by something far stronger.

He continued to surge into her as she thrashed beneath him. Nic nibbled on her neck, then sucked on her skin. Mindy's entire body stiffened and she let out a keening cry as a second release hit close on the heels of the first.

Nic's world narrowed. All he could see was her pulse fluttering in her neck. He rolled his hips and nudged her cervix. The second it kissed her center, he swelled. The change swept over his body. Nic couldn't stop it. In truth, he didn't want to.

"I'm sorry, but I can't resist," he murmured, then bit down on Mindy's neck.

Blood poured into his mouth. Nic swallowed it, greedily lapping her up, taking her essence into him. He was careful not to lose a drop.

Mindy whimpered and tried to pull away.

His growl stopped her. It was far too late to escape. His wolf had her now. It was determined to mark her, *inside and out*. But first it demanded her submission.

Mindy's body tensed.

Nic tightened his grip on her neck. A few seconds passed, then she stroked his head and relaxed beneath him. His wolf howled in triumph as Nic took more of her blood.

Instinct told him when he'd had enough. Nic stopped drinking and licked the tender bite until the blood quit flowing. Mindy was going to have one hell of a hickey, but it couldn't be helped.

Nic wanted her to taste him—to complete the mating ritual—but he knew she wasn't ready. His ragged breathing finally returned to normal, but his hips continued to flex as he spilled his seed inside her. Nic kissed her neck and nuzzled her cheek.

"Sorry, I lost control again. Being inside you makes me crazy with desire," he said.

Mindy touched his shadowed cheek. "I feel the same way," she whispered. "You make me want things I've never thought about. It's like a part of you is inside of me."

He glanced down and grinned.

Her heart flip-flopped. "You know what I mean."

"Yeah, I know." He rubbed his nose against hers.

"I guess this means we'll have to figure all this out together," she said.

"It won't be easy," he said.

Nic was still hard and heavy inside of her. She'd never known a man could have such endurance. That hadn't been her experience in the past. Of course Mindy only had her ex to compare him to, and it wasn't a fair comparison.

"We seem to end up naked every time we get together," she said.

He kissed her throat. "There are worse ways to end up. Take my word for it."

Mindy shoved at his chest.

Nic laughed and sat up, taking her with him since their bodies were still connected.

"I think you've ruined me for other men," Mindy joked, though it was the truth.

Something dark crossed Nic's handsome features and his eyes glittered. "It might be best if you avoid other men for a while."

Mindy arched a brow. "Is that so?"

His smile returned in a flash, but it didn't reach his eyes. "We need time to get to know one another. Can't really do that properly if you're seeing other men."

"Are you going to date other women?" she asked.

"No!" The certainty in his tone surprised her.

"So are you saying you want us to be exclusive?" Mindy couldn't conceal the hopeful note in her voice. She'd never been one to date around, or sleep around for that matter.

"If that's okay with you," he said, suddenly sounding less confident.

Mindy kissed his chin. "We could always give it a try. If it doesn't work out, at least we'll know for sure."

"Glad you see it my way."

For Nic, there was no longer any other option. His wolf had marked her. Claimed her for its own. It was what every member of the Moonlight Kin waited for, but not all found. She was his mate. The only woman he'd ever desire.

His elation was tempered by the knowledge that she didn't know what he was. How was he going to break the news to her without her wanting to get away from him?

He jerked one last time, then gradually deflated. He was still inside her. In a few more minutes, he'd be ready to go again. "I didn't hurt you, did I?"

"Hurt?" Mindy laughed. "Hurt isn't the word I'd use to describe what we did, but I'll admit you are an animal in the sack."

He flinched at how close to the truth she was.

"It's okay," she said. "The bite just surprised me." Mindy touched her neck. "I think you broke the skin."

He swept her hand into his own and brought her knuckles to his lips. Nic ran his tongue over each groove and then sucked her finger into his mouth. Her eyes widened, but she didn't pull away.

"Was the experience terrible?" he asked.

"Truth is, I kind of liked it," Mindy said. "Does that make me kinky?"

Nic chuckled. "Don't think so, but I'm glad you liked it," he said. "I didn't mean to bite so hard." It was a lie and the truth. Nic might not have intended to mark her when they first climbed into bed, but he hadn't exactly pushed his wolf down when it rose. "I'm afraid you're going to have quite a hickey."

Mindy's gaze locked on him. "Really? I've never had one of those."

"Never?" he asked, astonished.

She shook her head. "Never. My mom and dad would've killed me."

Nic chuckled and kissed her on the chin. "It's nice to know that I'm the only one who's ever marked you." He sighed. "I don't want to ruin the moment, but I have an early morning tomorrow." He needed to report to Aidan and tell him what had happened. Biting was serious business. It was never done casually because of the repercussions.

"You don't want to stay?" she asked.

"I'd love to, but if I do neither one of us will get any sleep tonight." He gave her a wolfish grin.

Mindy smiled back him. "I can't be mad when you look at me like that."

"Like what?" He slipped out of her.

"Like a naughty little boy who uses his cuteness to get out of trouble."

He leaned over and helped her up. "You think I'm cute?"

Mindy rolled her eyes. "You're gorgeous and you know it."

Nic knew he wasn't gorgeous, but it was nice that she thought so. He pulled on his clothes and saw a pink robe hanging on the back of the door. He grabbed it and held it open for Mindy. She slipped it on and secured it at her waist.

"Walk me to the door," he said.

When they stepped out into the hall, Nic caught the elusive odor again. It was stronger here. Stronger than it had been before. He didn't like it. The scent made his hackles rise.

"Do you have any other pets?" he asked.

"No, why?" she asked.

"I just..." He couldn't exactly tell her that he'd smelled something. "Just curious."

"Nope," she said. "You've met everyone."

They walked to the door. "Thank you for dinner and"—he grinned—"everything else."

"Thank you for everything else." She looked at him. The emotion he saw swimming in her brown eyes laid him low.

"When can I see you again?" Nic didn't want to wait. Now that his wolf had marked her, he wanted to be around her as much as possible. She wasn't officially his bondmate until he completed the ritual and had her take his blood, but as far as he and his beast were concerned, Mindy was theirs.

"How about tomorrow night?"

"Sounds good." He pulled her into his arms and kissed her swollen lips, tasting her one last time before releasing her. "I really have to go or you're going to end up on your back again. Though I'm not against using the wall."

Mindy pressed her lips together.

"Sleep well," he said.

"You too."

Nic stepped out onto her front porch. "See you tomorrow."

"Bye." Mindy slowly shut the front door.

Nic didn't move until he heard her throw the lock. The second she did, he covered the ground between her house and his truck. He refused to look back. Didn't dare.

It was taking every ounce of his strength to walk away. He inhaled to clear his head, and caught the strange scent on the wind. What was it? And why was it at Mindy's home?

He glanced at the house. Mindy had turned the lights off and there was no movement near the curtains. Nic decided to investigate.

He climbed into his truck and started the engine. Nic backed out of her driveway. He didn't plan to go far. Just down the road, so he could park his truck out of sight. He wanted to scout the area around Mindy's house without her knowing about it. It was the only way he'd be able to sleep tonight.

Nic found a place to pull over and stepped out of his truck. He lifted his head, allowing his wolf to surface.

It didn't take long to find the unfamiliar odor. He tracked it to the edge of the woods, where it simply disappeared. It wasn't possible. Scents faded, but they didn't disappear. Before he could figure out the puzzle, a new odor replaced the old one. This was one Nic was beginning to hate. He swore under his breath. *Some pups never learn.*

First her job and now back to her home. It shouldn't have surprised him given Weres' competitive natures, but Nic was astonished. Mindy had asked them to leave, and so had he. The brazen one knew he'd slept with her. He'd smelled Mindy on his skin. There was only one way her scent could've gotten there.

Nic let out a loud growl, warning the Weres to stay away, telling them without words that Mindy was off limits. Now that his wolf had claimed her, Nic was done playing with them.

If they jumped him or if either showed up at Mindy's house again, he'd consider it a direct challenge to his position in the pack. If that happened, they wouldn't be walking away.

14

Celina came home around ten o'clock and saw that she'd missed a call. She retrieved the message and heard Mindy's voice.

Her fingers tightened on the phone as Celina listened to the recording that confirmed her worst fears. Slade had been at Mindy's house. The message ended and she hung up.

Celina needed to call Mindy back and tell her the truth about what was going on. She'd chickened out of telling her earlier at work because Mindy had been so happy about her date with Nic. But now...

She punched in the number.

Slade walked into the apartment and slammed the door behind him. "Hang up the phone." The quiet intensity of his voice warned her not to argue.

Celina put the phone down. "Mindy called. She said that the hybrid was over at her house. She knows that I lied. It's only a matter of time before she finds out the truth," she said. "What were you doing over there?"

"Nothing," he snarled.

"Slade, don't lie to me," she said. "I've seen how you look at her. I'm not blind and I'm not stupid."

"You don't know what you're talking about." He moved deeper into the tattered apartment.

Celina hadn't imagined the attraction. She was hyper-aware of things like that. "Two Weres showed up at the clinic today after you left. They were sniffing after Mindy. She needs to know the truth," she said.

Hopefully it would scare her enough to make her want to have nothing to do with any of them. Maybe it would scare Mindy so much she'd leave town to join Izzy in New Orleans.

"Who were they?" he asked softly.

"Marco Faretti and some guy named Nic," she said. "It doesn't really matter. All that's important is that I warn her and that you stay away from her. I don't want you getting hurt."

"The Moonlight Kin are interfering with my plans," Slade said. "They have to be stopped."

Plans? "What do you mean?" she asked.

His claws slipped out as he waved off her question. "You're not going to tell your friend anything. And you're definitely not going to run her out of town," he said. "I'd be very unhappy with you, Celina, if you did that."

Celina ran a hand through her long brown hair. "I don't understand what makes Mindy so special. Why are the wolves circling her?"

"I wouldn't expect you to understand. You're human," Slade said.

"So is Mindy," Celina hissed.

"True, for now," he said. "Not all humans are created equal."

What was that supposed to mean? Didn't she give him everything that he needed? Didn't she cater to his every whim? What more did he want?

"What I desire you cannot give me," Slade said, his amber eyes glistening.

Panic struck swift and deep, sweeping aside her fear of him invading her mind. "How do you know unless you tell me what you need? Mindy is inexperienced. She doesn't even know your kind exists. She can't give you what you want, but I can."

He focused his fierce attention on her and stalked forward. "Can you? That's quite a boast, since you don't know what I want," he said.

"Yes, I do," she murmured.

"Are you absolutely certain?" Slade asked.

Celina nodded. "Yes," she said, backing up until she hit the wall.

Slade tilted his head and sniffed her neck.

She whimpered. Would this finally be the moment he claimed her? Marked her as his own? Celina trembled in anticipation.

A secretive smile canted his lips, then disappeared. "You know nothing about our kind," he said.

"I know everything important," Celina responded.

Slade laughed and grabbed her by the waist. He turned her away from him until Celina faced the wall. Claws scraped against her bare skin.

"Careful," she said. "You almost scratched me."

He ran his thumbs over the faded scars that marred her hips and lower back. "It's quite a collection of scratch marks you have here. I doubt one more set would be noticed."

Celina sobbed. "They meant nothing to me." It was a lie. "You know I love only you." She waited, hoping he'd return the sentiment, but silence met her. Crushed, Celina tried to move his hands away from the evidence of her other dalliances.

Slade's fingers tightened, almost to the point of pain. "Don't," he said, then stripped her jeans away.

Dressed only in her shirt and panties, Celina quivered in anticipation.

Slade pressed a kiss on her nape, then tore her underwear off.

She heard the hiss of a zipper. His jeans brushed against the back of her legs as they dropped to his knees.

Slade placed his hand between her shoulder blades and pressed down until she bent at the waist. He dipped a thick finger inside her. Celina whimpered and drove her hips back to push him deeper.

He smacked her bottom and tsked. "Behave or I won't give you what you want."

Celina swallowed hard and concentrated on slowing her breathing. She wanted him. Wanted this. *Wanted to be one of them.* She'd put up with his heavy-handed ways to achieve her dream.

The thick bulbous head slid between her thighs and parted her. Celina bit her lip. She'd been with a lot of wolves over the years, but never one as dominant as Slade.

Sure, he scared her sometimes, but that was to be expected given his feral nature. It didn't change how she felt about him or what she wanted from him.

"Please, Slade." Celina wiggled her bottom.

He laughed, the sound mirthless. "I had no idea humans could be so easily controlled."

"They aren't." Celina tried to keep from groaning as he slipped an inch inside her. Slade was so big, so thick, so incredibly hard. Her body craved him, while her thoughts bordered on mania.

The first time he'd taken her, she'd blacked out from the pleasure. In that moment, an addiction had formed. An addiction so powerful that she couldn't imagine ever breaking the habit.

"You won't get over me, unless I want you to," he murmured against her ear, then latched on to her lobe.

"You're pretty sure of yourself," she said.

Slade chuckled. "No, Celina, I'm sure of you," he whispered.

What did that mean? Before she could give it anymore thought, he thrust hard, burying himself inside her.

There was no gentleness in his taking. Slade slammed into her, rocking Celina onto her toes as he worked her body into a frenzy.

"Yes!" she screamed as he pounded her, his strong hands holding her tight and guiding her back to meet every thrust.

"I don't appreciate having my actions questioned, Celina," he said, spearing her deep. "Do you understand?"

She groaned. "Yes."

He reached around her body and found her hidden bundle of nerves. Instead of stroking it, Slade pinched her hard.

Celina sucked in a startled breath, then mewed. Her knees wobbled, then buckled beneath her. Slade caught her before she hit the floor, and held her up. He didn't break rhythm once as he continued to ride her.

"I want your word that you won't reveal the truth to Mindy. Do you hear me?" He shook her lightly. "You have no idea what's happening here."

Celina's mind was in meltdown. She couldn't focus on anything but the pleasure-filled pain of their coupling.

"Your word, Celina. I'll have it now!" He pressed down and his thumb twitched at such a speed that the breath left her lungs. He was thrusting so fast that she couldn't track his movements. It was a not-so- subtle reminder that he wasn't human.

"Say it!" Slade demanded.

He was asking her to choose between him and her friendship with Mindy. She couldn't do it.

Slade snarled and pumped harder.

Celina came apart in his arms. In the end, the decision was far too easy. "I'll do whatever you want," she gasped.

"Promise?" he asked, as he rutted like a beast.

"I swear!" Celina cried as shockwaves rocked her.

"Good girl." Slade stroked the soft curls at her apex, then gave them a quick pat. He wrapped another arm around her waist and lifted Celina off her feet, moving her boneless body around until she was draped over the arm of the couch.

At this angle, every thrust struck her heart. Slade impaled her, driving his point in over and over. Skin slapped skin as he picked up his pace once more.

Celina wanted him to empty himself inside her. Fill her womb with life. She'd stopped using birth control, but hadn't told him yet. She knew it was wrong to withhold that kind of information, but Celina was desperate and determined to keep Slade any way she could—even if that meant trapping him with a child.

She didn't see Slade's sly smile, but Celina heard him snort.

"You are so predictable, sweetheart," he said. "You almost make it too easy." Slade thrust a few more times, then grunted and emptied himself inside her.

15

Mindy awoke bright and early the next morning, feeling deliriously happy. Despite their unorthodox start, she and Nic had reached a turning point last night.

She glanced over to the spot he'd been lying in earlier and was surprised to see a flower had been placed on the pillow, along with a note. When had Nic come back? How had he gotten in? Why didn't he wake her?

Mindy picked the items up and smelled the bloom. She put the rose by her bedside, then opened the note. She grinned as she read it.

> *Had a great time last night. Promise I'm not a stalker. Just wanted to see you once more. Couldn't bring myself to wake you. You looked too peaceful. Make sure all your windows are locked before you go to bed tonight. I'll call you later. Can't wait to see you. Nic*

Mindy grabbed his pillow and brought it to her nose. She inhaled. His clean, rugged scent lingered on the pillowcase. Mindy groaned.

"You have it bad, girl," she murmured, then laughed.

She stretched, feeling the sore muscles in her body. Nic had been voracious last night and so had she. Obviously she was working hard to overcome her dry spell. Mindy giggled and threw the duvet cover back.

She heard whimpers coming from outside her door.

"I'll be there in a minute, guys. Let me grab a shower first."

Mindy showered and got ready quickly. Nic hadn't been kidding about that hickey. No amount of makeup would conceal it. She threw on a fresh pair of jeans and an oversized T-shirt, then rushed into the hall. She didn't want Tart to have an accident.

She grabbed the leash and quickly took the three-legged poodle out into the backyard to do her business. The sun had just crested the trees and the air was crisp and only hinting at the heat to come.

Once her dog was finished, Mindy led her back into the house and proceeded to feed the gang. Hannibal glared at her, but didn't turn his nose up at the moist offering.

Mindy stroked his head. "I'm sorry, buddy, but it was either you or Nic, and I just couldn't turn his offer down."

Hannibal sniffed and turned his butt toward her. "Fine." Mindy ignored her finicky cat and grabbed the jar of crickets she kept under the sink. "Sorry, guys," she said as she walked over to George's aquarium and sprinkled a few in with him.

She sealed the jar and placed it back under the sink. She'd just closed the cabinet when the phone rang. Mindy picked up the receiver, hoping to hear Nic's baritone voice on the other end of the line. Instead, it was Izzy.

"Mindy, are you okay?" Izzy asked. Zydeco music blared in the background.

What time was it in New Orleans? "Izzy, I can barely hear you. Where are you?"

"It doesn't matter," Izzy said. "You need to listen to me. You're in danger."

Mindy frowned. "What?"

"Darkness is closing in," she said. "The spirits told me."

She sighed. "Izzy, I don't know what that means." Mindy's great mood was slowly beginning to sour. This was one aspect of their relationship that she didn't miss.

"Just be careful," Izzy said. "He's close."

Did she mean Marco Faretti?

Mindy's heart pounded. She wasn't ready to go another round with Marco right now. She peeked out the curtains at her driveway, but didn't see any other car but hers. She let the curtain drop.

"Who's close?" Mindy asked, losing patience. "I need more information."

One zydeco song ended and another began. "I have to go," Izzy said.

"Not yet!" Mindy shouted. "Not until you explain what you mean."

"Just remember what I told you," Izzy said, then hung up.

Mindy cursed and stared at the phone. "As usual, you didn't say anything," she muttered.

She knew better than to be drawn into these conversations. Hadn't she learned her lesson a long time ago?

"I love you, but you're not going to ruin my day," she said, then placed the phone back on its cradle.

Mindy grabbed her keys and backpack, then stepped out onto the porch. "Behave yourselves," she said, then locked the front door.

She turned her face up to the sun, allowing the warmth to soak into her skin and chase the shadows away. Mindy smiled and skipped down the stairs.

As she stepped off the bottom one, her foot tangled on something solid and Mindy lost her balance. Her backpack went flying as she put her hands out to break her fall.

Mindy landed with a hard thud, scraping her palms. She hissed and rubbed the bleeding cuts onto her jeans, then checked to see what she'd stumbled over.

For a moment, Mindy's brain couldn't make sense of what she was seeing. When the picture finally registered, she scrambled back.

The pale, lifeless body had been mangled by something. Big chunks of flesh were missing from the chest and arms. His throat gaped open like his mouth. She forced herself to concentrate on the man's face.

"Please," she whimpered, praying it wasn't Nic.

Her horror intensified when she saw who was lying at the bottom of her front steps. Mindy's stomach lurched. It couldn't be. Oh no. She had to still be asleep.

Please let me be dreaming.

But Mindy knew she wasn't. The pain in her hands and knees was real. So was her sister's cryptic warning. She stared at the terror-stricken dead body of Marco Faretti. Nic's promise from last night came rushing back. He'd said he would take care of him. Was this what he meant?

Izzy had said he was close. You don't get much closer than when you sleep with someone.

I can't breathe. I can't breathe.

Mindy's heart hurt and her lungs burned. She couldn't be wrong about Nic. She just couldn't be. Izzy had to be mistaken. The euphoria she'd experienced a minute ago faded and doubts crept in. Mindy struggled to her feet.

She had to call the police, but what was she going to say? She didn't want to get Nic in trouble, but she couldn't lie. Not about something like this.

What if he *had* hurt Marco? Mindy didn't want to believe it. She'd always trusted her instincts. They'd never led her astray, but what if she was wrong and Izzy was right? No one else knew about Marco hassling her, except Nic and Celina. And there was no way Celina could've done this kind of damage. She wasn't sure how Nic could've caused these types of injuries.

Marco looked like he'd been ripped apart, starting from the throat all the way down through his intestines.

Could the hybrid have done this? He'd never shown any signs of aggression and there were no drag marks by the body. If the hybrid had attacked Marco, there'd be drag marks.

Why hadn't Tart barked when this was happening? Why hadn't she heard anything? The lack of noise meant Marco hadn't been killed here. He'd been dumped onto her sidewalk.

Would Nic do something like that knowing that she'd find the body? It seemed unlikely, but Mindy couldn't immediately come up with a better explanation.

Mindy's fingers trembled as she pulled her phone out of her pocket. The pain in her chest increased as she dialed 911.

She couldn't look at Marco any more. If she did, she was going to be sick. Mindy gave him a wide berth as she walked around the house to the back door and let herself in. She'd wait in here for the police. She saw Nic's business card on the kitchen counter and felt tears sting her eyes.

* * *

Nic smiled as the sun shone through his windshield. A cool breeze ruffled his hair as he drove into work. He'd overslept and was late for the first time in years, but Nic couldn't be upset because it was the best night's sleep he'd had in weeks. And he owed it all to Mindy MacDougal.

His grin widened as he thought about the woman who'd changed his life forever. There was still a lot to get past. Mindy would eventually have to learn the truth about him and the other Kin, but there was plenty of time to tell her.

Nic bounced in his seat as he turned down the hidden drive that led into the estate. He couldn't wait to tell Aidan the good news. Finding one's mate was cause for celebration amongst the Moonlight Kin. Nic looked forward to the hunt that would follow.

As he approached the security gate, Nic noticed that it was open. The skin on his neck prickled with unease. The gate was never left open. Alpha's orders. Nic continued down the long, tree-lined drive. As he drew nearer, he could hear voices and a commotion.

The trees parted and the estate came into view, along with a half-dozen police cars. Their lights were flashing, but their sirens were off.

What was going on?

Nic parked and turned off his engine. He'd just stepped out of the vehicle when he was approached by two officers. They asked him his name and told him to state his business.

Nic saw Aidan standing next to the front door. The Alpha looked at him and frowned.

"It's him," one of the officers who'd asked his name said.

"What's going on?" Nic asked.

An older police officer with thinning red hair and world-weary eyes stepped forward. "I'm Detective Markinson and that's Detective Daniels."

Though similar in age to Nic, Daniels' narrow face and jerky movements made him look like an over-caffeinated ferret.

"We'd like to ask you a few questions," Markinson said.

"About what?" Nic asked.

"It would be better if you could come down to the station and answer them there," Markinson said.

Nic's anxiety increased. "First I'd like to know what this is all about."

Aidan approached with a short mustached gentleman trotting along beside him. "This is Mr. La Croix's attorney. He'd like to have a word with his client before they follow you to the station."

It wasn't a request and both detectives knew it.

Markinson looked at Nic. "This is just a casual inquiry. Do you think you need an attorney present?"

Nic glanced at Aidan. The Alpha gave nothing away, but he had his answer. "That might be best until I know what's going on here."

Neither cop looked happy, but Markinson nodded and said, "See you down at the station."

Aidan jerked his head toward the house. The second the office door closed, the Alpha descended upon Nic. "We don't have much time," Aidan said. "What in the hell is going on?"

Nic shook his head. "I don't know."

"Where were you this morning?" Aidan asked.

"I overslept."

"Those are homicide detectives," Aidan said.

Mindy...

Nic's stomach plummeted and pain ripped through his chest. Fur rippled over his arm as his wolf struggled to break free. Its first instinct was to get to its mate.

Aidan growled. "Pull yourself together. The last thing we need is for you to shift in front of the police."

Nic struggled to breathe. Struggled to think as his primal side rode him hard. "I have to get to Mindy."

"Who's Mindy?" Aidan asked.

Their gazes met and clashed. "My mate," Nic snapped.

Aidan's dark brow rose, disappearing beneath his long black hair. "When did this happen?"

"Last night," Nic bit out. "I'd planned to inform you this morning." His big body swayed and Nic gripped the back of a chair. "She can't be dead."

Aidan's face blanked. He immediately reached for the phone and punched in a number. "You have a body coming in," he said to the person on the other end of the line. "I want to know everything about it. You know what to do." He hung up. "You have to go down to the station now. Leave your cell phone here in case they jump the gun and book you. Whatever you do, don't incriminate yourself."

Hard to do when you don't know what's going on, Nic thought, and handed Aidan the phone.

"Report back here the second you're finished," Aidan said. "That's an order. I don't want you to take any detours. No side trips. Am I clear?"

Nic nodded, and they left.

* * *

The Breakbend police station was set up like every other small-town police force. There were only three rooms: one for the head of the department, one for interrogation, and the last for everyone else.

Five desks were slammed together, each housing an ancient-looking computer. A jail cell built for ten people max had been shoved into the corner, out of the way. The bars were a constant reminder of where you were, in case you forgot.

Nic and his attorney walked into the station and were immediately met by Detective Markinson. He led them into the interrogation room and asked them to take a seat. The red light on the camera mounted to the ceiling came on. Detective Daniels followed them into the room and shut the door behind him.

They'd barely settled in when the detectives fired off the first round of questions.

"Do you know a Ms. Mindy MacDougal?" Daniels asked.

Nic glanced at his attorney. The man nodded for him to answer.

"Yes, is she all right?" he asked.

Neither detective answered, which only alarmed Nic more.

"How long have you been seeing her?" Daniels asked.

Nic rubbed the back of his neck. "We just met the other night."

"Have you slept with her?" Daniels asked.

Nic's jaw clenched. "I don't see how that is any of your business."

"We'll take that as a yes," Daniels said and glanced at Markinson.

"Do you know a Marco Faretti?" Markinson asked.

He hadn't. At least not until the other night. Nic didn't like where this was going. "Not personally," he said.

"But you do know who he is," Daniels said.

"Yes, I've seen him around recently," Nic said. What did this have to do with Mindy?

"I believe you've done more than see him," Daniels said. "Think hard."

"Is Mindy okay?" Nic asked again. He could barely keep his agitation under wraps. Had Marco hurt her?

"Why wouldn't she be?" Daniels asked.

"Please tell me. I need to know," Nic said. "Marco was hassling her the other night and stalking her at her job."

"Did you take care of him for her?" Markinson asked. "Did she ask for your help?"

The questions surprised Nic. "What's that supposed to mean?" He shifted in the hard seat, trying to get comfortable.

"She's a pretty girl," Daniels said. "I can see how a guy could lose his head over her and do something stupid. Something he might regret later."

The wolf rose before Nic could stop it. He knew the detective was baiting him, but he didn't like him using Mindy, using his mate.

"I don't know what you're talking about. I admit that I got into a scuffle with Marco at a bar. A scuffle he started, I might add. The next day I asked him to leave Mindy alone," he said. "That's the extent of my contact with him."

"How long have you lived in the area?" Markinson asked.

"Eleven years," Nic said.

"So you're familiar with the back roads and the woods," Markinson said.

Nic was more than familiar with the woods in the area, but he didn't think it was a good idea to let them know it. "I'm familiar with the roads I travel on regularly. As for the woods, I only go into them during hunting season."

"Are you sure you didn't run into him again?" Daniels asked, changing the subject. "Maybe he was sniffing around your girlfriend? Maybe she invited him over in between your visits? Ever think of that?"

Nic bared his teeth. "Get to the point."

His attorney put his hand on Nic's shoulder and squeezed. It was a warning to get his wolf under control.

"Mr. Faretti was found murdered on the steps of Ms. MacDougal's home this morning," Daniels said.

Nic shot to his feet. "What! Is Mindy okay? How long has he been dead?" What he really wanted to know was how he died. Marco might be a pup, but he was still a shifter. Weres didn't go down easily.

"We're trying to ascertain that now," Daniels said.

"As you can see by his explosive reaction to the news, Mr. La Croix had no idea that Mr. Faretti was dead," Nic's attorney said.

"Where were you this morning between three o'clock and six o'clock?" Daniels asked.

"In bed. Asleep," Nic said.

"Can anyone verify that?" Markinson asked.

Nic shook his head. "No," he said, "I was alone."

"So what you're saying is that you don't have an alibi," Daniels said.

"What I'm saying is I don't need one," Nic replied.

Daniels snorted. "For your sake, I hope you're right."

They continued questioning Nic, doing a variation of good cop, bad cop until he reached the end of his tether.

"Listen, I have told you everything I know. Asking me the same questions over and over isn't going to change my answers," Nic said.

"Mind if we get your fingerprints and DNA?" Markinson asked.

"Sorry, gentleman, but I'm not going to allow my client to participate in a fishing expedition," the attorney said. "Mr. La Croix has been more than cooperative, especially since the coroner hasn't had time to determine the cause of death yet. If you have any further questions for Mr. La Croix, please direct them to me." The attorney glanced at Nic. "Let's go."

Daniels scowled at the lawyer. Markinson didn't look at all surprised.

"We'll be in touch," Markinson said. "In the meantime, don't leave town."

"Hadn't planned to," Nic said. He was still trying to process what he'd been told. In the end, all that mattered to him was that Mindy was still alive.

Nic and his attorney returned to the estate. The interrogation had taken two hours. Two hours that were better spent checking on Mindy. The need to rush to her side was almost unbearable. The attorney ushered him into Aidan's office.

"Take a seat," Aidan said, then glanced at the attorney. "What happened?"

"Marco Faretti was murdered, or at least that's what they suspect right now," the lawyer said.

"Do they have any proof?" Aidan asked.

The attorney shook his head.

"Then why did they think you did it?" Aidan asked Nic.

"I guess I'm the most obvious suspect." Nic scrubbed a hand over his face. Mindy must be scared out of her mind. "Can I have my phone back?"

"What for?" Aidan asked.

"I want to call Mindy," he said. "Make sure she's okay."

"No!" Aidan snapped. "I don't want you talking to her. I don't want you anywhere near her until we know what's going on."

"She's my mate," Nic ground out. "That's not going to happen."

Aidan sat back, eyeing him closely. "I know there's been some tension between us. I hope that doesn't have anything to do with this current situation."

"It doesn't," Nic said.

"I take it your new mate is human," Aidan said. The answer was obvious, since no Kin would call in the human authorities over the death of one of their own.

Nic's jaw clenched.

"Does she know what you are?" Aidan asked.

"No," Nic said.

"That could be a problem," Aidan said.

"It wasn't for *your* mate," Nic snarled and glared at Aidan in direct challenge.

Aidan's amber eyes glowed until they were molten gold, and his incisors lengthened. He growled deep in his chest and rose to his feet. As he stared at Nic, the sound grew louder.

Nic didn't want to challenge the Alpha for his position. He wasn't interested in leading the pack. The only thing he wanted was to get to his mate's side to protect her. Nic forced his gaze down until he stared at the beige carpet.

Aidan continued to growl, then slowly sat back down. "You only get one pass," he said. "The next time you do that, I'll rip your throat out."

Nic swallowed hard. "Understood, Alpha."

Aidan clasped his hands together. "Now, I'm going to ask you one time and one time only," he said. "Did you kill the pup?"

Nic looked him in the eye. "No."

"Do you know who did?" Aidan asked.

"No idea," Nic said.

"Did they say how he was killed?" Aidan asked.

"No." Nic shook his head. "They were pretty tight-lipped about the details. Didn't give much out."

Aidan crossed his arms over his wide chest. "I should be getting a call from the coroner soon," he said. It paid to have wolves in the right positions. "Until I do, can you handle this situation on your own or do I need to step in?"

Nic's eyes flared.

Aidan snarled.

The attorney took a step back so he was no longer next to them.

"I'll handle it," Nic said. "Let me know what they find out." He had to get out of Aidan's office before his wolf got them into more trouble. On his way out, Nic ran into Jenna.

"Is it true that there's been a murder?" she asked.

"According to the police."

Her face paled. "Do we know who it is?"

"Marco Faretti," he said.

Her pale brow furrowed. "I don't think I know him."

"He doesn't live in town," Nic said.

Jenna stared at him, tilting her head from side to side. "You look different," she said.

Some of the rage seeped out of him. "I am different," Nic said softly.

He no longer felt anything for Jenna beyond friendly affection and abiding respect. How could he have believed that she was meant for him? He should've listened to his wolf. It knew all along.

"I have to go," he said. "My mate needs me."

Nic heard her swift intake of breath as he strode down the hall to the front door.

16

Mindy skipped class, but decided to go to work. She couldn't bring herself to stay around the house all day knowing that Marco's body had been lying outside at the bottom of her front steps.

She left out her back door and walked around the house. There was a crimson stain on the sidewalk where Marco had been. Her stomach soured as she climbed into her car.

She turned the key and the engine hummed smoothly. The lack of a ping reminded her that Nic had been there only a few hours earlier and they'd shared one of the best nights of her life.

Sadness rose inside of her. Where was Nic and what was he doing? Had the police contacted him yet? Had they arrested him? Would he ever forgive her if they had?

Mindy thought about Izzy's cryptic warning. She'd thought for sure her sister had been talking about Marco, but now...

She backed out of her driveway and drove into town. By the time Mindy reached Breakbend, her eyes were rimmed with red and her face was blotchy from crying. She parked behind the clinic and let herself inside. The cheerful light blue walls and photographs of satisfied customers did little to ease her pain.

Celina took one look at her and jumped out of her seat. "What happened? What's wrong? Did Nic do this?" she asked. "Is Izzy okay?"

Mindy sniffled and more tears appeared. "It's Marco."

Celina drew back in confusion. "Marco? What about Marco? I thought you didn't want anything to do with him. I told you that he was bad news."

Celina's face swam before Mindy's eyes. "He's dead," Mindy said. "I found his body on my sidewalk."

"What!" Celina shouted. "What happened?"

Mindy shook her head. "He was killed. Torn apart by something or someone. It was awful."

Celina's eyes widened. "When?"

"Sometime last night," she said. "I didn't hear anything."

"How?" Celina asked.

"I don't know," Mindy said. "He had to have been killed somewhere else and dumped in front of my house. Who would do that?"

Celina paled. "Oh, honey, are you okay?" She pulled Mindy into her arms and hugged her tight.

Mindy sniffed. "I don't know. I think I'm still in shock."

Celina reached for the box of tissues on her desk and handed them to Mindy. "I know you're scared, but why are you crying? This is Marco we're talking about. He was a jerk, remember?"

"I know, but I didn't want him dead," Mindy wailed.

"Did Nic spend the night?" Celina asked.

Mindy shook her head.

"Did you call him to let him know about Marco?" Celina asked.

"I can't," Mindy sobbed.

"Why not?" Celina asked.

"Because I had to tell the police about him and Marco getting into a fight the other night," Mindy said.

Celina pulled back. "Do you think Nic hurt Marco?"

Tears flowed down Mindy's cheeks. "Izzy called to warn me this morning. She was totally freaking out."

"To warn you about what?" Celina asked.

"Danger being nearby," Mindy said. "I don't know what to think anymore."

Celina studied her friend's blotchy face and tear-stained cheeks. She didn't look injured. Her gaze wandered lower until it reached a dark, angry smudge on the side of Mindy's neck.

At first she couldn't figure out what she was looking at. "What happened to your neck?" Celina moved Mindy's shirt aside to get a better look.

Mindy's hand shot up and covered the spot, but not before Celina saw the teeth marks in the wound.

"Nic got carried away last night and gave me a hickey," she said.

Celina's heart dropped. "Is that what he said it was?"

"What else would it be?" Mindy asked.

What else indeed...

In Celina's experience, wolves didn't get carried away. There were no accidents when it came to marking a female. They took mating very seriously and they never bit a neck without it meaning something.

"Take a seat," she said. "I'm going to get you a cup of tea, then I want you to start from the beginning and tell me everything. Okay?"

Mindy nodded. "Okay."

Celina's hands shook as she walked into the small kitchenette to make Mindy a cup of tea. That wasn't a hickey on her neck. A hickey wouldn't have broken the skin. It also wouldn't have teeth marks. Mindy was too naïve to know otherwise.

Nic had marked her. His *wolf* had marked her. In the eyes of the pack, Mindy was now one of them. How could this have happened? He'd only known her for a few days.

Resentment roiled inside Celina. Such a waste. The idiot didn't understand the significance of the mark. Couldn't appreciate the honor that had been bestowed upon her because she didn't know that the Moonlight Kin existed.

Celina tossed the ceramic cup into the sink, shattering it. She gripped the side of the sink and stared at the broken shards. It wasn't fair.

"Are you okay?" Mindy asked.

Celina bit the inside of her mouth, using the pain to focus her. "I'm fine," she said. "Just clumsy. I'll be right out with your tea."

If Slade hadn't made her promise not to tell Mindy the truth, she'd march into the other room right this instant and set her straight. But he had, so she couldn't.

Celina picked up another cup and put in a tea bag. While the tea steeped, she thought about Slade. He'd been hinting at marking her, but had put the act off repeatedly.

She had tried to be patient, tried to give him the time and space he needed, but seeing Mindy's mark brought clarity to her mind that hadn't existed before. Celina was done waiting.

Tonight, she'd push Slade for a commitment. If he balked, she'd tell him about Mindy's mark and ask him to move out.

Mind made up, Celina picked up the cup of tea and took it to Mindy. "This should make you feel better," she said, but her thoughts had already returned to Slade and the upcoming discussion they would have.

17

The only reason anyone would leave a dead body lying on someone's front lawn was if they meant to send a message.

The question was, who was the warning for? Him? Or Mindy?

It seemed more likely the warning had been meant for him, but Nic couldn't rule out the chance that it was meant for her. What could anyone possibly warn Mindy about?

He sped to her house, determined to check on her and make sure she was okay. Once he assured himself that she was unharmed, he'd sniff around to see what he could pick up. The cops were good, but their noses couldn't match one of the Kin's.

Nic was surprised to find Mindy's car gone when he arrived. Where could she be? He hadn't seen her at the police station. He didn't think she'd go to school or work, not after finding a body.

Mindy's car wasn't the only thing missing. The police were gone, too, but the crime-scene tape still surrounded the area near her front porch.

Nic rolled down his window and sniffed the air. He needed to make sure he was alone before he pulled over. Other than a few deer in the distance, he didn't detect anything of size. He guided the truck over to the side of the road and put it in park, then slipped out of the cab.

He listened to the sound of the wind. Nic stood perfectly still while the woods whispered their secrets. As soon as he was sure it was safe, he loped over to Mindy's yard and scented the area.

Death hit him instantly. It clung to the grass and soiled the dirt with its foul odor. The coppery scent of blood followed on death's heels. Marco may have been a pain in the ass, but he didn't deserve to die.

Nic slowly circled the area, sniffing every few feet to make sure he didn't miss anything. As he moved further out, he caught the elusive scent that had bothered him before. It was all over the yard. The strongest concentration hung in the air where the body had been. His wolf bristled. Nic followed the odor toward the woods.

Before he could reach the trees, Nic came across an odd *stain*. He circled the spot, smelling every inch of the diameter. The stain wasn't blood. Wasn't chemical. And it definitely wasn't man made.

Nic crouched down to examine the spot. He dipped a finger into the residue. The second the ashy substance hit his skin, it burned like acid. Nic ignored the pain long enough to sniff his finger. The stench of magic filled his nostrils and he stumbled back, landing on his butt.

It wasn't possible. Couldn't be. They were myth. Legends created to scare children into behaving.

There was only one creature Nic had heard of that left that kind of stain behind, and as far as he knew, it wasn't real.

The hair on the back of his neck rose, warning him that he was being watched. Nic didn't react. Instead, he wiped the ash off his finger, ignoring the blisters it had left behind.

Nic slowly scanned the area with his senses and detected—*nothing*. He rose to his feet. For the first time in his life, Nic knew what it felt like to be prey. He didn't like the sensation one bit and neither did his wolf.

He left the stain and headed toward his truck. Not once did Nic take his eyes off the woods, until he drove away. The idea that the bogeyman might be after Mindy terrified Nic and left him shaken. If he hadn't been certain about his growing feelings for her before, the deadly threat solidified them.

What had she gotten herself into? It was more imperative than ever that he find her. If what Nic had discovered was real, then Mindy wasn't safe. No one was.

Mindy nearly fell out of her seat when Nic burst into the animal clinic. Seeing him in person only added to her sense of guilt and confusion. She'd spent the morning at the police station giving them her statement. She'd had no choice but to tell them about Nic. That didn't mean she felt good about the decision.

His face was flushed and he was out of breath. His big body tensed when he saw her. She expected him to start yelling any second.

"Are you okay?" he asked.

The question surprised her. Didn't he want to know why she'd given the police his name?

Nic's gaze roamed over her, settling for a breath or two on her hickey before moving on.

"I'm fine," she said, finally finding her voice. "I'm sorry. I had no choice. I had to tell them."

"Doesn't matter," Nic said. "I'm just glad you're all right. I was so worried when the police stopped by my workplace and told me there'd been a murder. They didn't tell me who died." He pulled her into his arms and held her close. "I thought I'd lost you." Nic's voice cracked.

Mindy pushed out of his embrace. "I didn't want to get you into trouble, but I couldn't lie."

He grabbed her hand, threading his fingers between hers. "There's nothing to apologize for. You did the right thing."

"You're not mad?" She'd be mad if she were in his shoes.

Nic smiled. "No, honey. I'm relieved."

She stared at him. "It was horrible." Her voice quivered.

"I can imagine. I'm sorry you had to go through something like that alone," Nic said. "I wish I could've been there for you. I should've been there. I won't let you down again." His body quaked. "If only he had been there when I left."

"He wasn't?" Mindy asked, watching his face closely.

"No!" Nic frowned. "I would've noticed a dead body."

He took a deep, exasperated breath and his expression changed. Fury replaced concern. The switch was so abrupt that it left Mindy shaking. Nic gently moved her aside and rushed into the main part of the clinic.

"What are you doing?" she asked. "Nic, where are you going?" Mindy raced in after him.

Nic didn't stop until he reached the recovery area. Only a few animals were currently housed back there—a couple of dogs and two cats.

The second he entered the room, they all whimpered and clawed to get out of their cages. Nic ignored their reaction and moved deeper into the room. When he reached the largest cage, he crouched next to it.

"What happened to the animal inside this cage?" he asked. His tone was deadly serious. Mindy took a step back.

Celina came running into the room. Her eyes widened to the size of saucers when she saw Nic next to the empty cage.

Nic's gaze slid from Mindy to her friend. Rage returned, making it look like his blue eyes were glowing. "Where is it?" He pointed at the cage.

Celina's tawny face paled and her hand fluttered to her throat. "It's gone. I took it to a preserve and released it."

Mindy glanced at her. Why was Celina lying?

Nic could smell the lies emanating from Celina's skin. The sour odor stank up the room, but this was neither the time nor the place to confront her. Not in front of Mindy.

He should report to Aidan immediately. *And say what? I think the bogeyman is real?* Nic snorted. He wasn't about to present his findings to the Alpha until he had proof. An odd stain and a foul odor weren't enough. Not after everything that had happened this morning.

"Mindy, I think you should stay with me until the authorities find out who's responsible for Marco's death," he said.

Mindy slowly shook her head. "I can't do that."

Nic could see the fear shimmering in her brown eyes, smell it tainting her supple skin. And it broke his heart. "I know you're scared of me, especially after the morning you've had."

"I'm not scared," she said. "I just can't leave my animals alone."

He let her believe her own lies because Nic knew they were the only thing keeping her from falling apart. But there was no way he was going to leave her unprotected. She was his mate. It was his duty to take care of her. It was his honor, even if she didn't know it yet.

"Then you leave me no choice," Nic said. "I'll be over after you get off work."

Mindy's eyes widened. "Nic, you can't just barge into my life. A lot has happened. I need time to think."

"So you can convince yourself that I'm a murderer?" he asked. "I don't think so." Nic's gaze slid to Celina.

She took a step back.

"Tell her," he demanded. "You *know* she's safe with me. And you know why."

"She might," Mindy said. "But I don't."

Celina swallowed hard. "He's telling the truth," she said.

Mindy's head whipped around. She'd expected her friend to take her side of things. "How do you know?"

"I just do," Celina said.

"Well, forgive me if I don't take your word for it," she said.

"Mindy, someone left a body on your front lawn," Celina said. "Until we know who or what put it there"—she glared at Nic—"I don't want you being alone. Izzy would agree if she were here."

"But what if—"

"He didn't do it," Celina said. "Trust me."

"Do you know what you're asking?"

Celina sighed. "Yeah, I do," she said, glancing at Nic.

"Why do I feel like I'm not part of the conversation taking place?" Mindy asked.

Celina grabbed her hand. "Believe me, this is all about you," she said. "Nic had better protect you with his life."

"You know I will," he said, then sprang to his feet. He pressed a quick kiss on Mindy's mouth before she could protest, and strode out of the clinic.

Mindy watched him go, then glared at Celina. "Are you crazy? What if he killed Marco?"

Celina met her accusing gaze unflinchingly. "Do you believe that? Do you really believe that Nic is a murderer?"

Mindy opened her mouth to say yes, it was possible, but the words refused to come out. Her heart wouldn't let them. It just didn't believe that the same man who'd made love to her so tenderly, so passionately, had turned around the same night and killed a man. It didn't make sense.

Celina's gaze softened. "I know you haven't known him long, but I can tell you right now that he's serious about you. He's committed more deeply than you can imagine." She touched Mindy's hickey, then pulled her hand away.

Mindy sighed. "A hickey doesn't mean anything," she said. "Last night we talked about being exclusive, but with everything that's happened I don't think that's a good idea."

"You're wrong," Celina said. "You saw how scared he was when he came in here. That's not something he could've faked. Nic *will* protect you. His kind redefines loyalty. If you don't believe me, call Izzy and ask."

"Izzy has never met Nic," Mindy said. "Has she?"

"No, but she'll still *know*," Celina said.

Mindy looked at her. Really looked. For the first time in all the years she'd known her, Celina appeared fragile. Was it because of Slade? Or was it something else?

Before she took a leap based on blind faith, there was one question she needed answered. "Why did you lie to Nic about the hybrid?"

Celina's gaze dropped and sadness etched her face. "You'll understand why soon enough." She sighed. "When you do, it'll be clear why I couldn't let anything happen to him," she said, and walked away.

Izzy wasn't the only one who spoke in riddles.

18

Nic showed up at Mindy's house like he'd promised, and knocked on her front door. Mindy opened it and stared at him. He had a black duffle bag slung over his shoulder and wore a stained white T-shirt with his blue jeans. His hair was tousled and he was grinning.

She almost smiled back, but stopped herself. "I still don't think this is a good idea," she said.

Nic studied her small porch and shrugged. "I don't have a problem sleeping right here," he said.

Mindy was tempted to let him, but then her gaze strayed to the crimson stain she hadn't quite been able to get off with her power hose. What if whoever killed Marco came back while Nic was on the porch?

Her heart thundered in her chest. She wouldn't be able to live with herself if anything happened to him. Mindy glared at him, but Nic's smile only widened. His eyes fixed on the hickey, and the strangest thing happened. The spot heated.

Mindy brushed her hand over it, and something in Nic's blue eyes flared. She stepped back. "Come in."

Nic walked into the living room and dropped his duffle bag next to the couch.

"Can I get you anything to drink?" she asked.

"Water," Nic said.

Mindy went into the kitchen to retrieve a bottle. When she returned,

Nic was sprawled out across the couch, his wide shoulders and long legs eating up every square inch. He sat up when she handed him the water.

"Thanks," he said, then popped the cap and swallowed half the bottle in one gulp. "I know this isn't something you want to talk about, but I need to know if there's been anything strange going on lately."

"Define strange," she said. Her whole life was odd thanks to Izzy.

Nic set his bottled water down on the coffee table. "Let's start with the animal at the clinic," he said. "What was it and how did it get there?"

"It was a mutt. A big mutt, but a mutt nonetheless," she said. "I almost hit him with my car. When I first saw him, I thought he was dead."

"But it wasn't?"

Mindy shook her head. "No, but the animal was injured. Celina and I rushed it to the clinic, where Dr. Fields patched it up."

"What kind of mutt was it?" Nic asked.

"Wolf and something. Dr. Fields thought it had been bred with a Russian Bear dog, but the lab results were inconclusive," Mindy said. "Once it healed, Celina carted him off to the preserve."

Nic sat forward. "Are you sure?"

"As far as I know, that's what she did." Mindy couldn't meet his eyes when she was lying. Why was she protecting Celina, when her friend had tossed her to the wolves?

"Anything else unusual happen?" Nic asked. He didn't know why Mindy was lying, but he decided not to press her. He was afraid if he did she'd shut down.

She thought about his question and shook her head. "Not really. I don't think Izzy's warning from the wind counts."

"What?" Nic asked. What did she mean by that?

She blanched. "Nothing," she said.

Nic touched her hand. "You can tell me. I won't laugh."

Mindy stared at him in indecision. Nic thought she would refuse to answer, then she took a deep breath and slowly let it out.

"Remember how I told you my sister was eccentric?" she asked.

Nic nodded.

"Well, there's a little bit more to the story than that." Mindy sank into the chair. "Truth is, Izzy is odd. It's not just her fascination with monsters."

Nic inwardly cringed, but kept his expression neutral. He didn't want Mindy to see what effect her words had on him. He needed her to continue talking.

"Sometimes Izzy knows things before they happen," Mindy said, and glanced away.

"Are you saying your sister is psychic?" Nic asked.

"I know it sounds crazy," she said. "You don't have to believe me, but she called this morning and warned me that darkness was near. She gave me the impression that I was in danger."

Nic's heart stuttered in his chest. "Did she say from who?"

Mindy shook her head. "That's the problem with Izzy and her visions. They aren't always clear," she said. "I know you don't believe me."

"Actually, I do," Nic said. Her sister was a Sighted-One. Is that why the Darkling was here? He shook his head. No, that didn't make sense, since her sister was gone. Unless... "Do you have the same abilities as Izzy?"

"No." She gave him a humorless laugh. "There was only room for one whack-a-doodle in the family."

Nic could sense her pain. "You said Izzy believed in monsters."

She nodded.

"What did you mean by that?" Nic asked.

"When we were kids, Izzy used to tell me crazy stories about monsters walking through the mall. Used to scare me to death. Eventually, I outgrew the stories, but Izzy never did," Mindy said. "She swore she could see them. She said they were everywhere. Izzy was always so scared. I think that's why she partied so much in her teens. But no amount of alcohol could make them or her visions go away."

It must've been terrifying for her, Nic thought. Growing up as a Sighted-One without any guidance had to be a lonely existence. Had loneliness also contributed to Mindy's isolation?

"I'd like to fix you some dinner," he said, clearly surprising her.

"You don't have to do that," she said.

"I know I don't have to," Nic said. "I want to. You just stay here and put your feet up." He didn't wait for her to answer. He simply walked into the kitchen.

Mindy watched him go. She'd expected Nic to laugh, when she'd told him about Izzy, but he hadn't. There'd been compassion in his eyes, and what looked like concern. She sat back and had just kicked her feet up when the doorbell rang.

"I'll get it," she said. Mindy glanced through the peephole, then opened the door. "Detective Daniels, what are you doing here?"

"I was in the neighborhood," he said. "Thought I'd stop by and make sure you were okay."

"Thank you," Mindy said. "I'm fine."

He shuffled his feet on her porch. "I just received the coroner's report," he said.

Mindy's stomach dropped. This was it. What he said next could change everything. "What did it say?" she asked, not sure if she really wanted to know.

The detective watched her closely. "He ruled the death an animal attack. Said it most likely was a mountain lion."

"Really?" His answer shocked Mindy. Her surprise quickly morphed into relief. "I'm glad to hear Marco wasn't murdered."

The detective's lips thinned. It was evident that he didn't agree with the report. "I stopped by to tell you to be careful and to ask if you had anywhere else you could stay for a while. I don't like the idea of you being out here on your own," he said.

A hand grasped the side of the door, opening it wider. Nic appeared beside her shoulder. The detective stiffened and his brown eyes narrowed.

"She won't be alone," Nic said. "I'm here."

Detective Daniels gave him a hard cop stare, but Nic didn't seem intimidated in the least. The detective's gaze eventually returned to Mindy.

"You might want to take care with the crowd you're running with," he said. "Rumors around town say that the folks on the Fortier estate can be dangerous."

"I didn't think the police paid attention to gossip," Nic said, his voice lethal.

"Sometimes it pays to listen to whispers on the streets," Detective Daniels said. "You have a good night, Ms. MacDougal."

"You too."

Mindy shut the door. "That was weird."

"Did I hear him right? Did he say it was a mountain lion attack?" Nic asked.

"Yeah." Mindy's brow furrowed.

"But?" Nic asked, wondering why she didn't look convinced. "You don't believe him."

Mindy rubbed her neck. "No, I believe him. Why would he lie?"

"He wouldn't," Nic said, but the coroner would. "So what's bothering you?"

"Marco's body," she said. "How did it get in front of my house?"

"The cat must've dragged it there," he said.

Mindy stared at him. "That's just it. There weren't any drag marks."

Nic brushed her arm with his finger. "Are you sure? You were in shock when you found the body. Anybody would be. Is it possible you are mistaken?" He didn't want to put doubt in her mind, but Nic had no choice. The truth would have to stay buried until he could reveal all to her.

"I know I could be wrong, but I don't think I am." She rubbed her hands over her arms. "I know animals. Marco wasn't a little guy. Even a healthy-sized mountain lion would have had difficulty moving him. It would've had to drag him. If it couldn't, it would've sliced him open and eaten his stomach and intestines."

She was right. It wasn't a mountain lion that'd killed Marco. A cat couldn't take down a Were, but a Darkling could.

19

Celina drove home without knowing how she got there. Her thoughts were too preoccupied with how she was going to confront Slade. She wanted that bond. If Mindy had one in such a short time period, then there was no reason for she and Slade to wait.

She pulled into the weathered apartment complex and parked in her numbered spot. Slade didn't have a car, so there was no telling if he was home yet. Celina hoped he wasn't. She wanted to get the apartment arranged into a romantic setting before he arrived.

What if he didn't come home tonight?

He'd been spending more and more time away. Celina wondered, not for the first time, if he'd changed his mind. She couldn't allow that to happen.

She remembered the fury on Nic La Croix's handsome face when he'd asked about Slade. His anger scared her. Why did Nic want to know where he was? Did it have anything to do with Marco's murder? Was it because Slade had been sniffing around Mindy's house? Or was it because he wasn't part of the Moonlight Kin?

Wolves were highly territorial. Couple that with Nic leaving his mark on Mindy and you had a recipe for extreme violence.

A fresh wave of jealousy struck. Celina hated that Slade was so interested in Mindy, but she didn't want him harmed.

She got out of the car and walked to the tiny apartment she'd called home for the last few years. Gray paint peeled from the walls as she climbed the stairs to the second floor.

Celina opened the door and called out Slade's name. Her voice echoed in the silence. She didn't know how much time she had before he arrived, so she'd have to work fast.

She pulled out the candles from beneath her kitchen sink and lit them so that the warm glow softened the appearance of the tattered furniture.

Celina walked into her bedroom to search for her best lingerie. She placed the lacey outfit on the bed while she took a shower, then slipped it on beneath her jeans and green T-shirt. Celina went back into the kitchen and removed some chicken from the freezer so it had time to defrost.

Slade came home two hours later. He stopped in his tracks as he stepped through the front door. His gaze scanned the room, moving from the candles to the food on the table before settling on her.

"What's this?" he asked.

"I thought I'd do something nice for you," Celina said.

His amber eyes narrowed. "Why?"

"Do I need a reason?" Celina asked.

Slade smiled. "No, but I know you have one."

Celina exhaled. "Fine." She flipped on the lights.

"Do you know anything about a murder that occurred at Mindy's house last night?" she asked.

Slade glided deeper into the room, his molten eyes glittering.

"A body was dumped on her front lawn," Celina said. "She's terrified. Mindy came into work crying. I barely got her to calm down. I know I promised not to tell her, but I'm going to have to say something."

Slade shrugged as if it were inconsequential. "There is no reason for her to be afraid. No one's going to harm her."

"How do you know?" Celina asked. "Whatever killed Marco could still be lurking outside her house just waiting for an opportunity to get to her."

"Oh, I am certain it wants her. Just not for the reasons you suggest." He smiled.

"What's that supposed to mean?" she asked.

"People die every day, Celina. It's hardly a tragedy."

She put her hands on her hips. "You didn't answer my question."

"No." Slade laughed. "I didn't." He stalked around the apartment, moving as if he were caged and looking for a way out.

He hadn't denied anything, nor had he confessed. His evasive answers confused Celina and frightened her. Had he killed Marco? She didn't want to believe it, but Weres didn't live by the same laws as humans. She'd learned that over the years. Anyone familiar with the Moonlight Kin knew they were governed by a different set of rules. The punishment for breaking those rules was harsh. Had Slade broken the rules?

"You need to stay away from Mindy's house," she said. "It's not safe."

Slade's eyebrow arched. "I can't do that," he said.

"Why not?" Celina whined. Didn't the idiot understand that she was trying to save his life?

"Because I plan to claim her as my mate," Slade said casually.

"You can't do that!" Celina launched herself at him, pounding her fists on his chest.

Slade easily fended her off. "Stop it before you hurt yourself." He grabbed her wrists and pushed her down onto the couch until she was prone, then covered her body with his own.

"You promised," Celina gasped. "You said you'd claim me."

"I said no such thing," Slade said.

He hadn't. Celina had heard what she'd wanted to hear. Slade had used her...just like all the other Weres.

"If you'd bothered to investigate before you spread your thighs for every wolf around, you'd know that claiming doesn't work like that," he said.

"What do you mean?" She'd missed something. Something

important. Something Slade had been aware of since day one. Anger replaced some of her pain.

"One sniff and I knew you weren't my mate. Most wolves can scent whether a woman is their mate or not," he said. "There's a sweetness, a richness to her that runs beneath the surface."

"So this whole time you've been playing me?" she asked.

"Don't take it personally," Slade said. "In the beginning, I genuinely needed you."

Celina glared at him, then smiled. "You're too late," she hissed, thinking about Mindy's mark.

"What are you talking about?" Slade asked in confusion.

"You can't claim Mindy." Celina laughed maniacally. She wasn't the only one who hadn't been paying attention. Celina couldn't wait to see the look on Slade's face when he found out the truth.

Slade bared his teeth. "Why not?" He shook her, but it only made her laugh harder.

Celina's smile returned, this time wider. "Because she's already been claimed."

His amber eyes widened, then began to glow.

"That's right, Lover Boy, another wolf got to her first," Celina said. "I saw the mark on her neck with my own eyes. It's kind of hard to miss. Did I forget to mention that the Were who marked her is looking for you?"

"Who? Who did it? Tell me now, you stupid bitch!" Slade snarled, slamming her against the couch cushions.

"Nic La Croix," she said. "He's a big guy. I bet he's an even bigger Were. He won't be as easy to take down as Marco."

Slade's eyes narrowed until only tiny slivers of gold were visible. "You think you're so clever. You think you know what's going on, but you don't know anything." As he pinned her to the couch, a single claw extended from his finger.

"What are you doing?" Celina asked. "Slade, talk to me."

"What's wrong, Celina?" he asked. "Since the moment I met you,

you've been begging me to mark you. Change your mind?"

Her gaze fastened on the deadly claw. "Slade, honey, let's talk about this."

He shook his dark head. "There's nothing to talk about. I'm just giving you want you want," he said.

He was going to kill her. Celina could see it in his eyes. There was no warmth, no passion, only cold resolve. Celina struggled to break his grip.

"Slade, let me up. Stop playing around," she said.

He brought the claw to the inside of her wrist. If he sliced her the right way, it would look like a suicide and no one would suspect otherwise. Celina thought about Izzy's warning. She should've listened.

Slade ran the claw along her wrist, scratching her just deep enough for blood to surface on her skin. He leaned over and licked it off, then released her and rose from the couch. Slade walked toward the front door.

Celina was confused. She'd thought for sure that he was going to kill her. Maybe she was wrong about him? "Where are you going?" she asked.

"To get what I came to this world for," he said.

This world? What did he mean by that?

"You're just going to scratch me and leave?" Celina asked, though she no longer wanted him to stay.

"One scratch is all that is needed," Slade taunted.

"Needed for what?" Celina cried. "Mindy's mark was on her neck."

Slade's smile was slow to come, and when it did finally arrive, it made Celina shiver. "Enjoy what's left of your life."

Celina thought about Slade's parting shot as she polished off a bottle of wine. The scratch on her arm burned. She'd poured rubbing alcohol over it to clean the wound, but nothing stopped the pain.

She picked up her phone and drunk dialed Mindy. It was her fault that Slade wasn't here. If she hadn't flirted shamelessly with all the men, none of this would've happened.

Mindy picked up, her voice sleep-filled. "Hello?"

"You think you're so s-special," Celina slurred. "But you're not."

"Celina?" Mindy asked. "Have you been drinking?"

"No, I'm drunk," she said. "Wolves are circling you and you're too clueless to know it."

"What?" Mindy asked. "Celina, you're not making any sense. You should go to bed. We'll talk in the morning, when you've sobered up."

Celina balked. "You-you-you don't see what's right in front of you. You're blind to the truth," she said. "Izzy knew. Probably why she left."

"I'm going to hang up now, before one of us says something that we'll regret," Mindy said.

"Too late!" Celina snapped. The empty wine bottle toppled onto its side. "You have already ruined everything for me."

20

Mindy awoke blurry-eyed and confused the next morning. It had taken two hours to get back to sleep after she hung up with Celina. Her friend had said a lot of hurtful things, but Mindy knew it had been the alcohol talking.

What had gotten her friend so wound up was a mystery. A mystery Mindy planned to solve this morning.

She picked up the phone and punched in Celina's number. The phone rang five times, then her voicemail picked up. Odd, since Celina was an early riser. Was she screening her calls or too hung over to respond? It just didn't make sense.

Nothing about the last twenty-four hours made any sense. The outgoing message finished and was followed by a beep.

"Hey, Celina, it's Mindy." Words failed her. "We need to talk. I'll be over in an hour." Mindy hung up and wandered into the living room.

Nic was lying on the couch with an arm thrown over his eyes and his long legs propped up. His chest rose and fell evenly. He'd insisted on sleeping on the couch after Mindy told him that she had a perfectly good spare bed. Nic had smiled at her and said the only bed he wanted to sleep in was hers.

She tiptoed into the kitchen. Mindy had made it to the door when Nic said, "Morning beautiful."

Mindy stopped and glanced over her shoulder. His amazing eyes were fixed on her. Suddenly she wished she'd put on something nicer than her sweats.

"How'd you sleep?" she asked. No way had he been comfortable. Her couch had a lump in the middle of one of the cushions.

"Pretty good." He sat up and stretched.

"I'm going to make coffee," she said, watching the play of muscles beneath his shirt. "Want some?"

"That'd be great." He grinned. "But first I'm going to grab a shower."

Mindy nodded and slipped into the kitchen. Her fingers shook as she measured out the scoops and filled the tank. She pressed brew and walked back into the living room. She'd just finished feeding her gang when she heard whimpering outside.

The sound tugged at Mindy's heart. She threw the bolt on the front door and stepped out onto the porch. The hybrid was in the middle of her lawn, half-standing, half sitting. When he saw her, he dragged himself forward, his back legs limp beneath his big body.

"Oh no!" Mindy rushed off the porch and crouched down next to him. "What happened?" She scanned the canine from head to tail, but didn't immediately spot any blood. Had he been hit by a car again?

Mindy stood. She needed to get him into the car, get him to the clinic. "It's okay," she cooed, and stroked his head.

"Mindy, get away from him," Nic said.

She glanced toward the front door and saw Nic standing on the porch. He had a towel wrapped around his trim waist, his hair was slicked back, making it appear darker than it really was, and water dripped down his chest.

Normally a sight like that would disengage her brain, but something about his tone frightened her. "It's okay," she said. "He isn't wild."

Nic stepped down from the porch. "You're in mortal danger. Move away from him slowly."

She frowned. What did he mean by that? "I know he's big, but he's really a teddy bear. Trust me," she said.

Nic was breathing hard. Not from exertion, but from sheer terror.

Mindy didn't understand. He needed her to move away from the Darkling before it killed her. If it drew blood in any way, she was dead.

"Mindy, I need you to come to me." He took another step forward. "I know I'm asking a lot, but I need you to trust me one more time. That isn't what you think it is."

She stroked the massive creature's head. "It's a hybrid. A wolf dog," she said.

Nic moved closer. The first wave of magic licked his skin. He closed his eyes and let it roll over him. "No, honey, it's not. It's a Darkling."

"I don't know what that is." Mindy stared at him in confusion. "Nic, you're scaring me."

Before he could respond, the second wave of power struck. This time it hit like a tsunami, weakening his legs, driving him to his knees. Nic's head dropped back. "Oh goddess, no!" he cried as fur rippled over his arms and down his legs. The towel fell as his big body contorted. His wails quickly turned to howls.

Mindy stared in horror, not truly understanding what she was witnessing. No sign of Nic remained after the transformation. In his place stood a brindle-furred beast with a long snout, sharp claws, and massive teeth.

"Nic?"

The creature's head dropped and it stalked forward, baring its fangs and growling. Mindy knew this was it. She was about to be ripped to shreds. All the stories Izzy told her through the years came rushing back.

Izzy is right. There are monsters in the world.

The beast rushed her. Mindy closed her eyes. He hit her legs hard, sending her flying off to the side. Mindy landed in the grass and immediately rolled to her feet as the two animals came together in a clash of claws and teeth.

They tore at each other, ripping chunks of fur and flesh off. Blood covered their sides as they broke apart and attacked again and again. Mindy couldn't seem to tear her gaze away from the horrific sight.

She'd seen dogs fight, but their aggression had been nothing like this. These two creatures were trying to kill each other. Nic might actually die. Mindy's heart exploded in her chest. The thought of him dying left her bereft, left her more frightened than she'd been when she'd discovered Marco's body at the base of her steps.

Nic had to block Mindy's terrified expression out of his mind. One look at her face had told him that he'd lost her, but there was nothing he could do about that now. His heart had nearly stopped beating when he saw her so close to the Darkling.

All the stories about their abilities were true. The Darkling's magic had called to his wolf and demanded that it reveal itself.

Now Nic was in a fight for his life—for both their lives. He could feel his body weakening, but didn't dare let up.

The Darkling's magic wrapped around him, siphoning his power drop by drop. Soon he wouldn't have the strength to continue to fight.

He had to end this. Trouble was, they were evenly matched.

Blood dripped into his eyes and matted his fur. Nic stumbled, but somehow managed to stay on his feet. The Darkling struck again, tearing a furrow down his side. The magic burned like acid, eating at his skin.

Nic whimpered at Mindy. Tears streamed down her face. *Run!* he tried to shout, but all that came out was a fierce bark.

He swayed. He wouldn't last much longer. There was a reason why Darklings were the bogeymen of the Kin. Just stay awake long enough to get her to safety. His mate's safety was the only thing that mattered to him.

Nic latched on to the Darkling's leg and shook his head, trying to tear it off. The move didn't work, but it did leave his neck open for a counterattack.

Fear made Mindy finally move. Nic was hurt. Blood was everywhere. With the hybrid gripping his throat, he wouldn't last much longer. She had to do something. She scanned the yard for a weapon. There was nothing.

Mindy ran to the side of the house. The only thing there was a hose. She snatched it up and checked to make sure her power-washer nozzle was screwed on tight. As weapons went, it wasn't much.

She turned the water on and ran back to the front yard. Nic was lying on his side, but he hadn't completely given up. Mindy pointed the nozzle at the animals and squeezed the trigger.

Water blasted the hybrid in the face, shocking him enough to release Nic. He turned toward her and snarled. Mindy sprayed him again.

"Bad doggies!" The words brought out a giggle that threatened to release the hysteria Mindy held inside.

The hybrid snorted and shook his head, sending crimson droplets in every direction. Nic was trying to struggle to his feet, but couldn't seem to manage. The hybrid stalked Mindy. Nic threw his head back and howled. The sound was different, but she didn't have time to analyze the "hows" or the "whys."

"Stay back!" She held up the nozzle in front of her like it was a gun.

The beast hesitated, then kept coming.

"I'm warning you." She glanced over her shoulder to judge the distance to the door. Mindy didn't think she could make it to the house before he got her. "Don't move," she said, hoping he could understand her.

He kept coming.

A streak of bright orange ran past her legs. Hannibal's fur was raised, along with his tail. He yowled and spat at the hybrid, but it paid no attention to him.

That was until her cat launched himself onto the creature's back and clamped down on his ear. The hybrid snarled as Hannibal's claws dug into his fur, finding the tender skin beneath. He tried to shake the cat off, but the tabby held on tight.

The hybrid raised a claw to rip Hannibal away. Mindy blasted him in the face with the water before he could touch him. Water sprayed everywhere, including onto her cat. Hannibal leapt off the hybrid's back and ran into the house.

More howls filled the air. This time they weren't coming from Nic. The hybrid cocked its head to listen, then took off toward the woods.

When Mindy was sure that he was gone, she walked over to Nic. He was on his side, bleeding, and he didn't appear to be conscious. Mindy didn't want him in the house, but she couldn't bring herself to leave him out here.

She went into the house and got a beach towel, then laid it next to the beast. Mindy rolled "Nic" onto the towel and dragged him across the lawn. She was glad he was out cold, because there was no way to get him up the stairs without causing him more pain.

Mindy got him down the hall and into Tart's doggie cage. She was grateful that she'd decided to buy the largest one. If she hadn't, there was no way he would've fit. As soon as she had him inside, Mindy went into her bathroom to retrieve her first-aid kit.

Nic didn't stir as she cleaned his wounds and stitched him up. Mindy bandaged him quickly, then locked the cage. Blood covered her hands. Nic's blood. She even had a streak across her cheek.

She'd done everything she could think of to save him. For a second, she'd thought about taking him to the clinic, but Mindy quickly dismissed the idea. Nic wasn't an animal and he wasn't *human*.

Werewolf.

The insidious word whispered through her mind. Mindy's hands trembled. Werewolves weren't real. Monsters weren't real. This had to be a nightmare. Soon she'd wake up and Nic would be sleeping on the couch. Everything would go back to normal.

She stared at herself in the mirror. Nothing would be normal after today. Mindy couldn't go back to pretending that none of this was real. Nic was a monster. The kind of monster Izzy had warned her about.

He was also the man who'd saved her from Marco and Emmett. And the man who'd fixed her car. And the man who'd made love to her like she was the only woman on the planet who mattered to him. The question was, which one was the *real* Nic La Croix?

Mindy turned the water on in the shower as hot as she could stand it, then stripped out of her clothes and stepped under the spray. It hurt, but she didn't care. Mindy scrubbed and scrubbed until her skin glowed bright pink and there was no trace of blood swirling around her toes.

What was she going to do now?

She needed to call Celina, but she wasn't sure how much her friend knew. Nic had gone to a lot of trouble to keep his secret. Mindy couldn't betray his trust. He might have misled her, but he'd also saved her life. That counted for something.

21

Nic groaned and came to slowly. Every muscle in his body ached. He moved and felt a sharp pain in his side. He touched the spot and encountered gauze. What the hell happened to him?

He inhaled and caught Mindy's intoxicating aroma, then slowly opened his eyes. Bars came into view. Had he been arrested?

His hand slipped down, hitting bare skin. He was naked. That wasn't a good sign, if he was in jail. Nic blinked, trying to clear his vision and foggy head.

Something meowed.

Nic turned his head to find Mindy's one-eyed orange tabby, Hannibal, glaring at him. He scanned the bars again. They surrounded him. Not jail. A cage.

Fear enveloped him. Nic sat up quickly. His head banged against the top of the cage and he yelped. Hannibal sniffed at him, then turned tail and strolled silently out of the room. He looked around, but didn't recognize the bedroom. How had he gotten in here?

Mindy arrived in the doorway. A wary expression shadowed her soft features. "I thought I heard movement," she said. "Glad you're finally awake."

Nic shifted to sit up, but with his wide shoulders and large frame he couldn't move much. "What happened? How long have I been in here?" It was obvious that whatever occurred was bad—really bad, if he was locked inside a dog cage.

Mindy's eyes widened. "You don't remember?"

He shook his head and groaned again, clutching his temple. "No," he said. "How did I end up in here?"

She bit her lower lip. Despite his weakness and confusion, his body responded to the innocent act.

"I put you in there," she murmured. "Four hours ago."

The effect of her words was like being doused with cold water. Everything in him deflated. Four hours? A lot could happen in that time period.

"Why would you..." Memories of a garden hose and a fight came rushing back. "Mindy, I'm not sure what you think you saw—"

"Save your breath, Nic," she said. "I *know* what I saw."

The conviction in her voice cleared the last of the cobwebs out of his head. He had to do damage control. "I can explain," he said.

"No need," Mindy replied.

Nic's heart sank. "Let me out of here and I'll get my clothes and leave."

"Is it safe?" Her voice cracked. "I mean are you going to go all furry again?"

"You were never in any danger from me," he said softly. "I was serious when I said I'd protect you with my life."

Mindy unlocked the cage and opened the door. The second it swung wide, she stepped back out of reach.

Nic crawled and scooted, feeling every kink in his body start to relax. He was still in pain, but at least he was no longer cramping. He stood and stretched, unconcerned by his nudity. Nic inhaled, expecting to smell Mindy's fear, but there was none. Only quiet resolve. The kind of resolve one got when they had decided to cut their losses.

He had lost her. The one woman who meant everything to him. "Why didn't you run when you had the chance?" he asked.

Mindy scowled at him. "I couldn't."

"Why?" Nic needed to know. Her answer was vitally important to him.

"You needed my help," she said, and turned away.

He grabbed her hand to keep her from going. "You saw what I became. What made you think I needed your help?"

Mindy shrugged, but didn't try to pull away when he ran his thumb across her knuckles.

That is a good sign, isn't it?

"You were bleeding, Nic," she said. "Bad. It took me thirty minutes to get you stitched. You bled through two of the bandages."

He sensed her fear for the first time. Nic tasted it on the air, drew it into his lungs. Mindy hadn't been scared of him, at least after she got over the initial shock. She'd been scared *for* him. Hope glimmered inside him.

"I heal quickly," he said.

Their eyes met and clashed.

"He was going to kill you," she said softly. "I couldn't let that happen." Her confession ripped a hole in his gut.

"Neither could I," he whispered, willing her to understand.

Tears shimmered in Mindy's eyes. "Just because I saved you doesn't mean that I'm okay with any of this," she said. "I don't see how this can work. How we can work. We're two different species."

"It can and it will, if you just give us a chance," he said, believing it for the first time. Nic yanked Mindy into his arms and kissed her gently, tenderly. Her body softened, while his grew rigid.

Mindy pushed out of the embrace. "You're hurt," she said breathlessly.

Nic glanced down at the hard evidence of his desire. "Not that part of me."

"Nic, I can't do this right now," Mindy said. "I need time to process what's happened. To make sense of it all. It's not every day you find out that mon—"

"Monsters are real," he finished for her.

Mindy wasn't able to face him. "You understand. Don't you?"

He did, which was why it hurt so much. "I'll get my things," he said. Nic had to report to Aidan now that he had confirmation of the Darkling. "You take as much time as you need." He prayed she wouldn't take long, wouldn't take forever.

Watching him go was one of the hardest things Mindy had ever had to do. Nic looked so lost, so confused. Twice she found herself opening her mouth to call out and ask him to come back. But she didn't. She couldn't. Not until she sorted through her feelings.

As Nic drove away, Mindy picked up the phone and dialed Celina's number. She had a feeling this was what her friend had been trying to tell her last night when she called. If she knew Nic was different, why hadn't she just said so?

The phone rang and rang. Once more, the voicemail answered. "Celina, it's me again. I'm coming over."

The truth didn't hit Mindy until she was almost to Celina's apartment. Nic had said the hybrid was dangerous. Did he mean it was like him?

She'd never seen it look like anything but a canine. Celina had taken the hybrid home with her. Had she known what it was all along? Or had Celina been clueless like her?

Fear had her accelerating. Mindy couldn't believe that Celina would keep something so important from her. What did that say about their friendship?

The parking lot was full of emergency vehicles when Mindy arrived at the run-down apartment complex. *It could be anything*, she told herself, but she knew that it wasn't. She threw her car into park and jumped out as Celina came down the stairs on a gurney.

Mindy rushed forward, only to be cut off by the police. "That's my friend," she said. "You have to let me through."

"We can't," the officer said. "The medics think she's contagious."

"With what?" she demanded.

"Miss, I need you to take a step back," he said.

"Can you at least tell me where they're taking her?" she asked.

"Forest Mercy General," the officer said.

As the stretcher rolled by, Mindy got a close look at Celina's face. It was pale and streaked with makeup. Red blisters ringed her mouth and pink foam bubbled from her lips. Celina's body thrashed. If she hadn't been strapped in, she would've fallen off.

"Werewolves are everywhere!" she shouted. "Can't you see them? You're one of them," she blurted at the paramedic. "You don't love me! You just want to bite and scratch me!" Celina struggled some more. "I'm not a chew toy! Ahwoo! Ahwoo!" Her words faded into unintelligible growls and screams.

Mindy's stomach clenched. What happened to Celina? Was she going to be all right? Had the hybrid done that to her? How could it possibly have done this to Celina, when it had been around *her* house?

"Does she have rabies?" she asked the paramedic before he shut the ambulance door.

"We don't know," he said. "Do you know her?"

"Yes," she said. "She's a close friend and I work with her."

"Do you know if she's been bitten or scratched by anything in the past few days?" he asked.

Mindy opened her mouth, but no words would come out. She wanted to help Celina, but she couldn't tell them the truth. They'd think she was insane.

"I don't know," she answered honestly, but she knew someone who might. "We work at the animal clinic, so it's possible."

Mindy's hand covered the mark on her neck and her head swam, as the reality of what Nic was came crashing down upon her.

The officer reached for her. "Are you okay?" he asked.

"I'm-I'm..." She clutched her chest and nausea swamped her. Mindy ran to the back of her car and threw up. Was the same thing that was happening to Celina going to happen to her, too?

"Miss, do you need me to call another ambulance?"

Mindy hadn't heard the officer approach. She wiped her mouth with the back of her sleeve, then righted herself with the help of her car. "No, I'm okay now," she lied.

She climbed into her car and started the engine. Mindy pulled around the corner out of sight and stopped. She hugged herself as the ambulance drove by, sirens screeching. She needed to get to the hospital to find out what happened to Celina. Only then would she be able to say for certain that she'd be okay.

22

By the time Mindy reached the hospital and parked, she'd calmed down enough to think. She'd wanted time to process everything before she called Nic, but Celina's grave condition changed everything. She pulled her cell phone out of her purse and dialed Nic's number.

He answered on the first ring. "Mindy, now's not a good time." He sounded stressed.

"An ambulance took Celina away as I got to her apartment. She was foaming at the mouth and babbling about werewolves. They think she's contagious." She sniffled. "I thought you should know."

"Where are you?" he asked.

"I'm outside of Forest Mercy General," she said. "I'm going in now to see how she's doing."

"I'll get there as soon as I can." Nic disconnected the call.

"We have a problem," Nic said to Aidan.

"I heard," Aidan said. "Go! We'll deal with the Darkling later."

"Thanks." Nic bolted for the door.

"Nic!" Aidan's stern voice stopped him in his tracks.

He turned back to look at his Alpha.

"She'll be dead within two weeks," Aidan said.

His heart dropped. How could he tell Mindy that her friend was dying? If she connected the illness to the Darkling, she'd never let him near her again.

"You're certain that nothing can be done?" Nic asked. "Human medicine has advanced over the years."

Aidan's amber eyes softened. "Only Sighted-Ones can survive being marked by a Darkling," he said. "As you learned today, their magic is powerful—and lethal."

"Do you think there's a chance she's a Sighted-One?" Nic asked.

Aidan shook his head. "He wouldn't have left her if she was."

"What about Mindy?" Nic asked. "She's not a Sighted-One, yet the Darkling continued to pursue her. He showed up at her home repeatedly." He still couldn't believe that Darklings were real or how close to death Mindy had come. It left Nic shaken to his core.

Aidan shrugged and sat back in his seat. "Hard to say what its motives are. Darklings are nothing if not unpredictable. Perhaps it was drawn to her kindness or to something in her house?"

Blood drained from Nic's face. "Isabel," he said.

Aidan's brow furrowed. "Who's Isabel?"

"Mindy's sister," Nic said. "She told me that Izzy was Sighted. I didn't press her for more information at the time because it wasn't important."

Aidan came to his feet. "Where is Isabel now?"

"New Orleans," Nic said. "She should be safe, since the Darkling is here."

"We haven't been able to locate it," Aidan said. "It can hide its scent if it chooses to. We need a special tool to track it. One that can detect its magic. Until we have that in hand, we won't know where it is for sure."

"I doubt it would leave Mindy. It's stayed by her this whole time," Nic said. His wolf grumbled and struggled to break free. Even with the wounds inflicted upon it, it was ready to take the Darkling on again.

"I hope you're right," Aidan said. "For our sake and for Isabel's."

* * *

Nic arrived at the hospital. The second Mindy saw him, she rushed into his arms. He didn't care that a temporary need for solace was what drove her to him. Nic would accept any excuse to hold her.

"What did the doctors say?" he asked.

Tears spilled down her cheeks. "They won't let me see her. There's a big hazard sign outside her door." She pointed down the hall to the closed doors at the end.

"The hybrid had to have done this to her," Nic said.

Mindy shook her head. "I don't think so," she said. "I got the impression that Celina hadn't seen the hybrid in a while."

A doctor came out of the restricted hallway. Mindy rushed him. "How is Celina doing? Does she have rabies? Was she bitten?"

Rabies was lethal if it wasn't treated in time. Nic wanted to tell Mindy that Celina didn't have rabies, but he didn't think she'd listen to reason right now.

The doctor's pale brow lowered. "There's no sign of a bite, but we have located a scratch that appears to be infected."

"With rabies?" Mindy asked.

"No," the doctor said. "We haven't been able to identify the pathogen." His expression turned grave. "We're doing everything we can for her. Is there anything you can tell us? Anything at all that might help us narrow down the possibilities?"

Mindy stared at Nic accusingly and her lip quivered. "Sorry, I wish I could help," she said. "Is she going to make it?"

"It's too early to tell," the doctor said noncommittally. "But you may want to contact her family."

"She doesn't have any." Mindy turned to Nic after the doctor walked away. "I don't understand. If it's not rabies, then how could a scratch make Celina so sick?" She took a step back and touched the mark on her neck. "I have more than a scratch. You need to tell me if you think I'm going to get sick, too."

How could she think he'd be so careless with her life? "You're not going to get sick. Not from me."

Myriad emotions played across her face. In the end, Mindy didn't look entirely convinced that he was telling the truth. "You called the hybrid a Darkling. If it's something different than what you are, surely your people have cures or treatments against it."

"We are not the same species, though we do resemble one another," Nic said softly. "I would give anything to be able to help your friend, but there is nothing we can do for her."

Blood roared in Mindy's ears. What did Nic mean by that? "Are you saying Celina's going to die?"

Shadows filled his blue eyes and his face pinched with pain. "I'm sorry," he said. "Nothing can be done now."

Mindy shook her head. "I don't accept that. You may have given up on Celina, but I haven't." She grabbed her purse and walked down the sterile hall toward the elevators.

"Where are you going?" Nic asked. His long legs ate up the distance between them.

"I'm going to find the hybrid," she said. "If your people can't help her, then maybe he can."

Nic grabbed her arm and swung her around. "Are you insane? Did you see what that thing did to your friend?"

Mindy glared at his hand until he released her. "Yes," she said. "That's why I'm going."

"We haven't been able to find it," Nic said.

She pressed the button to call the elevator. "Maybe you've been looking in the wrong place."

The doors open and she stepped inside. Nic followed.

"Where do you plan to look?" he asked.

"I'm going to start with Celina's apartment," she said.

Celina's apartment had been sealed by the police. Mindy stared at the crime-scene tape.

"What now?" Nic asked.

She reached into her purse and pulled out a scalpel. "Now we go inside," Mindy said.

"That's illegal," he said.

Mindy glared at him. "I'm aware of that. You don't have to come in."

"You don't know what you're looking for," he said.

"Neither do you," she said.

She cut through the tape and opened the door. The scent of Darkling smacked Nic in the face and made his hackles rise.

"It was here," he said.

"Of course it was." Mindy stepped into the apartment. "Celina brought him home with her, before turning him over to the sanctuary."

"She lied about that," Nic said, glancing around the small space.

"I know," Mindy said quietly. "He's been coming around my house for a few days now."

"The scent is really strong," Nic said. "Like he was here recently. I'd say within the last few hours."

Mindy shook her head as she opened a cupboard. "That's impossible. I was here a few hours ago and so were the police. There was no one around. Not even her boyfriend, Slade."

"Slade?" Nic slowly turned to look at her. "Have you seen him?"

"No," Mindy said. "I expected him to show up at the hospital, but it's possible I missed him."

"What does he look like?" Nic asked.

"Dark hair, amber eyes, good-looking." She shrugged. "Celina's usual type." Mindy's eyes widened. "Do you think that Slade did this to her? Are he and the hybrid the same creature?"

"I can't say for certain," Nic said. "But it stands to reason."

Mindy clutched her stomach. "That makes no sense. Celina loved Slade. He knew that. She put up with all his crap."

"Darklings cannot feel *human* emotions," he said.

Mindy stiffened. "Are you telling me that you feel nothing for me? That all that tenderness was just an act?"

Nic rushed to her side. "No!" he barked. "I'm *not* a Darkling."

"I know you keep saying that," she said. "But I don't understand the difference."

Nic brushed her cheek. "The difference is that I love you."

Her eyes grew to the size of saucers and her breath seemed to stop. "I can't deal with that right now."

He did his best to hide the pain her rejection brought. "Let's check the bedroom, but I think he's gone."

They searched Celina's bedroom, but couldn't find any male clothes.

"Where do you think he went?" Mindy asked.

"Hopefully far, far away from this place," Nic said, praying it was true.

23

Jenna walked into Aidan's office. He put the phone down when he saw her. His gaze warmed as it settled on her swollen stomach.

"Did you know that Nic took a mate?" she asked.

Aidan slowly nodded.

"Were you going to tell me?" she asked.

Jenna made it sound like a simple question, but Aidan knew it was anything but. His bondmate never went the simple route.

"I only just learned about the situation when the police arrived," Aidan said. "There hasn't been time to have a true discussion."

Her long strawberry-blonde hair bounced as she lowered herself into the chair. "Don't you think we should've met her first?" Jenna paused. "Nic's tough on the outside, but he's tender-hearted on the inside. I don't want him to get hurt."

Aidan melted inside. "I understand, but as you recall, I didn't have much to do with the decision of taking you as my bondmate," he said. "My wolf was determined to claim you with or without my permission."

Her brow arched. "Are you saying that you didn't want me?"

His lips canted and his eyes narrowed. "The first time I laid eyes on those legs of yours, I wanted to bend you over my desk and wrap my fist around your long hair."

Aidan looked at her stomach pointedly. "Obviously that's something my wolf and I could agree on."

Jenna giggled. "You're incorrigible."

"Yes." He grinned. "But you love me anyway."

She heaved herself out of the chair. "I have to go. The baby is hungry again."

She'd been using that excuse every time she needed to raid the kitchen. Aidan had ordered the chef to prepare a shelf just for her.

"You coming?" She waddled toward the door.

"I'll be there in a minute," Aidan said. "I have to make a phone call first."

"Don't take too long," Jenna said. "Or there won't be anything left."

"I won't." Aidan waited for her to shut the door, then lifted the receiver. He hit speed dial and waited for the Lycanian High Council to answer.

"What do you need, Aidan?" Tristan asked, forgoing pleasantries.

"A Darkling has entered our realm. It has killed one of my pups and has infected a human woman," Aidan said. "She's been hospitalized."

Silence met his statement.

"Tristan?" Aidan asked.

"Do you know where it is now?" Tristan asked.

Aidan could hear drawers opening and closing, then the sound of a zipper. "Not for certain. It was in the woods outside of Telegraph Road, but we haven't been able to find it. I have my best trackers scouring the area. It's possible the Darkling has moved on," he said.

"Where?" Tristan asked.

Aidan thought about what Nic had told him. "Perhaps New Orleans."

"But you are not certain," Tristan said.

"No," Aidan replied. "It's able to mask its scent."

"Why would it go to that city and not another?" Tristan asked.

"There is a Sighted-One down there," Aidan said. "Isabel's related to the mate of one of my wolves."

There was more shuffling and a grunt. "Is the human woman in the hospital a Sighted-One?" Tristan asked.

"No," Aidan said softly.

"Then she will die," Tristan said matter-of-factly.

"I'm aware of that," Aidan said, gritting his teeth.

Tristan didn't care for humans and never hid his disdain for them. He'd shown up on Aidan's doorstep after he'd bondmated Jenna to ensure that the bond was real and that he'd bred true. Like other Elders, Tristan didn't like that two of the Alphas had chosen humans for mates. As if they'd had a choice in the matter. Aidan snorted.

"Stop gritting your teeth. I will begin the hunt now," Tristan said. "You may not sense me when I enter your territory."

Aidan could hear the smile in Tristan's voice. "I'll know you're here," he said. "Use caution with this one. The Darkling took down one of my biggest wolves. He's powerful."

Tristan laughed, the sound cold enough to freeze water. "So am I."

"Be sure to bring *Selene*," Aidan said.

"I never go anywhere without my sword. I'll use the lodestone to track him," Tristan said. "You'll know when it's done." He hung up.

Aidan dialed another number. This time the call went to his new assistant, Carson. "I want you to call all the wolves back to the estate. No one lives off property until the Darkling is found."

* * *

Four hours later, Tristan lingered in the woods outside of a small house off Telegraph Road. The scent of the Darkling was fading quickly, but he'd definitely been here. In this very spot.

Tristan ran his gloved hand over the ash stain, then studied the house again. It was small, well kept, with white walls and green window frames. He waited for the woman to leave her house, then broke inside.

The scent was nearly overpowering. A dog and cat rushed him, but one growl sent them scurrying away. Tristan followed the aroma down the hall. It led straight out the back door. He was about to leave when another scent caught his attention. This one lighter, almost citrusy in nature.

He stopped outside the door where the scent seemed the strongest, and inhaled. Tristan's head swam. He clutched the doorknob and twisted. The door creaked open and a comfortable bedroom came into view.

Tristan stepped inside and shut the door behind him. The citrusy scent filled the room. It was followed by a snap of magic. A Sighted-One had been here.

He scanned the area and saw a dresser shoved against the wall in the corner. There were framed photographs sitting on top of it.

He walked over and picked one up. There were two fair-haired girls smiling back at him. One had shoulder-length hair and looked a lot like the woman who'd driven off.

The other had a wild mane that didn't want to be tamed by the barrettes in her hair. Their arms were wrapped around each other, but the one on the left seemed distracted. Haunted.

"Isabel." He tasted her name on his tongue. The sound was as sharp and tangy as her scent.

Tristan ran his finger over the photo and smiled to himself. If he were a Darkling, he knew whom he'd pursue.

24

It had been a month since Celina's funeral. The doctors still had no idea what had killed her, so they'd burned her clothes and suggested cremation. Since that was what Celina had wanted, Mindy had complied.

She hadn't seen Nic since the funeral. Mindy had told him that she needed time to grieve, time to digest, time to decide what she was going to do next. She still hadn't gotten over the fact that the hybrid had killed Marco and Celina because of her.

Guilt weighed heavily upon her shoulders, though she was aware that there'd been nothing she could've done to stop him.

Nic stayed away, but Mindy thought she'd caught glimpses of him in his wolf form, patrolling the edge of the woods. Occasionally, there'd been a single flower left on her steps. When that happened, she was reminded how much she missed him.

She had no idea how or if a relationship between them would work, but Mindy would regret never giving it a try.

The phone rang and she flinched, debating whether to let voicemail get it. It continued to ring. Mindy sighed and walked into the other room.

"Hello?" she asked.

"Mindy?" Izzy replied.

"Where have you been?" Mindy asked. "I've been trying to reach you for over a month. I thought something had happened to you. I was planning to fly down to Louisiana to find you."

"I'm sorry," Izzy said. "It's been kind of crazy around here."

"Celina's dead, Izzy." Mindy choked up.

There was a pause on the line, then Izzy said, "I know."

"If you knew, then why didn't you call?" Mindy asked.

"I couldn't," Izzy said.

Mindy opened her mouth to rip into her sister, but stopped short before she said something she'd regret. "I'm sorry."

"Sorry for what?" Izzy asked.

"Sorry that I didn't believe you," Mindy said. For the first time in her life, she truly understood her sister. "How were you able to live with the knowledge that there's more in this world than what meets the eye?" she asked. "I'm struggling, Izzy. Really struggling."

"I wish I could hug you," Izzy said. "It took a while to get past thinking I was crazy. Once I did, it took even more time to understand that the monsters weren't *all* evil. They're a lot like humans in that respect, but they do tend to be more loyal. Not that I hang around any of them. It's better if they believe I can't see them."

"How are you doing?" Mindy asked. "Do you need money?"

"I'm fine," Izzy said, but her voice cracked when she said it.

"Izzy, do you need me to come down there?" Mindy asked. "I can be on the first flight out tomorrow morning."

"No, I can handle what's going on. Remember, I've been doing this my whole life," Izzy said. "Besides, you're safer there."

A tear streaked down Mindy's cheek. "You were right about evil being here, but are you certain it's gone?"

"Yes, I am," Izzy said without hesitation.

"Then why don't I feel safe?" Mindy asked.

"It'll take time to adjust to your new reality," Izzy said. "I'm sorry I brought darkness to our door. I'm sure you've figured it out by now, but in case you haven't, you should know that it was after me."

Mindy had figured that out over the past few weeks. It had been the only thing that had made sense. "There's no need to be sorry," she said. "We handled it."

"We?" Izzy asked.

"I met someone." Mindy paused as she searched for the right words. "Well, *something*. We had a good thing going before I found out what he was, before the Darkling killed Marco, before Celina died, and everything fell apart."

Izzy sighed. "The world is complicated," she said. "We don't always get what we want, but sometimes we get what we need."

Mindy snorted. "You did *not* just quasi-quote a song."

Izzy laughed. "Maybe, but seriously, I have to lay low for a while. I may be out of touch."

"I'm coming down to get you," Mindy said. She wasn't about to let the Darkling or anything else get her sister. She'd already lost a friend and the man she was falling in love with.

"No!" Izzy shouted. "It's better if you stay where you are. He'll protect you."

"You haven't met him," Mindy said.

"I don't need to," Izzy replied.

"What's going on, Isabel?" Mindy asked.

"I'm not sure," Izzy said. "I think I'm being followed."

"By the Darkling?"

"I'm not sure," Izzy said.

"You need to call the police! Call them this instant!" Mindy demanded. "I'll phone Nic, he'll know what to do."

"Is that his name?" Izzy asked.

People laughed in the background.

"Yes," Mindy said.

"Nice name," Izzy said.

The sound grew louder. "Izzy, where are you?"

"I'm in a bar, but I have to go. It's getting crowded. Stay safe. I'll be in touch when I can. And remember, he *will* protect you. Celina's spirit told me so." She hung up.

It was as close to a blessing as she'd ever get from her sister and from her dead friend.

Mindy's first reaction was to ignore Izzy's request to stay away and go to her aid, but she had no idea where her sister was staying or if she'd be there by the time she got to New Orleans. Was she being followed? If so, by whom? She prayed it wasn't the Darkling.

She plugged the phone into the charger and walked down the hall to the backdoor. Mindy opened it and stepped outside, then sat on the stairs. Darkness closed in around her. Had she ever felt this alone? Mindy couldn't recall.

In the distance, a lone wolf howled. The mournful sound echoed through the night and was answered by one much closer. Mindy stepped off the porch and scanned the tree line.

At first, she didn't see any movement, but as she continued to watch, a dark figure appeared out of the woods.

For a heartbeat, she thought it was the hybrid, then the animal came into focus. "Nic?"

Bones popped, muscles reshaped and fur faded, until the wolf was gone and Nic crouched in its place. He slowly stood, tall, trembling and fully erect. He didn't have a stich of clothing on as he hovered near the trees, and seemed completely at ease with his current state.

"I've missed you," Nic said.

"I've missed you too."

"Can we start over?" he asked.

She'd asked him the same question after their first night together. He'd said yes without hesitation. Could she?

Mindy turned and climbed the stairs. She stopped at the top of the porch and looked back. "You coming?"

Nic could hardly believe his ears, but he didn't have to be asked twice. He covered the distance between them in record time and pulled Mindy into his arms. His lips found hers tentatively at first, then he allowed the passion to ignite inside of him until they were both swept away.

EPILOGUE

Two months later...

"**A**re you sure you want to go through with this?" Nic asked. "You don't have to do this right now. We could wait until you have received word from Izzy. I know you're worried about her. We all are."

It was sweet of him to offer, but Mindy had made up her mind. There was no telling when she'd hear from Isabel. Her sister had made good on her promise to drop out of sight. No one had seen any sign of her, not even the man who'd been sent to New Orleans to find her.

She was still alive. Mindy could feel it, but Izzy wouldn't be in touch until she was ready. Besides, she'd given Mindy her blessing the last time they spoke.

Celina's death had taught Mindy that you couldn't put off happiness. You might not make it to that future moment, which was why she found herself standing in the middle of the woods surrounded by Nic's people.

"Let's do this," she said. Mindy took a deep breath.

"I'm right here with you." Nic smiled and squeezed her hand, then faced the pack. "I would like to present my bondmate to the Moonlight Kin."

Howls rose, growing in volume until the sound deafened.

Mindy's knees quivered as she stepped forward. *Don't throw up.*

Don't fall. Don't throw up. Don't fall. The howls stopped instantly. Even the air seemed to still, waiting for what would happen next.

"You can do this," Nic murmured. "It's just like we practiced." A long claw slid out from the tip of his finger. When it surpassed four inches, Nic sliced the side of his neck.

Mindy's first reaction was to want to press her hand to the wound to stave off the bleeding, but she didn't. Instead, she waited like they'd rehearsed.

Once the blood flowed steadily, Nic leaned down so she could reach him.

Mindy framed his face with her hands and gently pulled him toward her. Her stomach gurgled, but there was no going back now. She pressed her lips against the wound and sucked. The coppery flavor on her tongue seemed unnatural, but she kept going.

Nic's body tightened and his arms locked around her waist. "More," he ground out, and shuddered.

Mindy sucked harder. Blood poured down her throat. She swallowed convulsively. How much would she have to drink to complete the ritual? She didn't think she could stomach much more.

Nic stopped her with a tender touch. "That's enough." He stroked her hair.

Mindy drew back and wiped the blood off her mouth. It stained her hands and shirt.

"It is done!" Nic shouted, and grinned at the pack. His teeth seemed longer than usual and his blue eyes were glowing.

A huge black wolf stepped forward, shape-shifting as he did so. Aidan turned to face the rest of the pack. "Let us welcome our new member with a hunt."

The wolves howled joyously.

As Mindy listened to their baying, her limbs began to tingle. "What's happening?" she asked Nic.

"It has begun," he said. "You're strong. You can do this."

Heat swept through her body. Mindy cried out as her first bone snapped. The pain was excruciating and she dropped to her knees.

"It's only painful the first time," Nic said, brushing her arm.

More bones broke and pale fur rippled over her arms. Mindy screamed as the world dimmed around her, then suddenly sprang into sharp relief.

She looked around and everything glistened with a silvery-gray hue. It was night, but Mindy could see every detail as clear as day. A massive brindle wolf nudged her, then nipped at her haunches.

Mindy took off through the woods with the pack running along beside her. The wind whipped through her fur, bringing with it all the tantalizing secrets that the trees kept.

She yipped excitedly.

The brindle wolf nudged her again, this time away from the others. Mindy was reluctant to go, but there was no fighting him.

When they were alone in a meadow, the wolf brushed its mouth against hers, then sniffed and licked her hind end with renewed interest. Fire swept through Mindy's body again as muscle and bone reshaped, but this time the pain wasn't nearly as numbing.

Nude and trembling, Mindy looked down at Nic and brushed his head with her fingertips. "I'm not sure that I'm that kinky," she said.

He gave her a toothy smile and slowly shifted back into human form. "There will be plenty of time for that later, bondmate," he said mischievously.

Mindy couldn't wait.

\# \# \#

Moonlight Kin 4: Tristan

1

In New Orleans you'd better like your sushi deep-fried and your saxophone dipped in a coating of bluesy jazz, or you wouldn't survive long in the Big Easy.

Music rang out through the Jackson Square courtyard as street musicians turned up the volume and charm to compete for tourist dollars. Tonight the jazzy band at the end of the square attempted to lure their crowd away from a lone trumpet player and a violinist.

Along with the musicians, tarot and palm readers had already set up their tables, staggering them just enough to give the pretense of privacy.

Isabel "Izzy" MacDougal did a quick head count. There were ten tables in total. Her table would make eleven, but she only counted the ones in Jackson Square. Others would be set up along the side streets near Bourbon Street, hoping to catch the stray drunk ready to part with their hard-earned cash.

Izzy scanned the growing crowd as she unfolded her small card table and spread her purple shawl on top of it. She spotted her friend Everly Watts a few tables over and waved.

Everly waved back then returned to reading the woman seated across from her. Izzy had met the short, dark-haired Goth when she first arrived in New Orleans a month ago.

Despite resembling an anemic vampire, Everly was down to earth and turned out to be a good friend. Most nights she could be found at The Dungeon with all the other Goths and vampire wannabes in town. The pancake makeup disguised her sensitive nature and fierce intelligence, but nothing hid her street smarts.

Izzy smiled as a few people slowed to browse her table. They didn't notice that enterprising locals were shadowing them, waiting for them to drop their guard.

Not even dusk yet and the French Quarter already bursting at the seams with sunburned tourists and crafty pickpockets.

Izzy finished setting up and took a seat. She kept her expression open. Hard to do when she was continuously bombarded by impressions from the growing crowd, but she managed. Unlike some of the others situated around the square, Izzy had a true gift of Sight.

She snorted. Some gift.

She and Everly had glommed onto each other when Izzy discovered that Everly suffered from the same "gift" that she'd grown up with. It wasn't easy being psychic, especially in a world populated by skeptics and monsters.

Instead of growing up in a loving household like Isabel, Everly had been kicked out of her home when her *gifts* arrived. According to the petite Goth, she'd been living on her own ever since. She survived by taking on menial jobs and never staying in one place for too long. Another thing that they had in common.

Izzy shuffled her tarot cards and smiled at a passing group of women. The women wore flowery nametags across their chests, advertising a local conference.

"Would you like to know what your future holds, ladies?" she asked.

One of the women giggled, but the ash blonde stopped to chat. "Can you tell me if I'm going to meet someone soon?" she asked.

"Sure," Izzy said. "Take a seat."

The woman's hand clasped the back of the folding chair as she pulled it out to sit down.

"Lisa, you're not really going to waste your money on that crap, are you?" her friend asked.

Uncertainty filled the blonde's green eyes. Before she caved to peer pressure, Izzy flipped the first card over.

"He has dark hair," she said.

The woman scooted forward on her seat. "Really?"

"Yes," Izzy said. "And he's tall."

"Is his name Mike?" Lisa asked, peering into the cards in search of answers.

Izzy closed her eyes and concentrated. She saw the dark-haired man in her vision drop down to one knee in front of the blond woman.

"I see him proposing," Izzy said. "It's quite a ring."

Lisa squealed. "Oh my God! When?"

Izzy examined her vision. The leaves on the trees around the couple were orange and red, but no limbs were bare. "The fall." She opened her eyes. "He'll propose in the fall."

The woman whipped her head around to search for her friends. "Did you hear that? Mike is going to propose to me in the fall."

The skeptic among them simply shook her head in disgust. "Mike's a jerk," she muttered.

Izzy turned her attention away from the cards and stared at the woman. Her black aura came into view. The color startled her. On occasion when Izzy looked at people, shadow obscured their entire face. She had no idea what the darkness meant, but it always felt evil and frightened her.

This was different. The woman's dark aura didn't obscure her features. Izzy peered deeper, past the outer layer to see what caused the woman's pain.

A red-haired man appeared in her mind, then his image quickly faded into a tombstone with the name Thomas carved into its rigid gray face.

"I'm sorry about Thomas," Izzy said. "He really loved you."

The woman's face went from red to white, as the blood drained from her cheeks. "How did you know about him?" she whispered.

Izzy shrugged. She couldn't begin to explain where her gift came from and certainly not to someone who wasn't ready to listen.

"Think she's still a fraud?" Lisa asked as she plucked several bills out of her wallet and laid them on the table.

"Let's go," the skeptic said. "I need a drink."

The crowd swallowed them. More people approached her. Izzy got ten more readings done before her head threatened to explode.

The pain happened every night. She could only read for so long before her gift exerted too much pressure and her body gave out. At least she'd made enough to pay rent. All in all a good night.

Izzy was packing her things, when the first inkling of unease struck. She casually scanned the crowd, but no one seemed overly interested in her. She finished gathering her fortune-telling tools and shoved them into her backpack. She quickly folded her table and chairs then took them over to Everly.

"Can you keep these for me until tomorrow?" Izzy asked.

Everly's back stiffened, and she frowned. "Sure," she said, scanning the faces around them. "I feel it, too."

"It's okay," Izzy said. Whatever was out there didn't know about Everly—at least not yet. She'd lead it away before it detected her friend. "I'm going to head out. Catch you later."

Everly nodded, but she didn't relax. She continued to covertly scan the crowd.

Izzy weaved her way through the throng, cutting along Pere Antoine's alley before hanging a left toward St. Peter Street. She glanced up and down the sidewalk to be sure she wasn't being followed, then ducked into Yo Mama's Bar and Grill.

The bearded doorman greeted her with a friendly smile. Izzy grinned back then bounded up the stairs to where her friend Heather bartended.

A red light illuminated the small space. Two couches, a couple of long tables, dancing statues, and a small bar filled the room. Classic rock from an old jukebox blared out of speakers mounted in the ceiling. The place reminded her of a bordello, but it had *amazing* hamburgers.

Izzy's stomach growled. She wished she had time to order a burger, but she needed to use Heather's phone then get back to her apartment on Dumaine Street.

Heather had just popped the cap off a longneck, when she spotted Izzy. She smiled, then without saying a word, she grabbed her cell phone and tossed it to her. Izzy caught it easily, mouthed the word "thanks," and quickly called her sister, Mindy.

She didn't want to alarm her sister, but Izzy needed to let Mindy know that someone was following her and she might have to lay low for a while.

It would hurt to be out of touch with her sister, but Izzy didn't have much choice. The darkness she'd sensed in Breakbend, Oregon was here and getting closer. She'd felt its presence growing, and it terrified her.

Izzy finished up her call and handed the phone back to Heather. "Thanks," she said.

"Anytime," Heather said. "Catch you later?"

She shook her head. "Not tonight. I have a headache." Izzy rubbed her temples for emphasis.

"Catch you next time," Heather said then moved onto a waiting customer.

Izzy hurried down the stairs but stopped before she stepped out onto the sidewalk. The doorman watched her, but didn't say anything since this wasn't exactly new behavior from her.

"It's all clear," he said.

"Thanks." Izzy slipped out the door and headed toward Bourbon. She'd just passed Royal Street, when the sensation of being observed returned.

Izzy glanced over her shoulder but didn't see anyone. Didn't see anything out of the ordinary. Ordinary being a relative term in the

French Quarter. Nothing to alarm her, but Izzy knew he was there.

She *felt* him.

She wound her way through the heavy crowd, hoping to lose her pursuer on raucous Bourbon Street. With the sun going down, the mood on the street changed. Izzy turned down Dumaine Street.

The crowd thinned, and she caught sight of Louis Armstrong Park in the distance. The trees swayed as the sun dipped below the horizon and darkness took over. A shiver tracked down her spine.

This was their time. The time when they were most active. The time when the real monsters came out and hunted.

Izzy hurried along the uneven sidewalks. She heard music coming from Bourbon Street. The jumble of sounds and the collision of smells should've comforted her, but Izzy knew she wasn't alone.

She tripped over a raised concrete slab and fell forward. She grabbed the wrought iron fence that ran along the front of one of the old gentrified homes to keep from falling.

The metal felt good in her hand. Cool. Hard. Real. Real as the heavy footsteps coming up fast behind her. Izzy pushed away from the fence and sprinted on.

Her blood pumped so hard she could barely hear herself think. Izzy turned to see who approached and collided with a wall. She cursed under her breath and looked at the offending object in her way. It wasn't a wall at all. Somehow she'd buried her nose in a man's hard chest.

Strong hands grasped her arms. Whether to keep her from falling or prevent her from leaving, she didn't know. Izzy craned her neck to see who she'd run into. Her gaze collided with a pair of mercury-colored eyes, and she shivered, despite his handsome face.

Her body went from hot to cold to hot again. Staring in his eyes was like staring into the face of the Arctic. His white-blond hair and stern expression mirrored the harsh, unforgiving environment.

Izzy opened her mouth to apologize, but before she uttered a single syllable, the image of a white wolf obscured his striking features. She felt the blood drain from her face. He was one of *them*.

"Let me go," she said, struggling to break his grasp.

He didn't release her. Instead, the man's grip tightened. "You're being hunted," he said.

She knew that. Izzy had known that for days. Weird that he announced it like he wasn't the one hunting her.

The man had to be the biggest monster she'd ever seen. Given his size, he'd be unnaturally large for a werewolf, and that was saying something, since they leaned toward massive.

"Let me go or I'm going to scream," Izzy said.

"This is the French Quarter," he said. "No one will notice or care." His sensual lips tilted into a smirk.

Izzy wanted to knock that smirk right off his face.

As if reading her mind, his smile vanished. "If you don't come with me, you're going to die."

Despite the ominous and rather clichéd warning, Izzy had no intention of going anywhere with him. She'd seen his true form. She would be safer locked in a cage with a half-starved polar bear. Everything about this man screamed danger.

A trashcan lid banged at the end of the street. They both turned to see what had caused the noise. Izzy took his momentary distraction as a chance to get away. She twisted out of his hold and took off running.

She didn't get far. He was on her before she'd made it ten feet. Given his tremendous height and long legs it wasn't really a surprise, but she'd had to try.

A small crowd of men and women wandered by. Izzy flagged them down. As they slowed to a stop, the giant beside her swung her around, and his mouth descended upon hers.

Tristan needed her to shut up and listen, but short of gagging her, he had no way of making her comply. He'd expected to find a flighty, air-headed female, but Isabel was also far smarter than he'd anticipated. Manipulating her wasn't going to be easy. When she flagged the small crowd down, Tristan used the only thing he had on hand to silence her. Himself.

He spun her around in his arms and pulled her close. His mouth came down upon hers before she understood what was happening. The second their lips met, something unexpected occurred, something entirely unwanted.

Tristan's body hardened, and heat exploded inside of him. Urges that he viciously suppressed surfaced in an instant. His hands tightened on her shirt, and his arms locked. He felt her nipples harden against his chest a moment before her body melted into his.

Instead of keeping the embrace superficial, Tristan deepened it. He nipped Isabel's full bottom lip until she opened for him, then Tristan surged inside.

Sweetness exploded on his tongue. He'd never tasted anything like it, like her. It was at odds with the citrusy aroma wafting from her skin. Tristan wanted more, so he took it.

He sank his hand into the wild tangle of her blonde-and- purple hair then tilted her head to get better access. Whoops and laughter surrounded them, but he ignored it all as he thoroughly explored Isabel's mouth.

Her hands tightened on his shirt, hesitated a moment, then she kissed him back. Fire spread through his body, making every inch of him hard. They needed to find a room before he ended up stripping her naked right here. Tristan calculated the distance to the nearest hotel. If they left now, it wouldn't take long to reach it.

She's human. The thought filtered through his mind. The reminder chilled his ardor as effectively as dumping ice water down the front of his jeans.

Tristan reluctantly pulled back. His chest heaved as he drew in air, waiting for his head to clear.

Izzy's world continued to tilt off its axis, even after he ended the embrace. Despite his frosty exterior, the man's lips were scorching. Maybe he wasn't made of ice after all.

The crowd she'd flagged down had wandered off at some point, leaving them alone. In some part of her mind, Izzy had realized that they were leaving, but for the life of her, she hadn't been able to tear her mouth away. Izzy had been kissed before. Plenty of times. But never like this.

His hands were still locked around her waist, clutching her shirt. The heat of his palms seared her flesh and made her wonder what would happen if they were skin to skin. Spontaneous combustion came to mind.

He must've realized what he was doing because he jerked his hands away and stepped back, putting some distance between them. This time when he looked at her, he scowled, banking the heat that had simmered in his mercury-colored eyes.

Was he mad at her or himself? It didn't really matter. She wasn't going anywhere with him, even if her lips were tingling and other parts of her were making unreasonable demands.

The man might be angry, but he remained fully aware of their surroundings. "If you don't come with me willingly, I'm going to pick you up and carry you."

Izzy glared at him and scrambled out of reach. "You wouldn't dare."

Before the sound of her words died, the man hoisted her over his shoulder and took off running down the street. The sudden move jarred Izzy's ribs, driving the air from her lungs. It would serve him right if she threw up on him. And she would've, had she bothered to eat.

Izzy managed to drag a breath into her body. "Put me down this instant!" She smacked his back, but the man didn't notice. "Do you hear me?"

He grunted in response but didn't slow.

"I don't know who you think you are, but you're not going to get away with kidnapping me," Izzy said.

"Who is going to stop me?" He didn't even sound winded when he spoke. "You?" he asked.

She'd stop him. Just as soon as she managed to catch her breath and quell the nausea rising inside her.

They passed several revelers on the way to Louis Armstrong Park. No one paid attention to them, even when she cried for help. The sight of a man carrying a woman over his shoulder wasn't unusual in this part of town.

The music faded as they moved farther and farther away. Soon, they'd be isolated. Izzy couldn't allow that to happen. Every investigative procedure show she'd ever watched said never leave with your attacker.

Of course, they never mentioned what to do if your attacker picked you up and carried you away.

"Put me down," she said. "I want to walk."

His thumb stroked over the back of her thigh. Every muscle inside of Izzy stiffened, while other parts melted—thanks to that stupid kiss. She pressed her lips together. She could still taste him. And an insane part of her that she refused to acknowledge wanted more.

"I mean it," Izzy said. "Put me down, or I'm going to hurl on you." She gagged to prove she wasn't bluffing.

His footsteps faltered. Guess he didn't want to be vomited on. "You cannot get away," he said.

Probably true, but it wouldn't stop her from trying.

"Let me go, and we'll forget this ever happened," Izzy said.

He shook his head, sending his long blond hair into his face. "I'm afraid that's not an option," he said.

Izzy saw her last chance to escape. She took a deep breath to scream again. The man leapt over six feet, dropping her down onto his hard shoulder. The move knocked the wind out of her again. No doubt that was his intention.

She gasped. "Jerk!" Izzy couldn't see his obnoxious smile, but she felt his shoulders shake with laughter. He'd pay for that.

For a human, Isabel MacDougal had a lot of spirit. Most women would be screaming their heads off by now. Oh sure, she'd tried to get help, but she hadn't fought him.

A woman afraid for her life would've ripped the hair from his head, which told Tristan that she wasn't as afraid of him as she claimed to be.

He kept running, moving them deeper into the shadows. He still sensed the Darkling's magic thanks to the lodestone around his neck, but it was fainter now.

Tristan didn't want to think about how close Isabel had come to being captured by the Darkling. He'd barely managed to reach her first.

He sniffed the air. Other than a few homeless people and some unsavory types, the park was empty. He kept moving. With enough distance between them, they wouldn't be disturbed. Eventually Tristan stopped and set Isabel down.

She wobbled then staggered a few feet away. "What do you plan to do to me now that you've abducted me?" she asked.

Tristan arched a brow. "I'm not going to attack you, if that's what you're thinking."

"You already did," she reminded him.

His eyes narrowed. "I kissed you. It's not the same."

Her pale brow furrowed. "Why did you kiss me?"

Good question. Tristan had been wondering the same thing, since now it seemed like such a mistake. It would be easy to say that he'd been trying to keep her silent. That had been the catalyst behind his actions, but the truth was Tristan didn't care if she screamed. He would've taken her with him anyway. Then there was the kiss itself... and what happened afterward.

Not liking the direction his thoughts were taking, he glared at her. Something about her mouth captured his attention. Even now, her full lips drew his reluctant gaze. They were moist, red, and oh so soft. Even her taste had been different than he'd expected.

Perhaps she wore something to enhance their appearance, enhance their flavor?

Tristan might stretch the truth with others, but he never lied to himself. That honeysuckle flavor was all her own, and damned if he didn't want more.

His frowned deepened. That wasn't going to happen. He shouldn't have touched her in the first place. It wasn't part of his plan.

Tristan didn't need to be thinking about her lips or her succulent taste. He was here to kill a Darkling, and nothing more. If he kept Isabel alive in the process, then great, but her continued existence wasn't necessary for accomplishing his mission. At least not after she drew the Darkling out.

"I kissed you to save your life," Tristan said.

Isabel snorted in disbelief. "Right, sure you did."

"I did," he said, sounding defensive. "You're in danger."

She cocked her head and looked at him. "From who? As far as I can tell, you're the only threat to my safety."

Tristan didn't like his actions being questioned. She should just thank him and be grateful he'd arrived when he had. "Someone is hunting you."

"That didn't answer my question, Frosty," she said.

She was smart and oddly attractive despite the awful purple in her hair. "No, I didn't," Tristan said. "And my name is not Frosty."

"Whatever, Ice." Isabel rolled her eyes. "Are you always a jerk, or am I just special?"

Tristan approached her until he loomed above her. "You'd do well to remember what I am," he said softly.

She bit her lower lip.

His gaze dropped to her mouth of its own volition, and something dark rose inside of him. Her tongue darted out to wet her lips. Tristan's jaw clenched.

The memory of their kiss came charging back, and his entire body tensed to the point of pain. He curled his hands into fists to keep from grabbing her.

"I know what you are. It's not like I can ever forget," Isabel said. "I see the real you every time I look at you."

Tristan jerked his head back. He knew Sighted-Ones could see the beast lurking beneath their human forms. It was one of the things that made them so valuable to the Darklings, but it unsettled him to know a human had such ability. It would make hiding from them impossible.

The only thing that kept them from being a direct threat to the Moonlight Kin was the fact that most humans wouldn't believe them. If that were to change...then people like Isabel MacDougal would need to be eliminated.

The thought left Tristan decidedly uneasy, but he refused to look at why. Instead, he focused on her colorful hair.

"A simple thank-you would've been enough," he said.

Her brow rose at the same time as her smart mouth dropped open. "You expect me to thank you, Marshmallow? After what you did? Are you insane?" she asked.

Tristan gritted his teeth. He was not used to sparring with sharp-tongued, purple-haired hoydens who didn't know what was good for them.

As the Enforcer for the Lycanian Elders, people respected and feared him. Known for his cold countenance and unwavering tenacity, Tristan took great pride in his position. The impression he made had never bothered him until now. Of course up until now, it had never been thrown in his face.

"I am as sane as you are," he snarled, moving his face closer to hers. "The only difference is I have a stronger sense of self-preservation. You, Ms. Purple Hair, have a death wish."

Isabel put her hands on her hips and glared at him. "And you, Snowball, can suck my big toe!"

Did he really think she was that stupid? Only a fool would trust one of them with their lives. They were the monsters, the creatures that came out of the night to swallow you up.

Either that or he had an overinflated opinion of his kissing abilities. Izzy glanced at his harsh mouth. Okay, maybe he deserved some bragging rights on that front, but that wasn't the point.

"Listen, I'm not sure who you think I am, but you have the wrong girl." Izzy hoped he didn't notice the tremor in her voice.

"Scents don't lie," he said.

Izzy swallowed hard. "Well this time your *schnoz* is wrong. So why don't you just be a good frost giant and run along?"

His mercury eyes glistened, then he slowly blinked. "Is there something wrong with your hearing?" He snapped his finger next to her ear.

Izzy flushed and shoved his hand away. "No, is there something wrong with *yours*?"

He stiffened. "I can hear things you never knew existed," he said through clenched teeth.

"Good for you, Snowflake, but you're still wrong about me," she said, more boldly than she felt.

The voices that had been in the distance grew louder. Perhaps if they got close enough, Izzy could scream for help. She had no doubt the giant of a man beside her wouldn't like the attention.

His silver eyes narrowed. "Don't even think about it," he hissed.

"Think about what?" she asked innocently.

"Whatever was going through your little purple head," he said.

"I didn't say anything, Whiteout," Izzy said.

"You didn't have to," he snarled.

The man raised his head and sniffed the air. The canine move startled her.

"Your pursuer has changed directions," he said after another moment.

Izzy smiled. "Great! Then I guess I'll see you around, Snow Drift."

"My name is Tristan Chevalier." He flashed astonishingly white teeth. "I suggest you remember it. You'll be hearing it a lot."

She took a step back. "I don't want to know your name."

Her confession brought out a frown, but Tristan didn't comment. "Whether you like it or not, we are stuck together." He held up a hand. "At least for the time being."

"Yeah." Izzy shook her head. "I don't think so. I'm a solo act. Besides, how do you know that I'm the one being hunted? It might be after you," she said.

"Oh, it would definitely like to kill me," Tristan said nonchalantly. "Of that there is no doubt."

"I know the feeling, Frosty," Izzy muttered.

Tristan scowled. "But I will not give it or you the opportunity."

She believed him. Izzy couldn't imagine much taking Tristan down. "If you're so big and bad, why do you need me?" she asked. "It's not like I can help. I'm crap in a fight. Just ask my sister."

Tristan cocked his head. "There wasn't time to ask Mindy," he said.

Fear engulfed Izzy. How did Tristan know about her sister? She didn't like the look he gave her. "How do you know Mindy?" she asked, bracing for his answer.

This time his smile left her chilled to the bone. "If she hasn't already, she will soon mate with one of the Moonlight Kin."

Izzy shook her head in denial. "My sister would never marry a monster."

Tristan's smile became colder, if that were even possible. "Not all monsters are created equal. I pray for your sake that you don't learn that firsthand."

Izzy shivered and glanced away. She needed to get to a phone to warn Mindy, then she needed to get out of town.

A police cruiser rolled to a stop behind Tristan. The officers climbed out of their car. This was it. This was her chance to get away from Frosty, the crazy snowman.

Tristan raised one powdery white brow and waited for her to answer.

"Forget it," she said, then in the next breath yelled for the police.

His head whipped around too late. The officers were already approaching them. Tristan cursed loudly and glared at her.

"You're a fool," he said, then took off across the park.

Izzy watched him go. Hopefully that would be the last time she saw him. An odd sense of disappointment followed the thought.

"Jeez, girl, it was just a kiss," she muttered then approached the police. "Thank goodness you guys got here when you did. I think he was going to mug me."

2

The police escorted Izzy home and checked her apartment. As they departed, they warned her to stay away from tourists.

Izzy waved goodbye, then quickly shut the door and locked it. She wasn't safe anymore. Not that she'd ever truly been, but she thought she'd have a little more time in New Orleans before she'd have to go.

She glanced around her studio. Other than a daybed, which served as both a couch and a place to sleep, there wasn't much in the place. Her foldable table and chair were with Everly.

The blood drained from Izzy's face. Oh gawd, she had to warn Everly about Tristan. It wasn't safe for her to stay either.

Izzy tossed clothes and her essentials into her tote bag. She was in the middle of packing when someone knocked on the door. Izzy's heart jumped into her throat.

Had Tristan found her already? Maybe the police had returned? Was it too much to hope for that they'd found Tristan and arrested him?

She grabbed the bat she kept next to the daybed and quietly tiptoed to the front door. Izzy peeked out the peephole and saw a dark-haired, handsome guy standing on her porch. She didn't recognize him. He looked young enough to be in college. Was he lost?

It wouldn't be the first time that someone knocked on her door by mistake, but after the night she'd had, Izzy wasn't taking any chances.

She checked again, this time using her gift. A swirl of darkness surrounded him, but Izzy didn't detect a beast. However, the darkness didn't bode well. She decided to ignore him and keep packing.

"Please, Isabel. I need to talk to you," he said. "I know you're in there."

He knew her name. How did he know her name?

Izzy cracked the door open, but didn't remove the chain. "Who are you, and what do you want?"

"Isabel?" he asked, as if he were unsure now that he got a look at her.

That gave her pause. "What do you want with her?" Izzy asked.

He stared at her. Like Frosty, this man was good-looking. The kind of guy most college-aged girls would welcome with open arms and open legs. Unlike Frosty, he seemed nervous.

"I came to warn you that you're in danger," he said. "Can I please come in?"

Gooseflesh rose on Izzy's arms, and she glanced behind him to make sure Tristan wasn't hiding in the bushes. The thought almost made her laugh. Almost.

"My name is..." He glanced around. "Stone," he said after a moment.

"Okay, *Stone*." Izzy emphasized his odd name so he'd know she didn't believe him. "What can I do for you?"

"It's not what you can do for me, it's what I can do for you," he said, surprising her. "I know this is going to sound crazy, but there are monsters after you."

"Monsters?" Izzy asked, trying to hide her shock. "Why would you say something like that?"

His amber gaze met hers, and he swallowed hard. "Because they're after me, too."

Izzy reared back in shock. No wonder he'd given her a fake name. He knew the truth. Stone opened his mouth to say more, but she held up a finger to stop him. "Wait." Izzy closed the door to unhook the chain then opened it again. "Please come in."

He flashed her a quick smile. "Thank you for the much- needed invitation," he said, then swept into the room.

Izzy ignored the odd churning sensation in her gut. There wasn't time to examine it. She had to get out of here.

"We don't have much time," he said, as if reading her mind. "I have reason to believe that you're being stalked."

Fear tightened her chest. She'd met her stalker already. What Izzy needed to know was if there were more of them hunting her.

"Have you seen or heard anything odd lately?" Stone asked.

Other than being kidnapped by an iceberg earlier, no, not lately. Izzy shook her head.

Stone scanned her small apartment, taking it all in with one glance. "You need to get some clothes together and come with me," he said.

Izzy wasn't going anywhere with him or anyone else. "How do you know about the monsters?" she asked.

"I sense them," Stone said. "Don't you?"

Yes, she did, but she rarely came across others like herself. Everly was the first person she'd met in years that had a true gift.

"That's why they want me so bad." Stone's head came up, and he turned toward the open door. "He's coming," he hissed. "We have to go now!"

"No," Izzy said. Although Stone seemed genuinely distressed, she didn't know this man. "I'll be okay on my own."

His eyes turned pleading. "I'm not kidding," Stone said. "He's coming. I can feel him like an itch beneath my skin."

An irritating rash... Definitely sounded like Tristan. "I feel him, too," she said calmly, though calm wasn't what Izzy felt at all. She wanted to smash the stupid butterflies flitting around in her stomach. "You should go, while you can."

Stone shook his dark head. "You don't understand the danger you're in," he said. "We should stick together."

She did, but there wasn't time to convince Stone. Izzy was well aware of what could happen to her if she let her guard down.

"The thing that's coming is a killer," Stone said.

Izzy knew that, too, since Tristan had admitted as much, though she wasn't sure how much was truth and how much was bluster. "Have you seen him?"

Stone shook his head.

"Well I have," she said. "You really need to go before he gets here."

Stone scanned her apartment. "Do you have a cell phone?" he asked.

"No." Izzy had always been afraid that the monsters would use it to track her, so she'd avoided them.

Stone pulled a cell phone out of the pocket of his jeans. He shoved the phone into her hands. "Take this. The number is in the address book, along with one where I can be reached. Once you find someplace to hide, call me and let me know that you're safe."

"I will," she said.

His gaze continued to dart toward the door. "Are you sure you won't come with me?"

"Positive," she said.

Stone looked as if he wanted to say more but instead shook his head. "I really have to go. If you run into trouble, call! I'll come and get you anywhere, anytime."

He bolted out the door before she had the chance to respond and disappeared down the street.

Izzy saw a streak of white flash by and knew exactly who was on his trail. She prayed that Stone was faster, but there wasn't anything she could do to help him. Izzy glanced back at her tote bag.

She had to get out of here before Frosty found her again. Izzy finished packing and left a note and some money on the counter for her landlord. She glanced at the small apartment she'd called home one last time, then shut the door.

Only one place she could think to go. She hoped Everly didn't mind the company. Ultimately, it didn't matter. If Tristan Chevalier found her, then he'd easily find Everly. Izzy wasn't about to leave Louisiana without warning her friend.

The scent of the Darkling burned Tristan's nostrils as he raced through the French Quarter in his wolf form. He was so close, he could almost taste the foul being on the air. The houses blurred as he poured on speed. The lodestone around his neck pulsed as it encountered a wave of dark magic.

Tristan shuddered and almost lost form, but somehow his great beast prevailed. He turned a corner, following the pull of the magic, and suddenly the Darkling's scent disappeared. The hair on his nape stood on end. Tristan stopped and dropped his nose to the ground.

A week's worth of city life smacked him in the face. He smelled spicy seafood, sweat, alcohol, and urine, but no Darkling. He raised his head and sniffed again, but the scent was gone. Had he opened a portal between the worlds and crossed over?

It shouldn't be possible without Tristan feeling it in the lodestone. Was this Darkling more powerful than the others? The thought left Tristan decidedly uneasy.

He circled back one more time just to make sure he hadn't missed anything, but his nose didn't lie. The Darkling was gone. Tristan growled in frustration and snapped at the air, then turned around and headed back the way he'd come.

When he'd been chasing the Darkling, he'd also picked up a familiar aroma. Isabel. Her strong scent let Tristan know that he had to have passed her during the chase or ran by her home. He retraced his steps until he encountered the honeysuckle and citrus aroma again. It was strange how quickly he'd associated the scent with Isabel.

Tristan stopped in front of a gray two-story mansion that had been converted into apartments. He put his nose to the ground and followed the sweet aroma wafting on the air until it ended at a closed door on the second floor.

Heat swept through him as Tristan allowed the change to take him. When it was over, he stood naked outside Isabel's home. He listened but couldn't hear a heartbeat inside.

Cold swept through him. Had the Darkling killed her?

Tristan's chest throbbed. He rubbed the spot, unnerved by the sudden wash of pain. He took a deep breath. Relief struck when he didn't encounter death's pungent odor.

He glanced up and down the street to make sure that no one was around. Then Tristan turned the knob, breaking the lock. He pushed the door open. It squeaked, before settling against the wall.

Tristan stepped inside and glanced around the small space. Compared to the vibrant woman who lived there, the place was lifeless. He walked deeper into the room and closed the door behind him.

There were no personal items that he saw, nothing to indicate that Isabel had ever lived here other than her scent. Two steps brought him to the daybed. Without thought, Tristan pulled the blanket off the bed and brought it to his nose.

He inhaled and smelled Isabel. He took her honeysuckle scent into his lungs and once again felt his beast rise. Tristan dropped the blanket and searched the rest of the studio apartment. The cabinets in the bathroom had been left open, indicating that Isabel had departed in haste.

Anger surged to the surface. The little fool was running from him. Didn't she know what would happen if she ran from his beast?

Tristan strode for the front door. As he yanked it open, he caught a scent of the Darkling. Fading now, but there was no mistaking the stench. A sense of urgency rose. He couldn't let the Darkling find Isabel before he did.

Thanks to her blanket, he'd be able to track her scent. Unfortunately, so would the Darkling. Tristan threw his head back as the change swept through him. Bones snapped, and his body reshaped into the perfect predator.

Isabel thought she could run from him, hide until he went away, but she was about to find out there was nowhere for her to go that he wouldn't find her.

3

No matter how fast he ran or how many false trails he laid, the white beast continued its relentless pursuit. Almost as if he were able to track his magic, which was impossible.

The Darkling had no choice but to open a portal into his realm. It was either that or fight to the death. He called out to the other side. Darkness thickened, then a tear in the fabric of this world shimmered a hundred yards in front of him.

He cursed as he ran for the entrance. The Darkling hadn't planned on returning without the female. He'd been so close. He had almost had the Sighted-One in his grasp, only to have her taken away.

The Darkling glanced back and saw a flash of white barreling toward him. He picked up speed. The houses in the French Quarter became a blur.

He passed a couple of humans stumbling down the sidewalk. His wake swept them off their feet. They tumbled into the street, their limbs tangling.

He hoped that would delay the Moonlight Kin pursuing him, but he should've known better. The wolf leapt over the downed humans and kept coming. He didn't even give them a second glance.

The Darkling frowned. This wolf wasn't like the others he'd encountered. They all cared about the humans, as if they were more than mere prey. This wolf was different. Single-minded. Dangerous.

The entrance to his perpetually dark world swirled before him. The Darkling saw the full moon glowing on the other side, illuminating the thick forest. Magic crackled in the air. Not much farther.

The white beast couldn't follow him, unless he wanted to die. The magic would take away his ability to shift into his wolf form and eventually kill him.

Only one wolf that he knew of had ever made it out alive, and he'd needed a portal rune stone to do it. His thievery had earned him a bounty on his head. Unfortunately, no Darkling had been able to locate him and claim the prize. Rumor had it he was dead.

The Darkling raced across the blackened ash that fell beneath the opening and jumped. He landed in his realm, his heart pounding in his chest, then turned to face the menace behind him.

The white wolf skidded to a halt, its nose nearly touching the entrance, and glared at him.

The Darkling laughed, but the sound came out as a shrill bark. He stood at the entrance taunting the beast, knowing full well he could do nothing about it.

Next time, he vowed, then trotted away.

4

Izzy sat back on Everly's lumpy burgundy couch to watch the sun rise. She'd only managed to get a couple hours of sleep, which was two more than her friend. Everly had been up all night doing God only knows what in her back room.

Black candles flickered from various candelabras, highlighting the empty eye sockets of a half dozen skulls scattered throughout the living room.

One of the skulls next to a hastily erected altar in the corner looked suspiciously real. Izzy didn't say anything, since this was New Orleans and nearly fifteen percent of the population practiced voodoo. She didn't think Everly fell into that category, but she couldn't say for certain.

The scent of frankincense choked the air. Everly said it helped her think. The scent gave Izzy a headache, but she didn't complain. She was too grateful to Everly for taking her in.

Her friend came out of the bedroom and sat across from her on a beanbag. Her dark brow furrowed in thought as she picked at her chipped black nail polish. The sun peeked through the dark purple curtains. Everly scowled when a ray hit her and got up to slam them shut. Darkness once more enveloped the room.

Izzy sighed and closed her eyes.

"Tell me again how you met him," Everly said.

"Which one?" Izzy asked without opening her eyes. She felt as if she could sleep for days.

"The snowy one," she said.

"I sensed him while I was reading cards in Jackson Square last night," she said, then paused. "At least I'm pretty sure it was him."

"I remember feeling him nearby," Everly said. "It made my skin crawl."

"Yeah, mine, too," Izzy said. So why hadn't her skin crawled when she ran into Tristan later?

"He wanted you to come with him?" Everly said.

Izzy sighed. "Yeah, they both did. The strange part was they said they wanted to help me for the exact same reason."

"Weird," she said.

"I know," Izzy said. "What are the chances?"

"Too high to be a coincidence," Everly said.

"That's what I thought," she said.

"One of them has to be lying."

Izzy glanced at her. "Well, one of them *is* a monster."

Everly bit her lip. "Good point," she said. "What are you going to do now?"

Izzy thought about it, but her tired, sluggish mind wouldn't cooperate. "I don't know."

If she were smart, she'd call her sister, Mindy, but Izzy didn't want to drag her into her drama. Besides, she'd left her baby sister to keep her safe. Phoning Mindy for help would defeat the purpose.

"Do you think he was telling the truth?" Everly asked.

"Which one?" Izzy asked, giving up on getting any sleep.

Everly shrugged. "Either one."

Izzy shook her head. "I don't know." She pursed her lips. "I suppose there could be a third player in the mix that I haven't met yet. Tristan had enough opportunities to kill me if he wanted," she said. "And Stone, he looked genuinely freaked out. I've seen that look before. It can't be faked. Not that I can blame him with Frosty on his trail. To be honest, I don't trust either one of them."

Everly giggled.

"What?" Izzy asked.

She smiled. "I think it's funny that you're calling Tristan silly names. I've never heard you do that when referring to one of them," Everly said. "Normally, you just call them all monsters. Hmm..."

Izzy sat up straighter. Hard to do on a lumpy couch that sagged in the middle. "He's still a monster," she said. "If you saw him, there'd be no doubt in your mind." She pictured Tristan's handsome face and godlike body. "Okay, he might fool you for a minute, but not for any longer."

Everly arched a dark, pierced brow. "I believe you," she said. "Just thought I'd point it out. In case you weren't aware that you were doing it." She crawled off the beanbag and walked over to an unlit candle. Everly pulled a lighter out of her pocket. The candle flared to life. "If you had to trust one of them, who would it be?"

Izzy considered the question. Her mind replayed the searing kiss she'd shared with Tristan. It had stirred her more than she'd cared to admit.

"Stone, definitely Stone," Izzy said. The kiss alone had proven how dangerous Tristan could be. "His fear was real, and I didn't see a beast lurking beneath the surface when I used my gift to look at him."

"Did your skin crawl?" Everly asked.

"No," she said, then added, "but I didn't feel comfortable around him. It might've been because I'd just gotten away from Tristan. When I'm stressed, my readings aren't as reliable."

"Maybe you're right about a third player being in town," Everly said.

"Maybe."

Everly tilted her dark head, sending black hair over one eye. "You said you didn't see a beast, when you looked at Stone, but you obviously saw something that freaked you out."

"Smoke," Izzy said. "Or maybe it was shadows. Whatever it was, it obscured his features for a moment. All I know for sure is that I didn't see a monster."

Everly stared at her for a long time.

"What?" Izzy asked.

"Not sure yet," Everly said.

"Listen, I appreciate you letting me stay here last night, but more than anything I came to warn you to get out of town," Izzy said.

Everly glanced at her nails. "I'm not going anywhere," she said.

"It's not safe," Izzy said. "It is only a matter of time before they find me—and you."

Everly leveled her gaze on her. "I'm tired of running from them," she said. "Aren't you?"

Yes, she was, but what other choice did she have?

"Not sure if you noticed, but they're everywhere," Everly said, sounding as tired as Izzy felt. "If they wanted me dead, we wouldn't be having this conversation. Lately, I'm beginning to think that they aren't all bad. I ran into one at the Dungeon the other night."

Izzy gasped. "Why didn't you tell me?"

Everly shrugged. "I wasn't sure how you'd handle the news."

Izzy touched her hand. "What happened?"

Everly pulled back. "That's just it. Nothing happened," she said. "He introduced himself then bought me a drink. We chatted for a while, then he left without asking for my number."

Was it her imagination, or did Everly sound *disappointed*? "Oh God, not you, too," Izzy said. "First Mindy, now you."

"What do you mean?" Everly crossed her arms over her chest.

"You liked him." She didn't bother to hide the accusation in her voice.

Everly's mouth dropped open. "I did not. He was just some guy."

"Liar," Izzy said. "Mindy said the same thing, then I had a vision about her and one of them. They were...let's just say I never want to see my sister doing that again." She stuck her tongue out and gagged.

Everly scowled at her. "Well you don't have to worry about that." She sounded a little sad. "They don't seem to be into Goth girls." She grinned, flashing a set of vampire fangs, but the smile didn't reach her brown eyes.

Izzy scooted to the edge of the couch. "I'm sorry, Ev."

"Don't be. I'm not," she said.

"If we were dealing with the usual kind of monsters, I wouldn't be concerned," Izzy said. "But this is something different. I can feel it."

"Me, too, but—" Everly clutched her head and her eyes widened in alarm. She opened her mouth, but nothing came out.

Izzy jumped to her feet and rushed across the small room. "What's wrong?" She shook Everly's shoulder, but she didn't respond. "Everly!" she shouted. "Help!"

Tristan followed Isabel's scent through the French Quarter, ignoring the steady stream of incense and spicy foods wafting on the air. He continued east, leaving the Quarter behind him.

He'd found her easily enough last night. He just hoped that she was still in the same spot.

Tristan glanced at the sun peeking through the space between houses.

It was already warm, and the sun wasn't even high in the sky yet. He should've grabbed Isabel last night, but he'd been exhausted. She had been, too.

Her scent grew stronger as he approached a run-down mansion squatting on the corner of *seen better days*.

White paint peeled from the side of the house, exposing the yellowed layers beneath. The walkway leading to the front door had cracked and split, thanks to gnarled tree roots, and threatened to swallow anyone foolish enough to traverse it. The building looked even worse in the daylight than it had the previous evening.

Tristan inhaled. Isabel was in there somewhere. Her delicious scent perfumed the air. He trotted around to the back of the house and saw a clothesline sagging under the weight of too many items. The line had been stretched across the yard.

He scanned the line. No way would he get into those jeans. No man should. But the sweats might fit. Tristan shifted, taking human form once more. He had just grabbed the sweats off the line when a plump woman carrying a laundry basket rounded the corner.

"Well hello there." She grinned and didn't even pretend not to stare at his bare backside.

Tristan knew the kind of effect he had on human females. He pictured Isabel's sour expression. Correction, most human females. He was proud of his form—both of them. He saw no reason to rush covering himself.

"Good morning," he said, slowly stepping into the sweats. They were tighter than he would've liked, but better than nothing.

Her smile widened. "I think I liked you better without them, but I suppose you can't run around here naked. You'll cause a riot." The woman winked.

Tristan grinned at her. "We wouldn't want that," he said. "Mind if I keep these for a while?"

She chuckled. "Darlin', you can keep them as long as you like, if you promise to come back and model them sometime."

He ran a hand over his bare chest, lingering on his washboard abs. She giggled louder.

"I just might have to do that when I'm finished with my business in town," Tristan said, making sure to stroke her arm as he brushed past her.

The woman played at fanning her face. "Ew-wee, is it hot out here."

Tristan chuckled. His smile faded the second he turned his back on the woman. He strode across the lawn to the rear door and opened it. He heard shouting coming from down the hall and instantly recognized the voice.

"Help!" Isabel said. "Somebody help me!"

The back door slammed behind him as Tristan rushed down the hall. He reached the last door on the right and kicked it in. The door cracked as it came off its wood frame and fell into the room.

Isabel screamed.

Tristan shoved it aside and ducked beneath the doorframe, expecting to see the Darkling. He crouched low, ready to fight. His gaze darted around the small space in search of the enemy, but there was none.

The only people there were Isabel and an unconscious woman. He looked at her in confusion. Isabel clutched her chest and breathed hard while she hovered over the small female.

"What are you doing?" she shouted. "Are you insane?"

He'd come in to save her, but it was obvious now that she didn't need saving. Tristan ignored the fear that had been pumping through him. When she'd screamed, he'd thought... It didn't matter what he'd thought. He'd been wrong.

He took in the situation with one glance then asked, "What happened?"

Isabel glared at him.

"I cannot help you if you do not tell me what's going on." Tristan drew closer to get a better look but didn't see any obvious injuries. "Is she hurt?"

He extended his hand to check the woman's temperature, since he couldn't smell anything due to the stench coming from the incense.

"I thought she was seizing, but now I'm sure she's having a vision," Isabel said.

Tristan jerked his hand back before he touched her. "What kind of vision?"

"Sugar plums and fairies," Isabel retorted. "You know, the usual."

He frowned in confusion.

Her expression soured, and she sighed. "Visions of any kind are rarely good. It's always about the future."

Tristan took a step back. He'd never been around anyone like this and had never experienced a Sighted-One in action firsthand. Something about the whole thing seemed *unnatural*.

"What's the matter with you?" Isabel asked.

"Nothing," he said.

"Then why are you freaked out?" she asked. "It's not like a cold. You can't catch a vision."

Tristan stiffened. "I cannot catch human diseases or illnesses," he said. "My kind is immune."

"Lucky you," she said.

His mood darkened. He'd come in here expecting to find danger, not a pissed-off woman and her unconscious friend. Tristan was used to action, not waiting around.

"What do you want me to do?" He needed to do something. Boil water. Fetch blankets. Run to the convenience store. Anything.

Isabel huffed. "Since you're here, you can help me get her on the couch." She didn't sound happy.

He picked up the tiny female.

"Be careful," she warned.

He scowled at her. "I am." Tristan gently laid her on the couch.

Isabel followed on his heels, keeping a close eye on him.

"What now?" Tristan asked.

"Now, we wait," she said.

Tristan hated waiting. He'd never been good at it, unless he was hunting.

Isabel took a seat beside her friend.

He either had to stand or... He glanced at the beanbag. Not happening. It was either that or the floor. Tristan straightened the door then jammed it in place. He glared at the beanbag, then with a long suffering sigh, sat. The bag deflated under his weight.

Izzy had nearly had a coronary when Tristan kicked the door in. The only thing that prevented it was her concern for Everly.

How had he found her so quickly? She'd thought for sure it would take him at least a couple days, and by then she'd be long gone.

Izzy glanced at him, trying to ignore the display of muscles that rippled every time he shifted his big frame on the bag to get comfortable.

If the situation weren't so serious, it would be comical.

Where was his shirt? And where did he get those sweats?

Heaven help her, they didn't leave much to the imagination. He caught her watching him. His expression said he knew exactly what she'd been thinking.

Izzy blushed and glanced away. She didn't like how off balance he made her feel. One minute she was attracted to him, the next she wanted to punch him in the face.

She didn't think Tristan was doing it on purpose. After all, he couldn't help how he looked, but she had no doubt he'd use his appearance to his advantage if it meant getting what he wanted.

"What are you doing here?" she asked.

"I would think that would be obvious," he said.

Izzy brushed the hair back from Everly's face. Her friend didn't seem to notice. "I told you, I'm not going with you."

"I'm afraid things have changed," he said.

"Really?" she asked. "You mean in the last eight hours?"

Tristan nodded. "Yes."

"Listen." Izzy forced herself to face him. "I'm sure you mean well in your own weird way." She had no idea if that was the truth or not, but Izzy thought it best that he think so. "But I'd rather be on my own."

His cool gaze moved past her to settle on Everly. "Then why are you here?"

Izzy thrust her chin out. "My place was getting crowded. I needed somewhere to stay," she said pointedly. "I also came here to warn my friend."

A pale brow arched. "About what?" he asked, all but daring her to admit the truth.

Izzy snorted. "I would think that would be obvious," she said, parroting his words back at him.

Tristan glared at her then slowly glanced around the room. His eyes widened when his gaze landed on the skulls. He struggled to his feet and walked over to examine them closer. Tristan lingered over the one that looked real near the altar.

"Where did she get this?" he asked, his voice low and menacing.

"No idea," Izzy said. "You'll have to ask her when she wakes up."

He continued to explore the items in the room. "What is all this?"

Izzy shrugged. "It's Everly's *collection*. She likes dark things."

He studied her friend with new intensity.

Izzy didn't like how Tristan looked at her. "She's defenseless," she snapped, moving her body in front of her friend.

Tristan balked. "You both are," he said. "You just don't realize it yet."

Everly groaned, and her eyelashes fluttered. Then she suddenly bolted upright and started to speak.

Darkness comes on silent feet. Only the light can open the door.

"What is she talking about?" Tristan asked, putting down the skull in his hand.

Izzy shook her head. "I don't know." She waved her fingers in front of Everly's face, but her friend didn't blink. "Whatever it is, it's part of her vision."

Two from different worlds will join as one. Bodies intertwined.

Izzy's eyes widened. She glanced at Tristan in time to see his lips flatten into a straight line. He looked about as happy as she felt. Surely, Everly wasn't talking about...about...sex. Was she?

"Visions can mean almost anything," Izzy said. "They aren't necessarily literal." She wasn't sure whom she was trying to convince, Tristan or herself.

As she stared at him, Tristan's mercury gaze shifted to hers. He looked straight into her soul. A shiver spread through her, and she broke eye contact.

There was no way she'd sleep with a monster. Not even a pretty one that resembled a Norse god. Not going to happen.

Trust as one you must to break the spell of darkness. For the door is open and cannot be closed until the Sighted-One crosses over, and the dead will rise to join her.

Izzy felt her face pale. That didn't sound good. Where was the door that Everly was talking about? Was it physical or metaphorical? And what would happen once Izzy got to the other side? It was one thing to see and communicate with Spirit. Quite another to make the dead rise.

Everly groaned and dropped back onto the couch. A moment later, her eyes fluttered opened and awareness returned.

"Hey," Izzy said. "You okay?"

Tristan stepped back and leaned against the wall.

Everly touched her head and winced. "I think so. How long was I out?"

"Long enough to scare the crap out of me," Izzy said. "I almost called an ambulance."

"I'm glad you didn't," Everly said. "They would've locked me up in a padded room. Help me sit up."

Izzy grabbed her hand and helped her swing her legs over the edge of the couch.

The second Everly caught sight of Tristan, her charcoal-lined eyes widened. "It's you," she said. "You were in my vision."

Tristan tensed, then pushed away from the wall and slowly walked toward them.

Everly straightened and stared directly at him.

A growl rumbled from his chest as their gazes met and clashed.

Izzy jumped, but Everly didn't even flinch.

"Knock it off, Snowman," Izzy said, not feeling nearly as brave as she pretended.

Tristan's jaw clenched, but he stopped posturing and took a seat once more.

The dark-haired woman should be terrified of him, but Tristan sensed no fear. She'd said she knew him from her vision. He wondered what exactly she'd seen. He didn't like being left out of the loop.

Tristan didn't know what to make of Isabel's tiny friend, but he did know one thing—there was no way in hades that he and Isabel were going to be lovers. He didn't sleep with humans. Ever! Tristan was an aggressive lover, and they were too *breakable.* They also carried inferior genes compared to the Moonlight Kin.

Of course, one look at Isabel's horrified expression and Tristan knew that wasn't something he'd ever have to worry about.

Good, he thought. *That made two of them.*

Isabel glanced at him then back to Everly. "What did you see?" she asked in a low voice.

Everly continued to stare at him. Then she slowly met her friend's startled gaze. "He can hear every word you say. Doesn't matter if you whisper. Does it?" she asked him.

Tristan stared at her. "No."

"Did you see our deaths?" Isabel asked and swallowed hard.

Everly bit her lip, and her brow furrowed. "Not the kind you're talking about."

Isabel frowned in confusion. "What other kinds of deaths are there?"

"There's true death, then there's everything else," Everly said.

Tristan inhaled. The truth...and a lie. What wasn't she telling them?

"Are you sure you're feeling okay?" Isabel asked. "You're acting weird, and for you that's saying something."

Everly's gaze slipped back to Tristan. "You're not what I imagined. In my vision you were... *taller.*"

He crossed his long legs. "I am six foot five," he said.

She wasn't at all what he'd anticipated either. Something about the dark little imp made him decidedly uncomfortable. Her brown eyes held humor and knowledge. Tristan dismissed the humor, but he wanted the knowledge she hid.

There was more to Isabel's friend than she revealed, but Tristan didn't have time to uncover all her secrets. Right now, he only needed to know the answer to one.

"Introduce me," she said to Isabel, before he asked.

"You don't want to meet him," she said. "It's better if you don't know him."

Everly glanced at her. "Yes, I do. Especially now."

Isabel looked as if she were about to argue, until Everly clutched her temple again. "Fine," she said. "Everly Watts, this is Tristan Chevalier, but everyone calls him Frosty."

"Not everyone," he said through gritted teeth. Only Isabel would dare to do such a thing. He would allow no other the luxury.

Everly nodded but didn't hold out her hand.

Smart woman. Or was she simply afraid to touch him? Humans had odd ideas about his kind. Most worked in Moonlight Kin favor, but some showed nothing but ignorance. Tristan didn't think this woman was stupid. Quite the opposite. Her scent told him that she wasn't afraid.

"So where do you want to take my friend?" Everly asked, abruptly changing the subject.

"That's not your concern," he said. "Where'd you get the wolf skull?"

"That's not a wolf," Isabel said. "It's human."

"Correction," Tristan said. "He was in human *form* when he died, but he was not human."

Isabel studied the skull. "How can you tell? It looks just like the others."

"Dead or alive, I can smell my own kind," Tristan said. "Now where did you get it, Everly Watts?"

Everly crossed her arms and sat back. "I didn't kill him if that's what you're asking."

Tristan scooted forward. He had wondered if she had, but wasn't surprised that she hadn't. Female hunters weren't common, but they did exist. The east coast Alpha, Damon Laroche, had mated with one such woman.

"Then who did?" he asked. Tristan would hunt them down once he eliminated the Darkling threat.

Everly scoffed. "I'm not about to tell you that. You'd kill them," she said.

"Yes, I would." Tristan smiled, showing more teeth than necessary. That was his job, and he was very good at it.

Isabel stared at Everly. "You knew the skull came from one of them, and you kept it anyway? Are you nuts?"

"Not crazy," Tristan said, answering for her. "But not particularly bright, since my kind can smell their own."

Everly stiffened and glared at him. This time she didn't look away until Isabel shook her. "You might've mentioned his resemblance to one of the Avengers."

"It wasn't Loki, so I didn't think it was important," Izzy said.

Everly laughed. "I see why you like him."

Isabel's mouth dropped open. A plethora of emotions rushed across her face. "I don't like him. Why would you say that? He's a monster."

Tristan tensed. Humans had called him many things over the years. Nothing really fazed him anymore—or so he thought. *She's human. She means nothing to me*, he reminded himself.

Her cheeks reddened. "No offense," Isabel added hastily.

"None taken," Tristan said nonchalantly, ignoring the churning in his gut. "Your friend was about to tell me where she got the skull."

"No, she wasn't," Everly said. "So drop it."

He surged forward. "If there is someone out there hunting Moonlight Kin, then I need to know about it."

"Hunting what?" Isabel asked.

"That's what they call themselves," Everly said. "I thought you knew."

"Of course." It was obvious she hadn't.

Tristan was within striking distance. He didn't make a habit of attacking women. In fact, he avoided it whenever possible. But his loyalty was to his people, not to humans. This woman needed to be reminded of the fact.

"I'm only going to ask nicely one last time," Tristan said. "Where did you get the skull?"

Everly glowered. "It was a gift."

"For what purpose?" he asked. Getting her to respond was like pulling teeth from a mule.

She thought about the question for a moment. No doubt trying to decide whether to lie. It would do her no good. He'd scent a lie immediately.

Everly sighed. "I use it to detect your presence," she said.

Tristan's nostrils flared. That was not what he'd expected her to say. Such a thing shouldn't be possible, but the ramifications of the admission were not lost on him. This woman was more dangerous than he first thought.

Somehow she'd turned a Moonlight Kin skull into a tracking device. If the Hunters learned about it, about her, they'd go to great lengths to get their hands on her. What if she'd already shared the knowledge? He needed to find out.

"How have you used this knowledge?" If she said that she gave the information to the Hunters, then Tristan was going to have to kill her or have the local Alpha take care of the job.

He glanced at Isabel. She would never forgive him if he murdered her friend, but what choice did he have?

"The skull is for *personal* use," Everly said. "I do not share what I know. It helps me avoid your kind."

"Why didn't you tell me about this?" Isabel asked, sounding hurt. "I could've used one of those myself."

"And exactly how did you plan to get one?" Tristan asked. Had he completely misjudged her? Was she talking about killing, too?

Isabel rolled her eyes. "I'll start by melting ice."

Tristan gave her a droll look and shook his head. He should've known.

Everly touched her arm. "You need to go with him," she said.

"Okay, now I know there's something wrong with you," Izzy said. "Because the friend I know would never suggest anything so insane, especially knowing full well what he is."

Everly's dark eyes filled with compassion. "I've seen the future," she said.

"I know," Izzy said. "We heard. Though a lot of it didn't make sense, and you don't seem to be in a hurry to elaborate."

Tristan rested his elbows on his knees. "What exactly did you see?"

Everly's dark gaze landed on him. "I don't think you're ready to hear what I saw. I don't think either of you are, but it doesn't matter." She pushed her hair away from her face. "I've seen what's going to happen... to us all. You can't outrun fate. None of us can."

A shiver tracked down Tristan's spine.

5

I zzy hugged Everly goodbye then stepped into the hall.

"You will see her again," Tristan said.

She hoped he was right, but thus far Izzy hadn't had any visions of the future. Did that mean she didn't have a future to see?

Izzy frowned.

"Come," Tristan said, but didn't reach for her.

"Where are we going?" she asked.

His guarded expression made her think he wouldn't answer, but then Tristan surprised her. "I must present myself to the Alpha of this area. He can aid us in finding shelter."

"Why do I have to go with you?" Izzy asked.

"Because you have shown that you cannot be trusted out of my sight." He smirked.

Once again Izzy had the overwhelming urge to slap the smartass expression right off his face. She'd try it if he weren't so tall.

Tristan laughed.

"What?" she asked.

"Sometimes you are so easy to read," he said.

Izzy tilted her head to get a better look at him. "I'll keep that in mind the next time I think about hitting you," she said.

"You'd only hurt yourself," Tristan said.

"Of course you would say something like that," she said, then muttered under her breath, "arrogant jerk." He was right. Hitting someone that solid would probably break her hand.

Tristan chuckled. "You mustn't be concerned about your friend's visions," he said.

Izzy stopped on the sidewalk. "I'm not. Why would you bring that up?"

He shrugged his broad shoulders. "I thought perhaps that was what you were upset about."

"No," she said. "I'm upset because you won't leave me alone and insist on disrupting my life. Hint. Hint. Hint."

"Oh," he said. "I'm glad to be mistaken. Better to be thinking that than the possibility of us having sex."

Her eyes rounded. "I wasn't thinking about having sex with you." Izzy's gaze automatically dropped to the bulge straining the front of his sweatpants. He needed to change clothes.

"Good." Tristan gave her a knowing smirk. "You can rest assured it's never going to happen."

Angry with herself for being distracted by his perfect body, Izzy rounded on him. "Damn right it's not!" she snapped. "So just get that mental picture out of your head." And she'd do the same just as soon as he got dressed.

They continued down the sidewalk toward the French Quarter, weaving their way through the growing crowds. Despite it being morning, the tourists were already out enjoying the delights the quarter offered.

"I have no idea what you're thinking, but sex with you never even crossed my mind. Nor would it ever with a *human*," Tristan said in disgust.

Izzy stopped again. "What's that supposed to mean?"

Tristan paused, his gaze scanning the people around them. "I do not sleep with inferior species," he said, giving her body a once over.

Izzy's mouth gaped. "Who are you calling inferior, Snowflake?"

His haughty expression spoke volumes. "You are human. Are you not?"

Anger rose out of nowhere. "How dare you!" Izzy shouted. "I am not a monster."

Tristan's jaw clenched, and he stepped forward until there was no space between their bodies. "Neither am I!" he snarled.

Izzy snorted. "I'm not the one who goes fuzzy once a month."

"I am *never* fuzzy!" he groused.

Izzy took one look at his affronted expression and laughed in his face. It was the wrong thing to do, but she couldn't help it. A picture of Tristan as a big, fuzzy, white dog popped into her mind, and she just could not shake the image.

"Take it back," he said softly.

"No." She crossed her arms.

"I said, take it back," Tristan hissed.

"No." Izzy shook her head. "Not until you do."

His heated gaze dropped to her mouth, and the tension between them changed in an instant. Suddenly the New Orleans heat was nothing compared to the simmering air around them. Tristan looked at her as if he wanted to eat her alive, and not in a *wolfie* kind of way.

When he stared at her like that, Izzy forgot all about him being a werewolf and saw him as a man. Their kiss came back in vivid detail. Izzy's traitorous body softened and swayed toward him, drawn by something primal.

Tristan's gaze grew hooded, and he crowded even closer. Heat poured off his body, along with a spicy scent that was unique to him alone. He unclenched his hands and reached for her.

If he touched her, she'd lose it, lose herself. *No! Don't let him kiss you again.* No matter how bad she wanted to feel his lips upon hers. Izzy's eyes widened as the insane thought struck, and she took a step back.

"We can't." She held out her hand to stop him and encountered a wall of warm marble. Izzy's fingers trembled as she pulled her hand away from his bare chest. Was it her imagination or had the color of Tristan's eyes changed? "I'm inferior, remember?"

Tristan took a deep breath, and his body shuddered. It took supreme effort to tear his gaze away from the temptation her mouth presented. It had been hours since he'd claimed Isabel's lips, but Tristan still tasted the honeysuckle on his tongue.

He thought about Everly's vision. She had to be wrong. There were many ways for information to be interpreted. It didn't have to be sex, though he couldn't think of any other way that bodies intertwined. And damn if that didn't make him hard.

Tristan glanced down at the front of his pants and cursed. He wasn't a little man. The snug sweats he wore hid nothing.

Isabel followed his gaze. If it were possible, her eyes widened even more. She couldn't seem to tear her attention away, which wasn't helping his current condition at all. His nostrils flared. Her warm scent filled his lungs.

She was still scared, but beneath the fear Tristan smelled something else. Something utterly enticing and overwhelmingly feminine. Isabel may not like him, but part of her desired him.

And damn if that didn't make his job that much harder.

Tristan's gaze raked Isabel. He could see the definite outline of a feminine figure underneath her long skirt and loose blouse. Hell, even if he couldn't, he'd felt her body pressed to his when he had kissed her. In that moment, whether she knew it or not, she'd surrendered.

The beast inside him roared to life. Tristan shook his head and grabbed hold of his shadow side. He couldn't afford for his beast to escape. It didn't think like he did. Didn't reason. It acted on instinct. And right now its instincts were telling it to take.

"Come," he said. "We need to hurry."

He needed to get to Pierre La Fontaine's home in the Garden District. If for no other reason than to get a break from Isabel's company and regain his footing.

She had him thinking about things Tristan rarely contemplated. Work was his mistress, not wayward females whose sense of self-preservation was questionable at best.

He led her through the French Quarter to Canal Street then hung a right. Trolleys ran down St. Charles Avenue to the Garden District, along with buses, but Tristan didn't care to wait for a bus. He preferred the open air of the trolley.

The trolley wouldn't take them all the way to Pierre's house due to the construction in the area, but it would get them close enough. Once he checked in with the Alpha, he'd retrieve his truck.

Tristan waited for Isabel to board, then he climbed on after her. There weren't any seats available, until he walked over to a couple of young men and stared at them. They suddenly jumped up and offered him their wooden seat.

He grabbed Isabel by the elbow and guided her onto the bench. She scowled at him, which was becoming an unwelcome habit. He much preferred her teasing. When she did that, Isabel reminded Tristan of his little brother, François.

He too had been a free spirit, floating through life without a care in the world. That was why it had been so easy for the lone wolf to kill him.

François had been so trusting, so innocent that when the wolf attacked, he'd been helpless to defend himself. His death had changed Tristan's life forever—changed Tristan forever. The loss had turned him into what he was now. The cold distance kept the pain at bay.

Tristan glanced at her. Isabel and François really were so much alike that at times the similarity scared him. When that happened, he pushed her away using cruelty to make her withdraw.

He pictured his brother's mangled body. Would Isabel meet the same fate?

The thought left him feeling decidedly uncomfortable. Tristan closed his eyes and clutched the window frame of the trolley until the wood moaned beneath his grip, then he slowly released it along with the bad memories. He didn't like thinking about the past. There was nothing he could do about it, but he could change the future.

Tristan glanced out the window. "This is our stop," he said.

Isabel waited for a couple people to pass, then stood.

Tristan followed her off the trolley then indicated to the far side of the street where a massive mansion took up half the block.

"Guess you guys don't know the meaning of the word 'subtle,'" she said.

Most Alphas didn't, but that wasn't how he lived. Tristan pictured his favorite home, an adobe nestled in the foothills of the high New Mexican desert. The place was warm, welcoming, and peaceful. Perfect for relaxing and clearing his head after a job.

"When you have to house an entire pack, you need a lot of space," he said dryly.

Isabel froze on the sidewalk. Her hazel eyes widened, then widened again until they swallowed her face. "There's a whole pack of monsters inside there."

It wasn't a question, but Tristan answered it as such anyway. "Yes, there is an entire pack of wolves in there," he said. "Southern Moonlight Kin to be exact. They don't take kindly to being called monsters, so I suggest you be on your best behavior, unless you want to end up on the menu."

She blanched and swayed before his eyes.

Tristan grabbed her before she fainted. He'd meant to scare her a little, but he didn't want Isabel so scared that she couldn't function.

He didn't like her viewing him and his people as monsters, even though it was best if she did. Why it bothered Tristan so much, he couldn't say. He'd never been bothered by such a thing before.

She's human, he reminded himself. *Humans are weak. They believe they are the apex predators. They're wrong.*

Isabel turned green, and she looked as if she were going to be sick.

A pang of guilt struck. "I was just kidding," Tristan said. "I will not allow anything to happen to you."

The moment the words left his mouth, Tristan knew they were the truth. She had a smart mouth and he might want to strangle her at times, but he wouldn't let anyone harm her.

Isabel's gaze searched his face, then she glanced back at the house.

"I swear," Tristan said. He'd vow anything to take away her fear. "Now come."

He led her to the front of the mansion, where they were met by a couple of Pierre's guards. The two men stepped forward and sniffed them. Their eyes narrowed when they caught Isabel's human scent.

"I need to speak to Pierre," Tristan said.

"Who shall we say is calling?" the wolf on the left asked, watching them both closely.

"Tell him that Tristan Chevalier, Enforcer for the Lycanian Elders, is in need of his assistance."

The wolf on the right paled and took a step back. His gaze immediately dropped to the porch floor. The man on the left was slower, but he eventually followed suit.

Isabel looked at them then glanced at Tristan. This time there was confusion in her eyes.

Better that than fear, Tristan thought.

The man on the right pressed the doorbell and waited. A moment later, a short wolf dressed in an expensive suit popped his head out the door. When he caught sight of Tristan, he shoved the other two wolves out of the way and bowed.

"Sorry to have kept you waiting, Enforcer," he said. "Please come inside and bring your little..." –he sniffed and his nose wrinkled like he'd smelled something bad— "*friend* with you."

"After you." Tristan ushered Isabel ahead of him.

The second they entered the foyer, her eyes widened and her mouth dropped open. Tristan had nearly done the same thing the first time he'd seen the inside of the Southern Alpha's home.

Entering the mansion was like stepping back into the seventeen hundreds. Everything had been meticulously restored to its original grandeur.

"Tristan, my friend," a booming voice said. "What brings you to my humble abode?"

The question almost made Tristan laugh, since there was nothing humble about Pierre's abode, or the Alpha himself for that matter.

Izzy continued to reel from the news that Tristan was some kind of assassin. Her tumultuous thoughts were interrupted when a dark-haired man with lightly tanned skin came silently gliding down the staircase. Had he not spoken, Izzy wouldn't have known that he was there.

No, she mentally corrected. There'd be no way to miss him. His presence filled the space, adding to its opulence.

Izzy stared, unable to look away. She had never seen anyone quite so beautiful. The man's finely sculpted face could only be called pretty. How he managed it without looking feminine in the process was a mystery.

Tristan gave her an admonishing look then glanced back to the man. "I'm sure you're aware of what has brought me to your fair city," he said.

The man stopped before them and smiled. The move seemed too practiced for her liking.

Yet, Izzy felt that smile all the way to her toes when he directed the wattage at her. Was it hot in here? She resisted the urge to tug on her collar.

"Aren't you going to introduce us?" the man asked, stepping closer to her.

Tristan looked as if he was about to refuse the request, then thought better of it. Why he cared one way or the other, Izzy didn't know, since he'd made his views on humans perfectly clear.

"Isabel MacDougal, I'd like you to meet Pierre La Fontaine, Alpha of the Southern Moonlight Kin pack," Tristan said.

So this was the biggest monster in town. Izzy stared at him until an image of his dark beast replaced his perfect features. He didn't seem to notice, or maybe he had better manners than her.

Pierre took her hand before she offered it and kissed the back of her knuckles in such a way that Izzy had no doubt he'd done it hundreds of times before. A shiver tracked down her spine, but somehow she kept her hand from trembling.

While Tristan exuded an air of ice, this man was nothing but sweltering heat and hot summer nights. He used his smoldering good looks to full advantage.

Izzy couldn't imagine many women turned him down once he crooked his finger in their direction. No doubt with one look, he could make panties drop from fifty paces.

"A pleasure," Pierre said. "I can't remember the last time a Sighted-One graced my doorstep."

Tristan cleared his throat and insinuated himself between them, forcing Pierre to release her.

Pierre's amber gaze lit with speculation. "Perhaps, Enforcer, we should talk in private."

"That would be best," Tristan said. "What I have to say calls for discretion."

"If you don't mind waiting in the parlor, Isabel." Pierre pointed to a room off to the left. "I'll have refreshments brought to you."

Despite the polite offer, it wasn't a request. "Sure," she said. "Take all the time you need. I'll just go in there and fluff my petticoats."

Pierre frowned in confusion.

Tristan laughed. "She's a delight, isn't she?"

The Alpha watched her. "She's certainly...interesting," he said.

Izzy walked into the parlor. Two navy-blue settees had been arranged in the middle of the room, facing each other. There were wooden side tables of various sizes and shapes spaced throughout the parlor, along with several chairs and stools.

Some of the tables held board games, while others housed lamps. All were covered in lace of some type or another. Everything looked so old and expensive that Izzy was afraid to sit down.

A minute later, the man who'd met them at the door came in, carrying a tray with a pitcher of lemonade and some finger sandwiches on it. The idea that wolves served finger sandwiches struck her as funny, but Izzy didn't laugh. She didn't think he'd appreciate her sense of humor.

The man set the tray down on a small side table then turned to her. "I thought instead of breakfast that you'd prefer a sandwich. If you need anything else," he said, "just ring that bell." He pointed to a cloth lever hanging from the ceiling next to the door.

"Thanks," she said. "I'm sure I'll be fine." Izzy waited for him to leave then checked the sandwiches. As soon as she realized they were turkey and ham, she tucked into them. She hadn't eaten last night or this morning. Right now, anything looked good.

Izzy wandered around the room while she ate, a glass of lemonade in one hand and a sandwich in the other. She had no idea how long Tristan's explanation would take, but Izzy hoped they'd be out of here soon. She didn't want to be in this house any longer than necessary.

She stopped near a window and stared out at the vast lawn. The lush green space had been carefully manicured to project an image of southern refinement. If people only knew who their neighbor really was, they'd be horrified.

Izzy had just turned to retrace her steps when she heard Tristan's voice. She stopped to listen. Where was it coming from? The window was shut. She was alone in the room, and the thick walls wouldn't carry sound.

Tristan spoke again. There was no mistaking the deep timbre of his voice.

She followed the sound to a heating vent behind a nearby table. Izzy glanced over her shoulder to make sure the door was closed then moved closer.

It was wrong to eavesdrop, but Izzy was genuinely curious what he and Pierre were talking about. She grabbed a small stool and took a seat. Izzy placed her food and drink on the table, so if anyone came in unexpectedly it would look like she was enjoying her meal.

"Never thought I'd see the day that you'd be slumming it with a human," Pierre said. "Even one as attractive as her."

She stiffened but listened for Tristan's response. Whatever he said, it was too low for her to hear. Izzy scooted the stool closer.

"Have you located the Darkling?" Pierre asked.

"I almost had him, but he opened a portal and got away," Tristan said. "He's after the woman. Of that there is no doubt."

"Ah," Pierre said. "That explains why you brought her here. You know if you took away the purple streaks from her hair and changed her formless clothes, she wouldn't be bad to gaze upon."

Tristan mumbled, but his next words were frighteningly clear. "She's a means to an end," he said. "Nothing more."

"Oh," Pierre said. "I thought perhaps there was something going on between you two. There seemed to be—"

"No!" Tristan cut off whatever he was going to say. "You know I do not mix with humans. All I see is bait when I look at her. Bait to catch the Darkling."

His cold words left Izzy chilled to the bone. She shouldn't be surprised. Tristan had said from the outset that he didn't care for humans, yet somehow she'd convinced herself that the frigid exterior was just a front.

She'd been a fool.

Izzy stood. She didn't need to hear anymore. She thought of Stone's offer of help. Would it still stand? She glanced once more at the closed door.

At any moment, Tristan might return. Izzy needed to contact Stone, if for no other reason than to tell him that he was safe because the monster was with her. They *all* were.

She pulled out the cell phone he'd given her and turned it on. Izzy found the number and sent a quick text. Less than a minute later, she received a response.

I'll help you get away. Just tell me where you are.

Izzy replied. *I'm someplace you can't help me. I'll let you know if and when we leave.*

Take care of yourself. The monsters aren't to be trusted.

Izzy knew that better than most. Tristan had just squashed the tiny bit of doubt lingering inside of her. She turned the phone off and shoved it into her purse. Izzy looked at her half-eaten sandwich. Suddenly she wasn't hungry anymore.

* * *

Tristan sat across from Pierre in his ornate office. He'd never seen so much gilded gold outside of a Parisian palace. He didn't like the way the Alpha looked at him. It was as if he knew something that Tristan did not.

"We need a place to stay. Preferably someplace remote, so that I will know when the Darkling draws near," he said.

"No problem. I know just the place." Pierre sat back. "How does the woman feel about being used as bait?"

Tristan shrugged casually. "I hadn't planned to tell her."

Pierre watched him closely. "What if something happens to her?"

Tristan's gut clenched. Nothing was going to happen to Isabel.

"You cannot always protect bait," Pierre said. "Accidents happen."

Tristan flinched.

"Are you sure there is nothing going on between you two?" Pierre asked. "I've never seen you so wound up."

"Positive," Tristan's vehement response didn't have the effect he'd hoped.

Pierre grinned, looking positively enthralled by the whole conversation. "You say that the woman is a means to an end, yet she carries your scent."

Tristan blanched. "I had no choice but to touch her," he said. "When I first encountered her, she refused to come with me."

Pierre's face hardened, along with all the muscles in his body. "When you say touch, what exactly do you mean?"

There was one hard-and-fast rule within the Moonlight Kin. A woman could be coerced, but never be forced into physical intimacy. Doing such a thing was an automatic death sentence for any Were.

Tristan had gladly carried that sentence out a few times over the years, which was why he gnashed his teeth at the Alpha's insinuation. "I had to pick her up and carry her someplace private so we could talk. That's how my scent got on her."

Pierre relaxed a fraction. "It seemed…stronger."

He thought about the kiss, and his whole body tensed. There was no sense in lying to the Alpha. They had ways of ferreting out information. "She forced me to kiss her."

If Pierre's eyebrows rose any higher, they'd disappear beneath his hairline. "How exactly did Isabel do that?" he asked. "Did she hold you at gunpoint?"

Tristan knew what he thought. It would be what any Alpha of the Moonlight Kin would think, when it came to him. Tristan wasn't known for being emotionally or physically demonstrative, unless he killed someone. And even then, emotions rarely played a part. He wasn't the type to keep females around.

Contrary to what they all believed, Tristan wasn't a glacier and he wasn't gay. He had needs just like any other male. He just rarely acted upon them.

Instead, Tristan focused on the job. It took a special breed of wolf to hunt down your own kind and kill them without mercy. It wasn't something he enjoyed, but Tristan was exceedingly good at the job. There were a few other Enforcers, but none were better.

Pierre continued to stare at him until he squirmed in his seat.

"She wouldn't shut up," Tristan said, trying to make the Alpha understand. "When she wasn't threatening to scream, she tore into me. Since I didn't have a gag, I improvised. That was all. The kiss meant nothing." The lie slipped out before he could stop it.

Pierre's amber eyes glistened. "That's some improvisation on your part. I would've never thought you had it in you."

"It's been a while, but kissing is not something one forgets how to do," he said mockingly.

"Wish I could've been there to see that," Pierre said.

"What did she do when you kissed her?"

Tristan's mind blanked. "I don't understand the question."

Pierre's lips canted, and his eyes crinkled in amusement. "Did Isabel smack you? She would've had every right to do so, since I have no doubt you kissed her without permission."

Tristan hesitated. Where was Pierre going with this line of questioning? "No, she didn't strike me, though Isabel did look like she wanted to," he said.

Why hadn't she hit him? She'd had plenty of opportunity. Tristan hadn't exactly been as unaffected by the kiss as he claimed. He wished the Alpha wasn't so amused by the situation, but Pierre had always had an annoying sense of humor.

"Did she scream or try to run away?" he asked.

Tristan shook his head. "No, she didn't do anything like that."

"Hmm..." Pierre said. "Interesting." He leaned forward. "I have one final question."

"Then ask, so I can put us both out of our misery," Tristan said impatiently.

Pierre chuckled. "Did she kiss you back?"

Yes, the word whispered through Tristan's mind, leaving confusion in its wake.

He straightened in his seat. "You don't know her. Isabel may look soft and tempting, but her tongue spews acid," Tristan said. "I am lucky to have flesh left on my bones."

A grin parted Pierre's face. "So she *did* kiss you back. Fascinating, don't you think?"

"Did you not hear what I said?" Tristan ran a hand through his long white hair. "There is nothing interesting about this situation," he said. "Isabel can be utterly infuriating, when she wants to be. Which is most of the time, I might add."

"Yes, I can see that," Pierre said. "Isabel." Her name rolled off his lips.

The seductive tone made Tristan's hackles rise. "That is her name," he said.

Pierre carefully blanked his expression. "It is indeed. Perhaps I need to speak with Isabel once more. I feel that I prematurely formed my opinion of her."

Tristan's muscles flexed as he gripped the arms of the chair. "I've told you everything," he said.

The Alpha gave him a knowing look. "I have absolutely no doubt, but women can be quite elusive when they want to be," he said. "There's obviously more to Isabel than meets the eye."

Something akin to panic struck. Pierre was renowned for his charm and his many conquests. Women of all ages responded to his devilish good looks. Isabel hadn't been immune. Tristan had seen her pupils dilate and heard her pulse jump when she looked at him. He didn't want the Alpha anywhere near her.

"I assure you that she will show you no respect whatsoever," Tristan said, trying to dissuade Pierre. "You are wasting your breath."

"If you don't mind, I'll be the judge of that." Pierre rose from behind his desk.

Tristan stood, too.

"Please, have a seat," he said. "This shouldn't take long." Pierre winked at him. "Or perhaps it will. One never knows what kind of mischief one can get up to in the parlor."

A deep growl rumbled out of Tristan as his wolf surged to the surface.

The Alpha stopped and gave him a hard look, one that all but dared him to continue.

Tristan clenched his hands at his sides.

"Sit, Enforcer," Pierre said. "Or I'll make you sit."

For one insane moment, Tristan considered challenging the Alpha. The thought must've shown on his face because Pierre's amber eyes widened.

"I won't harm her," he said.

Tristan wanted to stop him, but he couldn't forbid the visit without starting a major incident. He'd never wanted to be Alpha. Tristan didn't want the responsibility of caring for so many wolves. So what had gotten into him? Isabel's face flashed in his mind. He knew she was trouble, and this proved it.

Pierre laughed, and then the Alpha stepped into the hall.

It took every fiber of Tristan's being to nod and sit back down.

Pierre made sure to shut the door behind him, so there would be no chance of Tristan hearing what was going on. That didn't stop Tristan from trying to listen. He'd give the Alpha ten minutes. If he didn't return within that time, then Tristan would go after him.

The door opened behind Izzy. She turned, expecting to see Tristan, but instead found the darkly handsome Pierre La Fontaine staring at her. He noted the missing sandwiches on the platter.

"I trust they were to your liking," he said, indicating to the food.

"They were fine. Thanks," Izzy said, rubbing her arms. Where was Tristan? She wanted out of here. Now!

"I'd like to have a word with you before Tristan joins us. Which I have no doubt will be very soon." Pierre grinned.

What was so funny? Izzy hoped Pierre skipped the niceties and got straight to the point. He didn't know that she'd heard them talking, so if he lied, she'd know.

"Please, have a seat." Pierre pointed to one of the expensive-looking settees.

Izzy hesitated then perched on the edge of the seat. Instead of taking a seat opposite her, Pierre sat down next to her. Izzy immediately scooted away.

She checked to see if the move had insulted him, but his smile only widened. Izzy angled herself in such a way that she kept him and the door in sight.

Pierre noticed but didn't comment though for a second Izzy thought she heard him laugh. The sound was there and gone before she could be sure.

"What did you want to talk about?" she asked to hurry things along.

She knew exactly what the monsters had planned for her.

"What do you think of Tristan?" Pierre leaned back and draped his arm over the back of the settee.

Izzy blinked. The question surprised her so much that it took her a full minute to answer. "What do you mean?"

This time Pierre did laugh. "I'm just curious what you think of him. Feel free to speak candidly. You are safe within these walls."

Yeah, but what would happen when she left the house?

"He's fine," she said noncommittally.

"You can do better than that," he said.

"Okay, he's bossy and thinks he knows everything." She had no idea what Pierre was after, and until she figured it out Izzy wasn't about to be too direct.

"So the kiss wasn't that good," Pierre said.

Izzy's eyes widened in shock. Heat spread from her face to the rest of her body. Why had Tristan told Pierre about their kiss?

She sputtered as words clustered in her mouth and tangled on her tongue. "I-I-I." Izzy cleared her throat. "I'm not sure what that has to do with anything."

Pierre took pity on her. "I've known Tristan Chevalier for years. He's never been one to play with..." –he paused— "anything."

Play? What did he mean by that? Izzy had no clue, but it hardly mattered since she'd heard exactly what Tristan had planned for her.

"Perhaps he's trying to soften me up before he delivers bad news," she said.

"Perhaps," Pierre said. "But I've never known Tristan to care about such things."

"I'm not sure what you want me to say," she said.

Pierre tilted his head. "You are a unique woman," he said, surprising her once again. He rose from the settee and walked to the door, where he paused. "Contrary to his appearance, Tristan wasn't always made of ice. There was a time when he was a lot like you."

Izzy couldn't imagine Tristan ever being like her.

"Thank you for…" Pierre's brow furrowed, and his voice trailed off.

"What?" Izzy asked, more confused than ever.

"For thawing him a little," Pierre said, then opened the door.

Tristan stood in the hall, his hand raised to knock on the parlor door. He had an unreadable expression on his face.

Pierre grinned. "Right on time I see."

As if on cue, Tristan scowled. "Let's go, Isabel," he said. "I have the keys to the cabin. Thank you again for your assistance, Alpha. I will let the Lycanian Elders know of your aid."

Pierre laughed. "You do that."

6

Izzy waited until Tristan climbed behind the wheel of his silver F150 pickup truck and pulled out into traffic before she confronted him. She hadn't planned to bring the subject up, but Pierre's questions had rattled her, and Tristan had been acting distant ever since they'd left the house. Frankly, the whole situation pissed her off.

Tristan had no right to be angry or pouty or however snowmen acted when they got their carrot noses out of joint. Izzy was the one being taken advantage of. She wasn't the one in the wrong. He was.

"So," she said, itching for a fight. "How exactly do you plan to use me as bait?"

To his credit, he didn't flinch, but his glacial features tightened.

Didn't think I knew about your little plan, did you?

"Did Pierre tell you that?" he asked.

"Does it matter how I found out?" Izzy wasn't about to let him know that she'd eavesdropped on their conversation. There was confessing and then there was *confessing*.

Tristan exhaled. "The Darkling wants you. We have to give it what it wants," he said. "There is no other way to draw it out."

Izzy crossed her arms. The move pushed her breasts up. "Do I get a say in any of this?"

He glanced at her chest, then his expression hardened. "No," he said then returned his attention to the road.

He doesn't care about you, remember?

"Well I'm sorry to rain on your party, Snowflake, but you're just going to have to find the monster without me," she said. "Because I have no intention of helping you."

Izzy might've helped him, if he'd bothered to ask, but he hadn't. Instead, he'd planned to deceive her.

"The Darkling doesn't want me," Tristan said. "It wants you. It followed you here from Oregon. It knows you're here. It won't give up until I stop it."

"Sounds like you need me more than I need you," Izzy said. "That must suck for you."

Tristan laughed, but the sound sent shivers down her spine. "It matters not," he said. "You *will* help me."

"I will not," she parroted.

Izzy stared out the window. She didn't like anyone giving her orders. She'd had her fill of them when her parents had her locked up in the asylum.

"You either help me or everyone you love will die," Tristan said. "Just like your friend, Celina Gibson."

Her head whipped around in surprise. At the same time, a wave of pain struck. Mindy had told her about Celina's death. Told her about Slade, the man who'd killed her. Izzy had already known that her best friend had passed because she'd caught a glimpse of her spirit shortly after her death.

Izzy didn't like having the incident thrown in her face. And she damn sure didn't like being threatened. She'd done everything she could to lead the danger away. It just hadn't been enough.

She glared at Tristan. She'd known he was stubborn and beyond uptight, but Izzy hadn't thought he was capable of killing innocents. She'd really read him wrong. Or perhaps, she'd read him right the first time. He was a monster after all.

A strange calm came over her. Izzy loosened her seatbelt to face him. "Don't threaten my family," she snarled. "I may not be as strong as you, but I will find a way to stop you."

Tristan's hands clutched the wheel until his knuckles turned white. "It's not me who is threatening their existence," he said.

"Then who is?" she snapped. "Because it sure as hell sounds like you talking."

"The Darkling," he said with impatience.

"Is that supposed to mean something to me?" Izzy asked. He'd mentioned she was being hunted. Why differentiate the Moonlight Kin from the Darklings? All monsters were the same, weren't they?

Izzy had lied when she'd told Mindy that the monsters were just like humans. They weren't. They were far worse.

Her sister had mentioned something about a Darkling. What did she say? The music had been so loud and Izzy had still been reeling over Celina's death, so she hadn't asked a lot of questions. Now she wished she had.

"Yes, the word should mean something to you," he said through gritted teeth.

"Well it doesn't," she said just to aggravate him. "Right now the only person threatening me and my family is you."

She faced the window once more. Izzy had to get away from Tristan. It had been a mistake to think she was in any way safe around him. Tristan might claim he'd protect her, but after that statement there was no way she'd ever trust him. They were no longer just talking about her life.

"Where are we going?" she asked, so she could tell Stone. At this point, he was her only hope of getting out of this mess alive.

If Tristan thought she'd put herself in danger to help him kill someone—to help him period—he was wrong. Izzy had no intention of getting in the middle of this monster war. Let them wipe each other out. It would make her life much easier if they did.

She glanced at Tristan and pictured him covered in blood. Instead of relief, the thought brought only sadness.

He put his blinker on and took the Barataria Boulevard exit toward

Jean Lafitte Park. The traffic thinned as he continued down the road.

Eventually, Tristan turned right. It looked as if he were driving into the woods, but it turned out to be a poorly maintained gravel road. The truck bounced as it hit the potholes, jarring Izzy.

Trees scraped the side of the doors as they squeezed their way along the unmarked road. Izzy heard Tristan curse under his breath as a particularly large branch scratched his truck.

So he did care about one thing, she thought. Typical guy.

Tristan turned left onto a game trail. It certainly wasn't a road. The overgrowth was even worse, though she didn't know how that was possible given what they'd just driven through. Tristan drove over downed limbs and squeezed his way through the woods. At one point, he had to cross a murky stream.

His curses grew louder. Most were aimed at Pierre.

Izzy said nothing. Instead, she paid attention to the route they were taking. Somehow she'd have to explain to Stone where they were located. It wouldn't be easy without street signs. Hopefully he was from around here and would know what she meant. Because as far as Izzy could tell, they were in the middle of the woods next to the swamp, which in Louisiana could be just about anywhere.

Tristan had said what he'd said to anger Isabel. If she were angry with him, then she'd keep her distance. The spot in the center of his chest ached. Tristan ignored it. What he was doing was for the best—for both of them.

She was human. He was Moonlight Kin. Their worlds were never meant to intertwine.

He thought about Damon Laroche and Aidan Fortier. Both Alphas had taken human females as mates. They'd even managed to breed true, but that didn't mean the Lycanian Elders and the rest of the packs wanted consorting with humans to become habit. Aidan's parting words to him came rushing back.

Once the wolf makes its decision, there's nothing you can do to change its mind.

Tristan shuddered. It would not happen to him. He'd make sure of it. Contrary to what the Alpha believed, Tristan controlled his wolf, not the other way around.

The cabin came into view, or at least what was left of it. Like a lot of structures built in and around New Orleans, this one had been lifted off the ground to protect it from flooding. Too bad the move didn't protect it from the elements.

There was no paint left on the walls, except a thin strip of haint blue around the windows and on the front door. He'd bet his fur that the front porch roof had also been painted the same aqua blue color. Something clinked in the tree beside him. Tristan glanced at the branches. They were covered in bottles.

Like the haint blue painted on the house, the bottle tree was there to ward off evil spirits. It was a Gullah tradition, but obviously the Kin saw no need to get rid of it. Tristan stared at the blue bottles covering the tree and shook his head. He'd never been superstitious. He should remove them, but they could use all the help they could get.

Tristan turned off the engine. A frown marred Isabel's soft features as she stared at the shack.

"I'm sure it looks better on the inside," he said, hoping it was true. Wolves were used to roughing it. In their beast form, indoor plumbing and lighting wasn't a concern.

Isabel glanced at him. "Doesn't matter. I won't be here long."

What did she mean by that? He wanted to ask, but was afraid of her answer.

Just like on the night Aidan warned him about his wolf, Tristan felt as if someone walked over his grave.

His wolf snarled inside him. Tristan ignored his beast and opened the truck door. He climbed out and immediately sank two inches into the mud. Lovely, he thought, then raised his nose to the wind.

Tristan wanted to get a good scent of the area so he'd know the second something entered his territory. He smelled stagnant water, along with fresh. The rich aroma of green plants and lurking predators came next.

His gaze moved through the trees to the water beyond. Beneath that surface lurked at least one gator, quite possibly a few. He glanced at Isabel.

"Stay away from the water," he said, then grabbed his bag and hers from behind the seat and headed for the cabin.

The place looked as if a strong wind would bring it crashing down upon their heads. Izzy didn't want to think about how many creepy crawlies had made their way inside.

Did it even have a bathroom?

The thought of having to traipse into the woods to do her business left her uneasy. Tristan may be a woodland creature, but Izzy was not.

He climbed the stairs. The sweats molded to his tight butt like a second skin. There wasn't an inch of fat on him. Everly was right. Tristan did resemble one of the Avengers.

Izzy sighed. It would be so much easier if he were an eyesore. As much as she wanted to hide out in the truck, she had to go inside. Tristan opened the front door and disappeared into the dark interior.

She waited, but he didn't come back out. Izzy pulled her phone out of her purse and quickly dialed Stone. The phone rang and rang, but he didn't pick up.

"Where are you?" she muttered. Her eyes remained locked on the front door.

Izzy saw a flash of white and quickly turned the phone off and put it away. She didn't want Tristan to know that she had it. No doubt he'd take it away. She'd just have to try to get in touch with Stone later, when Tristan wasn't around.

That thought brought her up short. What if he was serious about not letting her out of his sight? It didn't matter. He had to go to sleep sometime or take a shower. Izzy would figure something out.

She shoved the door open and climbed out of the truck. Izzy tiptoed through the mud, though it didn't do her or her shoes much good. She glanced at the mud covering the toes and scowled.

When she reached the front door, Izzy slipped her shoes off and turned them upside down. At least if something crawled inside them, it would fall out when she lifted them up. She hoped.

Izzy pulled the screen door open and stepped inside. Tristan was right. It did look better on the inside than on the outside, but it was still only a one-room cabin.

A large quilt-covered bed had been shoved against the back wall. At the foot of the bed sat a small table with two chairs. The opposite wall held a couch. Perched beside it was an overflowing bookshelf. Whoever lived here liked to read, which surprised her.

A kitchenette, which consisted of a stove, a sink, and a couple of cabinets, had been tucked in a corner next to a small fridge. Izzy scanned the space, but didn't immediately spot a bathroom.

"Don't worry." Tristan pushed what she thought was the back door open. "The bathroom is in here. The place has a generator and its own well."

Good to know, Izzy thought.

"I'm going to take a shower," he said. "If you're hungry, Pierre keeps the kitchen fully stocked."

"I'm fine. I'll just..." –Izzy searched for a quick distraction— "read a book."

He hesitated then shook his head. "I'll be out shortly. Try not to get into any trouble."

Izzy waited until she heard the water come on, then slipped out onto the front porch. She pulled her cellphone out and called Stone again. This time, he picked up.

"Isabel?"

"It's me," she whispered. "You told me to call once we settled into a spot. I don't have long. The shifter is in the shower. I'm in a cabin in the middle of nowhere. I need you to get me out."

"Describe it," he said.

"Woods, mosquitos, and swamp," she said. "There weren't any road signs once we turned off."

Stone grew quiet. "I'm going to need a little more info."

Izzy glanced over her shoulder, but the bathroom door was still closed. "We turned right before we got into Jean Lafitte Park, then took a road that was barely visible. We made one or two more turns, then crossed a creek. I'm sorry. I've always had a bad sense of direction, especially when there aren't street signs."

"It'll be okay," he said. "We have time. He's not going to hurt you as long as you're of use to him. You've given me enough information. I'll be able to find you. Just stay put. You did the right thing by calling me."

Before she could ask when he was coming, Stone disconnected. Izzy turned the phone off and dropped it into her purse. She came back in the cabin as the bathroom door opened and Tristan stepped out.

Water dripped down his bare chest, and his hair was slicked back away from his chiseled face. He'd wrapped a towel around his trim waist, which only accentuated his rippling muscles. For a moment, she forgot how to breathe.

Tristan scanned the cabin. "Who were you talking to, Isabel?" he asked as he finger combed his long, white hair.

Izzy flinched but managed to keep her composure. "No one," she said. "Why do you ask?" Her voice squeaked.

Tristan's silver eyes narrowed. "I heard you speaking to someone. I'm a wolf, remember?"

Oh God! How much had he heard? Izzy didn't know and couldn't ask. Maybe he just suspected and hoped she'd confess. She needed to stay calm.

He stalked forward.

Izzy's heart skipped, and her mouth went dry. She couldn't seem to tear her gaze away from his moist flesh. This close she could smell the soap he'd used.

Tristan stopped in front of her and sniffed the air, then his expression darkened. "You're lying," he said. "Who was here?"

The accusation snapped her out of her momentary fascination. "No one," Izzy said, which was the truth. As far as she knew, they were alone. "I doubt there's another soul around here for miles."

Tristan walked past her and stepped out onto the porch. His skin glistened in the afternoon light, making him appear even more ethereal. His head lifted and he inhaled deeply, taking in the scents from various directions. When he finished, his shoulders relaxed, but Tristan's expression remained impassive as he came back inside.

A water droplet slipped down the center of his chest then glided over the ridges of his abdomen before seeping into the towel around his hips. Izzy licked her lips, suddenly thirsty.

It took her a moment to pick up on the silence. When she did, Izzy glanced up. Tristan's body was rigid. He didn't appear to be breathing at all. The heat in his mercury eyes looked hot enough to melt steel.

Izzy cleared her throat. "You should probably get dressed," she said.

Tristan took a step forward. "Who were you talking to, Isabel?" She'd lied when he'd asked her the first time, but he didn't know why. He couldn't sense anyone nearby, but that didn't mean they weren't there. When you were dealing with magic, you couldn't be too careful.

The heat from her body increased as he closed the distance between them. So did his. Isabel shouldn't look at him like she wanted to eat him up. She shouldn't be admiring his appearance at all. But she had been. There was no mistaking the hunger in her gaze or the longing.

Tristan crowded her until she backed against the front door. The pulse jumped in her neck. He slapped his hands down beside her head, caging her. If she weren't human, he would strip her and take her right here. But she was.

His chest brushed hers. Tristan felt her nipples pebble just like they had last night when he'd kissed her. Isabel's rich scent grew stronger. He wanted to roll in it—or at least his wolf did. His nostrils flared. Her desire wrapped around him, hardening every inch of his body.

"Tell me the truth," he said. He made sure they continued to touch, even though it was sheer torture.

Tristan had meant to intimidate her into telling the truth. He had always been good at holding himself separate from his duties, but Isabel's sweet citrusy scent was doing strange things to his head.

She glared at him. "I was talking to myself. Okay?" Isabel put her hands on his chest and pushed, but she didn't put much power behind the move. Instead, her fingers lingered on his hot skin and stroked across his pecs.

Tristan quivered. Did she realize what she was doing? He wasn't sure, until she did it again.

Isabel's eyes widened in surprise as his body responded to her caress. The woman was playing with fire. Her hands moved over to his arms, encircling his biceps.

It wouldn't take much effort to rip the clothes off her. Even now, Tristan tried to work out the easiest way to bare her.

She stroked the length of his arm.

Tristan froze, torn between wanting more and moving out of reach. It had been a long time since he'd taken a woman to his bed. Too long, given his state of arousal from a simple touch. Maybe later he'd go out and find a willing she-wolf to take the edge off.

"What are you doing?" he asked.

Isabel's mouth opened then closed. "I don't know. I just couldn't stop myself."

That was the truth. Tristan didn't need his wolf to know it. "If you keep touching me like that, you're going to end up flat on your back in that bed," he said.

Isabel yanked her hand back as if she'd been burned.

Tristan told himself that he wasn't disappointed, but the damn ache in the middle of his chest told a different story.

7

Izzy had managed to distract him—and herself. She had no idea how long it would last. Tristan struck her as the tenacious type. Why had she touched him?

Sure, when he wasn't scowling, Tristan was quite handsome in a god-like way. Not all women went for that type of guy. She glanced at his bare chest and wide shoulders. Okay, only someone blind wouldn't notice all those muscles.

When he'd cornered her, she hadn't been able to see anything but his beautiful chest. With the heat pouring off him and his muscles right in front of her face, she just couldn't resist.

Once she touched him, Izzy hadn't been able to pull her hand away. His skin was smooth like marble but hot to the touch. When he'd trembled beneath her fingertips, she'd thought she had imagined it. Izzy had touched him again to be sure.

The second time, he'd quivered and that rich spicy aroma of his skin had increased. She'd actually grown dizzy. Or maybe she'd just forgotten to breathe.

Izzy had gone on dates with good-looking men, but none had anything on Tristan. He was in a category all his own.

Tristan may not care for humans, but some part of him was attracted to her. If Izzy had needed any more proof, her doubts evaporated when she caught sight of the towel around his waist. There was no denying the hard ridge of arousal lifting the front of it.

It took every fiber of her being to tear her gaze away, but not before she saw Tristan's pained expression. "I'll give you some privacy to get dressed," she said.

He nodded and waited for her to leave.

Izzy stepped out onto the front porch and pressed a hand to her head. It had been so long since she'd touched anyone in a sexual way.

Mindy thought she was wild and slept around, but Izzy hadn't done that since her late teens. Even then, it had been out of rebellion and self-loathing.

Those days were long behind her, but that didn't mean she was dead inside. Even though she didn't want to, Izzy found herself responding to Tristan. Her physical reaction to his nearness had nothing to do with logic and everything to do with primal need.

How could you hate someone and want them at the same time?

She didn't know, but Izzy couldn't deny the truth any longer. She may not like Tristan, but part of her wanted him. A part of her that she hadn't allowed to surface for a long time.

Izzy glanced at the closed screen door but didn't spot Tristan. She hoped they didn't have to spend too much time here. She had no idea what would happen if they did.

Scratch that. Izzy knew exactly what would happen if they were trapped together for too long. It was the same thing that almost happened a minute ago.

They might hate each other and themselves afterwards, but they'd eventually give in to the physical attraction simmering between them.

Izzy thought about the hard ridge under that towel and felt her body moisten. He'd been so big and so beautifully formed. Such a waste.

She closed her eyes and sent up a silent prayer that Stone found her before she and Tristan did something they'd both regret.

Tristan's hands shook as he pulled on a shirt and a pair of shorts. He couldn't believe how close he'd come to taking her. He decided to back off from his line of questioning, at least until he had himself together.

Tristan walked into the small kitchenette and opened the cupboard.

Cans of various items filled the shelves, along with flour and everything else needed for baking. He pulled items out and placed them on the small counter.

"What are you doing?" Isabel asked as she came in from outside.

"Making an early dinner," he said.

She frowned.

"What?" Tristan asked.

Isabel shrugged. "I just never imagined you in a kitchen cooking."

Tristan laughed. "Why? Because I'm a guy?"

She came closer. "No, that's not it. I just thought..."

His brow arched. "Thought what?"

"That you'd become fuzzy and go out and catch a rabbit or something," she said.

He balked and went back to organizing the gumbo ingredients to make sure he had everything he needed. "Would you prefer to eat rabbit?"

His wolf rose in an instant, eager to get her what she wanted. Shocked by its behavior, Tristan shoved the beast back down.

Isabel leaned against the table. "No."

Tristan went back to prepping. It bothered him that she had such bad impressions of his kind, of him. Sure, he hadn't helped change her views, but given her experiences throughout life, she should've known better.

He opened the refrigerator to find it fully stocked like the cabinets. Tristan pulled out chicken, green peppers, onions, and carrots, then found a cutting board. He made quick work of dicing the chicken.

"Do you need any help?" Isabel asked.

Tristan glanced at her but kept cutting. She thought he was such a wild beast that he'd simply shift into his other form and go catch fresh meat. Why should he let her help?

Helping may loosen her tongue.

"Do you know how to make biscuits?" he asked.

Isabel shook her head. "I'm not really much of a cook," she said.

"Check the drawers to see if there's a peeler. If you find one, then start in on the carrots," he said.

She did as he asked. A moment later, she found a peeler and picked up the bundle of carrots. Isabel grabbed a paper towel then went and sat at the table. There she peeled the carrots.

Together they worked in silence until everything was prepared, then Isabel stepped back as Tristan browned the chicken in a pot. Once he finished, he tossed in the diced onion, peppers, and carrots. He found chicken broth and Cajun seasoning in the cupboard and added them to the mix.

"This needs to cook for a while," he said. "Thanks for your help."

He opened the refrigerator and pulled out a beer. "Want one?" he asked. Thanks to his fast metabolism, Tristan couldn't get drunk, but he did like the taste.

Izzy nodded. A beer sounded good.

Tristan grabbed another bottle and placed it on the table in front of her. Before she touched it, he twisted off the cap.

"Thanks," she said. This whole thing struck her as surreal, especially seeing him in a vintage rock T-shirt and shorts.

Izzy had never imagined Tristan dressed so casually or cooking anything. The act was so...so...*normal*. It was another reminder of how little she knew about him. She picked up the beer and tipped it into her mouth. It wasn't her beverage of choice, but at least it was cold and wet.

"Where did you learn how to cook?" she asked when he took a seat across from her.

Tristan stared at her.

For a minute, Izzy didn't think he was going to answer.

He took a drink of his beer then set the bottle down. "Mom taught me and my brother, when we were young."

Why she was surprised that he had a mom and a brother, Izzy didn't know. It wasn't like monsters were hatched from eggs. She guessed she'd never given their origins much thought.

"How old is your brother?" she asked.

Tristan's expression darkened. "Who were you speaking with earlier, Isabel?"

The change in subject gave her mental whiplash. If Tristan didn't want to talk about his family, then he shouldn't have brought the subject up.

"I told you. I was talking to myself," she said and glanced away.

"You're a terrible liar," he said. Before she responded, he added, "I have to stir the gumbo."

Izzy took another strong pull off her beer. This time the taste didn't burn as bad. She waited for Tristan to return to the table, but he didn't. Instead, he put the spoon down next to the pot and walked out the front door.

She sighed. It was only late afternoon. There was no way they were going to make it all night if they kept going like this. Izzy pushed the chair back and followed him.

She shouldered screen door and stepped out onto the porch. "What are you doing?" she asked.

Tristan didn't look at her. "I'm making sure our location hasn't been compromised."

Izzy tensed then forced herself to relax. "I doubt anyone could find us here. Wherever here is," she said.

His sharp gaze didn't miss a thing. "Not without help anyway."

She put her bottle down, so he wouldn't see her hands tremble. "Are you from around here?"

Tristan slowly pulled his gaze away from her and went back to scanning the woods. "No, but I come here often enough to be familiar with the area."

"Pierre called you an Enforcer," she said. "What does that mean exactly?"

Tristan's shoulders tensed. "I'm sort of like a cop," he said. "I hunt people who break the law."

"Hunt?" she asked. "Like a bounty hunter?"

He nodded. "Yes," he said. "But there are no bounties involved."

"So you take them to jail?" she asked. Izzy didn't know werewolves had a prison.

This time Tristan did look at her, and he slowly shook his head. "No jail."

"Then what—" Izzy's eyes widened. "You kill them? All of them?"

"I am an Enforcer for my people. It is my job to protect them from exposure and threats," he said. "I am very good at my job."

He'd insinuated that he was going to kill the Darkling, but Izzy hadn't really believed him. Deep down she didn't want to because that would mean that the person she was attracted to was a heartless killer.

"It sounds like you're an assassin, not a cop," she said quietly. Please let her have misunderstood.

"There is not a distinction between the two with the Moonlight Kin," he said, then turned his back on her.

Tristan hated seeing that disappointed look in her eyes. He'd never lied to Isabel about what he was. She'd known from the start he hunted the Darkling. But seeing the disbelief, the disillusionment, then eventual acceptance of the truth shattered something inside him.

He wasn't ashamed of what he did. His job was important, even if she didn't fully understand their ways. Tristan stared at the woods, unseeing. He still smelled her, but her sweet, delicious aroma had soured.

It's for the best, he told himself.

Tristan surveyed the area one last time then walked past her. He didn't look at Isabel. He couldn't. Tristan didn't need to in order to know what she thought. To her, he was, and always would be, an uncaring, unfeeling monster.

They ate dinner in tense silence. The second she finished her bowl, Isabel jumped to her feet. "I'm going to get ready for bed."

She took her bowl to the sink and rushed off to the bathroom before Tristan could respond. A moment later, he heard the shower come on.

Tristan finished his meal then walked into the kitchen to clean up.

As he washed the dishes and put the leftover gumbo in the fridge, he heard splashing.

Despite his best efforts, Tristan couldn't help but picture Isabel standing naked under the spray. Her firm breasts and supple thighs covered in water. Her wild blond hair with purple highlights slicked back. Would her skin still hold the warm musky scent that perfumed the air every time he drew near?

Tristan felt his body harden again. It had been doing that a lot around her. He needed to figure out a way to stop it, especially after their last conversation. Isabel would never understand him or his people. She was too human.

Another sound came from the bathroom. His ears perked. Was she singing?

Before he knew what he was doing, Tristan moved closer to the bathroom door. He listened to the off-key warbling and couldn't help but smile.

Did Isabel always sing in the shower? He'd like to think that she did. He pictured her using her hand as a microphone as she wailed out the latest pop song. It was...cute.

The singing stopped and the shower ended. Tristan hurried back over to the sink. He wasn't about to be caught lurking outside the bathroom door. Even he knew that was creepy. He went back to cleaning the last of the dishes.

Five minutes later, the bathroom door opened and a cloud of steam came out. Isabel followed, wearing nothing but a long T-shirt. The shirt left her firm thighs and pink painted toes visible. It also left little to his already strained imagination. As he watched, her nipples crinkled. He could see the rosy outline through the front of her white shirt.

He'd been right when he'd guessed that the baggy clothes she wore hid some serious curves. Isabel was built like a wet dream. She was soft where she needed to be soft and full where it counted.

The plate in his hand cracked under the force of his grip. "You aren't going to wear that, are you?"

Isabel glanced down at the front of her shirt, then back at him. "Everything is covered."

Not everything. Not nearly enough.

"Don't you have sweats or something you can put on?" he asked.

She put her hand on her hip, which only emphasized her trim waist. "Don't know if you noticed, but there's no air-conditioning here. It's too hot to wear sweats," she said. "If you don't like what I'm wearing, you don't have to look."

Oh, but he did. That was the problem. Tristan couldn't help but stare at her. There was too much bare skin visible for him to ignore. He tossed the broken plate in the trash and turned in time to see Isabel stop at the foot of the bed. Her shoulders stiffened, and her sweet scent curdled.

"What's wrong?" He scanned the bed to make sure a spider hadn't crawled onto it.

"Um..." She glanced over her shoulder at him. "We need to talk about the sleeping arrangements."

Tristan hadn't thought about there only being one bed. Pierre had conveniently forgotten to mention the fact. He'd have to have a word with the Alpha before he left town. The lumpy couch was too short for his large frame, but he couldn't exactly make her sleep there.

"I'll take the couch," he heard himself say.

8

Tristan knew it was going to be a long night as he listened to Isabel toss and turn, trying to get comfortable.

He wondered, not for the first time, if she had trouble sleeping because he was so nearby. He certainly was having trouble, and it only got worse, when he pictured Isabel in that sheer T-shirt.

He punched his pillow and turned over toward the window. If he sat up, he'd have a good view out to the front of the cabin. Not that he needed it. His incredible hearing had already picked up the gators sloshing around in the water and a few deer passing through.

Tristan closed his eyes and forced himself to sleep. He needed to get some rest. He'd just dozed off when Isabel whimpered. Tristan shot to his feet, prepared to face whatever had disturbed her, but he found the room empty.

He glanced over at Isabel. She thrashed against the covers, her limbs tangling in the sheets. A thin layer of sweat glistened on her pale skin. She whimpered again then let out a bloodcurdling scream.

Tristan leapt across the room, landing next to the bed. Isabel bolted upright and stared out the window. Her eyes were wide, but her gaze remained unfocused. His beast rose and he scanned the darkness, but didn't spot anything.

He watched helplessly as tears streamed down her cheeks. Tristan didn't know what to do.

"It's okay," he said awkwardly. "I'm here. You're safe. I'll be right back."

He bolted outside and quickly circled the house to ensure there wasn't a threat. When Tristan was sure they were alone, he went back in.

Isabel glanced his way, and her brow furrowed in confusion. "Did you find it?" she asked.

"Find what?" he asked.

"The monster," she whispered, then glanced out the window and screamed again.

Tristan rushed to her side and pulled her into his arms. There wasn't anything there, but he searched again to ease her fears.

"Please don't let it get me," she begged.

"Shh... You're safe," he said, lowering his voice. "I won't let anything harm you."

Isabel fought his hold for a minute then slowly relaxed. She blinked a couple times, and her eyes cleared. A moment later, she frowned. "Tristan?"

"I'm right here," he said, gently rocking her.

"What are you doing?" she asked.

"You were having a bad dream," he said. At least he hoped that's all it was. Tristan glanced back out at the darkness and felt his wolf pace restlessly inside of him.

Isabel ducked her head, but not before he saw her face blossom with color. "Sorry I woke you," she said. "I should've warned you that I have a lot of nightmares."

"It's okay." Tristan wished he could go into her dreams and slay the monsters plaguing her, even if they looked exactly like him. "You all right now?"

She nodded.

Tristan slowly released her and rose off the bed. Before he took a step back, Isabel grabbed his wrist.

"Don't go," she said, her panicked gaze searching the darkness.

"Not yet."

Tristan hesitated. She was awake now and aware of her surroundings. He should just go back to the couch. "I'll be right over there." He pointed.

"Please," she added. "Can you just stay for a little while?"

He sighed and put his knee back onto the bed, then sank down beside her. "I'll stay until you fall asleep."

"Thank you," she said.

Instead of turning her back to Tristan, she cuddled up next to him. Isabel's body fit perfectly against his larger frame. He felt every curve, every indent beneath that thin T-shirt.

Tristan tried to relax, but it was impossible lying next her. He remained rigid as she snuggled even closer and her breathing evened out. He had no idea how much time had passed. Tristan was about to slip off the bed and return to the couch when he felt tears hit his forearm.

Had he somehow woken her? It wasn't until he caught a glimpse of Isabel's blotchy face that he realized she was crying in her sleep.

A crack formed in his icy exterior as her tears fell. Tristan brushed her tangled hair back and made soothing sounds. The kind of sounds he hadn't made since childhood.

He couldn't bear to see Isabel like this. He wanted her fighting, yelling at him, anything but scared. Until this moment, Tristan had no idea she was in so much pain.

More and more of him thawed as the minutes ticked by. He continued to coo until her tears dried. As he stared at her, Tristan's control wavered.

He shouldn't touch her. It would only complicate things. Isabel didn't really want to be comforted by him, but that didn't stop him from pulling her into his arms. She snuffled, let out a long sigh, and relaxed.

Tristan held her tighter as something inside him broke. The wave of emotion that struck would've knocked him off his feet had he been standing. The emotion wasn't anything as superficial as lust. Though he definitely felt that, too. This was deeper and more profound.

Isabel's warm scent tickled his nostrils. Tristan waited for her breathing to even out, then he buried his nose in her hair. There it was again. Honeysuckle. Just like the night they'd met.

He would never admit it, but Tristan loved the scent. Loved that she smelled like summer and blooming flowers. It reminded him of his childhood. His grip on her tightened, as he wondered if she smelled like that *everywhere*.

He forced himself to relax. He didn't want to accidentally hurt her. Isabel nestled closer, and her hand brushed his shaft. Every muscle in Tristan's body tensed, and he groaned. She made it difficult to remain detached.

Despite his resolve, Tristan felt a bond forming between them. A bond that shouldn't exist and would only get in the way of his mission. His gaze shifted to the window. The Darkling was hiding somewhere out there.

Isabel was a distraction he could not afford. Tristan would need all his wits if he were going to defeat his enemy.

* * *

It had taken hours, but he'd eventually picked up on the Sighted-One's scent. The small cabin sat in the middle of the swamp like a fat toad on a log. There was no light shining from any of the windows, but she was in there.

They both were.

The wolf's stench clogged his nostrils, filling him with disgust. There was no way to get to her without going through him.

He circled the cabin, taking care to keep to the shadows. It wasn't hard given that he and the shadows were as one. He thought about burning them out, but couldn't take a chance that the woman might be harmed.

Waiting wasn't his strong suit. Heat rippled over his dark fur. The Darkling had felt the sensation before. He knew what it meant. The beast was watching.

He hadn't spotted him yet. If he had, there was no doubt in the Darkling's mind that he would've confronted him. After all, he'd chased him through the French Quarter, unconcerned that they'd attracted attention.

The Darkling lifted its nose and smelled the air. The muscles in his body tightened. Why were their scents entwining? He sniffed again to make sure he wasn't mistaken, but the odd mingling hadn't changed.

That shouldn't be possible without close contact. It would take more than being in a cabin together to create the aroma. Even a cabin that small. What was going on?

The possibilities that flitted through his mind left the Darkling enraged. There was a fine line between attraction and hate, but surely it hadn't been crossed so soon.

If that wolf had laid the Sighted-One, then he'd do more than kill it. He'd make that Kin suffer like no other. In the end, the wolf would beg for death.

* * *

Izzy awoke to find her nose buried in Tristan's neck. His arms were around her, holding her tenderly, and his chin rested on top of her head. To make matters worse, she'd snuggled up against him with her arm wrapped around his waist.

His breathing was even and relaxed, which seemed at odds with the hard ridge resting next to her hip. There was no way she could extricate herself without waking him.

She tried to remember how they'd gotten like this. A dream flashed in and out of focus. Izzy remembered tears... and asking him to stay. Tristan hadn't wanted to from what she recalled, but he'd done so anyway.

So he hadn't been the one to instigate this situation. She had. That just made everything worse. Izzy pulled the covers up over her head. The movement disturbed Tristan.

He dipped his nose to her hair and inhaled, then sighed loudly. A second later, his hips rocked, and she felt every inch of his morning erection.

Izzy closed her eyes and groaned.

Tristan stiffened beside her.

"Don't worry, you didn't disturb me. I was already awake," she said.

He pulled his arm out from under her, and her head dropped to the bed. A second later, he was off the mattress and halfway across the room. She stared at him from beneath her lashes. Tristan scrubbed a hand over his shadowed jaw.

"I'm going to catch a shower," he said. "Unless you want to go first."

Izzy pulled the covers down to her waist but couldn't meet his gaze. Instead, she focused on his shoulder. "That's okay. You go ahead."

Tristan gave her a curt nod and grabbed his tote. "When I get out, we'll grab something to eat, then get out of here."

"Where are we going?" Izzy thought for sure they'd spend their days hanging in the swamp, waiting for the monster to come.

"Into town," he said as if that were obvious. "We want to make sure the Darkling catches your scent."

Izzy didn't reply. What was the use? He'd told her yesterday that he'd planned to use her as bait. One night spent in his arms wasn't going to change his plans.

She waited for the door to close behind Tristan then wandered into the kitchen. Izzy put on some coffee and found a box of cereal. She pulled out two bowls and a couple of spoons. She left one out for Tristan, then filled hers and wandered back to the table.

Izzy slipped on some shorts. She felt too exposed in her T-shirt. Which was weird, since she hadn't felt that way last night. She thought about the moment she'd woken, wrapped in Tristan's strong arms.

For a few seconds, Izzy had forgotten all about monsters and being hunted. She'd forgotten all about being stuck in a cabin with a man who hated humans. She'd just been a woman, lying in a man's arms. And it had felt...*nice*. For once in her life, she had actually felt safe.

Izzy should've known the moment wouldn't last. Life as she knew it was a never-ending nightmare. Tristan's arrival wasn't going to change that.

Tristan couldn't seem to get her scent off his skin. It was like he'd absorbed part of her essence overnight. He scrubbed harder, but he still felt her warmth in his arms. He glanced down at his hard shaft and cursed under his breath.

This wasn't good.

He jerked the nozzle to cold and stood under the pelting spray. It helped with his body's physical response but did little to alleviate his growing need.

Damn her!

Tristan shut the water off and wrung his hair out. He didn't dare go out there in his current condition. He heard Isabel crunching on something and smelled the aroma of freshly brewed coffee wafting on the air.

He couldn't hide in the bathroom all day. Eventually he'd have to face her. It was best to do so head on before she got the wrong idea about them—about him.

Tristan pulled on a pair of jeans and a clean navy T-shirt, then yanked his hair back and tied it at his nape. He shaved quickly, while glaring at himself in the mirror.

Last night, he'd come close to doing something he'd absolutely regret. He'd have to make sure the opportunity didn't arise again because he wouldn't be strong enough to turn it down a second time.

9

The French Quarter bustled with tourists by the time Tristan parked his truck. He hadn't said much on the drive into New Orleans, and for that Izzy was grateful.

She was so embarrassed about last night that she'd rather pretend it didn't happen. Izzy unhooked her seatbelt and climbed out.

"What now?" she asked.

Tristan adjusted his sunglasses. "Now we mingle, so the Darkling has a chance to catch your scent."

"What happens if he does?" she asked, hoping there was more to the plan than that.

"It'll draw him out and allow me to get close to him," he said.

Izzy glanced around at the crowded sidewalks. "Tell me your plan isn't to kill him in front of all these people," she said.

Tristan snorted. "Hardly," he said. "I'll track him back to his lair, then I'll kill him."

Izzy rolled her eyes.

"What?" Tristan asked.

"Frosty, you make him sound like a Bond villain," she said. "I'll follow him back his lair." Izzy rubbed her hands together and cackled maniacally.

Tristan's expression eased.

For a second, she thought he might laugh, but then the moment passed.

"There's something really wrong with you," he said.

"At least I'm not a talking snowball," she said, then wandered down the sidewalk.

Tristan crossed his arms over his chest. "Where are you going?"

Izzy shrugged. "You said to wander. I'm wandering."

"I'll be close by," he said.

Her footsteps faltered. "You're not coming with me?"

"He won't approach you if I'm by your side," Tristan said, then disappeared in the crowd. Quite an impressive feat given his size.

Izzy hesitated then kept walking. Being bait sucked! As she window-shopped, she thought about last night. She hadn't expected Tristan to be so caring. When she'd woken up and thought she'd seen a monster outside her window, Izzy had expected him to ask her if she was okay, then go back to the couch. But he hadn't.

Instead, Tristan had climbed into bed beside her and held her until she fell asleep. Izzy didn't want to think about how good his arms had felt wrapped around her. Part of her hated that he'd made her feel safe. It only made his absence worse.

She kept walking. A couple times Izzy thought she caught a glimpse of Tristan in the window's reflection, but when she'd checked, he was nowhere to be found.

Izzy wandered another two blocks. The heat was already beginning to make her sweat. Most natives knew to get inside in the afternoon. Only the tourists were dumb enough to soldier on.

She turned a corner, and the skin on her nape prickled. Izzy allowed her senses to flare. The power she brushed against didn't feel like her snowman's. Was it the Darkling?

Izzy slowly scanned the area. What did a Darkling look like? Did it resemble a werewolf? A person? Or something altogether different? She should've asked.

She casually glanced at the faces around her, searching for some sign that would let her know that they weren't human. When that didn't yield anything, Izzy opened her power of Sight. The second she did, she saw Spirits fleeing from the next street over.

What could've frightened the dead? Izzy fought the urge to run with them.

She needed to find out what was going on. Izzy passed a couple of houses but didn't see anything unusual. She took a deep breath and kept going. Where was Tristan? Izzy crossed between two more houses. One of the homes had a massive trellis attached to the side of it. As she stepped past a trellis of honeysuckle, someone grabbed her.

Izzy opened her mouth to scream, but a palm came down over her face before she could. Fear stabbed her and her skin crawled. She struggled to break the man's tight grip. Everything inside of Izzy told her to get away.

"It's Stone," a low voice hissed. "Don't scream." He waited for her to nod, then he quickly pulled his hand away.

Izzy found Stone standing behind her. "What are you doing?" she whispered. "I thought you were—" She cut the words off before she finished the sentence. Izzy wasn't going to get into a conversation about a creature she knew nothing about. "You scared me to death," she said instead.

"Sorry." He scrubbed a hand through his disheveled hair. He'd shoved his wrinkled shirt into one side of his jeans, leaving the other half to flap on the outside. His red eyes showed just how little sleep he'd gotten. "I couldn't take the chance that the monster would hear you."

Izzy understood all too well the need for caution, given a wolf's keen senses. "Are you okay?" she asked, attempting to read him. She encountered a wall of darkness. "You look..." Tired. Wrecked. Stressed. None of those words properly described his current state.

"I'm fine." Stone frowned at her. "What are you doing? Why are you giving me that funny look?"

She'd been busted. "I tried to read you."

Stone became unnaturally still. "And?"

"I can't," Izzy said. "Why is that?"

Some of the tension in his body eased, and he scanned the sidewalks around them. "I've learned how to block people like us and the monsters. No one can sense me unless I want them to. If we had more time, I'd teach you how to do it."

The idea was beyond tempting to Izzy. What would life be like if she didn't have to worry about the monsters sensing her? It seemed like a fantasy...yet if what Stone said was true, then perhaps it was possible.

"Then how did you know I was here?" she asked in confusion.

Stone blinked. "You called me. Remember?"

"Oh, right," she said. Izzy had forgotten all about phoning Stone. She'd told him about the cabin, but how did he know she'd be here?

"You still want my help, don't you?" he asked.

His question interrupted her thoughts. "Yes, of course," she said.

Stone smiled. "Good," he said. "I thought for a minute that you'd changed your mind." Something about the grin reminded her of a shark.

You're seeing monsters everywhere now, she chastised.

Izzy hadn't changed her mind about getting away from Tristan. She thought about it. No, definitely not. Though leaving didn't seem nearly as urgent as it had yesterday afternoon.

"I've parked a few blocks over," Stone said. "If we can make it to my car, I think we can get away from him. The last time I saw him, he was several blocks away."

Izzy followed a few feet then stopped. *How did he know where Tristan was?* She didn't even know where he'd wandered off to.

"How did you see him without him knowing that you were there?" she asked.

Stone glanced back. "What?"

Izzy repeated the question.

His brow furrowed. "I told you. I'm able to block myself. Even if I hadn't been able to, I spotted his blond head above the crowd and went the other direction before he saw me."

It was possible. She'd managed to avoid Tristan, but not for long.

"Where are we going?" she asked.

"I have an apartment on the other side of town," he said. "We'll be safe there for a little while, but it's merely a temporary solution. There's only one sure way to get away from the monster for good."

"Do you mean blocking him?" she asked.

Stone stopped. The look he gave her sent a chill down Izzy's spine.

Her steps faltered. "What exactly are you referring to?"

"If you want to protect yourself, protect me, protect your friends, and your family, there is going to come a time when you have to choose sides. It's either us or the monsters."

Izzy stumbled back a step. "Are you talking about killing Tristan?" she asked, horrified by the notion.

Stone shook his head. "No, I'm talking about killing the monster before it kills us."

"I—I can't kill Tristan," she stuttered. "I can't kill anybody." But especially not him, even though Tristan had behaved like a careless jerk.

Stone gave her a hard stare. "We may not have a choice. You need to be prepared for that possibility," Stone said.

How could she prepare for something she couldn't comprehend? In all the years that Izzy had been running from the monsters, it never occurred to her to fight them head on. She pictured Tristan's face, pictured the concern that had been on it last night when he'd crawled into bed beside her. The idea of killing him left an odd ache in her chest.

"We have to go now," Stone said. "He's getting closer."

The first pulse from the lodestone around his neck nearly drove Tristan to his knees. It was like taking a direct strike from lightning.

The fact that it was so strong told him that the Darkling was nearby. His head whipped around, but Tristan didn't see Isabel.

Where had she gone?

He'd put enough distance between them to draw it out, but perhaps it had been too much. Fear embraced him as Tristan realized he might not reach her in time.

You can't always protect bait... Pierre's parting words struck deep.

Failure wasn't allowed to enter his mind. Just the thought of losing Isabel gutted him. Tristan didn't want to look too closely at why.

He followed the pulse of magic around the next block, but Isabel was nowhere to be seen. The lodestone throbbed like a toothache. Tristan turned left and ran another block.

As he rounded the corner, he saw a flash of purple hair in the distance. Isabel. He'd just taken a step toward her when he caught another movement. She wasn't alone. The man disappeared out of sight, and Isabel chased after him. Tristan's beast nearly burst from his body as he watched her run away.

Izzy followed Stone's brisk pace. Every step she took got heavier and heavier. It was as if her body didn't want her to leave, which was insane, since she'd been trying to get away from Tristan since they met.

She may not like Frosty, but she didn't want him dead. The thought made her heart hurt. As she ran, Izzy wondered just how many monsters Stone had killed. Suddenly, she wasn't sure going with him was the right thing to do.

He knows how to block them. Block you. If you could learn how to do that, it would change your life. Hell, it would give you back your life.

As much as she disagreed with his methods, Izzy had no choice but to go with him, at least until Stone taught her how to block. Then they'd part ways. Izzy wasn't a monster slayer and had no desire to be.

"How much farther?" she asked.

"We have another block and a half to go," Stone said, then his eyes widened. "He's right behind us. Run faster!"

Izzy turned to see Tristan sprinting toward them. He had a murderous expression upon his face. She glanced back to check on Stone, but he was long gone. So much for saving her.

Tristan's heart stopped. Fear had crippled him at first, but he'd been determined to reach her. When Isabel saw him and ran, Tristan's fear turned to anger. An unexpected wave of hurt followed his fury.

"Isabel, stop!" he shouted, easily closing the distance between them. There was no way a human could outrun one of the Moonlight Kin.

She skidded to a halt.

"What are you doing?" he asked. "Who was that man you were with?" He demanded answers. This time he wouldn't allow her to deflect the questions.

"He's just a friend," she said.

Tristan's beast didn't like the idea of another male hanging around her. "If he's just a friend, then why did you run?" he asked.

"He's like me, okay?" she said, defensively.

"Like you how?" Tristan asked.

"He's Sighted," Isabel said.

Tristan had never heard of a male being a Sighted-One, but he supposed it was possible. "What were you doing with him?"

Her brow furrowed. "Um..."

"Isabel?" He didn't bother to hide the warning in his voice.

She rounded on him. "If you must know, I was running away."

"From me?" Tristan reeled back. He'd wanted an honest answer. He just wasn't prepared for what he got.

"No, I ran from the other monsters," she said sarcastically.

His scowled deepened.

Isabel glared at him. "Can you really blame me, when it's obvious you don't care about anything but your mission?" she asked.

Tristan jerked as her words lashed him, scoring deep. He'd been so frightened for her. So scared he wouldn't reach her in time. He'd been a fool.

The warmth that had encased them last night evaporated. Tristan felt the cold inside of him return and openly embraced it. This was familiar. This was what he needed. He should've known there was no place for warmth, no place for her in his life.

"Thank you for the reminder." His words froze the air between them. "I'd temporarily lost sight of what was important."

Isabel blanched, and her color drained. "I didn't mean—"

His hard gaze stilled her words. "Yes, you did. Now let's go."

Izzy felt horrible. She'd purposely hurt him, which was something she never did to anyone. It was like Tristan brought out the worst in her. She stared out the truck window as they drove to the cabin.

Time only added to her sense of guilt. She hadn't really meant what she'd said to him. Izzy had been so shocked by Stone's suggestion and her reaction to it that she'd lashed out.

She glanced at Tristan. His stony expression never altered. She didn't think there was anything she could say that would make things better.

He didn't speak to her for the rest of the night. The silent treatment got on her nerves so bad that Izzy decided to head to bed.

She didn't know what time the vision struck. Izzy felt danger drawing nearer. She pushed back the haze that normally clouded her visions and gazed deeper. Izzy wanted to see what—or more appropriately who—was coming.

Her sense of dread grew. In her vision, Izzy saw trees all around. Trees with thick undergrowth. Trees that shook as the danger closed in on her. Hands parted the bushes.

Izzy turned and ran...straight into Tristan.

His hands closed around her arms.

Izzy glanced behind her, but there was no one there. Tristan's normally cold eyes shimmered like warm mercury. Before she could ask him to release her, his mouth claimed hers.

She remained tense in his arms for all of a minute, then Izzy's body melted. The heat between them flared even hotter as he deepened the embrace.

Tristan released her shoulders, and his hands dropped to her waist. He pulled her closer. Close enough for Izzy to feel a hard ridge. She gasped, and his tongue swirled around her mouth.

Izzy's heart stuttered, but this time it wasn't from fear. This time it came from desire. She pressed her hands to his chest then slid them up around his neck.

Tristan groaned and his fingers bit into her waist.

She couldn't seem to get close enough to him. Izzy stripped his clothes off. Her hands trembled as she made contact with his bare skin.

"Do you want me?" he asked against her lips.

"Yes," Izzy hissed.

Tristan nipped her bottom lip, then grabbed her T-shirt with both hands and tore it off her body. Izzy gasped as the rest of her clothes followed.

Within seconds she was naked and standing before him. Her body quivered as he cupped her sex to test her readiness.

"I will be here soon," he rasped. "It's only a matter of time before you welcome me inside."

What was he waiting for? She was naked and ready now. Izzy couldn't be more welcoming if she tried.

"Take off the rest of your clothes," she said.

Tristan smiled and shook his head. "Not yet," he murmured, nuzzling her neck. "You're not ready."

The moisture pooling between her thighs said otherwise. Izzy felt the brush of his lips, then sharp teeth scored her skin. Her nipples hardened, and she grew restless in his arms.

"I want you," she said, all but begging him to take her.

Tristan licked the spot at the base of her neck where it met her shoulder. "You only want this part of me." He guided her hand to the front of his jeans and left it resting on his erection.

Izzy shook her head. "No, you're wrong," she said. "I want all of you."

He pulled back just enough to look her in the eyes. "All of me?" he asked. "Are you sure?"

Izzy would swear to it, if it meant he'd get undressed. "Yes."

Tristan smiled at her, revealing his extended canines.

It took a second for Izzy's desire-fogged brain to register what she'd glimpsed. The moment she did, she jerked away.

Tristan's hard laugh filled the silence. "Told you," he said softly. "I won't touch you until you want all of me," he said, then turned to go.

"Wait!" Izzy shouted as the vision faded.

She blinked into the darkness, wondering if she'd spoken aloud. Her body was so aroused it ached. *Please be asleep.* She sent the silent prayer up into the ether.

Izzy turned her head toward the couch and found Tristan staring directly at her. His silvery eyes glowed in the dark. She inhaled sharply and caught a hint of her desire wafting on the air. If she smelled it, then it was a good bet that Tristan could, too.

The question was would he act upon it?

And if he did, would she stop him? The answer she received left Izzy blindsided.

Tristan continued to stare at her.

I want you, a little voice inside of her whispered.

He stiffened as if he'd heard her thought then slowly turned over, leaving her to stare at his pale back.

Izzy punched her pillow while cursing her visions. Normally they came true, but in this case, the chance of that happening was slim to none.

10

"Today we'll try again," Tristan said, taking a bite of bacon. "But this time I'm going to stick by your side, since you've made it clear that I can't trust you."

"I thought you said your presence would keep the Darkling away," she said.

He glanced at her, but his expression remained hard, unyielding. "There are other ways to draw it out. Ways I've avoided until now because of the discomfort they'd cause."

Discomfort? Izzy didn't like the sound of that. She stared at him across the kitchen table. "What exactly do you have in mind?"

"If it's worried that it's going to lose you to another wolf, it'll become desperate to grab you," he said.

"I don't understand." There was no warmth in Tristan's slate eyes.

He pushed his breakfast aside and walked around the kitchen table. He stopped in front of her.

"What are you doing?" Izzy craned her neck and scooted back, but there was nowhere for her to go.

He grabbed a fistful of her shirt and yanked her off her feet. Tristan's lips came down upon hers in a searing kiss. The kiss left Izzy breathless and shaken.

It took her a moment to recover and pull herself together. "What was that for?"

"To give you a taste of what's to come," he said, his voice hard and raspy. "Try to play along. It'll be more convincing that way." Tristan returned to his seat and finished eating his breakfast like nothing had happened.

Pain sliced Izzy. How could a kiss heat her to her toes and leave her so cold? Whatever softness she had witnessed from him the other night was now long gone. Tristan was back to being all business, and she was to blame.

She thought about Stone's warning again... *It's either them or us.*

Would this hunt come down to life or death? Izzy sure hoped not. What would happen if it did? The question left her nauseated.

Izzy shoved her breakfast aside. No longer hungry.

Tristan still felt her lips pressed against his. His anger had subsided, but not the hurt. He wanted to hurt Isabel back. Show her what it felt like. Glimpsing her pained expression, Tristan was confident he'd succeeded.

You did what you had to do, a little voice said.

So why did his actions feel so wrong? And why in hades did she always feel so right in his arms? If that kiss got any more convincing, they'd end up on the bed.

Tristan shoved his food away as Isabel stomped off to the bathroom. The second the door closed behind her, he ran a trembling hand through his hair. This whole situation was getting out of hand. Maybe he needed to call in another Enforcer to take over. There weren't many, but there were a few.

Even as the thought flitted through his mind, Tristan wouldn't do it. Just the idea of another wolf staying in the cabin with Isabel had his hackles rising.

"Get your head in the hunt," he muttered.

Thirty minutes later, the bathroom door opened and Isabel stepped out. "Ready," she said.

One look at her in that strappy purple sundress and the air rushed out of Tristan's lungs. She couldn't go out like that. Isabel couldn't go anywhere dressed that way.

The sundress plunged just low enough to give him and every other man a tantalizing view of the soft mounds filling the front of it. The dress nipped in at her waist, emphasizing how small it was, before flaring out at the hips.

Tristan's gaze traveled down before reversing direction.

The material ended just above her knee, showing off her shapely legs. Isabel was quite literally stunning.

It took Tristan a moment to recover. "What are you wearing?"

Isabel glanced down at her dress. "I would think that would be obvious," she said.

He clenched his jaw and tried again. "Why are you wearing that dress?" he asked.

Her blond brow arched. "You said we were going in town to draw the Darkling out. You said we were going to pretend to be a couple, or at least you implied as much," she said. "We can't really make someone jealous if we're dressed as slobs."

"I never dress like a slob," he said, insulted by the insinuation.

"Okay." Isabel rolled her eyes. "Maybe not sloppy, but definitely casual." She walked deeper into the room. "We won't attract attention if we're dressed like all the other tourists. We need to stand out."

She had a point, but Tristan didn't have to like it. He stared at her, trying to ignore the curves that were no longer hidden beneath baggy clothes. It was impossible. Without effort, Isabel had just turned a hard day into sheer torment.

"Give me a minute to change, and then we'll get out of here," he said.

The tension continued to build on the drive into town. Izzy caught Tristan admiring her legs a couple times and wondered if he even knew he was doing it.

The look on his face when she'd stepped out of the bathroom was one she wouldn't soon forget. Izzy had heard of people being stunned speechless, but she'd never witnessed it firsthand. And she'd certainly never expected to cause such an event.

Part of her felt unduly pleased that she'd been able to surprise him. That hadn't been Izzy's intent when she'd put the sundress on, but it was a nice byproduct.

They parked just off the French Quarter near Louis Armstrong Park then strolled toward Jackson Square. When they reached the square, Izzy spotted Everly's dark head near the west end.

Tristan scanned the people with quiet intensity.

"Mind if we stop at Everly's table?" she asked.

"I'm surprised she's up so early," he said.

"She probably hasn't been to bed yet," she said.

Tristan slipped his hand in hers. It should've been awkward, but for some reason the fit seemed natural.

"Lead the way," he said.

They walked hand and hand over to Everly. Her dark eyes widened when she caught sight of them and widened some more when she saw their joined hands. Her pierced brow arched.

"It's not what you think," Izzy said.

"Yes, it is." Tristan raised her hand up to his mouth and kissed the back of her knuckles.

She felt his tongue snake out to taste her. Heat spread from Izzy's hand down her arm before rocketing through her body. If it got any hotter, she'd have a heat stroke.

"What are you two up to?" A smile played across Everly's face as she indicated for them to sit down.

They took the seats in front of her table. To an outside observer they'd look like a couple of tourists getting their cards read. Only she and Tristan knew the truth.

Everly shuffled the tarot cards on her table then turned them over slowly. Her gaze focused intently on what they revealed.

"What are you doing?" Izzy asked, growing alarmed as the cards fell. She didn't want a reading, especially in front of Tristan. Goodness knows what the cards would say.

Everly grinned. "Thought it would be fun to see what's really happening here."

Izzy's jaw set. "I already told you," she said.

"You and I both know just how deceptive appearances can be." Everly stared at Tristan.

Izzy couldn't see his eyes narrow, but she felt his body tense and the grip on her hand tighten.

"You say one thing. He says another," Everly said. "I don't think either of you know the truth."

"What do you see?" Tristan asked, showing more teeth than necessary.

Everly flipped another card. The Lovers appeared. She tapped the card with her index finger. "That's the same thing I got in my vision," she said.

"But you *can* be wrong." Izzy heard panic and desperation in her voice. Seeing the card reminded her of the vision she'd had last night.

Everly glanced at her. "Sure, I can be." She paused. "But not twice."

"We are not sleeping together," Izzy blurted.

Tristan released her hand and placed his palm on the small of her back. His thumb made small circles at the base of her spine. If he was trying to relax her, it wasn't working.

"Now honey," he said, nuzzling her, "what starts in the bedroom, stays in the bedroom."

Two women passing by snickered and gave Tristan a once- over that made Izzy want to poke their eyes out. Couldn't they see his hand on her? Was she invisible? Didn't they notice her sitting next to him?

Before the next thought struck, Izzy stilled. Was it possible that she was *jealous*? How could that be? She didn't even *like* Tristan.

Everly kept turning the cards over, ignoring them both. The Devil card appeared. She frowned and flipped a few more over for clarification, but it only frustrated her more.

The Devil didn't necessarily mean something bad. It also indicated drastic change depending on the other cards around it.

Everly flipped the last card. Death.

Izzy gasped. Like the Devil card, the Death card didn't mean that someone was going to die. It could be the death of an old way of thinking or the death of an old way of life. It wasn't always literal... except it was next to the Devil card.

Everly's gaze met hers. "You have to be careful. Evil is nearby."

Nearby or sitting next to her, Izzy thought.

She glanced at Tristan. Frosty may be a pain in the rear with a questionable job, but as far as she could tell, he wasn't evil. This whole situation would be easier if he was bad, but Tristan wasn't. She'd been around him long enough to ascertain that much. Evil didn't fix omelets. Evil didn't hold someone in the middle of the night after they'd had a bad dream.

No, Snowflake wasn't evil, but his behavior left much to be desired. Perhaps that was what Everly picked up on.

"Thanks for the reading." Izzy pushed her chair back. She'd seen enough.

"I didn't do it just for you," Everly said. "What are you guys *really* doing here?"

"I wanted to make sure you were okay and to let you know that I was all right," Izzy said. "I also wanted to ask you again to get out of town."

Everly shook her dark head. She'd dyed the strands so black they appeared blue in the sunlight. "I told you before, I'm not going anywhere." Her gaze darted to the cards in front of her.

"Frosty says there's something worse than the monsters running around town." Izzy touched her hand. "Be careful, okay?"

Everly laughed. "Frosty?"

"Don't call me that," Tristan said.

"But it's okay if Izzy calls you that?" Everly asked.

Tristan's jaw tightened. "That's different," he said.

"I just bet it is." Everly laughed. "Don't worry, I will be careful," she said. "I think you're the one who needs to watch out. Trouble could be closer than you think." She gave Tristan a pointed stare.

Izzy snorted. "Tell me something I don't know."

"Okay," Everly said, taking her statement as a request. "You cannot change your fate on this one."

Gooseflesh prickled along Izzy's skin, despite the growing heat.

"Neither can I," Everly added softly. "When the time comes, remember that."

The resolve in her voice worried Izzy. She'd never heard that tone from Everly before. They needed to talk. There had to be something they could do to get out of this mess.

"Ready to mingle?" Tristan asked, kissing her cheek.

The move distracted her from her dark thoughts. "As I'll ever be," Izzy said.

Tristan tried not to show any reaction when the tarot cards were turned over. He didn't believe in those kinds of things, but Everly wasn't a normal reader. She was a Sighted-One, so he couldn't dismiss her findings out of hand.

It bothered him that she saw him and Isabel as lovers. Not because he couldn't imagine it anymore, but because he could. She'd worked her way under his skin and Tristan had no idea how to get Isabel out.

He touched the lodestone around his neck. Thus far, he hadn't felt even the slightest pulse. Perhaps the Darkling had left New Orleans. Wishful thinking on his part, since it hadn't gotten what it had come for.

Tristan glanced at Isabel. Her fair skin glowed in the sunlight. It was a stark contrast to her purple sundress, yet somehow as a whole it worked. Too well for his peace of mind.

Human males walked by with their necks craning to get a better look at her.

A growl rose from Tristan's chest before he could stop it. Isabel didn't seem to notice the men, but she certainly heard the growl. Her gaze cut to his, and her hazel eyes narrowed.

"What are you doing?" she whispered.

Tristan stared at her for a moment. "Making sure people mind their manners."

"What?" she asked in confusion.

She had been totally unaware of the attention. Isabel really didn't know what kind of effect she had on men, had on him. Tristan clasped her hand and tugged.

"This way," he said. They'd take a stroll along the river then circle back into the Quarter. He wanted to make sure Isabel's scent permeated the area and that she was highly visible. In that dress, he wouldn't have to worry about the latter.

Heads continued to turn as they strolled along the Mississippi River bank. Tristan tried to relax, but it was impossible with so many males sniffing around. Inside, his beast bared its teeth and snarled. Outside, Tristan pulled Isabel into his arms and kissed her often enough to send a message to the men around her.

Every time he kissed her, Isabel's gaze grew unfocused, and her luscious scent deepened. If only she weren't human. It would be far too easy to get used to this, get used to having her in his arms.

Tristan needed to think of something else, something to distract him and his beast from the urges pummeling his body. "How long have you known Everly?" he asked.

"Not long," she said. "I met her when I first hit town a month ago."

"She should leave," he said.

Isabel gave him a sad smile. "I know, but she won't. She told me she's tired of running," she said, her voice weary. "Can't say I blame her. It gets old."

"You sound tired, too," Tristan said.

"I am," she said. "But there's not a lot I can do about it. I'm more concerned with Everly's vision."

He was, too. Tristan tried to imagine what it would be like moving from place to place, knowing that you were constantly being pursued. The beast in him rose to the surface and growled.

Isabel laughed at him. "What's up with all the growling?" she asked.

"Sometimes my beast likes to voice its opinion at inopportune times," he said.

"Do you have conversations with it often?" she asked.

Tristan shook his head. "Not really. We rarely disagree with each other."

"Interesting," she said. "Where do you live?"

The change of subject surprised him. "I have homes in many places," he said. "My favorite is in New Mexico."

"Wow," she said. "I wouldn't have pictured you in the Southwest."

"Why?" His fingers lingered on her bare shoulder after he brushed her hair away from her face.

Isabel shrugged and casually stepped out of reach. "I don't know. You look more Nordic than Navajo," she said.

"I do have a Nordic heritage, but I prefer the sunshine and warmth over the cold and gray skies," he said.

"You don't look like you get a lot of sun," she said.

"I don't tan easily," he said wryly.

Isabel laughed.

"What's so funny?" Tristan asked.

She put her hand over her mouth to hide her smile. "I just pictured you in Bermuda shorts and a Hawaiian shirt, sitting on a turtle float in the middle of a pool."

"Is that so hard to imagine?" Tristan asked, liking the sound of her laughter, even if it was at his expense.

Isabel's shoulders shook. "Yes, it is, Frosty."

He laughed with her. "I must do a better job of distracting your smart mouth."

She flinched.

"What's the matter?" Tristan asked, unsure of what he'd said or done to cause the reaction.

"That's the first time I've heard a real laugh from you," she said. "I was beginning to think you'd never learned how to laugh."

"And you find the sound frightening?" he asked.

Isabel shook her head. "Just the opposite. It's quite nice and unexpected."

Tristan wasn't sure how to respond, so he didn't. He held her hand as he led them down to a docked riverboat.

"One of these days I'm going to take that ride." Isabel pointed to the boat.

Tristan had the sudden urge to get her tickets. *You're not here for fun.* For a moment, Tristan had forgotten why they were here. He'd been so caught up in touching her, kissing her, and holding her that he'd lost focus.

"Mind if we do it some other time?" he asked.

"You want to go, too?" she asked, surprised again.

Tristan glanced at the boat. He would enjoy the ride, if she were with him. "Sure," he said, then turned right so they were heading back into the quarter.

"How will we know if this works?" Isabel asked.

"He'll make a move." Just the thought of the Darkling trying to rip Isabel out of his hands made his beast snarl.

"You're doing it again," Isabel said.

"Sorry," Tristan said. "I didn't mean to. The necklace around my throat detects the Darkling's magic. I'll know he's coming long before we see him."

"Magic? As in Harry Potter or watch me pull a rabbit out of my hat?" Isabel pulled her hand out of his and stopped.

"Neither," he said.

"But you're telling me that magic is real," she said.

Tristan debated how to respond. He decided to be honest with her. "How else would you explain your abilities or what I'm able to become? The powers might be different, but they're nothing short of magic."

"But." She rubbed her forehead and took a deep breath. "I guess I never looked at it that way."

"I'm not surprised," he said. "You've spent your life running from us monsters. When you view an entire species that way, it's hard to see beyond your preconceived notions."

He was right. Izzy knew he was right, but it was a lot to take in. Her world had been filled with humans and monsters without anything in between. Now he was telling her there was even more to the world than she'd imagined.

Izzy had never once asked herself what was behind the ability to shift. She'd simply assumed they were all evil and left it at that.

Magic... just the word conjured all kinds of images in her mind.

She glanced at Tristan. "If you're magic, then why don't you feel your power pulsing in the necklace?"

Tristan opened his mouth and closed it again. "I'm not sure you're ready to hear the answer to that question," he said.

"Try me," she said.

"Like humans, there are both good and bad Moonlight Kin. We have far more gifts than humans could ever imagine, but we also have a shadow side," he said. "A very dark shadow side."

"You turn into wolves and the Darklings?" She took a step back. That would be bad. Very bad. Izzy wasn't sure what she'd do if Tristan said yes.

"No! Never that," he said. "I told you the truth when I said that the Darklings are from another world. Our shadow sides reside in another world. They do not belong here. Every time they've crossed into this world, they've caused bloodshed and conflict between humans and the Kin. Most humans don't distinguish between monsters. When pushed, they want to kill them all."

Guilt made Izzy look away, but she had to know more. She needed to know everything. "That doesn't explain why you can wear the necklace without it reacting."

He pursed his lips, and darned if he didn't look cute. She bet he made that same face when he was little. The look made her want to rise onto her tippy-toes and kiss him, but that would be inappropriate after what he'd just shared.

"Moonlight Kin magic is part of this world. This lodestone is designed to pick up the magic of creatures from other worlds," Tristan said. "Including our shadow side."

"If they're part of you, why can't you make them stay in their own world?" she asked.

"Can you make your shadow stop following you?" he asked.

Izzy looked down at her shadow. "I suppose not."

"Neither can we," he said.

Izzy's stomach rumbled.

Tristan grinned. "Hungry?"

"Sounds like it," she said. "I know right where to go."

Izzy led Tristan to St. Peter Street. She didn't stop until they reached Yo Mama's Bar & Grill.

"What's this place?" he asked, staring warily at the front of the building. "It looks..."

"Like a bordello?" she finished for him.

Tristan nodded. "I was going to say dive bar, but it resembles that, too."

"The décor is a bit of both, but it has the best burgers you'll ever eat in your life," she said.

They climbed the stairs and settled at a table near the small bar. Instead of sitting across from her, Tristan sat next to her, his leg brushing hers.

Every time he spoke, he leaned in close to her ear and brushed her sensitive lobe. At first Izzy thought he was doing it because the music was so loud, but he did it no matter what was playing on the jukebox. Was this part of their performance?

His actions left her feeling antsy and unsure. She tried to separate reality from make-believe, but the line blurred in her mind. It didn't help that Tristan played his role so convincingly.

Their burgers arrived, and they tucked into them. Izzy scarfed down half her burger before she noticed Tristan staring at her.

"What?" She wiped the ketchup off her fingers and hoped she didn't have more on her face.

"I love that you like to eat," he said. "Most human females don't."

Izzy put her napkin down. "That's not true. Most women *love* to eat.

They just don't for fear of getting fat."

He laughed. "You don't have to worry about that."

"I do," she said and grinned. "But my fear doesn't outweigh my love of food."

"I don't like skinny women," he said so low that Izzy almost missed the comment.

She wondered if Tristan even knew he'd spoken aloud.

"Can I have a bite of your burger?" he asked.

Izzy never shared her Yo Mama's burgers, but she couldn't bring herself to tell him no. "Sure." She put her burger down and waited for him to pick it up.

He didn't.

"I thought you said you wanted a bite," she said.

"I do," Tristan said.

Then what was he waiting for? Surely he didn't want her to feed him. Did he?

Izzy picked up her burger and brought it to his mouth. Ketchup and mayo dripped down her fingertips.

Tristan grinned and took a big bite. "It's good," he said after swallowing.

Izzy put the burger down and picked up her napkin, but before she used it, Tristan captured her hand. He brought her fingertips to his mouth and sucked on each one, licking them clean.

Every suck and every lick triggered a reaction in another part of her body. By the time he finished cleaning her hand off, the spot between her thighs was throbbing and Izzy was squirming in her seat.

"Thank you," she croaked.

Tristan's eyes sparkled. "Anytime," he said, his voice rough.

It wasn't until later, when they'd left the French Quarter, that Izzy remembered that there'd been no one in the bar to see their performance.

11

Izzy walked through town with the monster. They were holding hands and whispering into each other's ears like lovers.

Had she taken the wolf to her bed? Just the thought of her lying in the beast's arms made Stone crazy. What was she thinking?

The monster released her hand then slid his palm down to rest on the small of her back. It was a cozy act. The kind of act that implied intimate knowledge.

Fury filled him. Why would she beg him to take her away, then throw herself at the white beast? It made no sense. They laughed, then the monster leaned in and kissed her.

Stone waited to see what Izzy's reaction would be. He hoped for anger, but got breathlessness and fluster instead.

Was she setting him up?

Stone had thought her desire to escape was genuine, but watching them now, he wasn't so sure. He pressed the pre-programmed number on his phone.

Izzy didn't pick up. He hung up and tried again, but she didn't answer. She was too busy hanging on the beast's arm and flirting.

He couldn't let her do this. Not when he was so close. One way or another, Stone would have to stop the beast by her side. Failure was not an option.

Izzy's phone vibrated when she turned it on, indicating that she had a message. She'd kept the phone off after Stone had left her yesterday. She'd expected him to call eventually but hoped he'd take more time to come to his senses.

She glanced at her watch. It was still relatively early. The sun wouldn't go down for several more hours. She thought about how she and Tristan could pass the time. Instantly, a carnal image flashed in her mind.

Izzy glanced at Frosty. He hadn't said much since they'd gotten back to the cabin, but she had caught him looking at her a couple times. As per usual, she hadn't been able to read his expression. The man should play poker.

Her phone vibrated again. Izzy needed to deal with one problem at a time, starting with Stone. "I need to use the bathroom," she said.

Tristan glanced up from the paper he read. "Okay," he said.

Izzy picked up her purse and walked into the bathroom. They'd had such a nice day that she didn't want to do anything to ruin the mood. She shut the door and pulled out her phone, expecting to see a missed call. Instead, there were at least a half dozen text messages from Stone, each one angrier than the last.

Saw you in town today. What were you doing?

You said you wanted help getting away. Didn't look like you needed help to me.

How could you bring yourself to kiss a monster? What's wrong with you? He had his hands all over you and you looked like you loved every minute of it.

It's us against them or have you forgotten?

Makes me think you've been setting me up all along. Have you? I only wanted to help you. Why would you do something like that? Do you want the monsters to catch me?

You'll be sorry, if I find out that's what you've been doing all along. You don't know who you're messing with.

Is that why you didn't leave with me yesterday? You were too busy screwing a monster. Sick! Now I know why you didn't want me to hurt him.

I can no longer trust your judgment. Who knows what kind of magic he's worked on you. For your sake, I hope you're not around when I take out your boyfriend.

Wouldn't want you to get hurt by accident.

Izzy felt bile rise in her throat as she struggled to get control of her fear. She turned on the water, so Tristan wouldn't hear her texting Stone back.

I don't have to explain myself, but I will because you're obviously mental. Everything you saw today was... It wasn't what you think. The whole thing was an act.

But it hadn't felt like an act. A few times when Tristan had kissed her, it had actually felt real.

The whys are not important—just know that it was. Tristan is not my lover.

Everly's reading came rushing back to her. She saw them as lovers. Heck, even Izzy had seen them together in her vision. That didn't mean it would happen. It couldn't. Izzy's certainty wasn't nearly as strong as it had been in the beginning.

The more time she spent with Tristan, the easier it was to imagine them together. It would never last, but Izzy could no longer deny that she wanted him. If only for a night.

Stone's response was swift. *Looked like he was working his magic on you.*

Tristan had mentioned something about magic, but he'd made it sound like his was nothing special. Had he lied? The thought that he might have worried her. Worried her enough that Izzy was going to have to ask.

Izzy typed another message. *I believed that all monsters were the same. I was wrong. So are you.*

Tristan wasn't like any of the others she'd met over the years. In hindsight, most had left her alone. It had been her who'd run away, and only when she'd received a psychic warning.

You should go ahead without me. Get out of town while you can. I'll leave once I'm finished here.

Stone's response was immediate. *I am not going anywhere without you. Got it? So get your things packed. I'll be there soon.*

Izzy didn't need his help. His militant insistence frightened her. *I've changed my mind. I no longer want to go. Please, Stone, just leave.*

If you won't save yourself, I'll have to be the one to save you from yourself.

Stone's message made Izzy shiver. What was she going to do? His heart might be in the right place, but it was obvious that he wasn't stable.

Izzy felt sorry for him. She knew what it was like to feel like the only sane person in the world. Stone had been on his own for too long. Maybe he just needed time to cool off? Once he did, perhaps then he'd listen to reason.

She turned the phone off and dropped it back into her purse, then flushed the toilet. Izzy splashed some water on her face then walked back into the main room.

Tristan set his paper on the table, when she came out. "Everything okay?"

"Yeah," she said, hoping it was the truth.

Tristan noticed the change in Isabel's complexion. Despite the moisture clinging to the side of her hair, she looked pale. Certainly paler than she'd been when she walked into the bathroom.

He inhaled, catching a sharp scent that indicated fear. What had her so upset? He'd thought the day had gone as well as could be expected. She'd seemed fine a moment ago. Tristan pulled her into his arms as she walked past.

Isabel yelped. "What are you doing?" Her body remained tense for a moment, then she relaxed.

What was he doing? Sure, he wanted to know what was wrong, but he also had gotten used to touching her whenever he felt like it. There was no one here to see them, no one to perform for, but Tristan wasn't ready to stop the *act*.

"I know today was stressful," he said, rubbing his thumb along her spine, soothing the tense muscles.

She shrugged awkwardly. "It wasn't so bad," she said. "After a while I forgot we were pretending."

So had he.

"Toward the end, I thought we were actually having a good time," she said.

Tristan agreed. "Thanks for introducing me to Yo Mama's Bar and Grill," he said. The burgers had been delicious.

Isabel smiled. "I figured you'd like the hamburgers."

"I did indeed." He leaned in close to her ear. "We might have to do it all again tomorrow, including the lunch break."

Her scent changed subtly, growing warmer, richer, more intoxicating. Isabel probably wouldn't admit it, but she wasn't as adverse to the idea of pretending they were a couple as she'd been earlier.

Neither was Tristan.

Her delicious scent made him wonder exactly where she'd draw the line. Before he had the chance to change his mind, Tristan framed Isabel's face and kissed her. He made sure to linger over her lips, savoring her flavor.

At first, she was too shocked to respond, then her fingers sank into his hair and Isabel kissed him back. Tristan's whole body hardened beneath her. A sound rumbled out of his chest, and he pulled her even closer, deepening the embrace.

Their tongues brushed, then swirled, tasting, teasing, and delighting in the kiss. Tristan's hands dropped away from her face and slid down her bare arms, pausing only long enough to scrape the sides of her breasts.

Isabel gasped but made no move to stop him. Encouraged, Tristan continued his exploration. He kneaded his way down her arms before grasping her lush bottom.

Tristan squeezed and massaged until her luscious scent permeated the room, then he lifted her higher so she could straddle his thighs.

The move made her sundress bunch around her waist.

The material presented no barrier when he rocked his hips against her core. Isabel moaned and wiggled to get closer. Her blunt teeth latched onto his lower lip, and she tugged.

It was Tristan's turn to groan. Wolves loved to bite, especially during lovemaking. And there was no doubt that's where they were headed if he didn't put the brakes on. Tristan thought about it for half a second then surrendered to his beast.

He'd wanted to sink inside her since he first laid eyes on her photo back in Oregon. He'd told himself that she was human, that he should stay away, but despite appearances, Tristan wasn't a glacier. In fact, if he got any hotter, he'd melt the polar ice caps.

Tristan hooked Isabel under her legs and stood. He waited for her eyes to open and her vision to clear. "If you don't want this, you need to tell me now," he said.

Indecision crossed her face for a moment. "You know this isn't going to last," she said.

"I know." He ignored the pain that knifed his chest.

"Before I say yes, I need to know one thing," she said.

"What?" he asked, distracted by the feel of her in his arms.

"Are you using magic on me?" she asked.

"Why would you think that?" The question cooled some of the desire coursing through Tristan's veins.

Isabel took a deep breath and met his gaze. "I just wondered if that was why I wanted you so bad."

Tristan felt as if he was being ripped in two. On the one hand, he was angry that she'd accused him of doing something to her to get her into bed. On the other, he was elated to know that she wanted him.

"The only magic in this room is the kind conjured between a man and a woman," he said.

It took her a moment to understand, but when she did, her eyes widened and she kissed him.

It wasn't exactly the declaration Tristan hoped for, but it would have to do. He strode the short distance across the room to the bed. Tristan juggled Isabel in his arms and pulled the covers back, then he laid her down.

For a moment, all he could do was stare at her. Isabel's wild hair had fanned out around her head, and her purple sundress was wrapped around her waist, revealing a matching satin thong. Tristan smelled the moisture gathering between her thighs. The beast in him drooled.

This was a bad idea, but Izzy's body didn't care. All day long, she'd endured Tristan's gentle touches, his long drugging kisses, and his intimate nuzzling. By the time they'd left the Quarter, she'd been wound so tight she thought she'd burst.

Stone had accused her of taking Tristan as a lover. She hadn't lied, but she also hadn't told him the whole truth, which was that Izzy had been thinking about it. Thinking of little else. Now it looked like her wait was over.

Tristan grabbed his shirt and pulled it over his head. Muscles rippled in his arms and over his chest as he tossed it behind him onto the couch.

He truly was incredible. Izzy was pretty sure she'd never seen anything like him and doubted she would again. His fingers dropped to the front of his jeans. With a flick of his wrist, the button opened and his jeans split, revealing bare skin.

Izzy swallowed hard. He wasn't wearing underwear. Her imagination went wild as Tristan slid his zipper down. The hiss filled the silence, then his hard shaft spilled out of his pants.

How he'd kept it inside them was beyond her. It shouldn't have been anatomically possible to squeeze something so big into material so tight.

Tristan chuckled and slid his jeans down before kicking them aside. Naked, he stared at Izzy until she grew self-conscious. She wasn't ashamed of her body, but she was well aware she wasn't built like a god.

Izzy covered herself with her hands.

"No!" Tristan snapped. "I want to look at you. I've been imagining what you would look like with your dress hiked up around your waist all day."

The admission surprised her. "Really? But you don't like humans."

"And you don't like monsters," he replied, his gaze soaking her in.

"You're not a monster," Izzy murmured softly.

Tristan's dark gray eyes widened then quickly shuttered to hide his emotions. "You have no idea how beautiful you are, do you?" he asked. "Men were falling over themselves trying to catch your attention. It was very hard not to respond."

"As I recall, you growled at them," she said.

"For me, that counts as no response," he said.

Izzy laughed and sat up to untie the straps on her shoulders.

"Let me," he rasped. Tristan's hands trembled as he untied first one side of her sundress, then the other.

The material dropped, but the dress stayed in place—thanks to her ample chest. "There's a zipper in back," she said.

"I know." Tristan leaned over her and kissed her. Another hiss filled the air as her zipper came down.

Izzy had not felt his hand move. She'd been too busy trying to uncurl her toes. She hadn't worn a bra, since the dress had built in support. Now that the material pooled around her waist, Izzy wished that she had.

Tristan pulled back from the kiss to look at her. He shuddered. "Beautiful," he said, his attention locked on her engorged nipples. "Stay just like that." Before she could figure out what he was going to do next, Tristan dropped to his knees in front of her.

The position put him between her legs, but he couldn't get any closer without climbing onto the bed. He clasped her hands and tugged her forward, then he latched onto her nipple.

Fire shot through Izzy, spreading at an alarming rate. The flames leapt higher with each pull of his mouth. Tristan sucked her deep, laving her until Izzy thought she'd scream. She squirmed to get closer, but he wouldn't let her.

With infinite care, Tristan released the swollen bud then sucked the other one into his mouth.

Izzy clutched his head. She pulled his hair when the sensations got too much, but he didn't seem to notice or to mind. Every time Tristan swirled his tongue, she felt an answering flick between her thighs. Moisture trickled between her legs, soaking her thong. It wasn't enough. She needed more.

"Tristan," she gasped and tried to yank his head back.

He growled and kept feasting.

The pressure continued to build inside her. The steady throb left Izzy teetering on the edge of oblivion. "That's it," she said. "Just like that."

Right before she toppled over, he stopped.

Izzy growled in frustration.

Tristan's silvery gaze met hers, then he licked his lips. "You taste delicious. I can't wait to taste the rest of you." He slid his hands under her body until he got a hold of her dress, then tugged. The material slid out from under her, leaving Izzy in her thong.

"That's better," he said, scooting her closer to the edge of the bed. "Just one more thing." Tristan threaded his fingers into her thong and snapped the material in half. He pulled it aside and threw it onto the floor next to his jeans.

Izzy couldn't remember how to speak or to think. The look in Tristan's eyes left her breathless. She'd never had a man look at her the way he was right now. His gaze held so much hunger, so much passion—so much need.

"What now?" she croaked.

His lips tilted. For a second she saw a flash of extended canines poking out the side of his mouth. She should be frightened, but fear was the last thing on her mind.

"Now I savor," he said and slowly lowered his head between her thighs.

The first swipe of Tristan's rough tongue sent Izzy spiraling over the edge. Her fingers sank into his shoulders as she tried to ride out her orgasm.

It had been so long since she'd allowed any man close enough to touch her, much less make love to her. Izzy forgot how wonderful it could be.

Tristan lapped up her juices then dove in with gusto. His tongue swirled and teased, flicking her swollen flesh until it filled with blood once more.

"I can't," she gasped.

Izzy's thighs trembled and she tried to shut her legs, but Tristan wedged his shoulders between them to stop her.

"We're not done yet," he said, his chin moist from her release. "Not by a long shot." He licked his lips. "Mmm."

Tristan drove his tongue inside Isabel's tight channel. He'd never tasted anything so delicious, and it scared him that he might never again. He ate her, nibbling her flesh, until she writhed on the bed once more.

He sucked the bundle of nerves into his mouth and worried it with his sharp teeth, then plunged two fingers inside her. Her body clamped down on him. Isabel let out a harsh cry, then flew apart in his arms.

Tristan licked her, not wanting to miss an ounce of her juices, as her second release rippled through her. When the fluttering in her channel lessened, he slowly pulled his fingers out. Tristan waited until he had her attention, then he stuck them in his mouth and sucked them clean.

Isabel shuddered again, and her eyes clouded.

He rose to his feet. "You are everything I imagined and more," Tristan said. His shaft was so hard and engorged that it curved under the weight. Tristan wrapped his fist around his erection and stroked.

Isabel's gaze followed the movement, and she licked her lips.

Tristan traced her mouth with his finger. "I can't wait to feel you taking me here." He tapped her lower lip. "But first, I have to take the edge off." Tristan grabbed onto her waist and pulled Isabel fully onto the bed, so he could join her.

He dropped onto the bed. "Open for me," he said, his voice so gruff that he barely understood the words.

Isabel's legs dropped open. Moisture covered her swollen sex. He couldn't get over how responsive she was or how delicious she tasted.

Tristan settled between her thighs, letting her get used to his weight. Their gazes met and locked. He couldn't turn away if he wanted to. Tristan kissed her tenderly then positioned himself at her entrance.

As much as he wanted to thrust hard and bury himself inside her, Tristan didn't. Instead, he took it slow, giving Isabel's body time to adjust to his large size.

She was so tight, so blissfully snug that he wondered when she'd last been with a man. Just the thought of her being with another male, brought his beast surging to the surface. Tristan clamped down onto it, but it continued to stare out through his eyes.

If Isabel noticed, she didn't say anything. She also didn't look away. The move goaded his beast, challenging its dominance. He growled deep in his chest. Isabel ignored the threat and stroked his jaw. Tristan's control shattered and his hips rocked, sending him deeper inside of her.

Isabel gasped, and her body tightened.

"Sorry," he said.

"It's okay," she murmured. "It's just been a while for me."

Tristan gritted his teeth. "Me too."

She blinked in surprise.

"Is that so hard to believe?" he asked, trying to keep still when everything inside of him wanted to thrust.

Her brow furrowed. "I guess not." Isabel's body relaxed, allowing him to sink even deeper.

Between the warmth, the moisture, and the growing pressure, Tristan was in heaven—and hell. The scariest part of all was that he didn't want to leave.

Izzy felt stretched beyond her limits. Tristan was even bigger than he'd appeared, which was saying something. He rocked his hips, and pleasure shot from her core through her entire body.

"Do that again," she said.

"And again," he responded, then thrust harder.

Izzy moaned and wrapped her legs around his waist. Tristan must've taken it as encouragement because he began to move steadily in and out of her. The delicious motion spread through her entire body, leaving her aching for more.

Tristan stroked her jaw and kissed her. The ice in his mercury-colored eyes was gone. Now they shimmered with undisguised heat.

His hand slid down, then he hooked his arms under her knees. The move lifted Izzy's legs even higher and spread them at the same time. From this angle, Tristan bored straight into her soul.

Izzy mewed. Each thrust merged them together, taking him directly over the hidden bundle of nerves. He ground himself into her as he impaled her again and again. Tristan drove her body harder and harder until pleasure blinded her. She cried out from the overload and tried to wiggle out of his grasp.

Tristan's hands locked onto her shoulders, and Izzy saw his eyes shift to wolf. A growl rumbled from his throat right before his teeth locked onto her shoulder.

"I'm not going anywhere," she murmured, but she wasn't sure Tristan heard her.

His thrusts became more primal. His hips bucked, and he pounded into her.

Izzy thrashed as the pressure built inside of her. She couldn't stop the moans from escaping or the nonsensical pleas for release. Tristan licked her shoulder and let her go.

"Don't hold back," he snarled. "I want to hear you scream my name. Want to see your body flushed with passion. What to feel you embrace every inch of me." His speed increased.

Izzy unraveled in his arms. The pleasure was unlike anything she'd ever experienced. When she came, it was like a detonator went off inside her head. Everything exploded. Colors burst behind her eyes, and Izzy screamed Tristan's name. The world faded as the blast sent her tumbling over the edge.

Isabel's scream rang in his ears, and her tight sheath gripped him like a vise until Tristan could barely move. When had sex ever been like this?

Never, a little voice whispered.

He gazed upon her. She was perfect. Tristan felt his body tighten as her core continued to pulse. He didn't want the moment to end. This might be the only time they slept together. He rocked his hips to draw out her orgasm. Once the spasms eased, Tristan sought his own release.

He surged inside of her and felt his sac rise. Tristan built up a steady rhythm. He wouldn't last long. A ripple of pleasure struck, taking his breath away. He'd had sex plenty of times and never experienced anything like it.

Tristan stoked faster, reaching for completion. The pleasure inside him increased to the point of pain. Something was wrong, but he couldn't seem to stop. His movements became frenzied, and Tristan began to swell.

What were those stories he'd heard about Damon and Aidan, when they'd found their mates?

Realization dawned. It couldn't be. Horrified, Tristan tried to pull out of Isabel, but he couldn't. His shaft was too big. He rocked his hips back, but only managed to move an inch.

No! No! No! He wouldn't allow this to happen. Tristan tugged harder, but he didn't budge.

Isabel moaned and raked her nails down his back, oblivious to the physical changes taking place in him.

Tristan hissed at the mixture of pain and pleasure, then felt his canines lengthen. She was human. This couldn't happen to him. He was stronger, more focused than the others. Determined to outsmart fate, Tristan jerked his head to the side and bit his own arm.

Blood filled his mouth, but he didn't care. As long as he didn't bite her, he could get through this. All he had to do was achieve release.

Tristan locked a hand onto Isabel's hip and thrust harder. Pleasure erupted inside of him, and he swelled even more. Fire raced down

Tristan's spine, leaving him gasping for air.

The flames spread, and he bellowed. The first white-hot wave struck, and Tristan's body convulsed. His release went on forever and ever. Every time he thought his beast had finished, he'd spurt again and groan in blissful agony. Tristan had never experienced this level of blinding pleasure in his life.

Was this what sex would be like every time with Isabel? If so, he'd never survive.

Bondmate, the word echoed in his mind.

Tristan shook his head in denial. She couldn't be. He waited for the swelling to ease then quickly pulled out. Isabel's eyes were closed, but she had a smile on her face. He didn't want to ruin the moment, but Tristan was too shaken by what had occurred to stay in bed.

"I need to use the bathroom." He practically leapt off her.

Isabel cracked an eye open. "You must have to go bad."

He caught a glimpse of the hickey on her neck and stopped short. Had he broken the skin? Please goddess no. Tristan ran his tongue over his teeth, but didn't taste anyone's blood but his own.

"How's your shoulder?" he asked, hoping he hadn't hurt her.

"It's a little tender, but I'll live," she said.

"Don't worry, I didn't break the skin," he said.

"I wasn't worried. It kind of felt good." Isabel's lashes fluttered open all the way. Her smile slowly faded as she caught sight of him. "Are you okay? Your arm is bleeding."

Tristan put on his social mask. He wore it anytime he needed to avoid emotional entanglement. "It's nothing," he snapped and shoved his arm behind his back.

"Doesn't look like nothing to me, Frosty." She rolled onto her side to get a better look.

Tristan gritted his teeth. "I said it's nothing. Leave it alone."

Isabel's brow rose, but she didn't say anything else.

Tristan rushed into the bathroom.

He felt like an ass. He never rushed out of a woman's bed, but tonight he'd had no choice. Tristan stared at his reflection in the mirror. His wolf stared back.

"What were you thinking?" he muttered.

The wolf snarled and bared its teeth.

Tristan turned the water on and splashed it over his face. The cool liquid wasn't enough to diffuse the panic. He reached for the shower nozzle instead. Once he had the shower set to cold, Tristan took off the lodestone necklace and set it on the side of the sink, then stepped beneath the spray.

The water took his breath away but did little to ease the tension inside of him. He'd read the reports about Damon Laroche and Aidan Fortier. He'd even gone to check on them in person.

He'd been so certain that choosing humans for mates was due to their bloodline that he'd dismissed the cases as anomalies. But there'd been no mistaking what had happened with Isabel.

From all the reports Tristan had read and the wolves he'd interviewed, he knew that the only time a wolf locked inside a woman was when it found its mate. He liked Isabel. How could he not? But she was human. And humans weren't meant to mate with the Moonlight Kin. It was a fact his wolf would have to accept.

Izzy hadn't expected flowers or for Tristan to fix her dinner, but she'd thought he'd at least be polite enough to stick around for a few minutes after they'd had sex.

She pulled the blanket around her, feeling chilled despite the heat. Izzy didn't feel used. She'd entered into this with her eyes wide open. But she did feel cheap. Tristan must've thought the same. He'd barely been able to look at her. When he had met her gaze, he'd appeared positively panic-stricken.

It was obvious he had more than a few regrets about what they'd done.

The worst part was Izzy didn't. The sex was beyond a doubt the best she'd ever had. She'd tried to hold part of herself back, while keeping lust at the forefront, but it hadn't worked.

Despite her best efforts, feelings had worked their way into the equation. Unwelcome feelings. Feelings that would only end up hurting her, when it was time to walk away.

When did she start caring about him? She couldn't care about him. They weren't even the same species. For some reason that didn't seem to matter to her stupid, stupid heart.

Izzy had to get out of here. She couldn't face Tristan, not after what just happened.

His opinion of humans wasn't going to be changed by great sex, and she wasn't dumb enough to believe that what had occurred was anything other than a roll in the sack.

She listened to the shower. The sound sent pain slashing through her. It was as if he was washing the whole event away, washing her away. Maybe he was. If she were smart, she'd do the same.

Izzy glanced out the window. It was still daylight, but it wouldn't be for much longer. She slipped off the bed and quickly got dressed in a pair of sweats and a T-shirt.

Her gaze shot to the bathroom door. It was still closed, and the shower was still going. Izzy grabbed her purse. She quickly found her phone and hit the pre-programmed number.

The phone rang...outside the front door of the cabin.

Izzy looked up and found Stone standing in the doorway, glaring at her.

"Looks like I got here just in time," he said.

12

Izzy grabbed her tote bag and threw what little clothes she had inside it. "We need to hurry," she said. "Tristan will be out any minute."

"The car's unlocked," Stone said. "You go ahead. I'll be right out."

"Are you insane?" she asked. "Come on."

"Just go!" Stone snarled.

Izzy cursed under her breath and rushed outside. She threw her tote into the backseat of Stone's car and waited. When he didn't come out right away, she went back in.

"What are you doing?" she hissed.

"Taking care of the problem once and for all," he said.

The blood drained from Izzy's face. "You can't hurt him." Just the thought of Tristan being hurt left her feeling adrift.

"Yes, I can," Stone said.

Izzy grabbed his arm and swung him around to face her. "I didn't mean it like that. What I meant was I don't want you to hurt him." She didn't want to stay with Tristan any longer. It would just cause too much pain. But she darn sure didn't want to be part of any plan to hurt him. "Let's go."

His amber gaze hardened. "You wouldn't be saying that if you hadn't slept with him."

"How did you—"

Stone yanked her hair to the side.

Izzy slapped his hand away. "What are you doing?"

"Looking for bite marks," he said.

"Tristan didn't bite me," she said. At least not hard enough to break the skin. "He's not a vampire."

"That hickey on your neck says otherwise," Stone said. "You're a lucky lady. If he had bit you, there'd be no getting away from him."

What did he mean by that? And why didn't the idea frighten her more? "I don't know what you're talking about," Izzy said, glancing at the bathroom door. "Time to go." If Tristan found Stone in the cabin, there would be bloodshed.

"Go to the car, Izzy," Stone said.

She wasn't going anywhere.

"I don't want you to get hurt," he said.

Izzy put her hands on her hips. "I won't, if we leave now."

Stone's gaze locked on hers. "I have to slow him down so we can get away. If I don't, he'll be on us immediately."

"And just how do you intend to do that?" Izzy asked.

"I'll think of something." Stone glanced at the small knife rack in the kitchen.

Izzy followed his gaze. "Don't even think about it," she said.

"Wait in the car."

"If you're not out in one minute," Izzy said. "I'm leaving without you. I mean it."

Tristan stayed in the shower until his skin pruned. He couldn't hide in here all night. He'd have to face Isabel eventually. Better to do it sooner rather than later. He would simply go out and tell her that they'd made a mistake—that he'd made a mistake.

He shut the water off and grabbed a towel. He was drying himself when his head swam. Tristan clutched the sink and rubbed his temple. What was wrong with him? He didn't get sick. Ever.

Tristan glanced at the lodestone next to his hand. It glowed bright as a star. He cursed and picked it up. The Darkling had to be close. Really close. Tristan pulled the necklace on over his head. He instantly felt better, but the magic in the stone would only protect him for so long. He secured the towel around his waist then reached for the doorknob.

"Isabel," he called out.

There was no answer.

Maybe she'd fallen asleep. It wasn't late, but he had kept her busy for well over an hour.

"Isabel," Tristan said, then inhaled. The scent of dark magic filled his lungs. Fear enveloped him as he felt his muscles weaken.

He had to get out there and protect Isabel before the Darkling drained him completely. Tristan called to his wolf, but he couldn't shift. Not with the Darkling controlling his power. He tried again and managed to grow some claws.

Those deadly weapons and the lodestone around his neck would have to be enough until he got to his sword. Tristan shoved the bathroom door open and rushed out.

He saw the Darkling stumble as he drew nearer. Tristan didn't see Isabel. Where was she? Had it harmed her? He managed to rake the Darkling with his claws. Tristan heard a loud yip then saw a cast-iron pan coming at his head. He didn't have time to duck.

Colors exploded behind his eyes as the pan smashed into him. Tristan dropped to the floor. He tried to rise, but the Darkling hit him again. This time the colors dancing in his vision faded to black, along with the world around him. His only regret was that he hadn't been able to save Isabel.

Izzy heard a loud bang and rushed back into the house. She came through the door in time to see Stone approach Tristan. He had a butcher knife in his hand. Tristan was on the floor. Blood pooled around his head, and he wasn't moving.

How had Stone overpowered him so easily? She didn't think it was possible.

Stone raised the knife over his head and prepared to plunge it into Tristan's bare back.

Izzy rushed forward and shoved him aside. "What are you doing?

Can't you see that he's down? He's not going anywhere." Perhaps ever. Tears filled her eyes. All Izzy wanted to do was get away, so she wouldn't have to face the emotions Tristan stirred inside of her.

Rage filled Stone's amber eyes. "If I don't kill him, he'll just keep coming after us."

"You said you just wanted to slow him down," she said. "Was that a lie?"

His jaw clenched.

Izzy knelt down beside Tristan. "You told me that we were better than the monsters," she said, trying to swallow past the lump in her throat. He was still breathing, but his breaths were shallow. She hadn't meant for any of this to happen.

"We are," Stone said, yanking her to her feet.

"Then prove it!" Izzy shouted. "Come with me right now. If you don't, I'll know you're no better than them."

She glanced down. There was so much blood. It soaked his blond hair, turning it crimson. Izzy's stomach lurched.

"I'm going to be sick." She stumbled to the door, half faking and half telling the truth.

Stone swore loudly and dropped the knife. He grabbed her by the elbow and shouldered the screen door open. He led her down the stairs and over to the car.

"You're an idiot," he said. "You know that?"

"We need to call an ambulance," she said. "This whole thing has gone too far."

"You're not calling anybody. That's not a human in there. It's a monster." He shoved her in the passenger seat and slammed the door behind her. Stone ran around the front of the car and climbed behind the wheel. "Buckle up."

He threw the car into drive and mashed his foot down on the gas pedal. The car lurched and the tires spun, sending mud flying into the air.

Izzy scrambled to get her seatbelt on. "Do you think Tristan will be okay?" she asked.

Stone glared at her. "I sure as hell hope not," he said.

Her heart sank. "We need to call for help," she said.

"I told you no. Do you want to get the paramedics killed?"

"No," Izzy said. Would Tristan harm an innocent person? Normally, she'd say no, but there was nothing normal about this situation. Wounded animals often lashed out at the people trying to help them.

"Sit back and be quiet," Stone said. "I need to think."

Izzy just couldn't shake the image of Tristan lying on the cabin floor. "Pull over," she said. "I need to go back. I have to make sure he's okay."

"No," Stone said. "You need to calm down and think. What do you think would happen if you went back there right now?"

"I'd be able to check on him," she said. "Make sure he didn't have a concussion."

"Then what?" he asked. "You'd wait around until he figured out that you called me?"

She had called him. Izzy had only wanted help with getting away, but would Tristan see it that way once he recovered—if he recovered?

Izzy thought about what Tristan had told her about his job. He was paid to eliminate any and all threats to the Moonlight Kin. This move certainly put her in the threat category. Tristan didn't strike her as being very forgiving.

Perhaps the Death card had been referring to her death after all. Izzy pictured Tristan's cold slate eyes and felt fresh tears burn her eyes.

Stone looked at her. "Now you finally understand why I wanted to kill him."

Izzy glanced at him. "Just because I understand your reasoning doesn't mean that I agree with you," she said, angrily wiping the tears away before they could fall. "My name is Izzy, not Buffy. This isn't the movies. We're not Slayers."

His amber eyes narrowed. "Speak for yourself," Stone said, then clutched his head and groaned.

"Are you okay?" she asked.

"I'll be fine once we put more distance between us and the monster," he said.

She pointed to his bloody shirt. "Tristan wouldn't have done that to you if you hadn't attacked him."

"Stop giving the monster a name," he said.

"I didn't," Izzy said. "That is his name."

"You just couldn't keep your legs closed. Could you?" he asked in disgust.

Izzy's face flamed.

Stone hit the steering wheel with his fists. "I should've killed him when I had the chance."

He might already be dead. A wave of pain followed the insidious thought.

"Listen, I don't know what happened to you before we met, but I can tell that you're carrying a lot on your shoulders," she said.

Izzy had thought she and Stone were alike, two lost souls trapped in a world full of monsters. Now she knew that wasn't the case. Something had pushed him over the edge long before tonight.

She'd have to live with what she'd done to Tristan. If it turned out that he was dead, then she'd accept the consequences of her actions, even if that meant her death. If Tristan was still alive, then she'd cross that bridge when she got to it.

"I appreciate you getting me out of there, but I think when we get to town we should split up."

Stone yanked the car over to the side of the road. "We aren't going into town," he said.

Izzy's stomach pitched. "Where are we going?"

"To my house to lay low for the night," he said.

"I thought you said that you lived in an apartment in town," she said.

He glanced out the window. "That's what I told you at the time because I didn't know you." *Didn't trust you,* was left unsaid.

They drove to one of the wards that had been devastated by Hurricane Katrina. There'd been so many that Izzy wasn't sure which one they were in. Most of the people who'd lived in this one hadn't returned. The houses were still boarded up, and spray-painted signs covered many of the outer walls. It reminded Izzy of a warzone.

Stone drove down the deserted street to the last house at the end of the lane. He pulled into the driveway. Unlike the other homes they'd passed, this one's lawn was neatly trimmed, and plywood didn't cover the windows.

Flowerbeds lined the home's foundation, and the shutters around the windows were painted bright lavender. Stone didn't strike Izzy as a lavender kind of guy, but she didn't know him well.

"We should be safe here until tomorrow night," he said, killing the engine.

"What happens tomorrow night?" Izzy asked.

Stone looked at her. "We leave town for good." He swayed on his feet when he climbed out and had to catch the side of the door to steady himself.

"You sure you're okay?" she asked. "Do you want me to take a look at that wound?"

"I said I'm fine," he snapped, then moved toward the door.

The stench of death punched Izzy in the face the second she stepped out of the car. She nearly dropped her tote in an attempt to cover her nose.

"What's that?" she asked.

Stone's confused expression cleared. "Oh, an alligator wandered into the backyard. I had to kill it."

"Is it lying in the backyard now?" she asked. "Because that will only draw more of them. They can smell decomp from quite a distance."

"No, I shoved the corpse into the shed until I can dispose of it properly," he said, then continued toward the front door.

"Don't you mean carcass?" Izzy asked.

Stone hesitated. "Yeah, sure," he said, then added, "Stay out of the backyard. There might be more of them hanging around."

Izzy stayed by the car.

He noticed she wasn't beside him. "You coming?" Stone asked.

She looked at the decrepit neighborhood. It was almost dark. At first glance, it appeared abandoned, but that didn't mean there weren't gangs roaming around the area. And apparently alligators.

Stone waited for her next to the door.

Tonight, she was all out of options. Izzy hoisted her tote higher onto her shoulder and walked to the house. Stone stepped inside before she reached the porch and dropped his bag next to the door. He walked into the kitchen when Izzy reached the doorway.

The feminine touches on the outside carried on in the interior. Pink and lavender filled the small space, from the frilly curtains to the lace tablecloth. Photos of a blond woman and a fair-haired, freckle-faced little girl covered the walls.

Izzy walked over to one of the photos to take a closer look. "Who are they?" she asked.

Stone glanced at the photo. "My sister and her kid," he said.

"Really?" Izzy asked.

Both of the females had fair hair and blue eyes. Their features were soft, almost delicate. Stone had dark hair and amber eyes. Nothing about him gave Izzy the impression of soft.

"Yes," he said. "Your room is at the end of the hall on the left." Stone pointed down the only hall in the house.

"Thanks," Izzy said. She glanced one last time at the picture then walked down the hall. The home only had two bedrooms and a bath. She wondered where Stone's sister and her daughter were. Would they be coming back soon?

The thought of involving a child in this mess didn't sit well with Izzy. It was dangerous enough as an adult. She opened the door on the left and stepped into...a child's room.

The walls were a light pink like the curtains framing the window. The bedspread on the twin bed held the latest cartoon princess's likeness.

Next to the bed sat a small dresser that doubled as a bedside table. On top of the dresser was a lamp and another photo of the mother.

A small child-sized white desk was pushed against the opposite wall. Beside it was a trunk. Izzy assumed it was full of toys, since there wasn't a single one on the floor.

She stepped inside, shut the door, and rested her back against it. Izzy didn't like taking a child's room away from her. She needed to find out when they'd return. As long as it wasn't tonight, it wouldn't matter, because Izzy planned to be long gone tomorrow.

Izzy unzipped her tote and took out a wrinkled shirt to wear in the morning. Maybe if she hung it up overnight, the wrinkles would release. She opened the closet to get a hanger and found it bursting with clothes.

She shut the closet door and walked over to the dresser. Izzy opened each drawer to check inside. The drawers held socks, underwear, pajamas, everything a child would need on a trip.

In the bottom drawer, she even found a well-loved, stuffed brown bear. The kind of stuffed animal that a child kept with them at all times. Maybe they were coming back tonight after all.

Izzy closed the drawers and walked out the bedroom. "Stone?"

"In here," he said. Stone was bent over a pot on the stove. The contents were bubbling and hissing from the high heat.

Izzy couldn't tell what he was cooking, but it smelled funny. "Are your sister and niece coming back tonight?" she asked.

He shook his head. "No, why do you ask?" Stone picked up a spoon and stirred the contents of the pot. He brought the spoon up to his mouth and licked it. His eyes closed in ecstasy at the taste.

Izzy tried not to gag. "When do you expect them back?"

Stone's mouth tightened. "I don't know. In a few days," he said. "We'll be out of their hair by then, so stop worrying."

Their return wasn't what worried Izzy. It was the fact that it didn't look as if they'd left.

"Do they have another house?" she asked. That would explain not needing to pack.

"No," Stone said. "Not that I know of."

His response gave her pause. This was his sister he was talking about. Surely he'd know if she owned more than one property.

"Are you sure she doesn't mind us staying here?" Izzy asked.

Stone dropped the spoon into the pot. It hit the liquid with a *kerplunk* and sent droplets onto the stove. He turned to face her. "What's this all about?" he asked. "If I didn't know better, I'd say you weren't grateful that I rescued you."

"I—I am," she stammered. "I mean, I do appreciate it."

He looked as if he didn't believe her. "It's getting late. Unless you want something to eat, you should probably get some rest," he said.

Izzy smelled the food again. The odor seemed even worse than before. "No thanks. I'm not very hungry."

"Your loss," Stone said, then took another spoonful.

She had no intention of eating it, but she was curious. "What is it?" she asked.

Stone grinned at her. "Game," he said.

His response didn't exactly narrow it down, but it didn't matter. "Enjoy," Izzy said, then wandered back to the little girl's room.

Before she entered the room, Stone called her name. Izzy turned to find him standing at the entrance of the hall. "I'll stand guard in case the monsters find us. If you need anything, I'll be right outside the door."

Suddenly Izzy didn't feel as if she'd been rescued. She felt like a prisoner whose guard would be stationed at her door. Izzy didn't know what to say, so she nodded and stepped into the room.

The second she was out of sight, Izzy opened her mind to her gift. She needed to figure out what was happening. She closed her eyes and inhaled deeply. Her gift flowed out of her straight into something solid.

Izzy's eyes flew open. Something was blocking her, blocking it. Stone said he had the ability to block the monsters and people like her, but Izzy had only wanted to check in with the other side. She should've been able to get through to her spirit guides. Weird...

Maybe she was just tired. It had been a long evening, and she'd been through a lot. Izzy would try again later once she'd gotten some sleep—if she managed to sleep at all.

13

Tristan stepped out of the darkness. His mercury eyes glowed silver as his gaze swept over her. He was naked like the last time she'd seen him and gloriously aroused. Izzy licked her lips and scooted across the bed to make room for him.

"I'm so glad you're okay," she said. "I was worried that you wouldn't be."

"You've been a bad girl, Isabel," he said.

"I'm sorry that I left you," she murmured, meaning it. "I was just freaked out after... I don't expect you to understand. We both knew sleeping together was a mistake."

"You shouldn't have run from me." He stopped next to the bed.

Izzy patted the bed beside her. "If I could take it back, I would."

He smiled, flashing long canines, and took a seat. The bed dipped beneath his weight. "What am I going to do with you?" he asked.

"You can start by holding me," she said, unable to meet his gaze.

"Is that what you truly want?" he asked.

"Yes." Izzy nodded.

Tristan slid into bed beside her and pulled Izzy into his arms. His strength made her feel safe. He ran his hand down the side of her body and kissed her, lingering on her lips until her toes tingled.

"Open for me," he said as he pulled her under him.

Izzy did as he asked. She was so grateful that he was alive that she'd do anything to please him, even if that meant feeling foolish in the morning.

Tristan climbed between her thighs.

Izzy grasped his shoulders as he nudged her entrance.

She felt him swell even more. He'd done that the last time they were together. At the time, Izzy had been too far gone to take notice, but now she was fully aware.

"Is that normal?" she asked.

Tristan smiled. "For me it is." His teeth were even longer now and so sharp they could slice through steel.

"Maybe we should talk first," Izzy said. "I need to explain."

"A minute ago, you told me that you wanted me," Tristan said. "What's the matter, Isabel? Change your mind already?"

There was no warmth in his eyes when Izzy met his gaze. Only the cold stare of a killer.

"You betrayed me, Isabel." Blood began to drip down Tristan's face. "You left me to die," he snarled.

"I'm sorry." Tears welled in Izzy's eyes as blood hit her cheek. She tried to wipe it away, but there was too much.

Blood covered Tristan's white hair and obscured his features. "Do you know what happens to people who betray me and my kind?"

She shook her head.

His lip curled flashing his sharp teeth, then Tristan attacked.

Izzy awoke screaming. Her limbs thrashed as she struggled to get away. She reached for her throat, expecting to find it torn open. It wasn't. Her heart continued to thunder. She scanned the darkness for Tristan, but nothing looked familiar. All she knew for sure was that he was gone.

The door hit the wall, knocking a hole in the plaster. The light from the hallway temporarily blinded her. Stone rushed into the room, carrying a bunch of knives in his hand. By the time Izzy was able to focus, the knives were gone.

"Are you okay?" he asked, frantically searching the room.

"I'm fine," she said, quickly wiping her tears away. "I had a nightmare."

"Is that why you shouted the monster's name?" he asked.

For a second Stone's eyes glowed, but the flash was there and gone so fast that Izzy couldn't be sure her sleep-fogged brain hadn't invented the light.

She didn't remember calling out Tristan's name, but she did remember the horrible dream. "Sorry I woke you," Izzy said.

"You didn't," Stone replied. "Want to talk about it?"

She did, but not with him. Izzy plumped her pillow. "I'm really tired. I think I want to try to go back to sleep."

Stone looked as if he wanted to argue. "Sure," he said instead. "See you in the morning."

The moment he shut the door, Izzy curled into a ball, and hugged herself. She should never have left Tristan. The dream or vision proved it. Now more than ever she needed to know if he was okay. There had to be some way she could find out. Izzy couldn't leave town until she did.

The dream had allowed her to admit a hard truth. The feelings she had for Tristan weren't going away. She'd eventually have to face if she wanted to move on with her life.

In the dream, there'd been so much blood. He had to be all right. "Please be all right," she murmured.

"Izzy, did you say something?" Stone asked from the other side of the closed door.

How had he heard her?

Izzy closed her eyes a second before the door to her bedroom opened. She felt Stone's gaze upon her. Izzy kept her breathing even and didn't move. Her pulse throbbed in her throat, but there wasn't anything she could do about it. He stood in the doorway for what felt like an eternity, before he eventually closed the door.

It wasn't until she heard the click that Izzy released the breath she held.

* * *

Tristan groaned and rolled onto his back. He came to with his head pounding and a vague memory of being attacked by the Darkling. He tried to sit up and immediately fell back down. What had the Darkling hit him with, a truck?

He opened his eyes, and the first thing Tristan saw was Pierre's face. The Alpha stood over him with a concerned expression.

"*Mon ami*, I'm so glad you're back with us," he said. "You had me worried." Pierre held out his hand to help Tristan up. "You look like hell, by the way."

"Feel worse." It was a testament to how bad he felt that Tristan accepted the Alpha's assistance. He glanced around the cabin and noticed the darkness outside the window. How long had he been out? "Where's Isabel?" he croaked. The bed was still in disarray from the earlier lovemaking, but her things were gone.

Pierre's expression suddenly blanked. "I am sorry, my friend, but we haven't been able to find her. There were no signs of a struggle," he said. "But my wolves will continue to search."

No signs of a struggle? That would mean that Isabel had left voluntarily. Why would she do such a thing? Tristan thought about how he'd behaved after they'd made love and had a sinking feeling. The Darkling didn't have to take Isabel. Tristan had driven her away—straight into his enemy's arms.

He swallowed the bile rising in his throat. Its bitterness was nothing compared to the taste of shame. "The Darkling has her."

"Then why aren't you dead?" Pierre asked.

"Good question." Tristan had thought for sure the creature was going to kill him. It had to have been Isabel who saved him. It wasn't in a Darkling's nature to show mercy.

Pierre sniffed. "I don't mean to point out the obvious," he said. "But why does the cabin smell like sex, *mon ami*?"

"I don't have time for this crap," Tristan said.

Pierre grinned. "So you sleep with her. I thought as much," he said. "I just needed confirmation. Had it been the Darkling, you wouldn't be so defensive."

Tristan froze. Until that moment, it hadn't even crossed his mind that the Darkling might take Isabel against her will in that way. At least not until they'd crossed into his realm. He pictured her horrorstruck face and felt his lungs squeeze until he could barely breathe.

Not since he lost his brother had Tristan experienced terror on this level. The unwelcome emotion drove home just how much the little hoyden meant to him.

He rushed across the room and lifted the sheets to his nose. The musky scent of well-loved woman filled his lungs, along with the earthy aroma of Kin. The scent soothed his beast for a moment, but Tristan knew the emotion wouldn't last.

Pierre shook his head and gave him a sad smile. "The fact you are smelling that sheet in your hand proves she means something to you. I hope for your sake we are able to get her back."

Tristan's beast growled. The sound made Pierre and the young wolf who'd just entered the cabin freeze. Tristan felt his control weaken and his other push to the surface.

Pierre's eyes glowed as he faced Tristan. "This will not help," he said. "Get control of yourself."

White fur rippled over Tristan's arms, and claws sprang from his fingertips, as he struggled to cage his beast.

The Alpha growled, and black fur spread over his skin. "I understand what she is to you, even if you're not ready to admit it, but you must keep it together. You won't be able to save her if you don't."

Tristan yanked hard on his beast's leash. It reluctantly gave way, but not before it snapped at him. The fur faded back into his skin and his claws retracted. "Let me just gather my things."

"You might want to put on some clothes," Pierre said. "Can't exactly walk through town like that."

Tristan glanced down. The towel he'd been wearing was lying on the floor where he'd fallen. He shrugged and pulled on a pair of jeans, then grabbed a shirt. Tristan glanced around the cabin. He didn't want to leave, because there was always a chance that Isabel would return, though it was unlikely.

He packed his tote and gathered his weapons. He tucked the sword he'd named Selene into its sheath then glanced at Pierre. "What if—"

"One of my wolves will stay here just in case," he said, cutting Tristan off. "For now, let's head back into town to regroup and recover. You are in no condition to fight tonight."

Tristan hated to admit it, but Pierre was right. He just hoped the Darkling was in bad shape, too. Being near Selene had affected him, but to what degree?

"Can you drive?" Pierre asked.

Tristan scowled at him.

"I had to ask, since I have no idea how long you've been out," Pierre said.

Tristan glanced at the clock and frowned. He'd been out for several hours. That wasn't good. It said a lot about how powerful the Darkling was.

"Why did you come here?" he asked, wondering how Pierre knew he was in trouble.

Pierre hesitated. "I sensed the evil and felt your strength wane."

Tristan's brow furrowed. "How? I'm not one of your wolves."

Pierre grinned. "You don't have to be mine for me to detect you," he said. "You of all people should know that, Enforcer."

Tristan nodded, but the truth was he hadn't known that Pierre could do such a thing. Perhaps the Darkling wasn't the only creature cloaking its powers.

"I'll follow you," he said.

"Do keep up," Pierre said, then headed out the door.

Tristan spent the night tossing and turning at the Alpha's house. Normally when wolves surrounded him he slept well, but tonight sleep evaded him.

He kept picturing Isabel's face as she came apart in his arms. He'd never seen anything so beautiful in his life. He tried not to think about how hurt she'd looked when he'd fled to the bathroom.

Ashamed by his cowardice, Tristan sat up and scrubbed a hand over his face. Where was she? Was she still in this world or had she already slipped into the other? Wherever Isabel was, Tristan wanted her back, wanted to know that she was safe.

He should've taken her blood when he had the chance. If he had, Tristan would be able to track her anywhere. But if he had taken her blood during sex, he would've bound her to him. The thought should've disturbed him, but for some reason it didn't. He wanted to go back to that moment and do what he should've done from the start.

Tristan didn't think Isabel would've appreciated waking up to find herself bound to a werewolf, but that connection would have damn sure come in handy now. New Orleans was a big place, even bigger when you factored in all the parishes outside of the city proper. Then there were the swamps...

He lay back down and closed his eyes. With his Lycanian Elder job, Tristan had accepted long ago that he'd never have a mate. He'd vowed to stay clear of humans after Aidan and Damon had bound them and bred true. Now...well, nothing had really changed.

Even as the thought filtered through Tristan's mind, he knew that it wasn't true. He'd give his life to get Isabel back safely. If that Darkling was as powerful as he suspected, that might be what it took.

14

Izzy awoke to the sounds of birds chirping and a shower running. She turned over, expecting to see the cabin. Instead, she came face to face with a popular princess.

She pushed the covers away and glanced around. It took her a moment to remember where she was and how she got there. As soon as she did, her hopes fell.

Izzy had never been one for regrets, but when it came to Tristan Chevalier, she had more than a few. She wondered again if he was okay. There was no way of knowing for sure. The dream flashed in her mind. It had been horrific, but at least he'd been alive. Izzy clung to that aspect. She had to. It was either that or fall apart.

She threw the covers back and rolled out of bed. Izzy listened for the shower. It was still going, so she slipped out of the room. She found a pot of coffee sitting next to the stove.

For one crazy minute, Izzy considered stealing Stone's car, but she didn't think she could take it and get away before he caught up with her. She still had the phone he'd given her. Her best bet was to call Everly.

Izzy poured herself a cup of coffee and walked to the back door. A small porch had been attached to the rear of the house. The screened-in area held a couple of chairs and a small table. She turned the knob, expecting to find it locked, but the door opened.

She glanced down the hall, but the bathroom door remained closed and the water continued to run. Izzy stepped out onto the porch and shut the door behind her. She'd just pulled the phone out of her pocket when the breeze shifted and the stench hit her.

Izzy gagged. She'd forgotten all about the dead alligator. She blindly reached for the doorknob to go back inside, but an inner voice told her to stop. Izzy always listened to those voices. They rarely steered her wrong.

She peered into the yard. Like the front lawn, the back was well cared for and lined with flowerbeds. Other than a few birds, she didn't spot any movement. She'd never seen an alligator up close.

Curiosity got the best of her. Izzy shoved the phone into her pocket and put her coffee down on one of the chairs. She glanced back at the door and listened for footsteps, but didn't hear anything.

Izzy pushed the screen door open and took the two stairs down into the yard. The odor was stronger now. She checked to make sure the stench hadn't attracted more alligators.

She didn't see anything, but that didn't mean they weren't there. They were masters at hiding in plain sight.

Her inner voice urged her forward. The odor made her eyes water, but she kept going. When she neared the shed, her instincts screamed at her to stop. Izzy hesitated, but it was too late to turn back now. She was outside the door.

The tin structure was no more than ten by twenty in size. Rust covered the sides of two walls, thanks to the high humidity. The door to the shed was the kind that slid open. It would make a horrendous noise the second she touched it, alerting Stone.

Izzy stared at the door, studying it for what felt like an eternity. "Just open it," she muttered under her breath. "It's just the alligator." Why was her heart pounding? Why was she hesitating? Was it because Stone had told her to stay out of the backyard? Or was something else directing her?

She glanced one last time at the house. There was no sign of Stone, but he had to be done with his shower by now. Would he think that she was still asleep? He'd know she wasn't when she opened the door.

Izzy took a deep breath and grabbed the handle. The door screeched as she wrenched it aside. The shed's interior was dark. Sunlight barely penetrated the glom. Izzy waited for her eyes to adjust then scanned the space.

At first, all she spotted were tools for doing lawn work. She didn't see an alligator or anything else that would explain the gut-kicking, nausea-creating stench.

She looked again. The second time, she spotted a lump on the floor. The pile was too small to be an alligator and too large to be rags. It took a moment for Izzy's brain to register what her eyes were showing it. When it did, bile rose in her throat, choking her. She took one step back and vomited, then like a driver passing a bad car accident, Izzy looked again.

The woman's esophagus had been ripped out, and scratches covered the front of her body, leaving deep furrows in her clothes and flesh. Beside her was a smaller mass.

"No," she murmured. "Please no."

But her denial didn't change the facts. The smaller bundle resembled the little girl she'd seen in the photographs—or what was left of her. She'd been wrapped in a pink blanket, but the cloth didn't conceal the fact that half of her body was missing.

Not missing, Izzy thought. *Eaten. She'd been eaten.*

Izzy backed out of the shed and collided with a hard chest. Her legs nearly collapsed beneath her, and she let out a loud scream that was cut off by Stone's hand.

"You've been a bad girl, Izzy," he said. "I told you to stay out of the backyard. You should've listened."

Pain knifed through Izzy's chest, and she couldn't seem to breathe. She gasped and gasped until Stone grabbed her by the neck and led her to the middle of the yard.

The second he stopped, Izzy dropped to her knees. "What have you done?"

"What do you mean?" he asked, sounding genuinely perplexed.

"Stone, you need help. Serious help," she said. "This woman and her child weren't a threat." Had he somehow mistaken these two for werewolves? If so, he was further gone than she'd anticipated. "Why did you kill them?"

"I got hungry waiting for you," he said so matter-of-factly that it took Izzy a moment to comprehend.

"What?" Izzy glanced up at him. She couldn't have heard him correctly.

"Don't knock human flesh until you try it, Izzy," he said. "It's quite tasty, especially the young ones. They're tender and sweet." Stone stepped around her until he stood near her head. "I offered you some last night, but you were too good share a meal with me."

Izzy gulped. "That's what was cooking in the pot? A child?" Her stomach lurched, and she vomited again.

"You make me sound like I'm a monster," he said, his disgust evident.

"If you're capable of doing that to a defenseless woman and her child, then you are," she said, wiping her mouth with the back of her hand.

Stone glared at her. "You have no idea what I'm capable of," he said softly. "You'll change your tune once we get to my home."

Izzy staggered to her feet. "You said you lived here."

His lip curled. "You know I don't. I believe that's obvious now." He glanced over her shoulder toward the bodies. "I wouldn't live in this world if you paid me."

Her mouth watered and she swallowed hard, fighting the urge to throw up again. "This world? What are you talking about? Stone, let me get you help."

"You're not very bright," he said. "Doesn't really matter. I didn't fetch you for your brains. As long as your other parts are working, that's all that matters to my people."

Izzy scrambled back, searching for a way to escape. "What do you mean by *your* people?"

"Don't bother trying to run," Stone said. "I will catch you. I'm very fast, when I need to be."

Cold enveloped her, until Izzy felt oddly calm inside. It was the kind of calm that came when someone knew they were going to die and accepted the fact. "What do you plan to do with me?"

"I told you," he said. "I'm taking you to my world."

His words finally registered. "You're the Darkling that Tristan has been hunting," she said.

Stone laughed. "Finally she gets it."

Izzy shook her head. "You said you were like me."

"I lied," he said.

"But that doesn't make sense," she said.

"Why?"

"Because I can detect evil and see hidden beasts," she said. "It's part of my gift. You should've set off my internal alarms the second I got close to you."

"Ah, yes, your gift." Stone glanced around the yard. "I'm sure the fact that my magic is stronger than your 'gift' is unsettling. It's always a tough lesson to learn that your power isn't as strong as you thought it was. Don't feel too bad. Soon all humans will know that they are not the be all and end all of existence."

"What does that mean?" Izzy asked.

"It means we're coming," he said. "Soon this world and the women in it will be ours."

"You're insane." She took another step back. "Tristan is going to come for you," she said.

"I'm sure he will if he's still alive. I hit him pretty hard. Thanks again for helping me get close to him," Stone said.

Guilt over what she'd done swamped her. Izzy had been so stupid.

"By the time Tristan recovers, you and I will be long gone." He glanced up at the bright morning sky and winced. "You should probably enjoy the sunshine while you can. It doesn't exist where we're going."

The thought of living in constant darkness terrified her. Izzy would rather die than be trapped somewhere like that.

Stone sighed. "I know what you're thinking."

Did he or was this another lie? "You can read my mind." Izzy tried to clear her thoughts.

"I don't need to be able to read your mind. The look on your face told me that you were thinking about doing something stupid," he said. "Don't! Or I'll have to tie you up for the rest of the day."

"We're not leaving right now," she said. There was still time for her to escape. Izzy made sure her hope didn't show.

"No." Stone shook his head. "We'll leave tonight as planned." He took a step toward her.

She skittered back.

"Izzy, I may not have read your mind a minute ago, but that doesn't mean that I can't," Stone said. "Try to keep that in mind as you make your escape plans. Now come along. Looks like I'll have to tie you up after all."

"No," she said. "I won't go with you. There has to be someone in this neighborhood that will help me."

"The people in this neighborhood learned a long time ago to mind their own business and only count on themselves when there's trouble," he said. "You can scream if you want, but know this: if someone does come to your rescue, I'll kill them. Their death will be on your head. Do we understand each other?"

All too well, she thought. Izzy couldn't endanger anyone else. Stone had already proven that he could kill without remorse. One more death wouldn't matter.

He waited for her to answer.

"Yes," she said reluctantly.

"Good," Stone said. "Now come inside like a good little breeder and let me tie you up."

"What if I promise not to try to escape?" she asked.

Stone smiled at her. "We both know that would be a lie."

* * *

Tristan shifted into his wolf. He hadn't gotten much sleep, certainly not enough to recover from his injuries, but the shift would change all that.

Within seconds, he was back in his human form and heading to the shower. He stepped under the spray, and memories from the last time he'd been in the shower returned.

Tristan had been hiding from Isabel, unable to face her and the emotions she'd dredged up after they'd made love. At least now he accepted the fact that they had made love. As much as he wished otherwise, it wasn't just sex.

If only he hadn't run away, then none of this would've happened. Guilt assailed him. It joined the weight he carried from the past. Tristan couldn't do anything about those mistakes, but he could affect the future. At least he hoped he could.

Tristan closed his eyes and pictured Isabel lying on the bed, her multi-colored hair spread out around her head. Her lips had been swollen from his kisses, and she'd had the sleepy-eyed expression of a woman well loved. The satisfied expression vanished, the second he ran into the bathroom.

He ducked his head under the water, hoping it would wash away some of the regrets, but water was only so strong. It didn't have the power to cleanse one's soul.

Tristan hurried through his shower. He was done hiding from life. It was time to accept both the pain and the pleasure that came with this existence. He just hoped he had another chance to feel some of that pleasure with Isabel before it all ended.

The moment Tristan stepped out of the bathroom, he encountered Pierre's assistant. "The Alpha has issued an invitation for you to join him for breakfast in the sunroom," he said.

"I'll be right down," Tristan said.

Five minutes later, Tristan sat across from Pierre La Fontaine as the

Alpha's hired help served them breakfast in the enclosed veranda.

Ceiling fans churned the air lazily over a small four-seater table. It was set for two, letting Tristan know that the Alpha wanted this to be a private conversation.

Pierre waited for the staff to load up the plates in front of them and pour the coffees. "Feeling better?" he asked, after the staff exited the room and shut the door behind them.

Tristan shrugged. "I'm fit enough to take care of what needs to be done."

"For your sake, I hope so. What do you plan to do?" Pierre asked, taking a bite of blood sausage. Like most Weres, the Alpha preferred a high protein diet.

Tristan took a sip of his coffee. A hint of chicory hit his palate, and he nearly groaned in ecstasy. This town could do coffee. He'd give them that.

"I'm going after them," he said. He owed the Darkling for hitting him upside the head and nearly crushing his skull.

"That's a given," Pierre said, then took another bite. "What I want to know is where are you going to start your hunt?"

Tristan thought about it. He had to narrow the search area down. If he didn't, he'd never find them in time. If the Darkling managed to drag Isabel into his world, then there'd be no getting her back. The spot in the center of his chest throbbed. He rubbed it absently.

Pierre watched him but said nothing.

"When I first met Isabel, she hung out with a friend in Jackson Square," Tristan said. "The woman is also a Sighted-One."

Pierre's eyebrows shot to his dark hairline. "Why didn't you tell me? I could've had her picked up or at least watched."

"I've had my hands full," Tristan said.

The Alpha grinned. "Yes, you have."

Tristan growled.

"Knock it off," Pierre said. "Does the Darkling know about Isabel's friend?"

"I don't know," he said. "It depends on how long he's been stalking her. He didn't strike me as being very patient."

Pierre sat forward. "We can't let him get his hands on another Sighted-One."

"I agree," Tristan said. "But I don't think it's smart to grab Everly. If she's able, I do think Isabel will try to contact her. I need her to be there to get that call."

"That's a huge risk you're taking," Pierre said.

"I know," Tristan said.

"What if she leaves town?"

He shook his head. "Everly's not going anywhere. Isabel tried to warn her to get out of town, but she refused to leave."

Tristan pictured Everly. The fiery Goth with a Moonlight Kin skull in her house was hardheaded like Isabel, but she was also loyal. If it were possible, Everly would be the first person Isabel contacted. What if Isabel was injured and wasn't able to contact her? He couldn't think about that or he'd go insane.

"I don't like the idea of another Sighted-One running around town unprotected," Pierre said.

Tristan picked up his fork and played with his food. "I don't either," he said. "But Everly is stubborn."

"You said the same thing about your human," Pierre said.

"She's not *my* human," Tristan replied.

"The sheets in the cabin say otherwise," he said.

Tristan ignored the Alpha's bait. "Even if Isabel hasn't been in contact with her, Everly still might be able to help. From what I've seen, her gift is quite powerful. Possibly more powerful than Isabel's," he said. "Putting your wolves on her won't do any good. She'd know they were there. Everly has power objects in her home. Things that protect her and mask her presence."

"What kind of power objects?" Pierre put his fork down.

"It's not important," Tristan said. He needed Pierre's cooperation. If the Alpha found out about the skull, he'd pull his assistance and scoop up Everly immediately.

"Let me decide what is and is not important in my territory," Pierre said.

"I'll be more than happy to have this discussion once we get Isabel back," he said, letting his frustration show.

"I will not forget."

"You never do," Tristan muttered.

Pierre picked up his coffee cup and took a drink. "What makes you think Everly would help you?"

"She wouldn't, if it was just me asking," Tristan said. "But she'd definitely help Isabel. Of that I am certain."

Pierre sighed. "What can I do to help?"

"Have your wolves continue their search for Isabel's scent, but if they haven't found it by this evening, then call them in," Tristan said. "The Darkling will make his move tonight. That's when he's most powerful."

"Do you think you can take him?" Pierre asked, setting his cup down.

Tristan had the utmost confidence in his abilities, but he'd never encountered a being as powerful as this Darkling. He wasn't sure if he could beat him in a fight, even with his sword, Selene. "I may not be able to take him, but I will stop him. One way or the other."

Pierre's lips twitched. "Do me a favor," he said.

"What's that?" Tristan asked.

"Try not to get yourself killed," he said.

Tristan laughed. "I'll do my best."

"When are you going to approach the other Sighted-One?" he asked.

Tristan glanced at a clock on the wall. "Not for a few more hours. From what I gathered, she likes to stay out all night with the wannabe vampires."

Pierre's brow furrowed. "The what?"

Tristan picked up a piece of bacon and popped it in his mouth. "You know, the people who put in fake fangs and pretend to drink blood."

"This is a friend of Isabel's?" Pierre asked, his disgust evident from his expression.

"Yes," Tristan said. "Everly's definitely odd, but her concern for her friend is real."

Pierre dabbed the side of his mouth with his napkin. "I hope you know what you're doing," he said.

Tristan did too.

15

Izzy pulled against the extension cord Stone had bound her with, trying to break it. She only succeeded in cutting off her circulation. He'd tied her up in the little girl's room, so she had a constant reminder of what sat out in the shed.

The sun moved across the sky fast. It was only a matter of time before he came for her to take her to his realm. She had to get out of here. Izzy yanked, and pain shot through her wrists.

She wondered where Tristan was. Wondered if he was even alive. Stone had thanked her for helping him. Izzy's head dropped back and hit the wall with a *thunk*. How could she have been so stupid?

If Tristan was alive, the chances of him forgiving her were slim to none. She might not have helped attack him, but she had been in contact with Stone the whole time.

Please be alive…if for no other reason than to avenge me.

Izzy yanked at the cord again. It stretched, but held. Stone would have to untie her when he moved her. Wouldn't he? What if he didn't? Izzy needed to have her hands free in order to fight.

He's a werewolf, a little voice reminded her.

No, he was something far worse than the creatures she'd encountered over the years. Izzy racked her brain trying to remember what Tristan had told her about Darklings. Unfortunately, it wasn't much because she hadn't wanted to listen.

She had to think. There had to be a way out of this situation. She wasn't a damsel in distress. Okay, maybe she was, but there was no way Izzy would let him drag her anywhere. She'd rather die. At least if they found her body, her sister Mindy would know what happened to her.

The door opened. Stone stepped into the room holding... Izzy squinted. Was that a sandwich?

She thought about the little girl in the shed, and her stomach twisted. "I'm not hungry," she said.

"You have to eat something," he said. "The crossing is rough on the body. It's especially difficult for humans. Don't want you dying before you get there."

"Perhaps you didn't hear me. I said I wasn't hungry," she said. "I'll never be hungry enough to eat a child. Now get that away from me."

Stone scowled at her. "It's peanut butter and jelly." He walked into the room and placed the sandwich on the small dresser, then sat beside her on the bed.

Izzy scooted as far away from him as her bindings allowed.

"You have a choice here. You can either eat this sandwich on your own, or I'm going to hold your smart mouth open and force-feed it to you. Either way, you're going to eat."

"I can't eat with my hands tied." Izzy held her hands up for emphasis. "I can't even feel my fingers anymore."

Stone glanced at her hands, which were turning blue. "You shouldn't have been pulling on the cord," he said.

Izzy just stared at him.

"Fine," he said. "I'll untie you, but if you try to get away I'll make sure you can't move at all next time." Stone ran his finger down the side of her thigh.

She jerked her leg away. His touch made her skin crawl. "I need to use the bathroom," Izzy said.

Stone untied her and waited for her to climb off the bed. He walked her into the hall to the bathroom and pushed the door open.

"Go ahead," he said.

"I can't go while you're looking," she said.

"Then you mustn't have to go very bad," Stone said.

Izzy grimaced. She did have to go bad. She'd been holding it for over an hour. No way was she leaving this bathroom without relieving herself.

"Can you at least turn your back?" she asked.

Stone rolled his eyes. "Humans," he said. "You all have so many needless quirks."

"Humor me," she said.

"Fine." Stone turned his back. "But this is another thing you'll need to get over when we reach my realm."

Izzy kept an eye on him while she quickly relieved herself. She did not want him looking at her. Just the thought of him seeing her naked made her physically ill. There was no way she could let him take her to his world. Death was far preferable to whatever Stone had planned.

She had always assumed that *all* monsters operated like Stone. Then she'd met Tristan and her opinion changed. Izzy laughed to herself. Her opinion had more than changed. It had done a one-eighty. She'd gone from fleeing from the monsters to sleeping with them, except... Tristan wasn't a monster. Stone was.

She stared at his back. Izzy had hoped Stone would give her a moment of privacy so she could use her cellphone, but he'd been too smart for that. She washed her hands, then took a quick sip of water to ease her dry throat.

"All done," she said.

"Good," Stone said. "Now eat. I won't ask you again."

He walked her back into the bedroom and took a seat at the child's desk. Izzy sniffed the sandwich and lifted the bread to examine it.

Stone swore. "It's just peanut butter and jelly. For goddess' sake, just eat it!"

Izzy jumped at his raised voice. She took a tentative bite of the sandwich. It tasted normal, but that didn't mean he hadn't put something in it. *Please don't let it be ground-up little girl.*

Her stomach gurgled.

"Keep eating." Stone kept a close eye on her.

"Why are you doing this?" she asked.

"I told you. You're needed in my realm," he said.

"What's so special about my gift that you have to kidnap me for it?" she asked, taking another bite. Izzy would kill for a glass of milk, but she wasn't about to ask him for anything.

Stone stared at her for so long that she thought for sure he wasn't going to answer. "Nothing," he said.

Nothing? Not the answer she'd been expecting. "Then I don't understand why you went to so much trouble to get me." She set the sandwich down.

"Your gift is necessary, but not needed," Stone said cryptically.

"I don't understand," Izzy said.

"Don't expect you to," he said. "Now eat."

Izzy picked up the sandwich and took another bite. At least her stomach began to settle, though for how long was anyone's guess.

"You said earlier that it wasn't important that I be able to think quickly," she said.

Stone grinned. "That's right."

"Why?" she asked.

"Because you are only needed for breeding."

Izzy dropped the sandwich onto the plate. Her throat worked convulsively as she fought to keep the contents down. The plan was to breed her to monsters like himself.

She shook her head in denial, but Izzy knew from his pleased expression that Stone told the truth.

"I'm going to be sick." She jumped up off the bed and raced past him. Izzy barely made it to the toilet before she threw up her peanut butter and jelly sandwich.

She heaved and heaved until there was nothing left to expel. Izzy pushed off the toilet seat and grabbed onto the sink to pull herself up.

She glanced in the mirror. The color had bled from her face, leaving her pasty. Izzy splashed water on her face and rinsed her mouth.

Stone stood in the doorway, holding another sandwich. Had he made two? Or had he gone and made another one while she threw up?

Izzy glared at him. "I hope you don't expect me to eat that. Right now I can't keep anything down."

He simply stared at her as if she hadn't spoken.

"Did you hear me?" Izzy sneered.

Stone arched a brow. "Every word. Did you hear me?" He held the plate out to her. "The choice is yours."

Izzy snatched the plate out his hands. "You're an asshole."

Stone had her around the neck before Izzy blinked. The plate dropped onto the bathroom floor a second before he slammed her against the wall.

"I've had about enough of your mouth," he said. "I overlooked the fact that you spread your thighs for that monster. The only reason I didn't rip your womb out was because it's needed, but your tongue isn't." Stone squeezed, cutting off her air.

Izzy clawed at his hand, but he only squeezed harder. She choked, and black dots appeared before her eyes.

"Now you're going to pick that sandwich up and you're going to eat it all, then I'm going to tie you to the bed until we need to leave," he hissed. "Don't worry. It won't be long. Nod if you understand me."

She tried to move her head but couldn't.

His grip on her eased a fraction.

Izzy sucked in much-needed air.

"One word, one whisper, and I will rip your tongue out and eat it," Stone said. "Got it?"

Izzy nodded.

Stone released her.

She fell to her knees.

"Pick it up." Stone pointed to the sandwich.

Izzy's hands shook as she scooped the sandwich up and placed it back on the plate.

"Good girl," he said. "Now get up."

She staggered to her feet. Izzy caught sight of her reflection a moment before he shoved her out the door. Finger marks ringed her neck.

Izzy didn't fight when Stone tied her up. There'd be no escape—at least not alive. He hadn't meant to, but Stone had given her a weapon to use against him. Now all Izzy had to do was get him mad enough to kill her. Given her track record with the monsters, that shouldn't be too hard.

* * *

The door opened at three-thirty. Tristan had been debating whether to leave, when he heard the footsteps drawing nearer. Hope soared until he realized there was only one set. The key clicked in the lock, and the door swung open. Everly stepped into the living room.

"Where have you been?" he asked.

Everly yelped and pressed a hand to her throat. "What are you doing in my apartment?" she asked, her charcoal-lined eyes narrowing on him. "How did you get in?"

"The new door wasn't that strong." He glanced at the crack he'd left in it.

She scowled when she saw the damage to the door. "You're going to pay for that. Now what are you doing here?" She glanced around the space. "Where is Izzy?"

"She's the reason I'm here," Tristan said. "Have you heard from her?"

"What's happened?" she asked, ignoring his question.

"Nothing yet," he said, but that wouldn't be the case for long.

Everly pushed the door closed and walked deeper into the room. "Are you alone?"

"Yes." Tristan didn't tell her that the wolves already knew all about her. That would come later. Right now, he didn't want to spook her. "Have you heard from Isabel?"

Everly stared at him for the longest time then sighed. "No," she said. "I haven't spoken to her since I saw you guys in the square." She threw her bag down and took a seat across from him.

Tristan tried to hide his disappointment, but he mustn't have been too successful.

"What's happened to her?" Everly asked. "I thought you were protecting her."

He was supposed to be, but that hadn't worked out well. If he lost her for good, he'd live with the regret for the rest of his life.

"The evil that came to town has her," he said.

Everly didn't say anything. She zoned out for a moment, then her attention snapped back to him. "I can't sense her," she said, her voice thick with emotion.

"Does that mean she's dead?" Tristan's chest tightened to the point of pain. For a moment, he couldn't breathe, as Isabel's face and his brother's blurred together in his mind.

She shook her head. "I don't think so," Everly said. "I think she's on the other side of the river. Water mutes my powers."

Good to know, he thought, but he needed concrete info to find her.

"Tell me about this evil," she said.

Tristan wasn't sure how much he should say to her.

Everly's dark eyes narrowed. "Don't even think about lying, even by omission. The more I know about it, the more I can help."

"The thing is like my people, but not," he said cryptically. "Everyone and everything has a shadow side. Our shadow side doesn't live in this realm. It exists in another dimension."

"Okay," she said, her brow furrowing as she listened carefully.

"The Darklings—that's what we call them—can cross into this realm. When they do, they bring death and madness in their wake," he said.

Everly's lips pursed. "Is that why I couldn't pinpoint its location?"

"Perhaps," Tristan said. "They have powerful magic behind them. Magic that comes from their dark world."

"Magic? That shouldn't have mattered with me." She kicked off her boots and curled her feet beneath her. "Are they werewolves, or are they sorcerers?"

Tristan sat forward. "They're a bit of both. They use magic, but they shift into a wolf form."

"What does this thing want with Isabel?" she asked.

"Isabel isn't the only one it's after." He gave her a pointed stare.

Everly's eyes widened, and she gulped. "So what does this thing want with me and Isabel?"

Tristan shook his head. "Again, it's not just you two it's after. It's all women like you."

She frowned. "Like us?"

"Sighted-Ones," he said trying to be patient while his beast raged inside him. "The Darklings need women like you."

"Need us for what?" she asked.

She already knew the answer to the question, but she obviously needed to hear it said aloud.

"They want you for breeding purposes," he said. Tristan gripped the side of the chair until he heard the wood groan, then forced his fingers to ease. "They can only mate with Sighted-Ones. Normal women go mad if they're scratched or bitten by them, then they eventually die."

"What happens to a woman if one of these things takes her into their world?" she asked.

"Nothing, other than the obvious, if she's truly Sighted," he said.

"Lovely," she said. "How long has this thing had her?"

Tristan tensed. "He's had her since yesterday."

Everly shot out of her chair. "And you're just coming to me now?"

She had every right to be angry. He was angry, too. Tristan had failed Isabel when she needed him most. He snarled. No, he'd failed her before then.

"The Darkling tried to crush my skull in," he said. "And nearly succeeded. I have no idea why I'm alive, but I assume it's because of Isabel."

Everly put her hands on her hips. "So she saved you, but you couldn't save her."

That about summed it up, though there were extenuating circumstances.

Tristan ran a hand through his hair and scrubbed it over his face. Despite the shift, his head was still sore.

"Have you slept?" she asked, losing some of her fury.

"Not much," he said.

Everly sat back down. "What can I do?"

"I need you to use your gift to try to locate her," he said. "If that fails, I need you to let me know if you hear from her. I doubt the Darkling will simply let her call, but knowing Isabel, she'll wiggle out of his grasp. At least for a short while."

She watched him closely. "You love her, don't you?"

Tristan stiffened in his seat. "Don't be ridiculous."

"You're awful quick to deny it," she said. "But if you don't love her, then why go to so much trouble to find her?"

Because he didn't want Isabel to suffer in the Darkling world. Because he couldn't imagine never getting to see her again, even if it was from afar. Because she was his, and the Darkling had taken her from him.

"It's my job," Tristan said.

Everly smirked. "Liar. Didn't look like you were doing your job when I saw you guys in Jackson Square," she said.

"I was," he said.

She snorted. "You're not that good of an actor. You care for her."

"You don't know what you're talking about," he said.

"Actually, I do," Everly said. "You forget I had a vision about you guys, and there was a whole lot more going on than just encountering evil."

Tristan's jaw clenched. "Visions can be wrong."

"So you haven't slept with her?" Everly asked.

Heat spread across Tristan's face, and his gaze dropped.

Everly grinned. "That's what I thought. Job, my ass. You like her."

"Will you help me if I say I do?" He'd tell her anything to get her cooperation.

"No." She shook her dark head. "But I will help Isabel."

"Can you try to find her?" he asked.

Everly nodded and closed her eyes. She took several deep breaths, then the muscles in her face relaxed. Minutes passed, and nothing happened.

Tristan tried to be patient, but every minute that went by brought Isabel closer to being taken into the other realm. There was a slim chance that the Darkling had already crossed her over, but it was more likely he'd need time to heal from his injury.

Just the thought that she might be gone forever made his beast howl in agony.

What if this didn't work? What if he was too late?

Everly's eyes popped open. "What I'm seeing doesn't make any sense," she said.

"Tell me everything," he said. No clue was too small.

"I saw flashes of a child. She had fair hair like Isabel and held a stuffed bear," she said. "Like I told you, it doesn't make sense."

A child that looked like Isabel... It wasn't hard for Tristan to imagine such a thing. In fact, it was far too easy.

"Did you see anything else? Anything at all?" he asked.

"Destruction and water, but it could be anywhere in New Orleans. I'm sorry," she said. "If I get anything else, I'll let you know."

"Thanks for trying." Tristan rose. "I need you to do one more thing for me." He grabbed the sheath that held Selene and tucked the lodestone in the side of it.

Everly's eyes widened when she saw the sword, and she jumped off the beanbag. "I won't tell anyone, I swear," she said. "Please don't kill me."

Tristan glanced at the sword in his hand and frowned. "What are you talking about?"

She stopped inching toward the front door. "You're not going to kill me because I know too much?"

He grimaced. "No," Tristan said. "I was going to ask you to hold this until I shift into my other form. Once I do, I need you to tie it around my neck."

"Oh." She sounded oddly disappointed.

Tristan shook his head. Everly was a strange woman.

"Don't you think you'll attract too much attention in your other form?" she asked. "I know this is New Orleans, but even here a wolf running through town with a sword around his neck is bound to raise a few eyebrows."

"No doubt," he said, "but I have no choice. I need my other senses to find the Darkling. If by chance Isabel phones you, please call this number." Tristan pulled a business card out of his wallet and handed it to her.

Everly's eyes widened when she saw the name on the card.

"I take it you know Pierre La Fontaine," he said.

"Know him personally?" She shook her head. "No. But I do know of him."

"He'll know how to find me," Tristan said. "What you're about to see isn't something the Moonlight Kin share with humans. I'd appreciate it if you'd keep it to yourself."

Everly nodded and took a step back.

Fur rippled over Tristan's arms, and claws extended from his fingertips. He dropped to his knees, and his vision faded before quickly snapping back into the place.

In his beast form, the scents in Everly's house were even stronger, especially the scent of death. He glanced over his shoulder at the Moonlight Kin skull on the bookshelf.

Everly followed his gaze and hurried over to cover it with a cloth. "Don't move," she said. Her fingers shook as she slipped the sheath over his head then put the sword inside it. "Do you need me to open the door?"

Tristan barked.

She flinched but hurried to the door and opened it.

He was about to step through when she blocked his exit. Tristan growled.

Everly thumped him on the head. "Knock it off," she said.

Shocked by her actions, Tristan didn't do anything for a moment. Then his gaze rose, though not very far since they were close to eye level in this form.

"Save my friend," Everly said. "I know you love her, even if *you* don't know you love her."

Fortunately, Tristan couldn't speak in this form. He had vocal capabilities if he performed a partial shift, but not a full one. For once he was grateful for that fact, since he wasn't sure what he'd say.

He barked at her again.

This time Everly stepped aside and let him leave. Tristan raced out the back door, hitting the screen with his shoulder. The world around him came alive, but the one scent he wanted to smell more than any other remained elusive.

Tristan weaved his way through the side streets, avoiding the more touristy areas, but it would take a while to make his way out of town.

Every mile or so Tristan would glance down to see if the lodestone glowed. At one point the lodestone did, but the magic stopped abruptly. The water from the lakes and rivers dampened the signal just like it had Everly's gift.

Tristan tried to ignore the sun's rapid descent. He raised his head and sniffed the air. *Where are you?* He couldn't lose Isabel. He didn't think he'd survive another loss of that magnitude.

16

Stone came for Izzy as the sun dipped below the trees. It wasn't dark yet, but it would be soon. He pulled out a knife and cut through the extension cord binding her hands.

"Time to go," he said.

Izzy clenched her hands to get feeling back into her fingers. She'd need to be able to use her limbs if she stood any chance of escaping. She rolled off the bed.

"Grab your things and anything else you might want from this realm," he said. "We don't have the same things in our world."

"What do you have there?" she asked.

"You'll see." Stone grinned.

Izzy didn't want anything from this house. The place held nothing but death. She grabbed her tote and threw it over her shoulder.

Stone stood in the doorway and waited for her to exit. They reached the front door. There was a gas can sitting on the side table next to the couch. He grabbed it and began to slosh the contents all over the house.

Izzy grabbed his arm. "What are you doing?"

"Getting rid of the evidence, unless you want your fingerprints found at a crime scene," he said.

"What if they had family?" Izzy asked. "This might be all the family has left to hold onto."

Stone shrugged. "I'm sure you're trying to make a point of some kind, but it doesn't change what I need to do." He went back to pouring the gas around the house.

The sick feeling returned. Izzy clutched her stomach. Somewhere a family missed their daughter and granddaughter. After today, a father would never see his daughter again.

She turned and rushed out the door. Stone was on her before she'd made it across the lawn.

"Where are you going, Isabel?" he asked, blocking her escape.

"Anywhere!" she snapped. "As long as it's away from you." Izzy caught the odor of smoke a second before she saw the flames rise.

"Get in the car," Stone said. "We don't want to be here when the fire department arrives."

Stone drove her in the same direction as the cabin she'd stayed at with Tristan. Izzy saw the exit for Jean Lafitte Park and was surprised when Stone took it.

If Tristan was alive, would he still be in the area? Izzy's mind raced with ways she could contact him.

Frosty, where are you?? she thought. *I need you.*

Stone didn't take the road toward the cabin. Instead, he continued on until they arrived at a swamp tour boat dock. He pulled his car to the end of the road and parked.

"We'll have to walk from here," he said.

The trees leading into the swamp were thick with undergrowth. All kinds of things could be hiding in those weeds. Was it too much to hope that an alligator got Stone?

Izzy glanced at him. He'd probably kill it and eat it. As she lifted her tote, it hit the cellphone in her pocket. She needed to call Everly. Heck, she needed to phone Mindy and say goodbye.

"This way," Stone said, walking toward a fallen tree that concealed a rugged path.

She followed, but Izzy continued to search for a way to escape. She wondered if werewolves were afraid of the water like cats. If so, she would take her chances with the gators.

Even as the thought slipped through her mind, Izzy heard something large splash in the water. She stared at the murky inlet that ran along the path.

"Don't worry," Stone said. "I won't let it get you."

"Being gator bait is preferable to what you have in mind for me," she said.

He laughed. "I won't be one of the ones vying for you," Stone said.

"Good!" she said.

Stone smiled. "You might wish that I was by the time the breeding challenge is over."

Izzy stumbled on a root. "Breeding challenge?"

"Yeah." Stone ran a hand through his short black hair. "When an eligible female arrives in our world, males come from all around to see who can breed her. They each get a shot at the woman until one of them succeeds in impregnating her. The last woman had to endure forty warriors before she was with child." He shrugged. "Nearly killed her. With any luck, it'll take you a hundred."

Izzy's stomach gurgled. She had just enough time to step off the path before she vomited onto the leaves of a plant.

"Not this again," he said as if the whole thing bored him. "You're only delaying the inevitable."

She threw up again then rubbed her mouth with the back of her sleeve.

Stone grabbed a water bottle out of his small tote and handed it to her. "Rinse your mouth. I don't want to have to smell that, too. You already smell *funny*."

She swished water in her mouth then dug into her tote for a mint. She popped it onto her tongue. With any luck, she'd choke on it.

Izzy knew she needed a shower. He didn't have to point it out. "I don't stink," she said affronted.

"Yes, you do," he said. "You smell like that wolf."

She couldn't smell anything, but it made Izzy unduly pleased that

Stone thought she smelled like Tristan.

They continued down the trail until they reached a small clearing. At first, Izzy thought the clearing was natural. Once they got closer it was obvious that someone had cleared the area. What wasn't so obvious was how, since none of the trees were cut.

The area reminded Izzy of the crop circle photos she'd seen online. It wasn't as elegant, but there were striking similarities. Did that mean that Darklings were showing up around the world? The people hoping for aliens were going to be very disappointed if that were the case.

Stone pulled out a weird sphere from his bag. He placed it in the center of the clearing and stepped back. "This will take a little while."

"Take your time," she said. "I'm not in a hurry."

The shadows lengthened around them and her heart sank. Tristan wasn't coming. No one was. She was on her own, and she had no one to blame but herself.

"Since we have time, can I call my sister and my friend to say goodbye?" she asked.

"Sure," Stone said. "But if you say anything to warn them, I'll come back to kill Mindy and your friend. Do you understand?"

Izzy frowned. "You know my sister?" The idea terrified her.

"How do you think I found you?" he asked. "I could've killed her anytime, and would have had I known she wasn't a Sighted-One."

She shuddered at how close Mindy had come to dying. Izzy had to do something to protect her. "I'll come with you willingly if you swear to leave my sister alone."

Stone's brow arched in surprise. "Really?"

"Yes," Izzy said. "I want your word."

He laughed. "Sure."

"No, I mean it," Izzy said, advancing on him.

"I swear I won't touch Mindy," he said. Stone didn't bother to mention that it would be difficult to get to her now that she'd mated with one of the wolves.

Izzy studied his face. "Okay."

Stone chuckled at how gullible she was. Izzy pulled out the phone he'd given her and punched in a number. He heard voicemail pick up.

She deflated before his eyes. "Hey, Mindy, it's me. I just wanted to tell you..." She sighed. "I just wanted to say that I love you very much, and I hope you have a long and happy life." Izzy choked on a sob. "I've got to go. Take care of yourself." She disconnected the call.

"I imagine that's disappointing," Stone said. "Your last chance to speak with your sister and she's not home. She's probably with that wolf of hers."

Izzy turned on him. Her eyes narrowed, and her expression became a mask of pure hatred. "I hope so," she snarled. "At least then she'll be safe from the likes of you."

"You'd better make your other phone call while I'm still feeling generous. The energy is building. Soon the portal will open, and this disgusting world will be gone."

Her fingers trembled as she punched in the last number. It rang and rang, then a harried voice came on the line.

"Everly?" Izzy asked.

"Oh my God! Where are you?" Everly asked.

Izzy gave a pained laugh. "You wouldn't believe me if I told you," she said.

"He's there with you, isn't he?" she asked.

Izzy's face paled. "I don't know what you're talking about."

"Tristan came by earlier looking for you," Everly said.

This time Izzy did sob aloud. "He's alive?"

Her palpable relief pissed Stone off. He'd really thought Izzy was better than that. He should've known that wasn't the case.

"Of course Tristan's alive," she said. "Why wouldn't he be?"

"It's a long story," Izzy said. "All that matters is that he is." Her eyes widened as Stone approached. "Listen, Everly, I just wanted to call to say goodbye. You take care and get out of town."

Stone grabbed her hand before she hung up. "Don't be like that," he said. "Invite her to the party. The more the merrier, I always say."

"No!" Izzy struggled in his grasp. "Run, Everly! Run!"

Stone struck her with the back of his hand, knocking her to the ground. The loud thwack carried over the line. Izzy's grip on the phone gave way. He put the receiver up to his ear.

"You still there?" he asked.

Silence greeted him. He wanted to laugh.

"I can hear you breathing. You might as well answer me, especially if you want your friend to live," he said.

"I'm here," Everly said.

"Good," Stone said. "We're at the tour dock in Lafitte Park. Go past the fallen tree, and you'll see the trail." He glanced at Izzy, who staggered to her feet. "Oh, and come alone, or she's dead."

Izzy screamed for Everly to stay away, but Stone had already hung up.

"You bastard!" She rushed him. Her fists pummeled his chest and grazed his face.

Stone dropped the phone onto the ground and stomped on it.

"No!" Izzy renewed her efforts, but it didn't do her any good.

He countered every blow, waiting for her to wear herself out. It took longer than he expected, but eventually she dropped to the ground.

"I'm going to kill you," she said softly.

"I have no doubt you'd like to," he said. "But we both know you're no match for me. Even your boyfriend wasn't strong enough to take me."

Their gazes met. "He would've been had you not sucker hit him with a pan."

"Believe that if you must, but my people are stronger than the Moonlight Kin. It's why they fear us so," he said. "I really should've killed him when I had the chance."

She hoped that Everly was smart enough to stay home, but even as the thought flitted through Izzy's mind, she knew her friend would come. It wasn't in Everly's nature to run.

Izzy thought of Tristan. He'd been to Everly's house. He was looking for her, but it was unlikely that he'd find her in time. She was just grateful he was alive. It would give Izzy something to hold on to, something to dream about while she walked through hell in the Darkling world.

The air around them thickened.

The leaves swirled *vertically*, defying basic physics. "What's happening?" Izzy asked.

"The doorway is opening," Stone said.

"Then let's go," she said. "We don't need to wait for Everly. She'll delay us needlessly."

Stone chuckled. "Two Sighted-Ones are far better than one. Don't you think?"

He knew. "How?"

"I've been following your trail for a while," he said. "One night I thought I had you, but when I got nearer I realized it wasn't your power I'd been picking up. It was another's. She's a lot more powerful than you. Probably why I hadn't been able to detect her before." He swirled his hands, making odd patterns in the air. "I only caught a glimpse of her, but it was enough to know that I was dealing with two Sighted-Ones. When I return to my world, I will be honored as a hero."

"You're going to be a hero for kidnapping two women?" Izzy asked. "Your world must have pretty low standards, if that's the title you get for such a despicable act."

"For finding two Sighted-Ones," he corrected. "No one in my world has done such a thing. I will be rewarded for my bravery."

Izzy snorted. "Bravery? You're a coward," she said. "You hide in the shadows. You attack the innocent. You don't fight fair because you know you'll lose."

He hit her again.

This time Izzy didn't fall. "Truth hurts, doesn't it?"

Stone shook his head. "You really aren't bright. If you were, you wouldn't test me this way."

Dark fur rippled over his skin, and his jaw cracked. The bone extended until his human mouth disappeared and a muzzle replaced it. His clothes ripped and fell to the ground. He kept growing and mutating, until a monster stood before her.

Izzy had seen Moonlight Kin in their beast forms. They'd been larger than real wolves, but had maintained the general shape of the animals. Stone didn't. He looked like something out of a bear-themed horror movie.

She scrambled away. "Stay back." Izzy grabbed a stick and swung it at him.

His claws extended, and he sliced the wood in half as if it were a ripe peach. With lightning speed, he struck her, scratching Izzy down her arm. Blood welled on her skin. The wound burned like fire, but she wouldn't give Stone the satisfaction of knowing he'd hurt her.

He slowly shifted back to human form. Sweat covered Stone's naked body, and he was panting from the exertion. He glanced at her arm and grinned, flashing teeth too long for his mouth.

"Now you have to come with me," he said in a garbled voice. "If you stay, that scratch will lead to madness and death. That's what happened to your sister's friend, Celina Gibson."

"Her boyfriend killed her," she said.

"I know," Stone said. "I didn't want to do it, but she got too clingy, and since she wasn't a Sighted-One, I didn't have a lot of use for her." He snorted. "Other than the obvious. Celina was so needy that she let me do whatever I wanted to her."

Izzy glanced down at the wound. The furrows were just deep enough to bleed. "You infected me like you infected Celina?"

Mindy had told her all about Celina's death. It hadn't come as a shock, since Izzy had seen her friend's spirit prior to the phone call. At the time, Izzy hadn't been too surprised, given her friend's dangerous lifestyle, but now she felt horrible for what Celina had gone through. Not only had she been used, but she'd been betrayed.

"In a fashion," he said, then pulled out a clean pair of clothes from his tote.

The sense of evil emanating from him overwhelmed her. "Celina's boyfriend's name was Slade." They couldn't be the same person.

His smug expression said they were. "Slade, Stone, I really don't care what you all call me," he said. "It's unimportant as long as it doesn't interfere with my mission."

Izzy clutched the wound. If she was going to die anyway, then maybe she could take him with her. She turned and ran for the water. The blood would attract the gators. With any luck, they would take Stone out at the same time.

"What are you doing?" he shouted. "Come back here!"

She ran faster. The branches and bushes pulled at her clothes, slowing her down, but Izzy saw water up ahead. This was it. She was almost there. Just a few more feet and the bayou would take her into its watery embrace.

It felt like a truck hit her from behind. Izzy sailed through the air then landed hard, knocking the wind out of her.

"I told you that you couldn't get away," he snarled and yanked her to her feet. "Don't try anything stupid like that again, or I'll knock you out and throw you through the portal."

Izzy tasted blood in her mouth as Stone dragged her back to the clearing. The leaves were swirling faster now, and the darkness at the center of the mass grew. Soon it would be big enough for them to fit through.

17

Everly stared in shock at the phone in her hand. Had she just heard Izzy die?

Izzy told her to run, but the guy had sounded serious when he'd threatened her friend's life. What should she do?

She glanced down and spotted the business card Tristan had given her. The thought of phoning them terrified Everly, but the thought of losing Izzy was even more frightening.

Everly picked up the card and punched the number into the phone. It rang twice, then someone picked up.

"La Fontaine residence," the man said. "How may I help you?"

"I'm—I'm..."

"Is this a crank call?" he asked. "If so, you should know that we have caller ID."

Everly swallowed hard. "No!" she said. "My—my name is Everly. I'm a friend of Izzy MacDougal's."

"Hold please," he said.

A strong male voice came on the line a second later. "This is Pierre La Fontaine. Whom am I speaking with?"

"I'm a friend of Izzy's," she said.

"You must be Everly," Pierre said.

She jolted at the mention of her name. How did he know about her? Everly pictured Tristan and swore under her breath.

"Listen, I don't have a lot of time," she said. "I just heard from Izzy. She's in big trouble. If I don't meet her, she's going to die."

"Where did she tell you to go?" he asked.

Everly quickly filled him in.

"You did the right thing by calling," Pierre said. "Sit tight. I'll send some of my men over to guard you."

"What?" Her voice rose before she could stop it. "I don't need a guard. I need to get to my friend before the psycho she's with does something crazy to her."

"He won't harm her," Pierre said.

The deepness of his voice sank into her bones, making her body relax a little. Everly wanted to believe him. He sounded like the voice of authority, but the truth was she didn't know this man, this creature. She wasn't about to take a chance and risk her friend's life, when she knew she could save her.

"I've got to go," she said. "I know what needs to be done. My path is clear."

"Don't hang up!" Pierre shouted, but it was too late.

Everly pushed the disconnect button and grabbed her keys. She didn't know how long it would take him to notify Tristan or to get wolves to her house, so she had to hurry.

"Hang on, Izzy," she murmured, then snatched her gris-gris before running out the door.

Tristan was searching a few miles from the cabin when he heard the wolves howl. He knew what the sound meant. They'd found Isabel. His heart jumped then began to race. Was she alive? He couldn't imagine that the Darkling would kill her—at least not on purpose or without provocation.

His chest squeezed. In the short time he'd known Isabel, Tristan had discovered just how annoying and adorable she could be. Darklings weren't capable of feeling human affection. What if Isabel had spouted off to the Darkling? Fear embraced him. He had to get back to Pierre's house.

Tristan had run a half a mile and was about to turn toward town when he caught Everly's distinctive scent wafting on the air. The only way he could've smelled her was if she was nearby. What was she doing out here? It didn't matter. He had to get back to town. The spicy scent faded.

He took a few more steps then stopped. There was no reason for Everly to be in this area. Tristan sniffed the air. Her scent was faint now. He shook his head and snorted to clear his lungs. When he inhaled again, the scent wasn't just faint. It was moving.

There were only so many directions Everly could be going this far out of town. Tristan kept his nose in the air and followed her scent. Instead of heading toward New Orleans, it led him deeper into the bayou.

Something wasn't right.

The howls came again. This time they were closer, but they were still miles away. Everly's arrival along with the wolves couldn't be a coincidence. Tristan focused on her and prayed to the goddess that Everly didn't drive too fast.

A gaping mouth of darkness stared at Izzy. When Stone had said he came from a world without sunlight, she'd hoped he'd exaggerated. The darkness was so complete it swallowed the light.

Izzy couldn't spend the rest of her life in there. She wouldn't survive. She glanced at Stone/Slade. He grinned now that the portal was open.

He must've sensed her watching because he turned to her. "Are you ready to leave this horrid place?"

"No." Izzy stepped back. At least Everly had been smart enough to stay away. It wasn't much of a consolation, but it was a small victory.

"Come now," Stone said. "Don't be shy. There are a lot of warriors eager to meet you."

Izzy shook her head and ran. She wouldn't get far, but she wasn't about to make it easy on him. Stone caught her and swept her off her feet. Izzy kicked and hit him with all her strength, but he held her easily.

"Let me go!" she cried.

Stone had a bemused expression on his face. "You need to take a deep breath. It's going to hurt."

Her head swam, and her vision dimmed.

"Put her down!" The shout came from behind them.

Stone turned, giving Izzy a clear view of Everly.

"Get out of here!" she shouted. "Run!"

But Everly didn't run. She stood her ground, glaring at Stone. If she noticed the dark opening—and there was no way she could miss it—she didn't acknowledge it. "I said, put her down."

Stone grinned. "I'm so glad you could join us," he said.

"You won't be, when I get done with you," Everly said.

He laughed. "You think your power is stronger than mine?" Stone put Izzy down but didn't release her.

Everly smiled, flashing her vampire fangs, but there was no warmth in her brown eyes. "Not my power," she said. "But the one who's coming for you will be more than your match." She hiked her thumb over her shoulder.

"He won't get here in time," Stone said. "Now be a good little girl and come with me." He grabbed Izzy by the hair and dragged her toward the portal.

She cried out in pain and struggled, but her resistance was useless against his overpowering strength.

"No!" Everly screamed and raced forward.

"Stay back," Izzy shouted, but Everly ignored her and dove for Izzy's legs.

Stone pulled hard to break her grip.

Everly held onto Izzy for dear life.

Izzy felt like a human tug-of-war rope. "Everly, let go! You have to get out of here."

"No," she said. "I can't let him take you."

Tristan saw the ash on the road before he found Everly's car. He touched the hood. Heat rose from the engine. She hadn't been gone long. He scented the area a second before the lodestone flared, indicating dark magic nearby.

He rushed into the woods. Everly and Isabel's scent appeared along with the Darkling's foul odor. Screams and cries rang out. Tristan followed the sound, shifting into human form as he ran.

The leaves parted and Tristan stepped out of the woods, clutching Selene in his hand. He stopped when he caught sight of what was happening. The lodestone pulsed again. Despite its strength, Tristan felt the Darkling steadily siphoning his power. He didn't have much time.

Tristan ran toward the women. He couldn't get a clear shot at the Darkling without the possibility of harming Isabel or Everly. He swung the sword and caught the Darkling in the side. The blade struck true.

The Darkling screamed in agony and staggered back. He dropped Isabel in the process. The move was so unexpected that Everly fell onto her back. She quickly scrambled away on her hands and knees. Isabel didn't move.

It was then that Tristan saw the bruises on her neck and the blood on her arm. The perfect finger placements around Isabel's slender throat made the weapon used easily identifiable. A red haze covered Tristan's vision. It had dared to harm what was his.

Fear filled the Darkling's amber eyes, as he touched the blood and brought it up to his face. He glanced at the sword in Tristan's hand and put even more distance between them.

"That's right," Tristan said. "This isn't a normal sword. It's made for killing your kind."

"I should've finished you when I had the chance," the Darkling said, staying out of reach.

"Yes, you should have," Tristan said. "Go to your friend, Isabel." He never took his eyes off the Darkling.

"Move and I'll gut you," the Darkling said.

"Tristan, stay back," Isabel said. "He's infected me. I'm going to die."

"I won't allow that to happen," Tristan said, glancing at the scratch.

Pain filled Isabel's hazel eyes. "It's too late. Get Everly out of here."

"I will not be leaving without you," Tristan said.

Isabel sniffled. "But I betrayed you."

"That makes us even," Tristan said, then shifted his attention back to the Darkling. "This is between you and I."

The Darkling laughed. "This has nothing to do with you, Kin. Leave now, and I might let you live."

Tristan grinned, flashing sharp, white teeth. "We know that's not going to happen."

"Have it your way." The Darkling held out a hand. Power flowed from his body.

Tristan felt the first wave strike him. The pain nearly knocked him to his knees.

"Come here, beast," the Darkling said, crooking a finger.

"No!" Tristan shouted, but it was already too late. The shift was upon him.

Fur rippled over Tristan's flesh as his beast rose to the surface. The enchanted sword dropped to the ground, useless in his paws. He threw his head back and howled in anguish. Others nearby mirrored the lonesome sound.

The Darkling's head rose, and his eyes scanned the tree line. "Time to go," he snarled and grabbed Isabel, pulling her toward the opening.

Tristan felt his strength drain. Being this close to the Darkling and the opening to the other realm sucked the life right out of him. He wouldn't be conscious for much longer. Tristan leapt, covering the distance between them.

He landed on Isabel, knocking her out of the Darkling's hands. Tristan growled and snapped at him, daring him to try to take her.

Isabel shoved at his fur to try to get away.

Tristan didn't move.

The Darkling took a step forward.

Tristan bared his teeth and growled low in his chest.

The Darkling hesitated then kept coming.

Tristan lowered his head and grabbed Isabel by the throat. He sank his fangs into her flesh where her shoulder met her neck. Blood filled his mouth. It was sweeter than anything he'd ever tasted. He swallowed as much as he could then licked the spot to seal the wound. When Tristan was sure the bleeding had slowed, he released Isabel.

Tears streamed down her cheeks as she clutched her throat and scurried away. Tristan couldn't bear to see the pain of betrayal in her eyes. It hurt too much. But he held no regrets.

The Darkling roared in anger. "What have you done? You can't! She's mine!"

Wrong! Isabel was his. And he'd just proven it. Tristan shook his head to clear it.

The Darkling snarled. "You think biting her is going to stop me?" He ran toward Isabel, who tried to reach Everly's side. The blood flowing from his wound didn't slow him.

No! Tristan shouted inside his mind as he watched in horror. He tried to cut the Darkling off, but he was too weak to catch him.

Tristan staggered forward. He wasn't going to make it.

The Darkling made a grab for Isabel.

"Remember what I told you!" Everly shouted, then shoved Isabel out of the way.

Instead of scooping Isabel up, the Darkling had no choice but to grab Everly or leave empty-handed. The momentum he'd built as he crossed the clearing carried them through the portal opening.

Tristan sprinted toward the portal. If he reached it in time, it would mean his death, but he'd gladly sacrifice his life if it meant saving Isabel's friend for her. After all, she'd saved Isabel for him.

He jumped as the portal snapped shut. The momentum carried him forward into a tree trunk. Tristan hit headfirst. He heard a loud crunch, then the world faded to black.

Izzy stared in horror at Tristan's lifeless form. Everly was gone, and Tristan might be dead. They'd both sacrificed themselves for her. Tears filled her eyes as Izzy struggled to gain her footing. As soon as she was steady enough to move, she rushed to his side.

Blood trickled out Tristan's nose and muzzle.

She dropped to her knees and gently pulled his head onto her lap. When she saw his chest rise, the tears flowed down her cheeks. At least he was alive, but Izzy had no idea how badly he was hurt. Tristan hadn't returned to his human form.

Izzy took off her shirt to put pressure on his bleeding. She kept her eyes on the woods. Would Stone come back for her?

Blood seeped through her shirt. If Tristan didn't wake up soon, she'd drag him to the road. "Please, come back to me," she murmured. "I need you."

Izzy heard a twig snap. Her heart slammed into her ribcage, trying to kick its way out. She glanced around and spotted Tristan's sword. She gently laid his head aside and crawled over to it. Izzy had just wrapped her hand around the handle when wolves poured out of the woods.

She screamed and scurried back to Tristan. "Stay back!" she shouted, swinging the sword wildly around her.

One wolf stepped away from the others. He barked once, and the others grew silent. The air around him shimmered. One moment a black wolf stood in the middle of the clearing, the next Pierre La Fontaine stared at her.

It said a lot about Izzy's state of mind that she didn't even care that he was naked. "Stay back." She kept one hand on Tristan and the other firmly wrapped around the sword.

"Isabel, it's me," Pierre said. "We're not here to harm you."

"I sa—said stay back," she cried.

Pierre held his hands up and motioned for the wolves to move back. Once they were far enough away, he dropped down into a crouch.

"He's in bad shape," he said, indicating to Tristan. "He needs my help."

Izzy glanced at Tristan. He was still breathing, but his breaths were shallow and he was still bleeding badly. "He tried to save me."

Pierre glanced at the wound on the side of her neck. "Did Tristan do that to you?"

Izzy's brow furrowed. "What?"

"Did he bite you?" he asked.

"Yes," she said. "Stone got really mad after Tristan bit me."

"I bet he did," Pierre said. "Where's your friend, Everly?"

Fresh tears filled her eyes until Pierre's image wavered. "He took her," she whispered. "She shoved me out of the way, and he took her instead."

Sadness filled Pierre's amber eyes. "I'm sorry," he said softly, then murmured in French.

Izzy didn't speak the language, but something about the cadence of his voice made her muscles relax. The sword seemed heavier than it had been a moment ago. Her arm trembled and dropped.

"No!" she said, but there was no fighting Pierre's steady voice.

"It's okay." He slowly moved closer as he continued to talk to her.

Izzy's eyes drooped, and the sword fell to the ground.

Pierre moved with lightning speed. He grabbed the weapon, then tossed the sword to someone behind him and still managed to catch her before she fell over.

"It's okay," he said. "You'll be okay."

Izzy had a hard time understanding him. His words were slurring in her mind.

He turned his head to address the others. "Someone get over here and get Tristan. I have his mate."

18

Izzy awoke in a strange room. The antique furnishings were ornate and exquisitely chosen. She was in a comfy bed with plush linens. A vase full of flowers sat on the bedside table, along with a glass of water.

She tried to recall how she'd gotten there, but came up blank. The door opened, and Tristan stepped inside. Everything came crashing back to Izzy in an instant.

"How are you feeling?" he asked, but didn't meet her gaze. Instead, he leaned against the doorway.

Izzy sat up. "Okay, I guess," she said. "How are you?"

Tristan shrugged. "My head hurts, but I'll live."

"Everly is gone. Isn't she?"

His jaw clenched, and all warmth left his expression. "Yes."

"Can we get her back?" Izzy asked.

Tristan shook his head and winced, then touched the side of his temple. "No."

"Stone told me what he had planned for me on the other side," she said. "It was horrifying. The thought of Everly..." Izzy voice cracked.

"I'm sorry," Tristan said. "I tried to save her. I just wasn't fast enough. I thought if I could get to her, I could toss her back through the opening before it sealed shut."

Izzy frowned. "You told me you couldn't survive in the Darkling world," she said. "Was that true?"

"Yes," he bit out.

"So you would've died had you leapt into their world." The truth punched Izzy in the chest, leaving her winded.

"I might have been able to save her for you," Tristan said, avoiding the truth.

And if he had, it would've cost him his life.

Izzy played with the ends of the comforter. "Everly pushed me out of the way," she said quietly.

"I saw her," he said. "She did it to save you."

She closed her eyes. "Why would she do that? She had to have known what would happen."

"You were her friend," he said.

Her eyes flew open, and she glared at him. "I still am," Izzy snapped.

Tristan nodded. "I think she knew all along what was going to occur. We just didn't listen."

"What happens now?" she asked.

He stared at a spot on the wall. Izzy got the distinct impression that he did it so he wouldn't have to look at her. The thought hurt.

"You'll return to your life with your sister," he said. "And I'll return to mine."

Pain blossomed inside her, but she refused to show it. She wasn't sure why she was surprised. After all, they'd been forced to work together. No sense drawing the situation out. It was already uncomfortable enough.

"I'm..." She cleared her throat. "I'm going to need a ride."

Tristan glanced at her. "It's already been arranged."

"Are you going to take me back?" she asked, knowing the answer before he replied.

"No," Tristan said. "I have... I have things I need to do."

"Of course," she said, unable to keep the bitterness from her voice. "Well, thanks for stopping by. I'm glad you're okay."

Tristan opened his mouth to say something more, then closed it and left the room.

Izzy stayed strong until the door clicked then she let herself fall apart. When she was done wallowing in the pity pool, she threw the covers off and jumped into the shower. Izzy was surprised to find fresh clothes waiting for her when she got out.

They must really want to get rid of her. Or maybe Tristan did.

Well she'd never been one to overstay her welcome. She looked around the room one last time. Nothing of hers was there, so she left.

Pierre La Fontaine waited for her at the bottom of the stairs. Tristan was nowhere in sight. She guessed they'd said their goodbyes earlier. Izzy painted a smile on her face as she approached the Alpha.

"Glad to see you're feeling better," he said.

Izzy rubbed her arms. "Thanks for putting me up. I—uh, guess I'd better be going. Thank you again for—everything."

"Take care of yourself, Ms. MacDougal," he said. Pierre's expression remained pleasant, but he didn't bother to hide the concern in his amber eyes.

Izzy nodded and walked out of the house. A car idled near the curb to take her to the airport. She glanced back one last time at the house, hoping to spot Tristan, but he was nowhere in sight. Her heart broke as she slipped into the car and it drove away.

Tristan pulled the curtains back and watched the black sedan take Isabel away. He had to let her go. It was the right thing to do. She hadn't asked for his bite. Hadn't wanted it. He wouldn't force himself upon her. He'd already done enough damage.

"Are you going to stand there all night?" Pierre asked, coming up beside him.

"Perhaps," Tristan said.

"She's your mate," Pierre said gently.

Tristan's lip curled. "No," he said. "She isn't. I bit her to protect her."

Pierre had the audacity to laugh in his face. "Is that what you think happened? I was wondering what load of bull you were telling yourself."

He scowled. "I know that's what happened. I was there. You weren't."

Pierre shook his head and walked over to an antique cabinet. He pulled out a bottle of port. "Want a glass?"

Tristan shrugged. "Sure."

Pierre poured two glasses and handed him one. Tristan started to take a sip but stopped short when the Alpha raised his glass.

"Here's to beautiful women," he said. "The ones in our lives and the ones we let get away."

Tristan glared at him.

Pierre clinked his glass then took a sip. "Funny thing about wolves," he said, "they don't do anything they don't want to do."

"She's not my bondmate," Tristan said then tossed the contents of the glass back. The port burned his throat but did little to ease his tension.

"That bite tells a different story," Pierre said, taking another dainty sip. "You really should savor rare things." He glanced at his glass, but Tristan wasn't sure he discussed the port.

Tristan set his glass down on the side table. "The bite didn't happen during sex, so she's not going to become Kin."

Pierre nodded. "Perhaps not," he said. "You're probably in the clear. You can go back to doing what you do without having to worry about your...Isabel." He finished his port and set his glass down beside Tristan's.

Tristan turned back to the window as Pierre wandered toward the door. The Alpha's footsteps halted. Tristan knew his leaving was too good to be true.

"I do wonder though," Pierre said.

He sighed and turned to face the Alpha once more. "About what?"

"About what did happen during sex," he said.

"That is none of your business," Tristan snarled. He opened his mouth to deliver another scathing response, but Pierre held up his hand to stop him.

"I don't want details," Pierre said in exasperation. "I'm just giving you something to think about."

"Pierre," Tristan ground his name out between clenched teeth.

"Fine," Pierre said. "I'll leave you with one final thought. Isabel may not be your bondmate and she probably won't shift during the next full moon, but if you locked inside of her during sex, then there's a very good chance she's carrying your pup."

Blood drained from Tristan's face, and he grabbed hold of the windowsill to keep from falling over. Was that possible? Had he impregnated Isabel? Just the thought left him light-headed.

Pierre laughed. "You look like you need another drink." He walked over and grabbed the port, then refilled their glasses. "You'll only know for sure if you go after her."

Tristan grabbed the glass and drank the port like it was a shot, then rushed past Pierre. He heard the Alpha laughing as he took the stairs two at a time.

"Thought that might change things," Pierre shouted. "Have a nice flight."

* * *

Izzy had been back in Oregon for over three weeks. Tristan had showed up shortly after she arrived, but she had refused to speak with him. Seeing him hurt too much. Everywhere she turned Izzy got a constant reminder of what she'd lost.

Her sister Mindy was so blissfully in love that it was sickening. She was happy for her. Truly happy, but nothing made someone hurting more miserable than hanging around a happy couple.

She continued to mourn Everly but had accepted that there was nothing she could've done to save her. That didn't make her feel any less guilty, but it had brought a modicum of peace.

Mindy had been badgering her for the past two days to come over to the estate where she lived with Nic, her new husband. Izzy tried to digest the fact that her little sister was married. So much had changed in such a short period of time.

And it wasn't just her sister's life. Izzy had changed, too. Now when she saw the monsters, she didn't go the other direction. Not all of them were bad. Most were just trying to get by. Her stomach gurgled. Izzy hadn't been feeling very well lately, but Mindy's cheerful persistence eventually wore her down.

She'd agreed to go to Aidan's place with one stipulation. Tristan wasn't allowed to be there. Her sister readily agreed, which was why Izzy found herself in a car heading toward the estate.

She sat in silence as they drove past the big gates guarding the entrance. Through the trees, Izzy thought she caught glimpses of movement, but she wasn't sure.

The car stopped in front of a magnificent mansion. Mindy turned to her. "What do you think?"

Izzy looked at the house. "It's very pretty."

"Come on." Mindy tugged her hand. "You'll like it more once you see the inside."

She didn't need to like the house. It wasn't like she'd be living here, but she humored Mindy all the same. Izzy felt eyes upon her as she exited the car.

She didn't see anyone, but they were there. A few times during the week, Izzy swore she'd sensed Tristan in her mind, but that was impossible. They didn't have that kind of connection.

Just the thought of Frosty brought a wave of sadness. Izzy pushed it aside and smiled, but it didn't fool Mindy.

"I'm fine," she said. "I swear."

"I'm not buying it," Mindy said, "but I appreciate the effort."

Okay, she wasn't fine. Far from it. But Izzy would be eventually. It would just take time. *A few years should do it*, she thought.

If only Mindy would wait. Her sister had already talked about setting Izzy up. Just the thought of a strange man touching her made Izzy's skin crawl. She couldn't imagine anyone holding her, but Tristan. She didn't tell her sister because frankly her behavior embarrassed her. Izzy had never been the type of girl to moon over any man.

A handsome man with shoulder-length black hair met them at the door. Next to him stood a willowy strawberry blonde with her arm wrapped around his back.

"Isabel," he said. "It's great to finally meet you. Mindy has told me so much about you. I'm Aidan." He held out his hand.

Izzy shook it. "Nice to meet you, too."

"This is my bondmate, Jenna," he said.

The woman stepped forward and shook her hand. "It's so nice to meet you," she said.

Aidan's nose twitched. He gave Izzy a funny look then glanced at Mindy and Nic.

"Something wrong?" Izzy asked.

"No," Aidan said, recovering quickly. "Please come inside. We have lunch prepared."

"You didn't need to go to any trouble," Izzy said, feeling uncomfortable by the attention. Though truth be told, she was hungry. More than hungry, ravenous.

"No trouble at all," Jenna said.

After a long leisurely lunch, Mindy gave Izzy a tour around the estate. Unlike Pierre's house, this one was super modern inside and high tech. She tried to picture Pierre going high tech and nearly laughed aloud. He liked his antiques too much to ever do that.

Thoughts about Pierre and New Orleans opened the floodgates on the emotions she'd been trying to suppress. Memories of her and Tristan strolling through Jackson Square filled her mind.

Izzy could almost feel him holding her hand and kissing her. He'd been pretending they were a couple at the time, but the kisses had felt real enough for her to forget for a while.

Her throat thickened. She shouldn't be thinking about Tristan or New Orleans. He wasn't there any longer. Izzy wasn't even sure if he was still in Oregon. Tristan had told her that he lived in the Southwest. Maybe he'd gone home.

Did he think about her and their time in the Big Easy? Did it matter?

Izzy swallowed past the lump in her throat. "Mindy, I'd like to go home now."

Concern filled her sister's brown eyes. "Sure," she said. "Let's just say goodbye to Aidan and Jenna before we leave."

As they drew near Aidan's office, they heard shouting coming from the other side of the door.

"I don't think we should interrupt him," Izzy said, turning to leave.

"I'm not going anywhere until I get to speak with her," a familiar male voice said.

"She doesn't want to see you," Aidan shouted.

Izzy froze. She knew that voice. Knew who it had come from. *Tristan.* Izzy glanced back at the closed door.

Words were quickly replaced by loud growls.

Izzy moved long before reason raised its ugly head to stop her. She pushed the door open and stepped inside the room. Two sets of glowing eyes turned on her at once.

"Knock it off, Frosty," she snapped.

The growling ceased. Aidan's dark brow shot to his hairline.

"What are you doing here?" Izzy asked, ignoring him and focusing on Tristan.

He inhaled, then his mercury-colored eyes narrowed. "We need to talk," Tristan said.

"There's nothing more to say," she said.

"You may have nothing to say, but I have plenty," he said.

Izzy told herself that she only agreed because she wanted to defuse the situation, but it was a lie. She'd missed him. Missed him so much that it hurt. Being near him made her heart lighter.

Tristan glared at Aidan then walked out the door. He didn't touch Izzy as they stepped off the back patio onto the grass, but he stayed close by her side.

A couple times Izzy caught him scowling at the other wolves they passed as they wandered down a trail in the woods. But she didn't say anything. Izzy simply waited.

She should have heard him out long ago, but she'd been afraid to.

Too afraid of what he might say. Izzy couldn't go on like this, though. It was too painful.

When they reached a small clearing, Tristan stopped. He shifted his feet and glanced around, but nothing held his interest for long.

What had him so nervous? she wondered.

"You said you wanted to talk," Izzy said. "So talk."

Tristan rubbed the back of his neck. She saw his gaze dart to the spot where he'd bitten her. It had healed, but the mark didn't look like it was ever going to go away.

Izzy had noticed a similar spot on Mindy's neck. When she'd asked her about it, her sister had been evasive. At the time she'd assumed it was sexual in nature, but now that she'd seen one on Jenna's throat, Izzy wasn't so sure.

He took a deep breath. "I missed you," Tristan said, surprising them both.

She'd missed him, too, but Izzy wasn't about to admit it. "Tristan, what are you really doing here? Does it have something to do with this bite?" She motioned toward her neck.

Tristan's lips thinned. "Yes, and no," he said.

"I think if you try you can be a little more vague," she said.

He laughed, breaking some of the tension between them. "I have missed that mouth of yours."

She gave him a wry glance. "You don't like humans, remember?"

"I remember," he said. "I also recall you don't care for monsters. Has that changed?"

Izzy laughed, but the sound held no warmth. "Yeah, it has." She caught the flare of hope in his eyes. "I didn't know what real monsters were until I met Stone, Slade, or whatever his name is."

Tristan brushed a lock of hair away from her face. "It doesn't matter what his name was, he's dead now."

Izzy blanched. "What do you mean he's dead?"

"The sword I struck him with wasn't a normal weapon," he said. "It was made specifically to kill his kind."

"What does that mean for Everly?" she asked, knowing her friend was now alone in the dark world.

Tristan chose his words carefully. "At least she won't have him to contend with."

Being this close to Isabel and not being able to touch her was sheer torture for Tristan. The proximity was bad enough, but couple that with the aroma coming from her skin and it was enough to make a wolf beg.

He had to tell her the truth about the bite, though it was minor compared to the other news he must share with her.

"You asked what the bite meant," he said.

"Yes," she said.

Tristan pulled her into his arms and kissed her. She pulled back to argue or protest. He wasn't sure which and didn't care. He continued kissing Isabel until she melted against his body. Tristan hardened instantly, wanting her more than he desired his next breath.

Reluctantly, he ended the kiss. Her eyes were glazed when she looked at him. Tristan waited until she focused. "That's what the bite means," he said. "It's what it will always mean, if you'll have me."

He kissed her again before she answered. Tristan was too afraid to hear her response. Couldn't bear the thought of her rejection.

Isabel tore her mouth away. "I can't think when you're kissing me," she said.

"That's the point," he murmured.

She laughed. "You know this probably isn't going to work, right?"

"It'll work," he said. "We will make it work."

Isabel pulled out of his embrace and continued walking until they reached a small clearing.

"You never answered me," Tristan said.

She looked over her shoulder and grinned at him. "I know."

Izzy's hands trembled as she grabbed the bottom of her shirt and pulled it over her head. She felt more than saw Tristan's gaze upon her. It burned her flesh everywhere it touched. She heard him growl behind her.

"What are you doing?" he asked.

"You mean you don't know?" she asked.

Tristan's long legs ate up the distance between them. When he neared, he whipped his shirt off and let it fall to the ground. His godlike beauty left her breathless.

"What now?" he asked, voice harsh.

Izzy wiggled out of her pants then automatically covered her stomach with her hands. "I'm a stress eater. I've put on a little weight since you last saw me."

His eyes flashed with banked emotion. "You're beautiful at any size."

She blushed. "Yeah, well, you won't say that if I continue my cookie dough affair."

Tristan shed his pants and slowly approached her. He gently placed his hand on the small mound she'd been trying to hide, covering it. "It's natural for women in your state to put on weight."

She frowned. "My state?"

"Yes," he said. "You're with child."

"I'm pregnant!" She didn't mean to shout the news. "I can't be pregnant. I'm on birth control, and we only had sex once."

Tristan grinned. "With my kind, once is enough, if everything else falls into place."

Izzy swayed. "This can't be happening!" She glanced down at the small mound and touched it with trembling fingertips. "What am I going to do?"

"Is having my child such a bad thing?" he asked quietly, but there was no mistaking the hurt in his eyes.

Izzy took a deep breath, then took another. She quickly evaluated what she felt. Shock, check. Panic, check. Fear, check. All natural emotions when someone found out they were going to have a baby. The one emotion that she expected to feel was missing. Izzy searched again. Nope, she didn't feel an ounce of regret.

"No," she said, pressing her hand to his chest. "It's not a bad thing."

Tristan shuddered beneath her fingertips.

"What happens now?" she asked.

He flashed a quick grin. "We finish what we started."

Tristan spread their clothes out on the ground then gently laid Isabel upon them. He'd never seen anything quite so beautiful in his life, and she was his.

He dropped to his knees at her feet and lifted her leg to tenderly kiss the inside of her ankle. Isabel sighed.

Tristan continued kissing her, taking care to avoid the areas she wanted him to visit the most. By the time he finished exploring every inch of her, Isabel mewed incoherently.

He grabbed her knees and gently parted her thighs, then settled between them. If he got any harder, Tristan was convinced he'd explode.

"Isabel," he said. "Look at me."

Her lashes fluttered, then their eyes met.

"You asked me about the bite earlier," he said.

She nodded.

"If I do it again when I take you, it'll have a different meaning," he said. Tristan had her full attention now.

"What will change?" she asked.

"For starters, it will bind us together," he said, knowing he was already bound to her with or without the final act. "So I need you to be sure, because there's no going back once it's done."

Isabel bit her lip, and her brow creased. "What's the rest of it?"

"What do you mean?" he asked.

"You said for starters, so there has to be more," she said. "Tell me everything."

Tristan hesitated. There was still time for her to change her mind. Tell him she wasn't ready for this, for him, and there'd be nothing he could do about it. The thought of not being around to raise his child made him ache, but Tristan would honor her wishes—even if it destroyed him to do so.

"If I bite you again, while we're making love, you'll become like me," he said, then braced himself for her rejection.

"I'll become a wolf?" she asked.

Tristan nodded. Isabel spent her whole life fearing and running from the monsters in the world. The last thing she'd want was to become one of them. This was it. He prepared for the worst.

"Will our child be like you?" she asked softly.

His gaze speared hers. "Yes." Tristan searched for any sign of disgust. There was none. "It'll also be a reflection of you...just as I am."

Her brow furrowed. "What do you mean?" she asked.

Tristan brushed her cheek with his knuckles. "You've brought out my humanity. Made me want to be more human, so that there would be a place for me in your world." He touched her heart. "And in here."

Tears pricked her eyes and she kissed him tenderly. "Then let's do this," Isabel said.

"You need to be sure." Tristan felt his beast rise. It wanted her, wanted their child, and it didn't care if she agreed.

She caressed his cheek. "I am sure. I've had a lot of time to think during the last few weeks. It seems like all I've done is think," she said. "The one thing that kept coming back again and again was you."

"I will give my life for you and our child," he murmured. "I will protect you both with my last breath."

"You already have, Frosty," she said. "You nearly died trying to protect us."

"And I'd gladly do so again." Tristan kissed her hard and entered her with one thrust. The feel of her tight channel surrounding him was like coming home. Isabel was his. And he was hers. Together they were a family.

Emotion welled inside him. Tristan looked away before she glimpsed the tears swimming in his eyes. It had been years since he'd had a family. Years spent wandering the country alone. Now Tristan had someone to come home to. Soon, he'd have two.

He placed his hand upon her abdomen and kissed Isabel lovingly. "Thank you," he said.

"For what?" she asked, placing her hand over his.

"For loving me enough to say yes," he said, then began to move.

Tristan made love to her, taking her body to new heights as he bound them together in the way of his people. He took her blood, savoring it for the gift that it was, then gave Isabel his in exchange. And when she fell apart in his arms and cried out in ecstasy, Tristan followed.

He'd follow her from this life into the next and anywhere else she decided to go. Because this human—*ex-human*—had stolen this wolf's heart.

EPILOGUE

Tristan and Isabel sat in Sticks, waiting for Mindy and Nic to arrive. The dive bar was hopping. Tables had been pushed aside to accommodate the dancers. Even with the added space, they overflowed into the aisles, kicking up sawdust as they moved to the music.

"If they don't get here soon," Isabel said, "I'm out of here." There was edginess to her movements as she scanned the crowd.

Tristan smiled and rubbed her lower back. "Hungry again?"

"Starving," she snapped.

Isabel had eaten two hours ago, but her stomach was already rumbling again. He stroked her rounded belly. She'd deliver in another month—thanks to Weres' short gestation periods. Until then, Tristan would fetch her whatever she wanted, whenever she wanted it.

"They'll be here soon," he said, hoping it was the truth. If not, then he'd leave a message at the bar to meet them at the restaurant.

Isabel looked around the crowded barroom and sighed.

Tristan tensed. "What's wrong? Is the baby okay?"

She touched his arm. "The baby's fine. I was just thinking about Everly. She'd never hang at Sticks, but she would've gotten a kick out of this place," she said.

He squeezed her hand. "I wish we could help her, but there's only been one wolf who has ever crossed into the Darkling world and lived to tell about it."

"Where is he now?" she asked, a hint of hope in her voice.

Hope that he was about to crush. "He's dead," Tristan said, fighting back impotent rage. He wanted to do something to help her, something to make the situation better, but he couldn't.

Isabel didn't bother to hide her disappointment.

"I'm sorry, love," he said.

"Me too," she said, then glanced at something behind him. "Mindy and Nic are here." Isabel pasted a smile on her face and wiggled her way off the barstool. She waddled across the room to hug her sister.

Tristan followed close behind, making sure none of the wolves jostled her. They gave her a wide berth, once they caught sight of him.

"Ready to go to dinner?" Mindy asked.

"I was ready an hour ago," Isabel said.

"Guess that means you don't want to stay for a drink," Mindy said.

"Unless you plan to do a shot, then no," Isabel said.

"Lookout! Pregnant cranky lady coming through," Mindy shouted.

Nic waved to his friend, Lucien.

The bartender smiled and waved back. His jovial mask faded the second the couples left the bar. Lucien overheard Tristan and his bondmate talking about her friend, Everly. She had been taken into the Darklings' world. He shuddered at the thought of a human being trapped there.

Tristan was right. There wasn't much that could be done to save her. But he was wrong about one thing. The wolf that made it out of the Darkling world wasn't dead. He was right here, hiding in plain sight.

Lucien knew firsthand the hell that existed on the other side. He'd barely managed to escape. If he hadn't stolen a portal rune stone, he wouldn't have succeeded.

It had taken months for him to recover his sanity. Months spent trapped between man and beast, raging against the darkness trying to envelop him.

He'd kept his past a secret from everyone, including his best friend, Nic. It had been safer that way—safer for everyone.

Once he'd recovered, Lucien vowed never to return. Not just because the Darklings put a price on his head, but because Lucien knew he wouldn't be so lucky next time.

He pulled the black stone out of his pocket and ran his thumb across the runes etched into the surface. Dark magic snapped at his fingertips, making them tingle. Lucien shoved the rock back into his pocket. Why had he kept it? He should've gotten rid of the stone long ago.

If what they'd said was true about Everly, then she was running out of time and he was the only one who could save her.

THANK YOU NOTE

Thank you for taking the time to read *Moonlight Kin Vol. 2*! If you enjoyed Nic and Tristan's stories, then please consider leaving a **REVIEW** to let other readers know. If you've already left a good review somewhere, drop me an email to let me know, so I can thank you personally. For more information about upcoming books--including *Moonlight Kin 5: Lucien*--access to free reads, and surprise giveaways, sign up now for my newsletter at: www.jordansummers.com.

PIT FIGHETERS: CAGE-Excerpt

PREFACE

*The Dark King stood at the window, staring out at the Walled City.
His people were dying.*

*He'd tried everything to save them, but with fewer and fewer females
born every year, nothing had worked. But just when he'd nearly given up
hope, his salvation—their salvation—had walked through the door.*

*Hades glanced over his shoulder at the human female who was now his
mate. He saw his newborn daughter squirm in Taylor's arms and snuffle
softly as she nursed. The sudden swell of love he felt for the Earthling
humbled him. It made the Dark King even more determined to see that
his warriors got the same chance at happiness and contentment that he'd
found.*

*He knew most Phantom Warriors would jump at the opportunity to go
to Earth to search for a mate...but not all. For a few stubborn individuals,
it would take a direct order.*

Hades grinned. No one disobeyed the Dark King.

1

Fighting with a lion shouldn't be this easy...

Chrysus, the black panther, dug his paws into the firm soil that packed the Pit floor. Spotting an opening, he lunged at the lion and caught him across the chest with a vicious swipe of his sharp claws.

His opponent roared in anger and surprise, the lion whipping around to swipe at the panther, missing him by a whisker. Chrysus leapt back, slamming into the crude cage that surrounded the fighting arena. The rusted enclosure clanged and groaned, straining metal echoing throughout the amphitheater before being muted by the fortress's stone walls.

Chrysus snorted. It was a rare day that anyone got a claw on a lion and he intended to relish the moment—from a distance.

He was so focused on the lion that Chrysus didn't hear the jaguar sneaking up behind him. The other cat grabbed him by the haunches and yanked his legs out from under him. Chrysus went down hard, getting a paw beneath him before his face hit the dirt.

Incensed at the two-against-one tactic, Chrysus twisted and slashed the jaguar's nose, bisecting his left nostril before the big, spotted cat leapt away. The panther scrambled to his feet and backed up until his tail hit the fence. From this position, Chrysus could keep both beasts in his line of sight. He should've known the lion wouldn't be so easily taken down.

Deep furrows from the panther's long, deadly claws scored the golden lion's massive chest. But if he was in pain, it wasn't obvious. The lion stared at him with unblinking amber eyes. Eyes that told him that he would wait all day and night for his chance at revenge.

The black panther's gaze moved to the jaguar, prowling from side to side. Blood dripped from his nose, creating a crimson mosaic on the hard ground. Beneath the spots covering his body, the cat's muscles quivered and its tail swished back and forth, as he searched for an opening.

The panther snarled and hunched down. Chrysus leapt into the air and collided with the two angry felines. They came together in a clash of claws and teeth. Exhaustion rode him hard as all three hit the ground in a heap.

The lion latched onto the panther's front leg and bit down to the bone. Chrysus snarled, but couldn't pull away without shredding flesh. When you were a Pit Fighter, embracing pain became second nature. He dug his claws deeper into the lion's sides, unable to get at the beast's throat through his thick mane.

The jaguar grabbed him from behind to drop him. A panther was no one's prey. Chrysus rolled, forcing the other two cats to roll with him. The move broke the lion's hold, allowing the panther to claw the jaguar across his belly and leap out of the way.

Every muscle in Chrysus's body hurt as he limped across the fighting field. He could feel blood running down his leg, pooling on his paw. He flexed his claws. Pain seared his flesh. He needed to shift, but the battle wasn't over yet. He turned in time to see the two cats stalk toward him.

A sudden roar came from the far side of the Pit. A roar that was unexpected, yet instantly recognizable. The sound made the fur rise on the panther's neck. Chrysus saw the jaguar and lion stiffen, all conflict instantly discarded as they turned to face the new arrival.

Hades, the Dark King, swaggered into the amphitheater and stopped at the entrance to the Pit. His bright blue gaze locked on the three cats, then he signaled for the warriors to join him. As he did so, something squirmed and squealed in his arms. Hades juggled the bundle, then gently clicked his tongue. None of the warriors ever expected to hear that sound come out of their King.

Fur receded from their bodies and their claws retracted. Within seconds, the three predatory cats were gone: exhausted, naked warriors stood in their place. Chrysus, Zeph, and Asher made their way across the Pit, gathering discarded items of clothing as they approached.

The Dark King's face shifted, the faint markings and features of a liger emerging. The auburn-haired little girl in his arms giggled and reached for his sensitive whiskers. She gave them a hard yank. Hades didn't even wince. He simply wiggled his nose, then shifted back.

"Peek-a-boo," he said.

His blue-eyed daughter giggled again and wrapped her tiny hand around his finger. She immediately pulled it into her mouth and sucked on it.

"I have to get you back to your mother," Hades mused. "You're hungry again."

Chrysus watched the exchange, unspeaking. He had little knowledge of Earth children's dietary needs, but knew that Phantom young ate continuously. Most Phantom Warrior males envied the Dark King for he possessed a well-endowed mate. She'd be able to feed fifty babies with her ample *assets*. And if the Dark King had his way, the Queen would whelp that many.

As Hades cooed over his little girl, Chrysus's chest twinged. He rubbed the spot and glanced away. He must've hit the ground harder than he realized. The child smiled at her father, causing the discomfort in his chest to increase.

"Are we needed for another mission, Sire?" Chrysus had been on more missions than he could count, but if the King needed him, he'd pull himself together and go.

All male Phantoms were warriors, but these Pit Fighters were in a different league. They'd been handpicked for their ruthlessness and cunning to be part of an elite team of fighters that the King sent out far ahead of his army.

Their motto: Take care of problems *before* they arise.

"Yes," Hades said simply. He juggled the baby once more, then settled her against his chest and stroked her back. "Once again, I require your service."

Chrysus nodded. "When do we leave?" he asked.

"You have two days," Hades said.

"And our destination?" Zeph asked.

For the first time, Hades' full attention moved from his daughter to the fighters. "Earth," he said.

Chrysus glanced at his brethren. Their expressions held the shock that he felt. "You…you want us to go to war with Earth, Sire?"

Phantoms had never invaded a planet without provocation.

"No," he said, then smiled ruefully. "Though sometimes I think that would make things easier for our people in the long run."

"Then is there someone on Earth you need us to eliminate?" Zeph asked.

Hades looked at them. "No."

Chrysus frowned. "Sire, I do not understand. Then what is our mission?"

Hades' blue gaze roamed over their faces. "I want you to have what I have."

Chrysus's eyes widened in alarm. He didn't mean…surely he wasn't talking about… He glanced at Zeph, who seemed rooted in place, but looked ready to run. As always, Asher remained cool and calm. Nothing rocked the six foot four, golden-haired lion shifter.

"Sire, what is it you wish us to have?" Asher asked.

Hades grinned. "A chance."

"At what?" Chrysus asked, more than a little confused.

"Happiness," Hades said.

Chrysus was suddenly aware of the silence of the pit. He could feel his heart pounding in his ears, and hear the breathing of his fellow fighters. And he knew of himself—as he knew was true of them—they would all rather be back in the throes of the fight than having this encounter with their King. None of them answered. There was no way to do so without ending up in a true Pit challenge. And no one went against the Dark King and lived.

The silence grew. Perhaps only seconds, but it felt like an age. They all knew this was not the way these discussions were meant to happen. The Dark King was accustomed to his fighters' immediate and enthusiastic obedience.

Instead, in the midst of the standstill, Chrysus heard himself—and could hardly believe hearing himself—begin, "But, Sire..."

A growl rumbled out of Hades' chest, threatening to morph into a full-blown roar.

His daughter sobbed.

The men took a step back and fanned out, as her wails grew in volume.

Their eyes widened as they glanced at each other.

What do we do? Chrysus mouthed.

Don't know, Zeph mouthed back. Spots appeared and disappeared on his arms.

Asher gave them a tense shrug.

The Dark King deflated. "Athena, don't cry. Daddy was just teasing." The cold gaze he shot to the warriors said otherwise. "You're going to Earth to look for mates."

Chrysus's chest tightened, making it hard to breathe. His two hearts felt like they were trying to break through his ribs. What was happening to him?

"But, Sire, we're Pit Fighters," Asher protested.

The lion's reaction surprised Chrysus. His commander was always the first to follow orders—and give them. He never questioned Hades. Ever.

"There is much training to be done here on Zaron," Asher continued.

"It can wait until you return," Hades said. "I've already spoken to

Helio. He volunteered to fill in while you're gone."

Asher frowned. "Helio is a child," he said. "He's a good warrior, but the bear is not ready to lead the rest of the Pit Fighters."

The Dark King's tawny brow arched. "Then it's a good thing I'm here," he said softly.

Chrysus's feline side bristled.

Asher took a step back and dropped his gaze to the ground. "I meant no disrespect, Sire."

"I know," Hades said. "It's the only reason you're still standing."

Asher blanched.

"I think what the commander meant, Sire, is that we're needed here," Chrysus said.

The tightness in his chest got worse. Was he dying? Chrysus didn't fear death. He considered the goddess a friend. But he'd never felt anything like this. Fear before a mission was normal. Fear kept him alive. But whatever this was, was dangerous. Unpredictable. This kind of emotion could get him killed.

"Breathe, warrior," Hades said. "The panic will pass in a moment."

Panic? Was that what this was? If so, Chrysus didn't like it one bit.

"You need to find mates. This proves it," Hades said. "Fighting for your people is honorable. You have my loyalty and gratitude because of your willing sacrifice. But you need more." He bounced Athena until she laughed. "Listen to that sound. It's the sound of happiness. The sound of contentment. I had no idea it was missing from my life until I met my mate."

The word 'mate' sent a shiver of unease through Chrysus. *Normal* Phantoms mated. There was nothing normal about the Pit Fighters. Sure, the Phantom people revered them for the sacrifices that they made on their behalf, but they also *feared* them.

Not even Pleasurers wanted the scarred assassins in their beds. It took double the credits to get them there and most kept their eyes closed during the sex act.

How in the worlds could the Dark King expect them to find mates on Earth? The sight of them would traumatize any female in her right mind.

Chrysus loved his fellow Pit Fighters like brothers. They were his family. The only family he needed. Didn't the King understand that?

"You have two days to prepare," Hades said. "I suggest you use them wisely."

"That's not enough time, Sire." There was no use arguing with the Dark King once he'd given an order, but Zeph still tried.

"Would you rather I make it one day?" Hades asked.

"No, Sire." Chrysus hit Zeph in the arm to silence him. "Two days is perfect. We'll be ready."

Hades laughed. "I doubt it," he said. "Now if you'll excuse me, I have to go find my mate. My daughter isn't the only one who's worked up an *appetite*."

The Dark King disappeared down the hall that led out of the Pit area.

Spotted fur sprouted from Zeph's arms. "What are we going to do?" he asked. "I don't want to go to Earth. Humans are so...fragile." He rubbed the newly healed skin on his nose and began to pace.

"What choice do we have?" Chrysus struggled to remain calm. He wasn't the only one shaken. Even Asher's hands trembled as he shoved them into his pockets.

"None," Asher snarled. "We have to go..." He hesitated, then suddenly smiled. "But not all missions end in success."

Chrysus saw a slow grin dawning on Zeph's face, and felt his own expression shift. An unspoken understanding passed between them. They'd go, make a show of trying, then return home.

Some of the tension fled from Chrysus. When he'd joined the team, he had accepted the fact that fighting, bleeding, and eventually dying for the safety of his people was the best that he could hope for out of life. Searching for a mate had never been part of the plan. Still wasn't.

"Do you think he's told the other fighters?" Zeph asked.

"Not yet," Asher said. "I'd wager we're first in line for this particular…*privilege*." He spat the last word.

Zeph nodded. "Should we warn them?"

Asher grimaced. "Not unless you want Hades to remove your head."

Chrysus ignored their bickering. He tried to picture himself on Earth. Tried to picture himself blending in with the human population. He couldn't. He felt far too savage, too scarred inside and out for that primitive planet. The thought of laying his paws on an Earthling female sent chills up his spine.

What if his claws came out? He imagined a moment's inattention, the ease and shame of injuring some helpless woman, and his entire being recoiled. For a Pit Fighter, there would be no greater dishonor.

"I'm not touching any of them," Chrysus said. "I won't take that chance."

"What are you talking about?" Zeph asked.

"The women. The Earthlings." Chrysus held his meaty hands up and slowly unsheathed his claws. "These hands aren't for touching human skin. They're for mauling. They're for killing. Sending us to Earth is a mistake."

"On that, we're in agreement," Asher said.

# # #

RELATED TITLES

Moonlight Kin 1: A Wolf's Tale
Moonlight Kin 2: Aidan's Mate
Moonlight Kin 5: Lucien (coming soon)

OTHER PARANORMAL TITLES

Phantom Warriors 1: Bacchus
Phantom Warriors 2: Saber-tooth
Phantom Warriors 3: Talon
Phantom Warriors 4: Arctos
Phantom Warriors 5: Linx
Phantom Warriors 6: Riot
Phantom Warriors 7: The Dark King
Phantom Warriors: Hawk's Slave
Phantom Warriors: Pit Fighters: Cage,
Atlantean's Quest 1: The Arrival
Atlantean's Quest 2: Exodus
Atlantean's Quest 3: Redemption
Atlantean's Quest 3.5: Atlantean Heat (Novella)
Atlantean's Quest 4: The Return, Paris After Dark

About the Author